FIRST COMES DEATH

AVRAH C. BAREN

Publication Date: April 15, 2024

Book design by Youness Elh

Edited by Corey Lamont

Published by Chaos Monster Publishing LLC

ISBN 979-8-9900546-0-8 (paperback)

ISBN 979-8-9900546-1-5 (ebook)

To the black hole documentary I watched when I was a kid. I don't remember what you were called, but you gave me nightmares until I learned that black holes couldn't emerge out of thin air to eat me alive. You inspired more nerdy fixations than you'll ever know.

Author's Note

This book discusses death and dying throughout the pages. It also features emotional manipulation from a guardian; drowning; a car crash from a bridge; mentions of homophobia; mention of nonconsensual touching; generational trauma; murder; revenge; being buried "alive"; consumption of alcohol; use of guns and knives; sex between consenting adults. There is also quite a lot of blood and gore. Please take care if you need.

1

DINA

Who by fire? And who by water?

The Yom Kippur poem echoed, ghostly in Dina's mind. An endless loop, pounding against her skull, her chest. In the ice-cold depths, she thought she could see the words written in the current. Floating upwards in the wake of each air bubble, ripped through clenched lips. They streamed, letter by letter through the cracks in the windshield as her car sank deeper into the brackish waters of the Chesapeake.

Who by water?

Me, she wanted to scream. *I will go by water.*

Fuck, I'm not ready to die.

Her panic narrowed to the tightness of her lungs. The pressure in her ears. The way all sound died in the brine, muting everything beyond her frantic heartbeat, the scattered thoughts of: *Hold on. Hold on. Hold on.*

She had long since ripped off her nails in the struggle to free herself of the seatbelt, so neatly crushed against her by the fractured limb of the guard rail. Had worked her arms to exhaustion trying to race the brown water filling the sedan to the brim. Now, they were nothing but dead weight against her sides, worn to the bone from the useless fight to break free, open the goddamn door, and swim for the surface.

Lungs burned. Another air bubble escaped. Writhing and clawing with bleeding hands. Tears swallowed by bay water. Screams devoured by punishing pressure and the animal instinct to keep her mouth shut and the air inside her body.

No no no no no.

The fucking seatbelt. It wouldn't budge. It had kept her from flying through the windshield and splattering her insides across the safety glass when the other car had slammed into her. Now it held her captive. A veritable kraken, pulling her ever downward.

She summoned another ounce of strength, grappled with the nylon, hands weakening as her vision narrowed from brown to black. Yanked and pulled and raged.

Who by water?

Shema Yisrael Adonai elohainu—

Hair floated around her like tendrils, the deep brown threads mixing with the silty waters. Where did the bay end and she begin?

A useless scream escaped and she inhaled, breathed in the bay. Choked and sucked in more, until her lungs sloshed with it.

Her grasp loosened as her struggles died.

Hands slid uselessly from the belt.

Lungs collapsed.

Thundering heartbeat no more than a memory hidden beyond dilating pupils, ice cold skin.

Who by water?

The guard rail slid free, and with it, the seatbelt.

But there was no more strength. The air bubbles had long since stopped floating to the surface.

Dina Adler went by water.

Seven days later, she opened her eyes.

2

Ivy

Dirt scattered out of Ivy's eyes. She'd been trying to blink them for a while now. To close out the sickening scurrying of ants and centipedes across her vision. She shuddered. Internally anyway. She might have been a statue for all the control she could exert over her own frozen form.

Fingers brushed against her ribs, wiped at her face. Cleared the heavy burden of grave dirt from her chest.

Thank fuck.

The paralysis had left her skin cold, bones heavy and stiff. Her body caked in thick layers of soil and blood and other substances she didn't want to think about.

The knife buried deep in her ribs was absent, yet she felt the memory of the metal tip sliding between her bones, burrowing into her heart, a ghoul left behind to carve her open again and again. It clawed and scraped. The way she kept willing herself to. To dig herself free.

Now. At last. Someone was doing it for her.

"Shit, Topher, are you sure?" a woman was saying, words murmured with the hush of secrecy, muted by the earth clogging Ivy's ears. "It hasn't happened since—"

"Just get them up. Trust me."

"But they're not even on your list," the first voice said, even as they brushed more dirt aside, lifted Ivy's body to a stiff, seated position. Her creaking bones held her in place, joints rigid and unyielding.

Memories sparked like the flashes of light in a club. Images imprinted on her eyelids. Her eyes were so fucking dry, unable to make out her surroundings. Something was still crawling behind one of her eyelids, sucking on the viscous surface. Tears welled up to expel the intruder.

"See? They're coming to."

Blink, damnit, Ivy thought. *Move, you fucking useless body.*

It took an eon. Every fiber of power she could muster. And then her eyelids closed, clearing away all remaining insects, snapped open again, synapses relinking and firing until the blurred, dark world took on shape and some memory of color. It took long moments to understand she had woken in the night, cold, humid air clinging to her hair and clothes. Warmer than the grave, but not by much.

She coughed. Sneezed. Smelled rotting pine needles, tasted stale dirt.

Two figures bent over her. She twitched.

Lenox!

Her hands stayed dead at her sides, refusing to lash out, no matter how she screamed at them to hit and scratch and fuck Lenox up for what he'd done.

"Give them some space," one of the figures said. They moved to either side of her shallow grave.

No, not Lenox. He and the rest of the crew must have fled hours ago while she'd been knocked out. Must have been confident about covering their tracks to leave her here in the woods, just spitting distance from Seattle's skyline. They hadn't even bothered to put her six feet under or toss her into a lake.

A short blade and a pitiful grave. No, they hadn't cared about another Jane Doe turning up. Not one bit. Hadn't even stuck around to make sure they'd done the job properly.

Fuck. She was in rough shape, even if she had somehow survived being run through with a knife. How had she not bled out? And why weren't these strangers carting her off to some hospital even now? Not that she loved that idea either.

Ivy warred against her motionless body, sensations returning bit by bit as her last moments with Lenox, with the crew, played endlessly in her head. The satisfaction in Lenox's cold, gray eyes as he watched the others handle his dirty work without a strand of his salt-and-pepper hair out of place. The vicious greed leaking through Jason's grin as he wedged the blade deep between her ribs.

She needed to get the fuck out of here, hunker down 'til she could come up with a plan. Wipe Lenox and the others from the face of the Earth for trying to murder her.

But she couldn't move.

The world shone silver and black, bled into a murky, gold dawn as Ivy bent one finger. Two. Brought her hand to her face in a useless attempt to wipe away the dirt. Her shirt stuck to her skin in a canvas of blood, rusted and caking.

One of the figures knelt closer. Patient, as if they had all the time in the world.

"Hey, what's your name?" they asked, words somewhat accented.

Ivy had to turn her whole head to look at them, eyes still misremembering how to swivel in their sockets. The dawn lit her companion's brown skin and silky black hair. Intelligent, black eyes. Over their shoulder, Ivy could just make out the turned-up dirt covering the other grave, silent under the shadow of death. The way hers should have been.

"I'm Lucia, she/her," the woman was saying. "That's Topher, they/them. What's your name? Do you remember?"

Ivy couldn't unstick her throat to work her vocal chords. What emerged was a terrible, coughing sound. A dead man's last gasp.

"Take your time," the person called Topher said.

If Ivy had all her faculties, she would have flipped them off. She wasn't a child.

But seriously, what the fuck? That knife had stuck *deep*. How had she not—

She felt along the crusted shirt, peeled it from the gaping wound with more ease than she would have expected. Crept her hands over the cotton tank top, wincing in anticipation of pressing into the puncture Jason had left with that jagged, awful knife.

Found blood-caked fabric with a rough edge. Shuddered when the pain remained absent. With relief or terror, she couldn't say.

"What," she croaked, "happened?"

Silence greeted her as the strangers exchanged looks. Ivy swiveled her head to Topher, who adjusted their septum piercing and scratched their mouse brown beard, looking uncomfortable.

"Well...you see...you died."

3

DINA

Dina crawled up the beach, every inch its own battle. She fought against her exhaustion and complaining muscles to put distance between herself and the shore. The thick air was cloying in its humidity. For a few panicked moments, she wondered if she'd merely imagined breaching the surface, swimming for the sliver of shoreline she spotted between parting waves. But gravity had far too much pull here. As did the drenched clothes chafing against her body.

She was above the water. And she'd made it to land. At last.

Sand scraped her cheeks, became a second, irritating skin. Each time she thought she'd finished vomiting up water, another convulsion came over her.

A final, pathetic squirm forward, and she flopped onto her back. Gray clouds greeted her, hanging low with the threat of rain. She lay gasping and coughing, eyes seeing and not seeing the shifting sky.

Drained. Terrified. But alive. Fuck, but she was alive.

A sob tore through her like a riptide and she curled up on her side, digging fingers into the sand, muffling her screams in her arm. Even on land, it felt like she was still under the water. Breathing air, yet drowning, the memory of the bay gushing into her car, pouring into her lungs, crashing like waves against the inside of her skull.

Maybe it would help if she could remember how she'd made it out of the car. How she'd fought her way back to the surface. But the only memory that stuck was the grim determination of her drive across the bridge, the way she'd fought to school the anxiety that rose with each passing mile that took her further from the coast, and ever closer to her parents' house in Northern Virginia.

A day at the Maryland beaches had seemed like a good idea at the time. All she'd wanted was a moment to walk the boardwalk and watch the waves. Nothing ever calmed her quite like a visit to the shore. A long drive for a such a short stay. But it would get her head in the right space before she told her parents that yes, their second child was *also* gay.

Then that car switched lanes on the Bay Bridge, knocking into hers, making her overcorrect into the guard rail. Metal screeching. Sickening nothing. Tires spinning through air, desperately seeking grip. The blank disbelief that she was flying off the bridge, towards her death.

And impact. Pain as her body lurched back into the seat. Terror as the guardrail pinned her in place, as the cracked windshield vomited water around her ankles, her lap, her shoulders.

She'd always hated that fucking bridge. Drove across with white knuckles and clenched teeth, and what good had that done in the end?

Now, flopped on the wet sand, nothing felt real. Nothing but the sick loop of the car driving off the bridge. Over and over and over.

The panicked sobs wracked through her until she was spent, until all she could do was lie there, staring at the sand, wondering why the only thing she could focus on was that she would be late for dinner. That she still needed to have "The Talk" with her parents.

What a joke. In her mid-twenties and still terrified of disappointing her parents after a near-death experience.

"Hey, hon, you okay?" someone shouted.

Dina struggled to sit up, every limb stiff and noncompliant. Something wet and furry and smelling of ocean water approached, and she found herself being licked by a warm, wet tongue. It was a testament to how out of it Dina was that she barely minded the dog's excited snuffling.

"Hey, stop that, you ratty dog," the mutt's owner called.

The dog retreated, brown tail wagging behind it, tongue lolling happily.

An older white man had approached and now hovered over her, squinting as he gripped a makeshift walking stick of driftwood. Now that Dina was somewhat upright, she could see the boneyard of trees all around, pale bark jutting from the sand like tombstones.

"The hell you doin' way out here?" he asked, all vowels and slurred consonants.

Dina coughed and wiped her salt-crusted hair from her eyes. The brown of it was completely obscured by all the sand she'd managed to accumulate, and her pale fingers were still puckered from their soak in the bay.

"Out where?" she asked, taking in the stretch of beach. It looked like pretty much anywhere along the Mid-Atlantic. She must have been swept out to the ocean, ended up downstream. Or however you described ocean currents. She'd never had a head for science. Barely even thought of it during her day-to-day as an accountant.

"South side of Little Hunting Island. What, you swallow too much sea water?"

Dina shook her head, as if it truly was full of water. "Little Hunting Island?"

"North of Tybee," the man elaborated. The longer they talked, the more worry slipped into his voice.

"But that's not..." she trailed off, eying the treacherous waves, gentle crests of gray and white lapping at the sand. How fast did water travel from the Chesapeake to the Carolinas? She'd have been long dead. Should have been. But she'd only been knocked out for a moment. Right?

The last of her breath, squeezing from her lungs, hissed through her memories.

"I think you need some help, hon. Can you walk?"

The man held out a wrinkled hand.

"Think so." Dina hobbled to her feet with his help. Swayed. The old man steadied her and brought her hand to the walking stick. Dina had always been slight, but she'd never been weak. Not like this.

"Think you need this more than I do."

Dina leaned heavily on the stick, letting the man guide her through the dunes and maze of skeletal trees. Back to a rusted out, once forest green pickup truck, parked right on the sand. The mutt hopped into the back, while she crawled into the passenger seat, legs shaking, too worn out to care if getting into a stranger's car was a stupid idea. Her mother would have a panic attack when Dina told her. *If* Dina told her.

The truck smelled of long days by the beach, old tobacco and salt. It turned over when the man put the key in the ignition, groaning, as if reluctant to be put to use. The motor growled as the man drove from the beach to a flat stretch of asphalt.

"Look, there's an urgent care, 'bout a half hour from here. I'm gonna take you there and have you looked over. Think you have a concussion or somethin'. Anyone I can call for you?"

The truck swerved as the man fished around for a cell phone. Dina squeezed her eyes shut against the unwelcome memory of the car falling through the air, into the bay. Breathed through her nose as the truck stayed on the pavement and the drive evened out.

Dina reached into her jean pocket, feeling the weight of her own phone. Took it out to confirm it'd been bricked from the extended soak in the Atlantic. She'd deal with that later.

The man's thumb hovered over the keypad expectantly.

"Uh, yeah it's..." she trailed off, willing the loose combination of 4's and 0's in her head to form the number she'd known her whole life. The landline her parents had kept long past its usefulness.

"Gimme a minute," she grunted, cradling her aching head in her hands. If her head could just clear, if the pounding and crashing inside her skull could just go away, instead of getting worse with each minute, maybe she'd be able to think straight.

"Sure, sure. Phone's here whenever you're ready," he said, placing the mobile in the cup holder, right beside an old soda bottle with something dark swirling around the bottom. Dina nearly vomited again, realizing it was a spit jar for chewing tobacco. Yikes.

"Where you from?" the man asked.

Dina struggled to string two thoughts together, to connect the maelstrom in her head to her vocal chords. Instead, she could only navigate a torrent of wordless wants. A familiar face. Her parents' kitchen, their glass mezuzah beneath her fingers as she brushed through the doorway on a visit home. Zev there to ruffle her hair and call her "kid". Maybe for now, she'd settle for dry clothes.

"You got a name at least?" the man asked, turning on the heat when Dina started shivering.

She swallowed a lump of phlegm and found her voice.

"Dina," she said. "Dina Adler."

"Well, Dina Adler, I'm Tom Jessup. And I'm gonna make sure you get to a doctor, and then we'll all figure out how to help you get home, alright?"

Home. She didn't think of the apartment she spent far too much money on, just outside of D.C. The room that smelled of curry and spices from the Thai restaurant below her window. She thought of cut grass and yellow shutters on cookie-cutter siding. A table set for four instead of three. Not that her parents had even acknowledged Zev's existence in years.

It surprised her to still think of that house as "home" when she'd known the conversation she was about to have might banish her from that place.

She supposed she should have arrived by now. Dinner would have started already, depending on how long she'd been knocked out. Her parents were probably phoning up the police, asking them to search for her sedan even though she'd only been missing a short while. Perhaps she'd learn to be grateful for their paranoia.

If she could just unscramble her thoughts, she could call them and reassure them that the dutiful daughter who called each and every night without fail was in one piece. She wouldn't think about everything that remained unsaid between them. She'd get home. Figure the rest out later.

The truck thrummed a comforting drone beneath her seat, vibrating through tired, washed-out limbs. The hum rose and rose, until she went from lolling easily against the headrest to rattling around in her own skull, the pressure seeming to squeeze her from the inside out.

When they crested a bump in the road, Dina jolted forward, clutching her head again. The buzzing became interminable.

"Do you hear that?" Dina gasped, fingers digging into the skin at her temples, though the pain was hardly a distraction.

Tom said something Dina didn't catch, the roar of noise surging through her, the rush of water vibrating her apart. She wrapped her arms around her ribs, desperate to hold her rattling bones in place, gripping the smallest atoms of herself and clutching them one by one as she shook and shattered apart.

The dog was barking loudly. Someone called her name, the tone and inflection all wrong. Unfamiliar as a ghost brushing past her ear. The solid seat of the truck became wisps, the world viscous, disappearing drop by drop, drained like rainwater down a gutter, all the texture and color leaching away.

Until nothing remained. Until Dina herself became nothing.

4

Ivy

The apartment complex Topher drove them to was so quaintly suburban Ivy could have laughed. All trimmed lawn and blue siding. A "Welcome to Riverside Suites" sign in looping script by the parking lot. She imagined this was what Hallmark movies looked like. The only thing stopping the wry mirth was the grave dirt still caked in her hair, embedded beneath her nails, and staining her clothes.

That, and the last words Topher spoke before ushering her into a rented sedan.

You died.

She pressed a hand to her chest for the millionth time, reassured when the steady beat of her heart pulsed against the dirty palm.

If this was death, it sure wasn't anything Ivy had ever pictured. No dark abyss, no freedom from the lightning-quick anger in her veins. Just stiff limbs, a mind that couldn't focus for shit, and skin that itched from soaking in dirt for too long.

Topher parked in the lot behind the apartment complex, right between a minivan and an SUV. Turned off the car and leaned back, regarding Ivy over their shoulder.

"You have questions, I'd bet," they said, adjusting a pair of round glasses that glinted in the light of a nearby streetlamp. The reflection made their expression difficult to discern. Ivy hated that she couldn't read them, map out whatever their intent was in bringing her to this place. Was it all another part of Lenox's plans to punish her? Pretend to save her before turning her over to a fate worse than a knife through the ribs?

She wasn't sure how long she sat there staring at Topher, thinking through every scenario that resulted in her making it out of this car in one piece. Letting the heat in her blood simmer and boil, wondering if she should simply jump out now, make a run for it before she could discover what Topher was hiding. Assuming her recently dead body would cooperate.

But Topher simply waited, as if they had all the time in the world.

Well, at least if they were here to torture her, they weren't in a rush. Ivy could work with that. Besides, they weren't wrong.

"Fucking hell," she burst out. "Of course I have questions." The words came out scratchy, throat and lungs still remembering how to work in tandem.

Topher nodded, nonplussed by her snarling. The woman, Lucia, kept trying to make eye contact with Topher, but after a while, gave up and crossed her arms, staring out the windshield.

"Wanna come in and take a shower first?" Topher asked. They had an air about them like a camp counselor handling a tantrum. The implication of that train of thought made Ivy bristle all the more.

"No, asshole. I want to know what the fuck you mean I fucking died."

"Looked to me like you got stabbed," Lucia contributed. "And if you're going to curse, you could at least be creative about it. And maybe think twice, since we pulled your sorry ass out of the ground."

Great. Another kindergarten teacher.

"No shit, I got stabbed," Ivy muttered. "I mean, how am I, like…here if I died? Not like you had a defibrillator or some shit on you."

"Don't think a defibrillator would have done much anyway," Topher said, continuing to ignore Lucia's obvious discomfort and the fact that Ivy was one wrong word away from scratching their eyes out. "Looked like you'd bled out a while ago. Though no more than a week if you're holding to the same patterns as the rest of us."

Ivy ground her teeth. Nothing these people said made any sense. And where the hell was Lenox and the rest of the crew? Watching from the dark windows of one of the apartments above, or reveling in her supposed death? What about Pete? He'd bled out too. She'd watched those blue eyes go empty and dead, silver hair soaked crimson from his slit throat. But if she'd come back from the beyond, what about him?

That other grave snagged on her train of thought. But there was only one way to find out for sure. And it wasn't by spending another second in the car.

"Fuck it," she said, opening the door with far more force than was necessary. At least she hadn't lost too much of her strength. "Okay, yeah I do want a shower. And a drink."

"Demanding," Lucia muttered.

"Give her a break," Topher said. "She's new to this."

"She's also got functioning ears," Ivy muttered, letting herself out of the car.

If these two were offering her a shower, either they were some randos who'd come across her body in the woods, or they were working for Lenox. If it was the latter, she'd be ready to pounce on Topher, grab them by the neck and use them as a shield until she could get her hands on something useful. Preferably a knife. If the former...well she was sick of sitting in filth. And she needed to regroup. Get her wits about her and figure out why she wasn't rotting in the ground.

She slammed the car door shut and waited for the others to follow suit, keeping her eyes trained on every minuscule twitch as their footsteps echoed on the asphalt.

"This way," Topher said before loping towards the apartment building. Inviting window plants and faux roman columns greeted them on either side of the entryway. Domestic under the warmth of an incandescent bulb. Nothing like the "home" Lenox had offered. The manor house that served to put a roof over everyone's heads as they planned the next arms deal and discussed which rival gang was getting too close to their territory. A house in which you kept your knives and guns close at hand unless you were idiot enough to trust everyone that lived there.

You overstepped, Ivy, Lenox had said. Calm as a spring day, gray eyes glinting with satisfaction while she gasped and lashed out against Jason's grip. As she struggled for air while the bigger man crushed her windpipe with his forearm.

You know the rules. You break them and we break you.

Simple as that. Didn't matter that Lenox had been her guardian for as long as she could remember. That she'd been his heir. She was no exception. And she'd tried to leave. In his book, there was no greater crime. So no. That hadn't been home.

This new place was too orderly for her liking, the inviting entryway spilling into a white-washed hallway with several closed doors. As Topher led her through, she tilted a painting askew, slathered dirt on the pristine walls, leaving her mark before the stifling building could swallow her whole.

So many closed, blue doors. Any of them might be hiding someone ready to put her back in the ground and make sure she stayed there. Her limbs still had that creaking stiffness, but each step woke up more muscles, more pliancy and speed. She kept her fists tight, her senses alert, ready to spin around and claw at the fool who tried to jump her.

But she made it up the flight of stairs to the second floor apartment without anyone bursting out to put a bullet in her brain.

Topher opened a blue door with a silver "2D" nailed to the front and called over their shoulder, "We're a shoes off house." As if she'd come over for charcuterie or whatever shit Topher and Lucia did when they weren't digging women out of the ground.

Ivy rolled her eyes, still vibrating with anticipation, but slipped out of her Docs after glancing around the apartment. No boogeymen hid behind the overstuffed couches as far as she could tell. Despite removing the shoes, her feet left a satisfying trail of soil on the clean, wooden floors.

"This way," Topher said, motioning her to follow as Lucia flopped into the loveseat. She didn't doubt there would be an interesting exchanging of words once she left the room.

But neither seemed as nervous about bringing Ivy in as she would have expected. Which was annoying. Usually the combination of her dozen or so ear piercings, undercut, and Resting Bitch Face was enough to make folks sweat.

The bathroom Topher showed her was…pink. All shades of it. From the toilet to the rose gold frame of the mirror. She raised a brow.

Topher shrugged. "AirBnb. Never know what you're gonna get. Not my choice of decor, but the water pressure's decent. Towels and clothes in the cabinet."

Without another word, they left, allowing Ivy a moment to herself. A moment to realize that clothes in the bathroom cabinet meant someone had known she or someone else might need them. Whatever was going on with Topher and Lucia, they hadn't found her by accident.

She waited a moment, cracked the door, and held her breath, listening to the whisper-yells of an argument ensuing.

"We don't have to save them all, Toph. Yeah, okay. You were right about her. But have you not noticed her entire attitude screams bloody murder? I don't know about you, but I don't want a knife in my back because you decided to bring home a loose cannon."

"She's just on edge. You were too when we met, remember?"

"That was different. She's...I dunno, Topher. Dangerous. I know you're trying to help but—"

"Look, we'll get her back on her feet. It's the least we can do. We've already got a head start in comparison to her."

"And the others? You really want to take the time to focus on this one when there are others who need us?"

"This is the job we picked, Luz."

The conversation seemed to dissolve into what Ivy imagined involved a lot of sighing and long stares communicating more than words. She closed the door, relieved a bit that she wasn't likely to get jumped by anyone any time soon, but just as confused as ever. There was no mention of Lenox or Pete. And these two appeared to believe what they'd told her. That she had died.

Then how the fuck am I standing here?

She forced in a deep breath before a panic could sink in and turn her vision black. Shook out her tense limbs.

Alright, Ivy, one step at a time. And step one is taking a damn shower.

She yanked her hair free of its bun, shocked to find the interior bits of straight black strands salvageable. It took a while to dismantle the dirt and blood encrusted garb meant to be her funeral attire. Everything was ruined, it didn't matter that the clothes had been black to begin with. Even if they weren't disgusting, Ivy didn't want to look at these clothes ever again. The fabric reeked of grave dirt, conjured the memory of low voices and cruel smiles as Lenox told her how disappointed he was. The ache and anger that those words could still hurt.

The worst part was the cotton tank top, still sticking to her torso with all manner of grit and grime. She winced as she peeled it away, dumped it on the floor, kicked it into the pile of other discarded clothes along with her bra.

She didn't look at the wound. Not even as she turned on the shower, hissing with relief when rivulets of water cut through the dirt, freeing pale skin from its tomb, waking muscular limbs. Not until the water ran cold and clear as it circled her feet, making the most of the high pressure of a shower more luxurious than any she'd ever had access to. Lenox kept such treasures for himself.

She was going to have to face it sooner or later.

Come on. You can do this.

Her hands crept up her ribs as she stared hard at the pink tile, groped for the ragged entryway of the dagger, waited for the searing, deep pain.

And found nothing. Only smooth, unbroken skin.

She squeezed her eyes shut. Gulped. Looked down at her torso.

Nothing. Not even a scar.

She leaned her forehead against the slick tile, shivering under the chilly water, uncaring as it cascaded down the back of her legs.

Fucking Lenox. The sneer on his brutish, square face as he ordered her execution. A thump as Pete's body fell to the concrete floor, hours before Lenox had finally decided to put her out of her misery. The gasp of metal finding the space between ribs, the way it stole her breath. The useless clawing of her hands on Jason's shirt, his throat, pulling out chunks of his blond hair. The thunk of shovels and dirt burying her inert flesh.

Ivy gasped in a breath, shaking from cold or rage, she wasn't sure. But she shut off the tap and retrieved a towel (pink of course), wrapping it around her shivering body as she considered the clean clothes Topher had left. She needed to know what their whispered conversation meant and how it fit into the fragmented memories of those last moments.

She pulled on the black tee and gray sweats that were far too wide, cinching them tight to her waist.

Topher didn't seem all that flustered about the fact that she was supposedly one of the walking dead. In fact, Lucia's only hang up appeared to be Ivy's charming personality. Not all that unusual really.

So she'd get some answers from them. Figure out why her body showed no signs of what should have been a death sentence. Plan her next steps.

But no matter how she viewed the situation, she'd been given a second chance.

Lenox was going to regret that.

5

IVY

The whiskey in Ivy's mason jar tasted like plastic, but the burn soothed her agitation all the same as she eyed the notebook in Topher's hand. One of those mottled black-and-white ones with an empty oval you could fill in on the cover. Across theirs someone had scribbled the words: "Handbook for the Recently Deceased."

Topher lifted their eyes from the notes they were scribbling down and gave her a tilted smile from their spot on the mauve couch. "It's a joke."

"Topher loves Beetlejuice," Lucia added, when Ivy only stared.

Ivy rolled her eyes. Fucking nerds. "Never seen it."

"Movie night," Topher sang, as if they were all old friends, making plans for the coming weekend. Plans that didn't involve theft or price tags on someone's head, or the removal of someone's lackey who'd wandered too close to Lenox's turf. No, Ivy had never had much time for movies.

She took another swig. Grimaced at the aftertaste as she settled further into the loveseat. No time for movies, but even *she* drank better whiskey than this. Jesus.

"So what does your handbook say about my sitch?" Ivy asked, holding the mason jar with the tips of her fingers and glaring at the contents, as if that might result in a better brand of booze.

"Well, if your experience follows the usual pattern, you died about seven days ago. Any minute now, we'll find out how your Resurrection is going to present itself."

Ivy glanced up, eyes darting between her two unlikely companions, sitting side by side in an odd recreation of a parent teacher conference. Not that Ivy had ever attended one of those.

"Resurrection? What are we? Glorified zombies?"

Lucia grimaced, but Topher chuckled. "Not quite. Unless you've suddenly developed an appetite for brains?" When Ivy frowned, they continued. "I prefer calling us 'The Resurrected'. Sounds more super-heroe-y."

"Sounds pretentious as fuck."

Topher shrugged. "The others haven't seemed to mind."

"And Topher just ignores the ones who do," Lucia said.

Topher ignored her.

"Others?" Ivy had made a thorough check of the hallway and bedrooms following her shower. Still no hint that Lucia and Topher were anything other than a couple of well-meaning, if confusing, people. Still, she took another look around the disgustingly pink living room.

"Not here," Lucia explained. Her arms had remained crossed since Ivy sat down. Now, she drummed her fingers on one arm, annoyed. Or nervous maybe.

She almost didn't ask. Didn't want to give any more of herself away than the situation required. But she owed Pete at least this much. She could afford a breath of vulnerability. Just for this.

"Did you find anyone else out there with me?"

Lucia went tight-lipped. That was answer enough.

"There was another grave," Topher said quietly. "But the body had decomposed more than yours, which meant the timing wasn't right for Resurrection. I'm sorry. Did you know them?"

"Not well," Ivy said without blinking. Even as she saw Pete's dead, blue eyes staring at the floor while Jason kicked her in the stomach again and again. She wasn't sure how long the abuse went on before he finally lifted her up, pinned her against the wall, and shoved a knife into her chest on Lenox's command.

"So how many of these Resurrected are there?" Ivy asked before she could let the memory take her. Before she could grieve the man who'd tried to get her out for good. Before she could remember him clapping a hand on her shoulder when she'd snuck him the acceptance letter for a trade school in New York.

Lucia took her cue and shook her head, allowing the conversation to move past the dead body in the proverbial trunk. "We don't know. The first time this happened, about four years ago, we were able to track down a lot of the others. But with this second wave—"

Ivy nearly choked on the next swig of whiskey. When she'd finished coughing and spluttering, she leaned forward.

"Wait, back up. You mean this is a *thing* that *happens*? Like...regularly?"

Topher shrugged. "Not regularly. Or predictably. But it happens all at once. The Resurrected that came back to life four years ago all died on the same day, within a few minutes of each other."

Ivy furrowed her brow. "But like...why? How?"

Topher looked thoughtful. "What do you know about black holes and quantum physics?"

Ivy stared. "Fuck dude, I didn't even finish high school. Give me a break."

"But you understand radiation, right?"

"Uh..."

"Think Chernobyl," Lucia provided. "Black holes—their accretion disks to be precise—emit radiation. Kind of like a nuclear plant explosion. But we think they're emitting more than radiation. We think they're producing tachyon particles."

Ivy felt like she'd been dropped into one of those nightmares where you didn't know the lines to the show you were starring in. "Uh...tachyon..."

"Tachyon particles," Lucia said, nodding. "They're these theoretical particles that travel faster than light and essentially travel in time. Scientists don't even believe they exist. They're purely theoretical."

"Right," Topher said, clearly satisfied that this had explained everything. Ivy thought it explained fuck all.

They continued, ignorant of the way Ivy was considering hurling the mason jar at their head. "From time to time, astrophysicists observe black hole anomalies. Flares, or bursts of energy coming from their accretion disks. And no one knows what happens as a result. Yeah, there's an uptick in radiation and they could be emitting more of these tachyon particles, but you wouldn't think it would affect anything here on Earth, right? But four years ago, at the same moment that anomaly occurred, scientists were able to observe these changes in gravitational waves, indicating something big was happening in one of these black holes. And the last time that happened, people came back from the dead."

Ivy waved her hands in front of her, rejecting this revelation. "Absolutely not. No way people came back from the dead four years ago and no one fucking noticed."

Lucia sighed. "It wasn't many of us. And most of us have kept quiet about it. Built new lives. Besides, who's going to believe you when you tell them you're alive after they saw you die from a snake bite?"

The woman immediately bit her lip, as if she'd said too much. Interesting.

Topher fumbled around for a moment and produced a laptop, opening it to spreadsheet full of random numbers. The file was labeled 'LIGO_GravWave_Events'.

"So, on a normal day in space," Topher continued, as if such a thing existed, "a black hole is emitting x-rays and bursts of gamma rays. Chewing up stars, while also amplifying the formation of new ones. There are whole observatories studying this stuff, right from *this* planet."

They gestured towards the spreadsheet, which was about as readable as hieroglyphics as far as Ivy was concerned.

"And this connects to my situation because…"

"Because if a black hole is emitting all this radiation on an ordinary day, if it's shooting out these tachyon particles on a normal day, what *can't* a black hole do when there's an anomaly of activity?" They shut the laptop with a dramatic snap.

Ivy shook her head, trying to keep up. "That makes no sense. How would that bring people back to life?"

"To quote the Doctor, 'Life's easy, a quirk of matter'."

Ivy blinked. "Uh…what doctor?"

Topher sighed, shoulders slumping. "You were supposed to say 'Doctor Who?'."

"Ignore them," Lucia said, barely sparing Topher a glance. "When they get on a nerdy tirade, there's no stopping them."

Topher opened their mouth, but Lucia jumped in before Topher could start on what looked to be another "nerdy tirade".

"Look, we don't fully understand why this happens. We have theories. Scientists don't even know if these tachyon particles exist. But what we *think* is happening is that those tachyon particles are arriving in bursts following these anomalies. And they could be playing with time, bringing people back to the moment right before they died. Healing them essentially, but with some weird flukes."

Ivy examined her hands. She hadn't grown any extra fingers, and she couldn't feel any extra toes. "What do you mean by flukes?"

Lucia shook her head. "We'll get into that. But what matters is that four years ago, a few dozen people or more—we're not sure—came back from the dead. The only thing they had in common was the fact that they'd died within minutes of each other. To put it in simple terms, Topher's been studying the patterns of radiation and gravity that came from outer space on the day *we* came back from the dead. An indicator that this theoretical burst of tachyons started messing with things on Earth. Recently, they saw some similar patterns going on and thought we were going to have another wave of Resurrections. And well, you're proof that they're right. So now we're going to try to find the others before—"

"Before they get too confused by the whole situation," Topher chimed back in.

Lucia barely blinked, but Ivy knew a nervous tic when she saw one. It was the ill-timed swallow. The way she played with a ring on her finger. Lucia and Topher might not be working with Lenox, but they had their own secrets.

Unlike these two, she knew how to hide behind a mask. She said nothing, kept her expression easily neutral.

"You'll have noticed that waking up from death can be rather disorienting," Topher continued, as if there'd been no strange pause in conversation. "We're here to ease the way into your new life. Get you connected to resources. Think of us as your mentors."

"So...you two," Ivy said, bracing herself with another disgusting swallow of whiskey, "are dead?"

"As a doorknob," Topher replied cheerfully.

Lucia frowned, clasping her hands together on her lap. "Not exactly. We're still mostly human as far as we can tell. Still breathe. Still get hurt. It's not the same as being dead. We died and came back."

"So literally undead," Ivy pointed out, rubbing at her temple. When was she going to wake from this nightmare? Not that the preceding years had been much better, but at least she'd understood the rules.

"I suppose," Lucia admitted with a noncommittal shrug.

"Like I said, 'the Resurrected' has a kinder ring to it," Topher added.

Ivy rolled her eyes. "If it's a duck, call it a fucking duck."

Lucia grimaced. The woman continued to nurse her immediate dislike of Ivy, but she could roll with the discomfort better than Topher's apparent ease.

"Well," Ivy said, finishing her drink and placing the mason jar on the table without bothering to find a coaster. "Thanks for the ride and the clothes. I'll be off."

"You can't go," Lucia said, eyes wide, brows narrowed in confusion. "You just woke up!"

"Yeah, and you're telling me I was dead and came back for round two. Well, since I'm still kicking, I've got business to attend to."

"Ivy," Topher said with a gentleness that crawled over Ivy's skin like centipedes in a grave. "For all intents and purposes, you're dead. You've been dead for a week. Whatever life you had has moved on without you. Your bank accounts are being closed, your apartment is being cleared out. Whatever you're trying to get back to isn't there."

"Assuming I had any of those things to begin with," Ivy said, standing and crossing to the door, already picturing the hoard of cash she'd squirreled away, deep beneath Meridian Playground, safe from the others. Even from Lenox, though she was meant to be handing over every penny to him for the gift of being kept in his good graces. For having a roof over her head and his so-called protection, even if it came with knives hiding around every corner.

Topher sighed. "You're right, I'm assuming a lot. What I mean is things are going to be different from whatever it is you're picturing. We've seen it happen before. You really want to attend your own memorial service? It really fucks with you."

"That happen to you?" Ivy asked, gripping the door with a sweaty palm. She doubted Lenox had thought to hold her a memorial after ordering her execution. What a farce that would have been. No one in attendance but a circle of people who wanted her dead so they could climb over her body to get closer to the top of the chain. To claim her spot as his heir.

"Maybe if you sit back down and stay a minute, I'll tell you. Maybe even give you all the details on how this works."

"Nah, thanks."

"Alright, suit yourself."

"Jesus dude, would you cut it with the kindergarten crap?" Ivy seethed, turning over her shoulder. She should have been out the door already. Why was she even bothering?

"There are things you don't know yet, Ivy. Things we can tell you. You're not ready to go it alone."

"Bullshit," she hissed.

Heat coiled in her veins, raced through her blood as though someone had poured melted ore across her skin, injected it into her veins. But instead of searing, the heat satisfied, lighting her flesh to match the rage in her heart, dripping down her arms and torso, molding to her like a carapace of armor.

"Fucking hell," Lucia whispered.

Topher paled a touch, but held Ivy's gaze.

Her forearm split from wrist to elbow. From the flesh, a long blade, the white of bone and sharp as any razor, broke free. Clattered to the floor. Glinted up at her and teased her to violence.

She stared at the thing, frozen. The whiskey sloshing around her stomach threatened to make a nasty return through her esophagus.

Had she really just seen that? *Done* that?

This isn't real, she thought, even as she leaned down to pick up the blade, heart in her throat.

The second her fingertips touched the hilt, it fit into her hand as though it was part of her once again. She tested the point with her thumb, swallowed a hiss when it drew blood. The wound stitched itself back together before she could even shove her thumb into her mouth.

This isn't real.

But she'd felt that cut. That dagger had come from her own body.

They're not bullshitting. I did come back from the dead. But there was no sorrow with the thought. She'd brought something special back from the grave.

A grin split her face. Wide and ruthless.

Well then.

"Ivy," Topher cautioned. "I know we just met, but whatever you're thinking, let's just take a breath, alright?"

Ivy slid her thumb across the flat of the blade, then pressed it to the inside of her forearm. Her skin engulfed the dagger once more.

It was perfect. Lenox would never see it coming.

"Ivy," Lucia called.

But she was already out the door, bursting out of the apartment, letting the night enfold her into open arms.

IN THE WATER

*T*he *current ebbs and flows. Sharp and tearing, and then gentle. Soothing. She rises with the crest of each wave, crashes into a million droplets. Here there is no hunger, no cold or fear. There is only the water.*

And the water carries her along, a strange traveler caught in gyrations and whirlpools. Floating in the sky with the clouds, falling to the ocean's surface with the rain. Barely aware of where she has ventured, not knowing when she will come together once more.

In the waves, she breaks apart, over and over, and somehow, inevitably pieces herself together again. The memory of a girl flung into a distant bay, who resurfaced once more by some fluke of nature. Even the water does not understand, nor does it try.

But here, the water grows colder. The crashing strength of the sea giving way to something smoother. Water with power for all its quietude. It is water that carves through rocks that have stood for eons. It brings life and soothes the soil. Water that carries stories from one shore to the next. And her with it.

6

IVY

Lenox's crew may have been too hasty to dig her a proper grave, but they certainly hadn't skimped when it came to stealing any earthly belongings she'd had on her person. Wallet, phone, hidden butterfly knife, all were gone by the time she'd woken up. The borrowed clothes on her back weren't much to start an afterlife with. But she'd made her way with less in her first life.

And stealing Topher's car keys while they and Lucia had been busy pouring drinks in the kitchen had helped immensely. She wouldn't be able to hold on to her new ride for long, especially since it was a rental. Topher had probably called the cops on her already. But she'd see how far she could get before they caught up.

She drove through the afternoon, until the sparse suburban houses gave way to apartment complexes and storefronts. Found a quiet street that was unlikely to host security cameras, and ditched the car.

It had been a long drive. Someone had dumped her body all the way west of Monroe for chrissakes. But it gave her time to think. To test how easily she could produce and disappear the bone dagger. Contemplate how best to use the advantage of her supposed death.

She walked the rest of the way to the mechanic shop Lenox favored. He'd bought the place years ago when he'd eked out his own territory after years of "doing other men's dirty work". Work that he subsequently delegated to others like Ivy as he bullied his way up the ladder of the underground. Didn't mean his hands had been any cleaner.

In the past decade, business had been booming. If someone needed guns or drugs, Lenox could negotiate a deal. He had a finger in every pie in the city, had even begun stretching his reach further afield, sending his crew to set up fronts in New York, Philly, anywhere he could get a foothold. He'd become a force to be reckoned with when it came to illegal trade.

But he kept the mechanic shop. It had been the perfect cover until recently. People would bring their cars to get fixed, and some would walk away with nothing more than a repaired vehicle with a brand new (stolen) catalytic converter. Others would come in for an oil change. If they also left with their trunk filled with unregistered weapons, or pharmaceuticals that weren't strictly legal, well, no one was the wiser.

In the past few months though, work had begun to dry up. The only customers they received were the ones looking for actual car repairs and "thank you for the new brakes, I'll be on my way". Ivy wasn't surprised when Lenox told her they had a mole leaking information to the police, building a case strong enough to bring Lenox's expanding empire crashing down around him.

She *was* surprised at how quickly he'd found out it was her, the heir to said empire.

She'd gotten greedy. It wasn't enough to shuck off her role as Lenox's heir, to walk away from a life of blood and constant paranoia. She'd wanted Lenox to pay for all those years. For the so-called childhood he'd given her. Long nights locked in a closet instead of simply being grounded. Getting brought along on jobs instead of attending clubs, playing soccer, any of the normal shit kids got to do.

She hadn't known anything different. And the second she realized there was more, she couldn't smother the burning hatred in her gut, the rage of wasted years hungry for retribution.

So while Pete helped her with school applications and forging a new identity—one Sarah Smith among many—she'd hatched another plan. She'd thought leaving anonymous tips to the police would be a surefire way of bringing Lenox down, making sure he could never reel her back in. It was supposed to be safe.

So much for that. She hadn't expected Lenox to buy the loyalty of one of the so-called "good cops". And she was an idiot for thinking she might ever be safe while Lenox still breathed.

Well, at least he'd given her a ticket out and an upper hand, even if that had never been his intent.

Walking with borrowed shoes left the bottoms of her feet blistered, and the clothes were strange against her skin. But it didn't matter. Not if she could wipe Lenox off the face of the planet.

This close to evening on a weekday, he'd be in the upstairs office, checking the books to keep the farce of a garage operating. Then he'd be down in the basement, checking numbers and crates for the real work. Maybe even planning out the next deal, the next hit. He might have some muscle around, but not much until he headed back to his fortified home in Ballard. It would be a tight window assuming the clock in the car was correct, but she'd make it just fine.

As the closed-up garage came into view, Ivy let the heat, the fury, pool through her veins, down her arms for the umpteenth time. Loosing daggers from sheaths of flesh to fit into both hands.

The universe had never been on her side 'til now. A gun would be better. Safer and faster. But she had a major advantage. Two really. Lenox and his crew thought she was dead. And they certainly wouldn't be expecting her to come back as a weapon.

I only became what you made me.

The whole "heir" thing had started when she was a teen. Lenox had survived a deal gone sour, but not without the bullet wounds to show for it. And not without an uncharacteristic fear for his own mortality.

Ivy could still smell the stink of sweat and blood, feel his clammy, wide hand on her shoulder after he'd called her to his bedside. It was the first time Ivy had noticed the bits of gray speckled through his muddy brown hair. The lines carving his forehead and the sides of his mouth.

They'll call me soft for picking you, Iv. You'll always have a target on your back, and you won't thank me for it. But I raised you, didn't I? You know how I think, how I'd keep this whole business afloat. You're smart enough not to start a turf war without cause. So it'll be you, Iv. You'll carry on if I die.

And those words had coiled around her like some facsimile of care. For years, it had been enough to be at the top of Lenox's chain of command. To think he might actually give a shit about this wayward, scrapheap girl he'd raised to be a fighter. To wield guns and knives with calm precision.

It all seemed like such bullshit now.

The windows of the garage were dark, though that didn't mean anything. Avoiding the security cameras was easier than breathing. She'd been doing it for years now. Not all the time, not enough to draw suspicion (or so she'd thought), but enough that it came naturally. In no time at all, she was inching along the outside facade, peeking inside, body low, eyes and ears in hyperdrive, and daggers ready.

Nothing moved. Not in the garage, nor the small office where customers came in with their car complaints, real or falsified.

She considered her options. There certainly wasn't a key under the mat to conveniently grant her access. Nor could she break a window. Too much noise. The only saving grace was that Lenox didn't pay for security by official means. Trusted in hired help over a security system that might alert the wrong cop, or even the one he'd bribed to look the other way.

The daggers called to her, waiting in her hands, ready to draw blood and end this dance once and for all. Useless if Lenox caught onto her before she could get close. She should have brought wire to pick the lock.

As if reacting to her thoughts, the dagger in her left hand shifted, shrinking to the size of a porcupine needle, the edge of the blade still winking sharp.

A grin grew, wicked and bright across her face. With careful movement, she approached the door. Stuck the point in the lock. If she was quick, she could take out whatever guard Lenox had on duty before anyone noticed. Then it would be a short trip down the steps. She'd spill his hot red blood across the ground. Pry off his shackle at last.

She jimmied the tool in the lock.

The door swung open before she could even work her magic. Simply pushed in, as if in welcome.

She froze, hair sticking up on her arms, the back of her neck, causing her undercut to feel unusually prickly. The cool night air became ice along her spine.

The fuck?

She shook off the hesitation after a moment and crept inside, making sure the door made no sound as it closed behind her. Listened for a moment, expecting the familiar murmur of voices to rise from beneath the rug hiding the entrance to the crew's real main office.

Quiet as the grave and emptier than a tomb. She would know.

With shaking hands, Ivy consumed the daggers back into her skin. Dragged the rug away. She didn't even bother being quiet when she tilted up the door hidden in the floor boards. Just swung it wide open and fished around for the light switch.

Nothing. No sound. No light. The rotten bastard must have stopped paying electricity.

It took a long time for Ivy's eyes to adjust to the faint light of sunset streaming in through the garage windows, just barely illuminating the ground floor office. But even when she was finally able to locate a packet of matches, even when she took in the interior of the hideout, gleaming red and orange in the match's light, it revealed what she already knew. The reason Lenox and the crew hadn't bothered hiding her body when they'd dumped her.

They were already long gone.

You thought you were clever? Lenox laughed. Just as he had after the crew had ambushed her and Pete, stuck a knife through his throat as they pinned her down.

You've never been clever, Ivy. Just stubborn, and idiotic enough to think that made you strong. I made you, kid. And I will break you apart for this.

She lit another match. Found a broken piece of a crate left behind in the move. Waited until the flames caught the wood and made sure the stairs would be its next kindling, leading bread crumbs of fuel upstairs.

And walked out without even bothering to close the door behind her.

Topher and Lucia barely batted an eye when Ivy let herself back into the apartment two hours later. Both were seated on opposite ends of the couch with laptops out, the screens tilted such that Ivy couldn't make out what was on them.

Topher closed theirs and put it on the coffee table, instead, picking up a half-filled pint glass of a pale looking beer.

"How's the car?" they asked, taking a swig.

Ivy flopped into the loveseat, tossing the keys to Topher, which they handily caught. She would have envied their unflappability if it weren't so irritating.

"In one piece. Though you seem the type to pay for that bullshit insurance rental companies are always bullying you into."

Topher shrugged. "You never know when someone might steal your car. Though I'm wondering why you decided to bring it back."

From the looks of it, they and Lucia had expected such an outcome. But it didn't mean Ivy hadn't been asking herself the same damn question the whole ride back. Once she'd vacated the abandoned front, she'd walked back to the car and sat behind the wheel, listening to the approach of sirens coming to put out the fire. Fighting the urge to take out the dregs of her anger on the car windows and mirrors since Lenox hadn't provided her with a suitable target.

It was all for nothing, Pete. You thought you were helping some fucked up girl unfuck her life. And it was all for nothing.

She'd already swung by her hiding spot to pick up her stash of cash. If she started now, took back roads, she could probably get a bit further before the police recognized her plates. Drive east and then...

And then?

Where would she even go? She didn't have a plan, not like before when she'd laid out the steps to her escape as carefully as a brick mason. And most of the plan had involved trying to stay alive for just one more day. One more. One more. Except the "one mores" had dried up.

It was sitting there, spiraling, that she reached for the dagger again, feeling the heat of it well up in her left arm. There had to be more to this new power that she could learn. Something more useful than just stabbing through the dark and hoping the point would catch Lenox at the jugular. She would make them pay for taking her life. Pitiful as it had been, it was hers, dammit. And Pete had deserved better than a slit throat for the sin of helping her.

"I need to know more," Ivy admitted at last. Revealing the ignorance was the same as opening up a chink in armor. She hated saying it aloud. But Topher and Lucia were all too eager to share their stories, seemed to crave the mentorship Ivy had rejected, to be made important because they had knowledge someone else didn't. For now, that was useful.

"What do you want to know?" Lucia asked, looking skeptical. Did she ever do anything but frown?

Ivy waved between the two of them. "What is all this? How did you even find me? What are your powers? Your limits? Tell me everything."

Lucia quirked her brow. "You wanted nothing to do with us. Why so eager all of a sudden?"

"This is my life now, isn't it? Shouldn't I want to know?"

"Just seemed you were ready to go about things on your own, leave us in the dust. Why the change of heart? Empty house not to your liking?"

"How did you—"

"I can guess. You're not the only one who's been through this." The tone was annoyed. Well, Ivy was plenty annoyed herself.

"Fine, I'm not a special snowflake," Ivy said, flapping a hand dismissively. "Now just tell me what the fuck is going on."

Lucia shut her mouth tight, nose flaring a bit. Ivy tended to have that effect on people. Usually it worked to her advantage. When people lost their patience, they were often more willing to slip up. This time she might have miscalculated.

Thankfully, Topher didn't disappoint. "Did you follow what Luz and I described before, about the tachyon particles?"

"Basically, a black hole did something weird and people started popping up out of their graves, yeah?"

Topher shrugged. "Pretty much. And when this happened four years ago, the people who came back developed powers related to how they died."

Can't argue with that.

She crossed her arms and leaned back into the chair. "And you figured out I was one of the so-called 'Resurrected'," she couldn't help rolling her eyes with the word, "how exactly?"

Topher opened their laptop and turned it towards Ivy. More rows of numbers she didn't understand.

"Uh…"

"Topher is a modeler," Lucia explained.

As if that was an explanation. Topher was pretty average looks wise. Had what one might describe as a dad bod. She couldn't imagine them walking a runway.

Seeing her confusion, Topher grinned. "I like equations. Mathematical models and trends. I stay as far from the catwalk as possible. But to answer your question, since the first round of Resurrected, I've tried to understand the pattern of the anomaly and who resurrected where. When we noticed the new blip, I decided to try it out."

"Huh, must be a good equation."

Topher turned the laptop back around and closed it again. "It still has plenty of kinks. Much of it is guesswork. That, and the Resurrected Law of Attraction."

"You made that up."

"I mean, obviously," Topher said, waving the Handbook for the Recently Deceased.

"Explain."

Topher looked at Lucia. "The Resurrected tend to have an inexplicable connection to each other. You'll feel it too, with time. We seem to stumble on each other even when we're not looking. Like atoms bouncing together and apart, or gravity pulling things towards each other. So we started looking on the outskirts of Seattle based on what the model was saying, and that Law of Attraction led us to a freshly dug grave. It was like…before we were even close enough to feel the tug we usually feel when another Resurrected is nearby, Luz and I both felt kind of drawn to that area of the woods. Honestly it was a huge relief when the bodies we found weren't *both* dead. That would have been awkward."

"Yeah, real awkward," Ivy grumbled, being one of the bodies in question.

"So that's the basics of how we come back and how we found you. What else do you want to know?"

Ivy felt for the dagger, the warm glow in her blood. Kept it locked in the skin but close enough to the surface for comfort. "Is there a limit to this?"

"Well, the Resurrected appear to...present in different ways. Someone who died in an explosion might be able to generate explosive heat or pressure for example. Your powers seems...shall we say, utilitarian. Lucia and I can help you figure out your limits. Our powers are different. However, I can tell you what else makes you different from a Single Lifer."

"And what's that, Professor?"

"Never finished my PhD, sadly," Topher said, taking another sip. Ivy rolled her eyes. Of course they were a fucking academic. "But we die differently now."

"What, like stake to the heart?"

"I mean that would definitely do it, but not what I meant. You can't die from the thing that killed you. It's as if your body is immune to it."

"So if someone tried to stab me..."

"You'd heal."

"And if I were burned alive?"

"I don't recommend it. But yeah, you'd die. We're not invincible. Not even close."

"And let's say I die again a different way. Would I come back with more powers?"

"Do you really want to find out?" Lucia asked, barely masking her disgust.

Ivy thought about it. She already had a huge advantage. If she chose the manner of her death though, she could hone her body into an indestructible weapon.

Then she remembered the grave, the sensation of being paralyzed under the dirt, insects crawling over her skin. Shuddered.

"Even if you tried, you'd have to plan it around an anomaly. And those are unpredictable."

Ivy shrugged. "All for the best. Wouldn't be my first choice."

Lucia narrowed her eyes, but kept her mouth shut.

"But how is a black hole giving people superpowers? Like how does this all work?" Ivy followed her instinct to pull the bone dagger free, contemplating the unnatural blade. She touched the tip to the coffee table, leaving an indent in the wood.

Topher sighed. "You're going to ruin my flawless AirBnB rating."

Ivy set the blade down and motioned for them to answer her question.

"Honestly?"

"Yeah, that'd be nice."

"Beyond what I've told you? Not a fucking clue," they said with a dissatisfying shrug. "We're not exactly astrophysicists by training. But we're trying to pass on the knowledge we *do* have to the new Resurrected. Make their second lives a bit easier. Encourage them to start over somewhere else and connect them to others like us."

Ivy nodded, an idea catching fuel in her head. Lenox and the others were on the run for now, but it wouldn't be long before they set up shop somewhere else in the world, somewhere he'd kept secret. He'd never talked back up plans in front of her, but he had to have one. Topher and Lucia had their network, but she had her own.

Keeping her face impassive, she asked, "And you two? How'd you die?"

"That's a bit rude," Lucia grumbled.

"You got to see me go from corpse to walking, talking zombie again. It's only fair," Ivy said, fingers sweeping an old scar along her brow. She prodded the side of her head, a faint ache pulsing through the bruise Jason had left when he knocked her down.

"Lucia's powers manifest through her connection to venom. I have an affinity for fire."

Topher snapped and a flame formed at the tips of their fingers. Flickered and went out. "I think that's all we need to share at the moment."

"Huh. Alright." It was a shame Topher didn't seem like a pyromaniac. That could have come in handy. "And what's up with this situation?" she asked, motioning between the two of them.

Lucia shrugged. "We just found each other."

Topher snorted. "That's putting it mildly. If I recall, you tried to kill me."

"Are you ever going to let that go? You were a walking fire hazard, and I thought you were going to burn my camp down."

"It wasn't on *purpose*," Topher insisted. "And you nearly paralyzed me to death."

How they could say those words and make it sound like an old married couple bickering, Ivy had no idea.

Lucia waved off the complaint. "Basically, Topher and I had a run in before either of us really figured out how our powers worked. I was camping out, trying to get by with the little cash I'd scraped together. They stumbled onto my campsite and we almost surprised each other to death."

"Thankfully," Topher continued, "we avoided a second untimely demise and pooled our limited resources to help each other get back on our feet. Figure out if there were others like us. Once we found more, things got easier."

The look they turned Ivy's way made her gut clench with suspicion. "So that's our story. Anything you'd care to share with the class yourself? We're good listeners you know," Topher offered. Again with the kindergarten shit.

Ivy stood and brought her mason jar, still sitting where she'd left it, to the kitchen island, pouring herself some more of the shitty whiskey. She took a swig, letting it burn to cover the heat trailing across her skin, to disguise the way she could feel more blades rippling under her flesh, eager to be embedded in someone's skull. Hopefully Lenox's.

She sat again. "Nah. But I want in."

"In?" Lucia asked, glancing at Topher.

"Yeah. On this whole shtick," Ivy said, waving her hand as if to encompass their whole operation.

Lucia narrowed her eyes. "Why?"

Ivy considered the other woman. They weren't going to be friends, but she could appreciate someone with the right amount of suspicion. "Fair question. But really, you should be asking what I can bring to your little home for the lost and undead."

An arched brow. "Which is? We don't exactly have room for a groupie."

As if.

"Well, my sunny disposition, of course," she answered, grinning.

When Lucia grimaced, Ivy continued. "Look, you said you're going to be looking for more of these Resurrected right? People like me who are popping out of the ground like daisies because of this black hole or whatnot? Well that's what I'm good at. Finding people who may not want to be found."

It wasn't too far from the work she'd been doing for Lenox. Shaking down the people who owed him something, rattling the others who'd crossed a line. And she could work on her own search in the meantime.

Topher sighed. "Ivy, we're here to help you get back on your feet. Bring you into a network of others so you can have the right resources. You don't need to spend your new life wandering with the likes of us."

"In case you haven't noticed, I didn't exactly end my first life on the best of terms with society in general. If I'm going to start over, it needs to be somewhere else. So just bring me along for the ride, and let me lend a hand. Sounds like you want to find these people sooner rather than later. Don't you want help finding all your wayward zombies?"

"We're not zombies," Lucia responded. But she didn't say no.

Topher considered and turned to Lucia. "She's got a point. We got lucky this time. I know the others are looking, but the more hands we have on deck, the more people we can help."

Lucia chewed her lip and gave Ivy an appraising look. "You don't seem the most philanthropic person. What are you getting out of all this?"

Ivy spread her arms wide, her grin a matching knife across her face. "Why, a chance to see the world. You said you move around a lot. Well, I've never even left Seattle. Let a girl live a little her second go around, huh?"

If Lenox had relocated, Ivy needed to know where his new headquarters would be, and she needed to keep her advantage. Lay low for a bit. Let the crew continue thinking they'd gotten rid of her while she tracked down the new center of operations and figured out how to tear it down, brick by brick.

She doubted Lucia and Topher would like that answer.

The pair shared one of their silent arguments. When Lucia stood with a scoff and threw up her hands, she knew she'd won.

"Well?" Ivy said, holding out a hand to Topher and holding their gaze.

They considered her for a moment. A swift calculation beneath the lackadaisical exterior. And then put their hand in hers.

"Welcome to the team then."

7

DINA

Dina clawed her way out of the water inch by painful inch, shivering under layers of clothes, heart thrumming from the effort. The soaked wood of the pier turned the climb near impossible. But desperation made for powerful motivation.

When at last she crawled, gasping onto the slippery dock, she flopped down, sobbing with relief against the cracked wood for long breaths.

Hysterics, her father would have called it. Though maybe given the situation, he'd be more forgiving.

Here she was, having the weirdest day of her life, and all she could think about was her father telling her not to cry.

The thought made a giggle break through the sobs.

Forget hysterics. I'm probably hysterical.

She sucked in a wet breath, inhaling soaked wood and mist, fought desperately against the tears and bubbles of laughter.

It was a long time later that she was able to drag herself into a kneeling position and take in her surroundings. A thick blanket of mist obscured the night sky. But if she squinted, she could make out the inky surface of the water she had just hauled herself out of. Hear the quiet lapping of gentle waves against the poles of the dock.

No sign of the truck, nor of Tom Jessup and his dog.

What's happening to me?

In the truck her body had shaken apart, drop by drop. That weird dreamlike state of crashing waves. And now here. A quiet shore with no one in sight. Had the water dragged her further south?

But how?

When no answers emerged from her own panicked thoughts, she shook her head. "Right. We need somewhere warm and dry." Somehow saying the words aloud made the world feel more solid. Gave her strength to rise on shaky legs and wobble towards the shore and the halo of a lone streetlamp that indicated a small town.

The mist swallowed the shapes of houses until they were nothing more than hulking shadows. The shores of Tybee had been gray, but this gray had texture, even in the dark. It breathed like something old, something one found in fairy tales.

"Nothing for it," she muttered. "God, if you're listening, I'd love some help."

The Almighty might have spared her from drowning, but she was going to need a hell of a lot more if she was going to figure out how to get home. Not to mention how she'd managed to pop up on two very different shorelines in a matter of moments.

I must be losing it.

She supposed she was overdue for a complete mental break. And maybe hers had come with a bought of vivid hallucinations.

Very *vivid hallucinations,* she corrected, tugging her soaked shirt and jacket as she shuffled forward.

She knocked on the first door she came to, too wet and cold to consider how she looked, wandering the streets of a strange town, still in the same clothes she'd worn when she'd fallen off the damn bridge.

Voices muttered in lilting tones from inside, and the green door swung inward to reveal a blonde woman with ruddy cheeks and a shocked expression on her face.

"Jesus, hen, what're ye doing out here this time of night?"

The Scottish accent was so thick it took Dina a moment to decipher it. They must have immigrated recently.

"I'm sorry for the trouble, but do you have a phone I could borrow?"

She needed a fair bit more than a phone, but it seemed a safe enough place to start.

"Is that an American?" a man's voice called from further inside the white-washed, plainly decorated home.

"Christ, well come in from the cold at least," the woman said, ushering Dina inside. She scurried down the hallway and returned with a towel. "Thought we'd had a break in the rain, but seems ye got caught in it. Are ye backpacking? Don't get many of yer lot here in the spring, but some folks are stubborn like that. Ye have any gear?"

Dina accepted the towel and peeled off her ruined sneakers and socks. Her feet were wrinkled from being waterlogged and she grimaced as she squelched across the carpet.

"No, no gear."

"What happened to ye then?"

"It's a little hard to explain. I really just need to call my folks and let them know I'm okay. Can I borrow your phone?"

The woman scratched her head. "Alright, but let's get ye something dry to wear while I figure out how to make international calls from ours."

The accent, the question about Americans, everything clicked into place. "Um...international?"

"Well yes, unless yer folks are around here? But I don't know any Americans living around this part of the loch. Did ye come up from Glasgow? London?"

Dina shook her head. Loch. Like Loch Ness. "Sorry um...where are we?"

"Christ, ye hit yer head?" the woman asked, tilting Dina's chin up like she was a child.

"I don't think so," Dina mumbled.

Though with the confusion of the last few hours and the misguided notion that she'd landed on Tybee Island only to then wake up in Scotland didn't bode well.

"Well, yer on the east bank of Loch Lomond," the woman said, helping Dina escape the denim jacket that was sticking to her under-layers.

Footsteps approached, and a man with gray hair that belied a smooth face appeared, wiping his chin on a napkin.

"Here, hen, I've got internet calling on my phone. Can call from here. The connection's a bit shite, but ye can try."

Dina took the proffered cell phone and stared at it blankly. The numbers and details of life before the fall swirled around her mind, refusing to form patterns. She could feel the vague shapes of information, but nothing more. Maybe she *had* hit her head.

"Oh, give her some space, Callum," the woman said, shooing her partner back to what Dina presumed was the kitchen.

She stood, frozen for long moments, squeezing her eyes closed, shivering in soaked jeans, dripping on a stranger's carpet, and trying to keep her panicked thoughts from pulling her under.

She rubbed her forehead, thumped it with her fist.

And remembered the wallet still inside her jacket, now hanging on a peg by the door.

She freed the soaked fabric, paisley green and blue, grimacing at the now useless collection of cards from ice cream and coffee shops, fishing around for a well-worn bit of paper.

The yellow notepad paper—ripped around two edges and bleeding blue ink—proved difficult to extract without tearing it further. As it was, it had gotten stuck to a business card from her favorite bookstore. But she managed to extricate it without damaging the familiar script. A lifeline in the storm of the past few hours.

If you call, I'll pick up. Any time, anywhere - Zev

This definitely counted in Dina's book. So, for the first time since Zev had left, Dina called her brother.

The first two calls went to voicemail. On the third, he picked up with a harried, "Yes, hello? This isn't a good time."

She could picture him running a hand through his version of the typical Adler brunette frizz, getting fingerprints all over the glasses he adjusted when he was agitated. Did he still have the habit?

"Zev," Dina choked out, such was the relief of hearing her big brother, who's voice alone made her feel ten all over again. Like she was asking him to bandage a scraped knee.

The line went silent. She tried again. It'd been years after all. He probably wouldn't recognize her voice. "Zev, it's Dina."

More silence. She checked the connection hadn't broken.

"Zev? Jesus, will you say something?"

"There's no way. Dina...Dina is that really you?"

"Yeah. Look, I'm sorry to call out of the blue like this, but I need your help. Something's happened to me. I think I was in an accident and now I'm somewhere in Scotland and nothing makes sense and—" She cut off abruptly, realizing she was babbling. That nothing she was saying was coherent, even to her.

She took a breath. Tried again.

"Look, I know you haven't spoken to Mom and Dad in ages, but I was supposed to be there for dinner tonight and they must be worried sick. I think I hit my head. My phone's dead and I can't remember their number and I just don't know what the fuck is happening. So like..." she didn't even know what to ask.

"Help?" was all she managed.

"You're in Scotland," Zev repeated, incredulous.

"Yeah, either that or I'm having one hell of a hallucination."

"Dina...you can't be in Scotland."

"Look, I'm just as confused as you are. And now I have to try to get some place with an airport and probably get my head checked and—"

"Dina...I'm at home."

"Yeah, I'm sorry, I wouldn't bug you except—"

"No, like *home* home. Dina...I'm at your shiva."

"What?" she whispered.

"Dina, you've been missing for two weeks. You've been declared dead."

8

DINA

Waiting for Zev to arrive felt like ripping out her nails one by one, all over again.

Not only had he struggled to leave the shiva without raising an alarm—they had both agreed that spreading the news that she was in fact *not* dead should wait until they figured out whatever nightmare Dina had found herself in—but storms had grounded all flights coming in from D.C.

Now, after two days of waiting, of trying to make herself useful to her unexpected hosts, Dina's wait was almost over.

A text came through to the phone Callum had lent her:

Had to stop for gas ETA 45 minutes

Dina sighed and took another scalding sip of tea, burrowing into one of the many wool sweaters she'd been offered. Callum and Maggie were off running errands and promised to be back before she and Zev took off again. He'd managed to book them a red-eye home. Over the course of the flight, they'd figure out how to break the news to their parents.

It made her stomach churn, thinking of her parents covering all the mirrors in the house, still mourning her apparent loss, but she was terrified of the prospect of alerting them to the reality of the situation when she barely understood it. How she'd drowned, but subsequently wound up on the shores of the Carolinas and Scotland.

Going home must have been a different kind of nightmare for Zev, she thought once more.

Zev hadn't been home since he'd come out. Since Levi and Frannie Adler had sat, staring at him blankly until he stood in the uncomfortable silence, packed his bags, and left for the West Coast. A new life that Dina could only imagine. Returning to Northern Virginia to sit shiva with her parents must have been awkward, at the very least.

And now she had yet another discussion to carefully plot out. One she had very few answers to.

She supposed the original confession would have to wait. Then again, maybe hearing their daughter was still alive would make them more amenable to the news she was gay.

Surprise! I'm alive! You want to know how? Well, me too! Also being in the closet has been a major obstacle to keeping a girlfriend, so let's talk about that.

Dina chewed her thumb and pulled her knees to her chin, ignoring the buzzing in her head. It had been persistent all morning long, and even the aspirin Maggie had given her couldn't convince it to give her some reprieve.

She tried to sequester it to a corner of her mind. Typed a quick reply to Zev, telling him she'd be waiting. Hesitated, then sent another:

Barely a second passed before the reply came through.

She added a rainbow emoji for good measure. As far as coming outs went, it wasn't much. But it wasn't nothing.

Dina put the phone down on the table before she could see his reply, too nauseous to look at the screen any longer. Besides, Zev would roll up soon. Maybe having a familiar person here, an adultier adult, would help her piece together what had happened to her since she'd crashed from the bridge.

Thoughts swirled around her head, frantic and useless. She'd missed weeks of work without explanation at this point. Though surely her firm would have been informed about the crash. And according to Zev, her bank accounts had been shut down, the funds transferred to their parents and himself. A sign that they still loved him in their own, screwed up way. She wasn't sure what the protocol was for restoring your assets after being incorrectly declared dead. And once she got home, could she really just melt back into her life, as if nothing had happened? Go back to accounting and ignoring her lack of a social life as if the crash didn't haunt her every waking hour? As if she couldn't feel the weight of the bay in her chest even now?

And she still hadn't the faintest clue how she'd ended up swept along to Tybee and now middle-of-nowhere Scotland. Her mind kept whirring around the problem, as if turning it over again would yield an answer. But there was none to be found.

But Zev would be there soon. This nightmare would be over. Maybe she could stay with him for a while. Meet the partner she'd learned about through a friend of a friend. Take a well-deserved leave of absence. If the talk with her parents went poorly, it'd probably be the best option anyway.

As she tried to calm the whirlpool in her head, the buzzing grew louder. She groaned and wobbled over to the overstuffed couch in the living room, curling up with her hands still clutching the mug. Maybe if she could just lie down for a bit.

The room spun around her and she squeezed her eyes shut, willing it to stop, willing her mind to settle, for the storm clouds in her head to clear and leave her in still water once more.

But the tempest only raged harder. Her body a mercurial thing, quivering around her the way it had in Tom's truck.

No no no. Not again. This can't be happening again.

Dina forced her eyes open when the cup slid from her fingers, crashing to the floor and spilling tea all over the carpet.

And somehow, as she took in her disappearing hand, the thought at the forefront of her mind was how terrible a guest she made, to take these strangers' kindness and return it with tea stained floors. It was better than thinking about how her fingers were disappearing in front of her eyes, wavering like mist until flesh and muscle and bone became indistinguishable from the air around her.

No, please, God. No, she prayed, a litany of her own, pitiful sounding without the structure of the Hebrew she only ever spoke in synagogue.

The buzzing became a monster, grasping her in its clutches, dragging her back to the briny depths, to the cage of the seatbelt and water rushing through the windshield. She became nothing once more. No matter how she curled into herself, willing her flesh to maintain its shape.

And just as the waves came crashing down, the water overtaking her, she heard the wheels of Zev's car pulling into the drive.

9

DINA

Growing up, Dina had been what Zev liked to call "the pure amalgamation of centuries of Jewish guilt and generational trauma". She never stepped a toe out of line, always came home with good grades, never once contemplated sneaking out at night to go to illicit parties.

Not like Zev. Always talking back to their parents, fighting—she realized later—to define himself outside of their "perfect" nuclear family. A family that had gone truly nuclear when he'd come out of the closet.

The third time Dina emerged from the water, somewhere in Liechtenstein with a lake whose name she couldn't pronounce, she made herself steal for the first time in her life. Guilt sat alongside the filched granola bar in her stomach and the clean clothes on her back, yanked from the line in someone's yard.

By her seventh resurfacing, she didn't even blink. Gave little thought to the department store dumpsters she fished in for something better suited to the spring weather in various parts of the world. She'd long since given up on knocking on strangers' doors. Not after the man who'd offered her a ride to town, only to pull over to the side of the road and put his hand on her thigh. Another new, rebellious experience when she'd punched him bloody and ran through the forest, grateful for the first time when the water rushed over her and stole her away.

Ever since her drowning, she'd become connected to the water somehow. It was impossible, but what other explanation was there? She'd drowned in the Bay and emerged as a part of the water, proof that God had a sense of humor after all. She counted every breath now, dreading when they would run out, when the water would consume her again.

But in the passing weeks, she'd discerned patterns in her resurfacing:

1) She appeared to be moving eastward. Eventually, she imagined she'd find herself back in the US, even if not anywhere near Virginia.

2) Those hideous headaches always predicted the next time the water would take her.

3) She was able to bring along whatever was attached to her body. Clothes, and whatever she had in her pockets. Though this meant her wallet and Callum's borrowed phone were long behind her on the edge of Loch Lomond.

4) She could hold onto her body longer when she resurfaced in lakes or ponds or other still waters. Sometimes days or even a week. But the oceans and rivers swallowed her quickly back up, eager to carry her onto their next destination.

She reviewed these facts in her head as she rummaged through the department store dumpster, as if they might give her any control over her life again. It helped her make sense of things, even if it didn't solve her major problems: the lack of consistent food and inability to get in touch with Zev. No one was eager to lend a woman, drenched with river water, a phone, and she could never scrounge up enough change to use one of the few remaining payphones in the world. There was no way to explain to her brother what was happening. Why she hadn't been waiting for him. No way to reach anyone. She was on her own.

These days, the people Dina passed often looked at her askance, like she belonged in an asylum. And maybe she did. Because the only thing she could think of to explain what was happening was that she really *had* died in that car crash. That this was some fucked up afterlife. If she dwelled on the thought too long, she might scream until her throat bled.

God, she wished she had Zev, had a way to reach him. To explain why she hadn't been there when he'd pulled up to fetch her home from Scotland, to be able to process all of this with someone else. She wondered what he'd told their parents. Were they still mourning her? Dina, the model daughter? Dina, the child they thought they knew? The girl who never would have stolen money left out for a waiter's tip so she could afford something to shovel into her mouth?

They certainly wouldn't have dreamed of her dumpster diving like this. But in this moment, she didn't much care, now that she'd finally found a pair of pants in the realm of her size and a green tank top. The leather bomber jacket was a treasure in the sea of fast fashion. Perfect for the late spring weather. And the pockets meant she'd be able to carry more with her as she scavenged for resources. Her empty stomach gnawed from the inside, its only contents a loaf of bread she'd managed to pilfer from a shop off the coast of some large river system in what appeared to be somewhere in France. Maybe Victor Hugo would appreciate the irony.

New clothes settled, she hauled herself out of the dumpster and walked down the street, away from the lake's edge. No matter how far she walked, the water would only pull her back, and yet the distance was soothing. Rebellious in a way that was still new to her. And she needed to figure out how to channel that rebellion into fixing this endless loop she was caught in. Maybe she hadn't drowned, but this was no life. She was nothing more than a shadow creature, haunting the world.

The pathway from the lake took Dina closer to town, and when the empty night became populated with strangers, she shoved her hands in her new jacket pockets, shoulders hunching towards her ears. She walked by a group of teens, laughing at something she couldn't understand. Folks walking their dogs. Others sitting on benches.

She eventually found a bar and slunk over to a seat in a dark corner. Somewhere she could watch without being watched. Somewhere, hopefully, the waitstaff wouldn't notice her as she gave her sore feet a break and figured out her next move.

It didn't last long.

A waitress approached and said something Dina didn't understand. Russian perhaps.

"I-I'm sorry I don't—"

"No drink, no sit," the woman said with a thick accent.

Dina dug into her pockets and produced a few euros she'd picked up, knowing immediately what the waitress' response would be.

"No money, no business." She made a shooing motion with her hands. From behind her, a burly man, likely the bouncer, observed the interaction with interest.

Dina stood and hurried back out, face red with shame. That she couldn't speak the language or pay with the right currency. That her hair was a dried out mess from so much time in the water, and she looked as unkempt and unslept as she felt.

Loneliness ached through her chest, twin to the horrid pressure of the water. And the more the water drew her away from home, the more she realized just how long that loneliness had sat in her. Because the more she circled in her own head, the more she became aware of the absences in her life. She'd told herself for years that being closeted didn't affect her relationship with her parents, with her friends. But the truth was she'd been a ghost even before the crash. All those "friends", girls to go to the movies with, coworkers to grab happy hour with, and not a one of them who she trusted with the truth. Not a one who she'd call, even now.

She shook her head, as if that would dislodge her gloom. She needed to focus on finding Zev, or at least a way of calling him. If she could get to him, get some sense of shelter, maybe she could face the reality that her so-called life had never really been living.

As she wandered down the streets of a town whose name she didn't even know, keeping an eye out for spare change and an ancient phone booth, footsteps sounded behind her, matching her own. She put her head down and walked faster.

So did the person behind her.

Dina rummaged around in her pockets for anything useful. She didn't even have a key to scrape across someone's skin, let alone a real weapon. Only some euros and her bunched up fists. And an imagined tug at the back of her neck, urging her to turn around.

The buzzing in her head beat a mismatched tempo to her hammering heartbeat, and Dina went warm with relief. Whatever was happening, the water would carry her away. And soon. Coming to her rescue instead of her detriment.

She turned and faced her stalker, who froze without even the slightest hint of surprise.

It was a white man with buzzed hair that shone platinum in the streetlights. He was dressed all in black, hands in the pockets of a long coat, dark, transparent eyes watching with removed interest. The edges of his silhouette were blurred almost, his skin so pale Dina could almost see right through it.

"Leave me alone," she said. Once, she might have given him the benefit of the doubt. Naively assumed he needed help or directions. She knew better by now. Not everyone was kind. Not everyone had good intentions. "I'd like to go about my night without being followed, thank you."

The man stared. After a moment, something clicked in Dina's head. She could have smacked herself. Of course. He didn't speak English. She was the stranger here.

She motioned away from herself with her hands, hoping that would translate well enough.

The man didn't move. Instead, he watched her with those flat, black eyes, which devoured the dim light, rather than reflect.

Dina took a step back. He, a step forward.

The tide rushed in her head. She fisted her hands by her sides, ready to throw a punch, even if she hadn't quite perfected the art. She breathed deep to steel herself.

From one breath to the next, the man was before her, clasping her arm, grip grinding into her muscle and bone so tight she whimpered.

The water raged in her blood.

Take me away, she begged for the second time since the water had become her only anchor.

"You shouldn't be here," the man hissed from beneath closed lips. Those eyes bore into her, the man's face clean of expression. Yet the light in his eyes seared with the heat of hatred.

"Abomination," he said with the voice of ghosts, accent indeterminable. For a flash, the visage of a pale man disappeared, swallowed by darkness that bent all light around it, devoured every ounce of it. And in its place dripped shadows. Pieces of a void leaking from his grip into her flesh, dripping down his eyes, running down his cheeks until nose, throat, eyes, were oblivion itself.

A scream rose and died in Dina's throat. The shadows crawled into her mouth, oozing down her throat like an oil slick. Worse than drowning. Worse than dying.

Please! she prayed, willing the wave to crash, the current to sweep her away.

And just as the monster poured into her, swallowed nearly every last breath, the waters rushed in, pulling her into nothing once more. But at least in the nothing, she was safe.

This time, the water didn't consume her consciousness. She felt the current move, and her with it. And with each droplet, each change of the tide, the void's last words haunted her.

"I will retrieve what was stolen."

10

IVY

Driving down to Portland wasn't exactly what Ivy had in mind when she'd pictured globetrotting with her new companions. But she couldn't argue when Topher said they'd prefer to check out some nearby cities and towns before hopping on a plane to explore other potential resurrections.

So it was back into the rental car and down the I5, still tucked into the deep cloud cover of the Pacific Northwest, until they'd pulled up to a cute, single-story house with a neat A-frame roof and warm brown siding.

Money didn't appear to be a concern for either of the Resurrected. At first, Ivy had been convinced the two of them were up to something shady to be able to afford everything. That she'd gone from one gang, steeped in politics and the exchanging of lives for riches, to another. The ease with which they'd produced faked docs—from the same unknown source that had generated their own—only solidified that worry. But when asked, Lucia explained that they both worked as software engineers, which meant they could work from pretty much anywhere. The shadiest thing they'd actually done so far was get her a fake ID and social security card.

And the apartment?

"On loan from someone like us," Topher had explained, making themself at home in a worn, faux leather recliner.

And now, weeks into their stay, the apartment was littered with dirty dishes and torn out pieces of notebook paper.

"So…has your algorithm sussed out where this Resurrected is yet?" Ivy asked for the millionth time.

If you asked her, they should have called it at least a week ago, moved onto a new city with other recently deceased options.

"As I've said before, it isn't an exact science," Topher said, eyes on their screen. Finishing up their day job from the look of it.

Ivy was beyond bored of waiting for something to happen between the lines of code. Of flipping through Topher's sparse Handbook for the Recently Deceased. Of browsing obituaries and news sites for hits on people who fit Topher and Lucia's short list of requirements:

1) Having died on March 21, just like her, and

2) Dying quickly via violent means or freak accident

Surprisingly, that didn't narrow things down all that much. It had been a stroke of luck they'd found her. Her death never would have hit the papers. No obituary to track down, no gravestone. She wondered how many others like her were out there. People they would never find except by accident, or Topher's supposed Law of Attraction.

"I feel like I've walked the length of Portland at least a hundred times trying to find your apostles, dude. I'm good at finding people who don't want to be found, but this is like *Where's Waldo* on steroids."

She'd even started taking the car out to the suburbs to check gravesites for something to do. Not an activity she especially enjoyed given the looks she got in some places for having piercings up the length of both ears and through her nose. Oh, and probably because she looked like your stereotypical, flaming dyke with her undercut, cuffed jeans, and carabiner of keys hanging from her belt loop. All of the above was fine in the city. Less so further out. But the trips also gave her time to poke around the Portland underground a bit.

"How's your precious algorithm supposed to work anyway?" she asked, swinging her legs over the recliner's arm and kicking her feet against the sides.

Everything in her itched to move on. Along with her lack of progress with the Resurrected, she'd also failed to find Lenox's trail. Not even a crumb left behind.

Well, almost. It had caught her by surprise yesterday when she'd spotted a familiar head of box-blonde hair turning down one of the aisles of the gas station in Hazeldale. She'd ducked into the chips aisle, waiting there for a heart-wrenching moment. But Rita Baxter hadn't batted an eye. Ivy wondered if she'd been told about her supposed murder. She hadn't even known the woman *lived* here.

Rita, oblivious to Ivy watching from a couple aisles over, gave Ivy time to take her in for the first time in years, count the new wrinkles around the woman's eyes and mouth. And to formulate half a plan before she followed her home, keeping a careful distance the whole drive, and memorizing the exterior of the pale yellow trailer she walked into.

Maybe the city wasn't completely useless to her after all.

"We just keep training the model as we get more information and hope it improves. Gets more specific with its predictions," Lucia said, also not bothering to glance at Ivy. For a moment, Ivy considered smashing a mug to see if that would garner more attention.

Perhaps Lucia sensed Ivy's violent intention, since she finally looked her way.

"It's like we're magnets, right? We all seem to be pulled towards each other. But imagine said magnet when it's not near anything magnetic. It's just static. But when you *are* near metal, it attracts. So we just have to keep going out and tracking down deaths, and hope we strike metal."

"I like that metaphor," Topher commented with a crooked smile.

"Thanks," Lucia said, returning to her screen.

Ivy stifled a groan.

"Hey, you tagged along because you said you could help. Maybe if you're that bored, you can try another lead. Earn your room and board."

"Sorry I'm not a big fancy coder hacking into the matrix," she grumbled, getting to her feet and yanking on her boots.

"Didn't think you'd actually listen," Lucia commented.

"I'm not. I'm going for a drink. I'll see you two later when you actually have a better target for me than some cemetery out in bum-fuck middle of nowhere."

She needed to clear her head before she tracked down a target of her own anyway. Ivy tugged on her black, leather jacket (thank you thrift store), grabbed her keys and borrowed funds (thank you Topher), and tromped out the door, head bent against the spitting rain. She hadn't mentioned her stash of cash to either of her new companions. Better to see how far their generosity extended.

When you trust someone, you hold a gun to your own head and place someone else's finger on the trigger, Lenox had told her once. Back when she was a scrawny kid, picking locks and stealing petty cash, all to make herself believe she was contributing to him and "the business". And in that manor house where plots were laid and grudges came to violent ends, it had been advice worth sticking to. Now, with a new crew, she wasn't about to hand that gun to Lucia or Topher.

As she walked, she contemplated her own "algorithm". The list of places she'd checked out based on the rumor mill of which dispensaries were fronts for something less legal. Seattle was her territory, but she knew how to look for the signs in other places well enough. And the places she'd checked had resulted in nothing more than a few offers of weed or a job that looked a lot like becoming a mercenary. Again.

Rita was her only option in this city. And she was going to need a stiff drink before that one.

Over the last few weeks, Ivy had made sure not to become a regular anywhere. Didn't want to be recognized by anyone before she lost the element of surprise. But if a bar had a rainbow flag waving, she went in.

Tonight, she risked revisiting Step On Her. It was early enough that the place didn't have much of a crowd beyond the odd happy hour group. The lights were still high, illuminating framed Playboy covers and pink, neon signs saying things like "Every night is dyke night".

Lively conversation echoed around the place, and Ivy allowed it to wash over her. There was a familiar comfort in being surrounded by other queer folks, and mostly women at that. Lenox's group had been tolerant in that respect. Well, more than some of the rival gangs in the area. But such mild tolerance had been possible because the others thought it made her more "manly" to be attracted to women. As if she'd ever wanted to be called such a word.

Pete was the only one who didn't crack jokes about wanting to watch her get it off with another woman. Not that his advice was any comfort.

You love who you love, Ivy. But for fuck's sake, don't love them too close if you want to make it in this world. If you want them to make it.

It wasn't a bad rule, not in their line of work. Pete was always there to buy her a drink when she ended yet another relationship because someone was getting too close. Because she'd spotted Jason or one of the others following her on her way to meet some girl.

Well, she wasn't nursing a breakup now, but she dearly wished Pete were there to buy her a drink anyway.

And what good are wishes? she wondered as she ordered her old fashioned.

According to Lenox, wishes were for girls with parents. Girls who stayed in school, went to university, got married and popped out babies. For people who already had enough of a leg up that they didn't even need the universe to interfere to have said wish granted. Not for her. Not for any of his crew. She could fault Lenox for many things. But on that account, he'd certainly had it right.

She found a quiet table in the corner, pushing her dark mood aside to focus on an even worse subject: Rita.

Really hoped it wouldn't come to this, she thought miserably.

She hadn't had any contact with the woman in years. Liked it that way. But if there was anyone she could make contact with, get information from, and leave again without blowing her cover well...it would be her.

Around the bar, everyone else was in far better spirits. Many had come with a friend or something more. No one seemed to be looking for a new lay this time of day. Shame. That would have really gotten her mind off things.

For a moment, as Ivy sipped the old fashioned far too quickly to really enjoy it, she let herself imagine another life. One where she and her friends would meet up in a place like this for a quiet drink. Where they would tease her about her inability to keep a girlfriend for longer than a few weeks. Where she had friends.

Topher and Lucia certainly weren't that. They tolerated her, and she them. That was it.

Ivy let the last of her drink burn away the dregs of her vision. That was the life of a stranger. She was making the most of the one she had instead. A life that screamed for revenge. For Lenox's blood on her knives and his lifeless eyes staring up from the bottom of her boot.

She left her empty glass on the table and went to the gender-neutral bathroom to splash water on her face and try to get her brain ready to face a woman she'd sworn she was done with.

But when she opened the door, the room wasn't as vacant as advertised.

A woman sat on the floor, knees curled to her chest, tendrils of damp, wavy, brown hair covering her face as she sobbed into her hands.

Crying always made Ivy uncomfortable. She never quite knew how to handle it when she couldn't remember the last time she'd allowed herself to cry. She tried backing out of the room unnoticed, but her boot scuffed on the floor and the other woman's head shot up with a start.

"Shit," she said. "Sorry, sorry, I know I'm not a customer, I just needed a minute."

Ivy hesitated. Then stepped inside, unsure why. She should walk away, let this woman find better emotional support than what she could provide.

But there was this warmth in her chest, like someone had pressed their palm to her skin.

So instead, she closed the door and leaned against it.

"You're good. I don't work here. But flattered that I look like I do."

"Aw crap. I'm hogging the toilet."

The woman scrabbled up from the ground, wiping at her puffy face with the cuffs of her soaked bomber jacket, the pale skin going even redder as she scrubbed. She must have been caught in the earlier downpour without an umbrella.

"Um..." Ivy scratched the back of her neck. "You okay? No. Shit. Dumb question. Clearly that's a 'no'."

The woman let out a watery laugh and moved to the sink, washing her hands and splashing water on her face. "Yeah. Definitely not okay. But I'll get out of your way. Don't worry about me. Plenty of places to have a cry around here."

Ivy shrugged. "Nah, it's fine. I don't really need to pee."

The woman raised a brow. "Are you also looking to curl up in the fetal position on the bathroom floor?"

"You know, I hear that's the best place to do it."

The laugh that emerged surprised the both of them. It was far drier this time. Musical even. And deep in Ivy's chest settled the desire to hear it again.

"I prefer a nest of blankets myself, but the bar didn't have any handy, so bathroom floor was the next best option."

"Any port in a storm," Ivy agreed with a shrug.

Another laugh. "Pretty sure that's an innuendo."

Ivy grimaced. "Ugh, is it?"

The woman dried her hands and tossed the paper towel in the trash.

"And here I thought you were trying to flirt with the pathetic girl crying on the bathroom floor."

"Who says I'm not?" Ivy replied automatically.

As if that's what this woman wanted right now. God, she was probably in here crying over someone else. Ivy hoped the earth would just swallow her up and shut her up for good.

Still, the way the stranger blushed made Ivy's breath catch, no matter the puffy eyes. Hard to regret bringing out an expression like that.

They stood there for a second. It wasn't quite awkward, and yet Ivy hadn't the faintest clue what to do or say next.

Then the woman winced like she had a headache. She recovered in a flash and gave Ivy a quiet smile.

"Well, anyway. I'll just…" she motioned towards the door Ivy was blocking.

"Oh shit. Yeah." Ivy moved out of her way. As the woman reached for the handle, words flew out of Ivy's mouth without her mind even allowing such a thing. "If someone needs punching, I'm happy to lend a hand."

The woman's smile widened, shoulders loosening a fraction. Ivy had done that. She couldn't remember the last time her presence had put someone at ease. Usually, she was responsible for the opposite.

"Thanks. I'll let you know if I need back-up."

And then she was out the door.

Ivy stood around the bathroom for a few minutes after that. She *really* didn't need to pee, but didn't want to look like a lunatic, following a random woman from the bar. Time dragged until she decided it wouldn't be creepy to leave. Maybe she'd offer to buy the woman a drink if it turned out she'd come to the bar alone. Lend her a dry jacket and see if she could get her to smile again. She could leave Rita for another day.

But when she re-entered the bar, the woman was gone.

Despite the booze warm in her gut, Ivy dragged her feet to her next destination, mind still at the bar, wondering what it would be like to ask a girl out for a drink without the strings of Lenox and the crew pulling her away from any serious relationship she might have considered. A girlfriend meant leverage, and she'd be damned if she'd ever supply that to the likes of Jason and the others.

'Til now, her dating life had consisted of one night stands. Summer flings. Carefully spaced out so no one ever caught on. A well laid plan. And now Ivy knew why a particular saying about those had stuck.

She brushed fingers to the inside of her wrist, pulling her sleeve up as she readied the bone knife, allowed the sharpness of it to sooth her.

Could have turned out worse, she thought, a grim smile playing across her lips.

She kept her gait nonchalant as she strolled up to the trailer. A gleeful part of her imagined breaking a few windows on her way. But she wasn't an idiot. A woman like Rita would be armed.

So she walked up to the front door and knocked.

A white woman in her fifties answered, that bottle-blonde hair less put together than Ivy remembered.

"Yes?" Rita said, all annoyance and exhaustion.

Her eyes flew wide as Ivy burst in, bone knife pressing to the other woman's throat hard enough to draw a drop of blood.

"Are we alone?" Ivy hissed.

The fear dissolved, swallowed by anger as Rita answered. "Yes, you bull-headed idiot. At least have the decency to close the door before you jump someone."

Ivy kicked the door closed without relinquishing her grip. "Drop the gun," she hissed.

A thump on the ground.

"Where's Lenox?"

Rita glared. "How the hell should I know?"

"You ran with him for far longer than I ever did. Don't tell me you have no idea where he'd slink off to if things went sideways in Seattle."

"You're supposed to be the heir," Rita growled. "If you don't know, how the fuck would I?"

Heir. The word stung with its weight. Years of shadowing Lenox's every step, hoping to earn approval, to be gifted a crumb of acknowledgement from the man who had taken her in as a kid. To be more than just an ordinary lackey. He had that effect on people. And she'd finally managed it. Was announced before the whole crew as the woman who would take over the whole business of running the gang if anything happened to Lenox. She could still feel the warm clasp of his hand around the back of her neck as he pulled her in for a congratulatory head butt. Could still picture Pete's frown, even as he clapped with all the others. God, how that frown had haunted her.

That was before he'd convinced her to want more. Before she'd dreamt of a life outside of the crew and its web of contracts and executions. Died trying to grasp it and got Pete killed for good measure.

She'd gotten complacent, sure no one would think to track her to the trade school she'd put her hidden cash towards. And things between her and the rest of Lenox's crew had changed slowly enough that Ivy hadn't caught wise. Left out of a meeting here, told about a plan belatedly there. She'd smelled a rat, but it was pride that had gotten the best of her. Confidence that her plan was solid, that she could scrape together a life she only ever caught glimpses of on TV.

Even when Lenox had confronted her about it, ordered Jason to smack her around in front of the whole crew, she'd had the audacity to fight back. To pull her knife and claw and scrape towards the life she wanted.

It hadn't stopped her from being stabbed.

Dying hadn't been a neat thing. Not in that moment when every breath seemed to stretch a millennia. Not when she'd still been conscious enough to watch as Jason brought Pete forward with his hands tied behind his back. To scream when he'd slit his throat. Wait for her turn to join him hours later after Lenox had made his point.

Thought you'd slither right on out of here? I know what to do with snakes, Ivy. And I know exactly *what to do with you.*

So no, he hadn't told her everything. Not in those final months at least.

"Not anymore," she muttered.

Rita smiled. "They told me you were dead, but you wriggled your way out, didn't you? If you were smart, you'd leave Lenox and his bullshit behind for good."

"Just tell me where he would go next. What were his backups if things went south? If he had to start over?"

Rita watched her for a moment. Then, "You gonna kill him?"

"That's certainly the plan," Ivy said, applying enough pressure to the blade to make the woman wince.

Rita worked her throat. "If you put that creepy ass knife away, I'll give you a list."

Ivy hesitated, then took a step back, still clasping the dagger's hilt. Rita's eyes flicked towards the blade then back to Ivy.

"You got a pen and paper?"

"I've got a phone." Ivy pulled it out, opened the notes app, and handed it to Rita, watching like a hawk as she typed for a while.

"He may have abandoned all his plans when I left," Rita warned. "You know how fucking paranoid the man is."

"I know," Ivy admitted. But it was a start, which was more than what she had now.

"Here." Rita handed back the phone and Ivy glanced over the list before pocketing it.

"Man deserves a knife in the eye," she said after a moment, dabbing the wound on her neck.

"I know."

Rita looked her over and gave a tilted smile. "Just make sure he doesn't put one in yours first."

11

DINA

When Dina resurfaced on the edge of Lake Michigan, she couldn't see the sky. Just the keen hazel eyes of the woman in the bathroom.

Maybe it was because it was the first person she'd really interacted with in weeks. Maybe it was because any friendly face was a balm after her encounter with whatever that thing had been. In her head, she'd begun referring to it as The Void. A monster.

Because it had to be a monster, right? No human could do something like that.

Then again, who am I to judge? she thought grimly as she swam to shore.

At least she was getting better at keeping her awareness about her when she got dragged back under. It made the whole thing less disorienting, even if losing control over her own physicality made her heart palpitate and her head spin with endless anxiety over where she would emerge next. If she would be there long enough to steal a decent meal. If it would be safe. Lake Michigan was cold enough. She didn't want to think about what would happen if she resurfaced somewhere further north.

She could feel the time passing now, even when she crossed great stretches of ocean. She was keeping to a pattern of resurfacing a few days after she went under, emerging ever eastward. Sometime soon, she would almost definitely return to the east coast. Anywhere close to home or her parents? Probably not, given her luck. There was no steering this connection. Wherever the water was flowing, that's where she'd end up.

So long as it's away from that thing, *I'll count it as a win for now,* she thought miserably.

Still, she'd been hoping to surface in Sacramento, somewhere up the river where she might feasibly track down Zev to explain what had happened, to ask for help. Popping up in Portland had been next to useless in that respect.

It was this thinking that saw her breaking into an office building somewhere in the depths of Chicago. It had taken a few days to scout out the right one. One that didn't have security cameras covering all entryways, nor an obvious alarm system. One old enough to probably still have a landline. And best of all, one with a slightly cracked window.

She was starting to think she was going to have to take a brick to someone's lovely office front when she spotted a perfect target. Unfortunately, it was on the second floor.

Dina glared up at the window. Maybe she *should* just smash in one of the lower windows with a rock. After days of walking around the city, flinching away from shadows and darting looks over her shoulder every few steps in case that monster had followed her somehow, she deserved to take the easier route.

She sighed and flexed her hands, walking over to the drain pipe instead.

The Jewish guilt is strong in this one, she thought, annoyed at her own qualms.

Her mother would probably say that her great great grandparents hadn't fled the pogroms for their descendent to become a thief and a hooligan. Or something to that effect. Who knew how her ancestors would be employed to try to convince her to go back to pretending she was straight.

So the drainpipe was really a compromise. She wrapped her fingers around the metal, found footing on the straps holding the pipe to the brick wall, and climbed. It wasn't long before her fingers burned from clenching metal and sweat rolled down her spine.

Her foot slipped. Heart jumped into her throat. Legs shook.

"Come on come on come on," she whispered to herself. She couldn't be more than a few feet from the ground, yet here she was having a full-blown panic attack.

But Zev was at the end of this climb. Or at least a chance of contacting him.

She breathed in deep through her teeth, cool night air soothing her lungs. Exhaled. Climbed with shaky limbs and a pounding heart.

The climb seemed eternal, Zev's imagined voice the only thing keeping her on the damn drainpipe. And then she was wrapping her fingers around the sill and clinging on for dear life as she pushed the pane wide enough to slip through. Nearly fell off completely as she tried to crawl in, grasping the sill so hard her knuckles went ghost white. Pulled herself through the gap. And landed in a gasping mess on the coarse carpet floor.

She lay there for a second, breathing hard. God, she was going to have to find a way to work out if she was going to keep living like this. As her heartbeat settled, so did the bruises and scrapes already forming from the climb and her inelegant tumble.

One of the fluorescent lights still flickered overhead, lighting the office cubicles in shades of greenish gray. She timed the pulses of light for a moment, the scent of carpet cleaner thick in the air, then crawled to her feet and began her search.

When the first few cubicles were empty of landlines, despair cut deep into her gut.

But then at last. The reception desk.

She picked up the phone, barely daring to breathe until she heard the tell-tale song of the line waiting for numbers to be pressed. Hesitation stilled her fingers for a moment, her parents' number resolving in her head again, the way other details and memories had after those first few terrifying days of her new, ghoulish life. But she needed to get a lay of the land first.

She called Zev four times before he picked up.

"What?" he growled, sounding harassed.

"Zev, it's me," she said.

The line went silent, but she waited, reminding herself to breathe. And then:

"You must be some sick fuck to try this act after all this time."

"Zev, I swear—"

"Do you know how messed up this is? Getting me to go all the way to the middle of nowhere Scotland and find an empty house? What do you want? Money? Because if so, you're barking up the wrong tree trying to scam a librarian."

"Wait, when did you become a librarian?"

"Did you not hear *anything* I just said?"

"Zev," she appealed. Every minute they spent on the phone, the water crept closer. "I'm not scamming you. It's me. I'll prove it."

"Try me," he huffed.

"When I was nine, I caught you having a bad trip with your friends the first time you ever tried shrooms. You told me the ceiling was melting and trying to attack you. And I helped you hide it from Mom and Dad when they got back from Orlando early and never told them a thing."

Another beat.

"Shit, I totally forgot about that."

"But you remember now?"

A rough sigh. "Yeah, Dina, I do."

And God. The warmth of hearing her name again. Of having her brother say it through the crackling line.

"What the fuck?" he continued. "What happened? Why weren't you there? And why are you calling from a Chicago number?"

"How'd you know it was Chicago?"

"Because Ben has a Chicago number," he said, as though that explained everything.

"Should I know who that is?"

When Zev didn't answer, she guessed. "Is he your partner?"

She waited, allowing Zev to decide how much he wanted to say. Screw her time limit, she needed to know this at least.

"Yeah," he said eventually. "Yeah he is. We've been together for three years now. I...you'd like him, D."

"If he's good to you, I'm sure I will," she said, eyes prickling.

Three years. She'd never even known his name.

"Do you have anyone?" Zev asked.

A face flashed in Dina's head. Hazel eyes and straight black hair. Lips with a scar toward the right corner. She swallowed, cheeks warm. Stupid.

And the buzzing in her head reminded her she needed to hurry this along.

"Do you want to ask about my dating life right now? Really?"

"Yeah, good point. So what the hell is going on? Did you run away? Why didn't you stay in Scotland and just wait for me? And dude, pretending to crash off the Bay Bridge? Pretty fucked up. I know Mom and Dad didn't react well when I came out, but Jesus."

"I really did crash, Zev. It wasn't faked. And I think..." she trailed off, swallowing hard. It was something she'd never spoken aloud. Something she'd barely admitted to herself. "Zev, I think I died."

A huffed laugh of surprise. "What, so you're a zombie?"

"I don't feel like eating brains, if that's what you're worried about," she said, rolling her eyes before she remembered he couldn't see her.

"Shit." A pause. Then, "SHIT. Okay, from the beginning. Tell me everything."

"It's going to sound insane, Zev. Like...you're gonna want to lock me in an asylum."

"Look, all I know is that you died, supposedly showed up in Scotland, and now you're calling from Chicago. I need *something*."

She took a deep breath.

"Okay. But promise you'll *try* to believe me? Promise?"

"Yeah, Dina. I've got you."

So she told him. Everything. As much as she'd figured out that was. Everything except for that awful moment with the Void. Now that she had a familiar voice in her ear, the whole encounter felt even more surreal than the rest of her experiences since the crash.

What if it had been a hallucination? Brought on by weeks of exhaustion and navigating a life over which she'd relinquished all control. She'd only been half joking about the asylum.

When she finished, the line stayed silent for so long she feared Zev had hung up on her word vomit.

"Zev?" she prompted.

"Give me a minute," he muttered. Dina imagined him pinching his nose. After a moment he continued. "Not gonna lie, D. This sounds insane."

"Well, I told you," she grumbled. "Look, I know. But what reason would I have to lie about this? Believe me, if I could just hop on a plane and come home, I'd already be at the airport."

"You sure this isn't some long overdue prank? Because it's not funny."

"Zev, I've been living off of half-discarded sandwiches and stolen wallets for weeks now. Trust me when I say this isn't remotely funny."

More silence. "Alright. And right now? Are you safe?"

Dina breathed a sigh of relief. Seemed like she'd finally activated 'protective big brother mode'. "Yes. For the moment."

"And you have no idea where you'll wind up next?"

"No. Somewhere further east, but that could be anywhere from the Mississippi to the Atlantic."

"And how long do you think you have in Chicago?"

She thought for a moment, touching her awareness to the edges. The subtle crashing of waves. "Not much longer. A few hours if I'm extremely lucky. You'd be surprised at how hard it was to get to a phone, Zev."

"Dude, you should have gone to the library. They'd probably let you borrow one."

She stood there for a moment, resisting the urge to smack herself in the face. "Are you serious?"

"Yes! Do you know how many unhoused people libraries see on a daily basis? You could even borrow a computer there."

When she didn't respond, he sighed. "To think, my own sister is completely unaware of the value of public libraries."

"Alright, alright. Well, I know now."

"Anyway, keep trying to get to a phone. If you're somewhere long enough, I can high tail it out there and try to help you out, or at least set you up with funds and stuff. We'll figure this out, okay?"

"So you believe me?" Dina asked.

"I mean, yeah. I guess I do. It's insane, but I'm just glad you're alive, D." He hesitated. "Have you called Mom and Dad?"

A bead of guilt tightened her throat. "No, not yet. I wasn't sure how to...They think I'm dead, right?"

"Yeah."

"Would they even believe me if I called? Believe us, if you're willing to talk to them?"

"I don't know."

"Then maybe the two of us should figure this out first. Before I come back from the dead."

He sighed. "Yeah. Unfortunately, I think that makes sense. And look, I'm not exactly rolling in cash, in case you didn't believe the librarian speech. But whatever you need, I'll do it. If there's a way to get you money, or Jesus, a waterproof phone—"

"Yeah, we'll figure that out. But I don't know what's happening, Zev. And I'm not here to ask you to put your life on hold. I just—"

"I'm your brother," he interrupted. "I've got you."

"I know," she breathed, allowing herself to believe that she could let someone else hold the weight of her world for a moment. Two if she was lucky. "Thank you."

"We'll figure this out, D. Just let me know where you are as often as you can and I'll find you. One of these days I'll have to catch up, right?"

"Right," she paused, unsure what else to say, but clinging to the phone like a lifeline. To Zev's voice on the line and the hope she wasn't as alone as she'd felt since even before the crash. The waves could take her right now, and it would be okay. Because she had Zev in her life again.

"So you're a bit fruity too, huh?" Zev asked without warning.

Dina burst out laughing.

"Fruity as a salad on the Fourth of July."

"That makes no sense."

"Yes, it does."

Zev snorted. "Whatever you need to tell yourself." The next pause had the weight of a storm cloud. "Do Mom and Dad—"

"I haven't told them. I was going to when I saw them but then...well...Now, it kind of seems like a lower priority."

"Well, thanks for telling me."

She chewed her lip. Then burst out, "I should have called sooner."

"Dina, you were a kid."

"But I haven't been a kid for a long time. I should have called. I was just...scared. And I wasn't ready to face the fact that I'd never felt right with any of the boys I dated or that I watched the Matrix for Trinity and no other reason."

"No other reason? Not the masterful plot? The sick look into technology and societal commentary?"

"I mean those things were great. But Trinity in all that leather?"

Zev laughed. "Can't relate on that one, sorry. But anyway, we'll get you sorted and then we can decide how to approach Mom and Dad. *If* you want to approach them, that is."

"I don't know anymore," she admitted. "I was so ready to rip the Band-Aid off and now...I'm so scared. I don't even want to think about it."

"Can't imagine why," Zev muttered. "But for what it's worth, you dying, or whatever it is that happened, it kind of...changed them."

"Changed how?"

"Like they spoke to me at your shiva. Dad even hugged me. It was awkward as fuck, but it was...nice. We text a bit now, which is strange but...not bad strange."

"That's," she swallowed hard. "That's great, Zev."

"Anyway, you don't have to tell them anything you don't want to. But know I love you. And that I think they've realized they care more about their kids being safe than about who they date. So however you want to communicate about it, that's what we'll do."

"Thanks, Z. I-I'm glad you're in my life again. Even if the circumstances—"

"Are completely fucked? Yeah, same, D."

They spent a bit longer working out a plan for the next time Dina could reach out. Zev wasn't lying when he said he made a bad scam. Between the funeral eating into his limited time off and stretching a moderate income to fit life in Sacramento, it would be hard for him to fly out and meet her last minute. Dina wondered how much the trip to Scotland had cost, a sour taste in her mouth. But if she was somewhere long enough, he could at least help her find a place to stay for starters.

Somewhere with an actual roof over her head and access to a landline. He'd send her a phone too, which would mean bank connections. And in the meantime, Dina would keep trying to direct her powers towards Sacramento so she could stay with him for as long as the water let her. She felt the weight of her burdensome existence shifting to settle on Zev, but he assured her it would be fine.

"I'll talk to Ben. Not about all of it, but he knows how things went when I came out, and he's been dying to meet you. I'm sure he won't mind us footing your bill while we figure this out."

"But what I'm stuck on is *how* do we figure it out, Zev? I don't have any control here. I can't seem to make it stop."

"Dude, I'm an all-knowing librarian. If there's one thing I know how to do, it's research."

She rolled her eyes. "An all-knowing librarian who used to shoot milk out of his nose at dinner because he thought his own jokes were that funny."

"Psh, they were absolutely that funny. Now, how long do you think you have? Can I book you a place nearby? Somewhere that doesn't need an ID?"

The buzzing had gotten louder over the course of their conversation, and Dina tried to mentally prepare herself for the undertow about to pull her down. "No. I'll be gone in an hour tops. I don't think it's worth it."

"Okay. Well I'll talk to you soon, okay? Hang in there. I love you."

They hadn't said those words to each other in many years, and never with any seriousness. Now he'd said it twice. Now, they carried weight and sincerity.

"I love you too," she said, and ended the call.

Somehow, the conversation, comforting as it was, left her even lonelier. Like a phantom limb she was newly aware was still missing.

She glanced around the empty office building, the dull gray of it seeping into her skin. It was warm at least, but right now the vacant cubicles made her skin crawl and her chest ache. So, bones heavy and heart sore, she shimmied back out of the office building to resume her endless wandering.

Not sure this was what they had in mind when they came up with the "wandering Jew" stereotype, she thought bitterly.

Still, maybe with resources she could view things in a different light. Work had never given her the breathing room to go very far from home. Maybe she should be enjoying her cross-continental travel.

But she wanted to be in Chicago because *she* had decided to visit. Not because she'd been dragged here through streams and droplets, barely conscious enough to track the journey.

She shoved her hands in her jacket pockets, shivering in the unexpected chill of late May. Another shock. According to Zev, the car crash had happened two months ago.

The low hum of panic unfurled in her veins and she forced in a deep breath.

Just figure out how to get to Zev, she told herself. *Get to him and you can figure the rest out later.*

Wind blew off the lake like a call to home. To return to the water so it might claim her.

Well, the water would have her one way or another. It could wait.

She turned down a street at random.

All the streetlamps burst bright. Then burnt out. Like an electrical shock had hit the grid, eclipsing the whole street in darkness.

A shiver ran down her back as she turned around, darting frantic looks around the parked cars and closed shop fronts. But at first glance, she was alone.

At second, a figure moved against the shadowy world.

Dina froze, breath stilling in her lungs. A warm pressure on her chest. If it was the Void—

She stepped back, foot catching on a loose bit of concrete, stumbling with a loud scattering of pebbles.

The figure straightened, immediately illuminated by a streetlamp that flashed back on.

Dina sighed. It wasn't him. The light fell on the silhouette of a teenage boy with brown skin and disheveled, black hair. He couldn't be much older than seventeen. Nineteen at most.

"Sorry, I didn't mean—" As Dina took in the street, she realized that it wasn't a streetlamp shining on the boy. All the lights were still out. No, the light was coming from the boy himself, crackling in the empty night like...lightning.

Dina gasped and stepped forward, but the boy took a matching step back, holding up a hand, sparkling like a firecracker.

Dina showed him her empty palms.

"Please, I'm not gonna hurt you. It's just...how are you...I mean-how-I mean...."

The more she stumbled over her words, the more the boy tensed, ready to sprint off. So she got to the point.

"I'm the same. I think. I mean, different but...I have this thing. With water. Is this...did you have this ability always? Or did you—"

"I was struck by lightning. Was hiking with friends," the boy finally said, voice quiet and unused. The trace of an Arabic accent.

He reluctantly lowered his hands, but the arcs of lightning still flared. "I died. I think. When I woke up, I could do this. My friends..."

"Didn't make it," Dina finished, heart breaking for this stranger. "How did you learn to control it?" she asked, swallowing hard against the budding hope. Answers at last. If he could control lightning, perhaps she could—

He shrugged. "Just always could. I can't explain it. Like breathing."

He looked her over, expression inscrutable beyond his crackling light. "You can't control it?"

Dina shook her head, miserable. A glimmer of hope, of insight at last, but nothing useful. Only the information that her situation wasn't as unique as she'd assumed.

So I did *die.*

"Sorry," the boy muttered. His head darted around like a twitching dog. "I have to go."

"Wait!" Dina reached for him, taking a few steps closer, but he retreated backwards, shaking his head.

"It'll find us if we stick together in one place for too long," the boy said.

"It?" Dina repeated, skin crawling, knowing somehow what he would say.

"The Shadows."

The Void.

"You've seen it too," Dina whispered.

She glanced over her shoulder, watching the shadows, ready for them to pull away from the nearby buildings, to form the body of a pale man with eyes that devoured. But they were alone.

"Do you know what—" she turned back to the boy, wondering how to convince him to stay so she could ask what he knew.

But the street was empty once more. The boy and his lightning were gone.

12

IVY

D.C. smelled of dog piss and money. It had taken far too long for Lucia and Ivy to convince Topher to give up Portland, followed by L.A. and Las Vegas, as lost causes for finding Resurrected. The only thing that ever convinced them to move on was Lucia reminding them that waiting any longer meant they were potentially making it more difficult to track down others.

And so, it turned out that the first time Ivy ever got on an airplane, it was crossing the majority of the United States. A nonstop flight that crossed sweeping plains and an ocean of clouds. She even saw the Grand Canyon, looking like a slim carving in the red rock miles away. Though, given the turbulence they hit going over the Rockies, Ivy could have lived without it. Topher had offered to hold her hand when they caught her praying beneath her breath to any god she could remember learning about. Even then, she refused. If she was going to die again—this time from falling out of the sky in a metal beast that simply was NOT designed to leave the ground no matter what anyone said—she'd go out with her fists raised, thank you very much.

But the plane had arrived without crash-landing in a flaming pile of metal. And so the three of them disembarked in Dulles to the welcome of thick, warm air and pictures of the American flag plastered around every corner. She was already regretting rushing Topher.

"Eugh," she said, wiping sweat from her forehead. They hadn't even *done* anything yet. Simply stepped out of the airport.

"Agreed," Lucia grumbled, tying her hair in a bun and pulling up the handle of her suitcase.

"Aw, come on. It's gonna do wonders for this Jewfro," Topher said, fanning their frizzy mop of curls. Ever the optimist.

Lucia exchanged a look with Ivy and rolled her eyes. A conspiratorial expression that warmed Ivy's chest. Just a touch.

"Come on, I don't want to keep Danny waiting," Topher said. They had a large backpacking pack on their back and a laptop bag on their front, looking a bit like a hipster turtle. Ivy considered tripping them, just to watch them squirm on their back. She smirked.

"Do I want to know what that look is for?" Topher asked, leading the way towards the sign for ride pick-ups. It was a mess of Ubers and personal vehicles, all vying to get to different groups with suitcases. Nightmare.

"Probably not," Ivy admitted.

"Figured. Alright, keep your eyes peeled for a blue CR-V."

"I thought you said all the Resurrected moved around all the time," Ivy commented as she tried to sort through the mess of cars in front of them. "Why not this dude?"

Topher had explained the existing network of nomadic Resurrected. A chunk of them had apartments or houses they let the others use while they were on the move. It was how Topher kept finding them free places to crash in just about every city. But apparently, Danny had put down roots.

Topher shrugged. "He used to. Got tired of it, I guess."

"You guess?"

"I don't ask too many questions if I don't have to."

"But you trust him enough to stay with him?"

Topher raised a brow. "Yeah, of course."

What must it be like, Ivy wondered, to trust another person so easily?

"Anyway, he's got an extra laptop and a good set up to get you up and running with coding bootcamp."

Ivy groaned.

"You gotta start contributing somehow," Lucia reminded her.

"I thought I was helping you hunt down the Resurrected."

Topher grimaced. "Would rather not use the words 'hunt down'. More like 'find'."

Ivy rolled her eyes. "Right, because this is a charity."

"Regardless," Topher continued. "Yes, it's helpful, but moving around like this all the time takes income. You could help with that by becoming a developer like me and Lucia." Topher got a faraway look for a second. "I wonder if merging and becoming a small business together would be better for taxes."

Ivy looked to Lucia for help, but the other woman just shrugged.

"There he is," Topher said, pointing at a blue SUV clawing its way through the chokehold of traffic.

The three of them loaded their bags into the trunk and Topher took the front, while Ivy and Lucia jumped in the back. Ivy rubbed her warm chest as the Black man in the driver's seat turned around and gave them a wave.

"Hey. I'm Danny."

His hair was short, with a fresh swish design shaved into the shorn sides. He was younger than the three of them, but there were already frown lines embedded on either side of his mouth. He turned around without waiting for a response and pulled out from the airport, making his painful way across the city and over to Eckington.

They kept the conversation minimal, Topher interrupting the silence to ask, "How are things?"

"Quiet," Danny answered. And that was that for the hour long ride to the apartment. It made Ivy want to crawl out of her skin.

Just as she was ready to throw herself out the door for relief, they pulled up outside of a brick apartment building and they all piled out, Danny leading them up to a cramped one bedroom on the third floor.

Great, Ivy thought glumly.

As if quality time with Lucia and Topher wasn't bad enough when they had separate rooms. She knew she shouldn't complain. There was a roof over her head, seemingly without any strings attached, and Danny showed them a fully stocked fridge. But this much together-ness was going to wear on her fast.

When Danny went back out to grab some beers, Ivy asked, "So why are we crashing with this guy again? Does he have intel or something? Why not another empty nest?"

Topher helped themself to some of the baby carrots in the fridge, crunching noisily before they answered. "We've been striking out so far, so I want to get a lay of the land. See if Danny's noticed any signs regular people wouldn't. We just don't usually get the opportunity to stay with the other Resurrected because no one stays in one place."

"Again. Why is that? I mean doesn't *anyone* figure out a way to go back to their old life? Or at least rebuild somewhere? Surely not everyone likes being a nomad."

Lucia and Topher exchanged a look, one Ivy was becoming increas-ingly familiar with.

"What?"

Lucia sighed. "It's just easier this way. No one wants to feel like a ghost in their own life."

She was biting the inside of her cheek. Her tell. Ivy had been stum-bling on them more and more, as if picking pebbles out of her shoes with each question.

"In any case, we won't be able to stay with Danny long," Topher said, popping another carrot in their mouth. "Don't want to overstay our welcome. If we don't have any luck this week, we'll move across town somewhere."

Their words seemed innocuous enough, but they came out measured, mimicking Lucia's weird tone.

Still, Ivy let the topic drop, relieved when Danny returned and interrupted Topher's lecture about the merits of learning a coding language. No matter what they said, Ivy simply didn't have a head for hacking or whatever it was they did for work. Shame she didn't. It might have made hunting Lenox down that much easier.

So far Rita's list of possible headquarters had been just about useless, and none of the woman's contacts had reached out yet. Hopefully some of the potential fronts in D.C. showed some sign of him. Lenox had kept her informed about the operations of other fronts when she was in his good graces, but the second he started doubting her, he would have uprooted them and taken over new locations. It was going to be Portland, L.A., Vegas, all over again. Walking the city to sniff out the smallest clue, keeping her head down so she wasn't found out first, and each moment, stoking the fervent hope that Lenox was here somewhere, setting up a new center of operations. The process was painfully slow, but she was used to lying in wait for her prey, a viper ready to lunge when the time was right. Before, she'd only ever hunted the people Lenox ordered hits on, bringing back anyone who'd been found in collusion with rival gangs, anyone who had information he needed. Now, she hunted for her own ends.

At least she didn't have to worry about Rita running her mouth on top of everything else. The woman was right about one thing, if you were smart enough to get out of the game, it was suicide to become a player again. No, Rita wouldn't be a problem. She was too interested in saving her own neck. Still, Ivy hoped she'd actually follow up on her promise to send any more leads her way.

The night passed awkwardly at best. When the others went to bed, Ivy made herself at home on the tiny porch, dangling her legs over the edge and watching the occasional dog walker or teen stride by, none of them aware of her presence.

The glass door slid open behind her and Danny walked out, freezing for a moment when he noticed her. He wore a silk durag and pajamas made up of boxers and a t-shirt with an anime kid throwing an uppercut.

"Sorry," he mumbled, about to edge out.

Ivy waved him over.

"Your house. I can leave if you want."

After a moment's hesitation, Danny joined her, settling into the lone plastic patio chair and stretching his long, spindly legs in front of him.

"Can't sleep?" he asked.

Ivy shrugged. Saying yes would be putting it mildly. Between her natural instinct to stay alert and the nightmares about being used as a human pincushion, her sleepless nights were adding up to one large weight of exhaustion.

"Don't take it personally. Your place is...nice."

Danny snorted. "I don't usually host."

She chuckled. "Never been a people person myself. Do you at least have any fun party tricks?"

He cracked a smile. For all his guardedness in the car, here in the quiet of night, he didn't seem to mind giving her a peek beyond that armor. She could appreciate that.

She grinned even wider when he held up an empty terracotta pot between his hands. And without twitching the tiniest muscle, crushed it.

Or...no. More like...condensed. The clay almost buckled into itself, the bits all clinging together in one tight ball of terra cotta. And then...began to float.

Danny held his hands wide and the mashed pile of shards drifted apart, floating like feathers in a breeze. Suspended between flat palms.

"Shit, dude," Ivy whispered.

"Car crash," he said, condensing the broken pot again and letting the pile fall to the ground. "I died on impact. And when I woke up, I could feel gravity. Force. I get to play with it."

He nodded to her.

"Fair's fair."

So she let the warmth creep down her veins, into her arms, and produced a dagger into each hand.

He let out a low, appreciative whistle. "Can I?"

She handed him a blade, hilt first. He turned it over this way and that, before handing it back.

"Seems useful."

Ivy reclaimed the daggers and sheathed them, rubbing the insides of her wrists.

"It has its charms."

What those charms were, he had the decency not to ask. She watched him for a moment as he turned his attention back to the street below. Then tilted her chin towards the door and asked, "You ever think about traveling around with those two?"

Danny shook his head. "Nah. I appreciate what they're doing, trying to find the people in this new wave. But..."

"But?" Ivy prompted. She'd spent months dancing around Topher and Lucia's tight-lipped answers. If Danny knew more, maybe she could get him to share.

He rubbed the back of his neck. "If you ask me, Topher is poking the bear. I don't want to be around when it wakes up to take a swipe."

Ivy raised a brow.

"What bear?"

Now it was Danny's turn to look surprised. "They haven't told you about him? Or 'it' I guess? I'm not sure it's even human."

"Uh...no dude. Obviously not."

Danny digested this in his chair, looking uncomfortable. "Maybe there's a reason. You should ask."

She huffed out an annoyed breath.

"Any time I call them out on something fishy, they just dodge the question like goddamn politicians. What's going on?"

She'd had enough secrets with Lenox. And sure, she had plenty of her own, but that was different. Topher and Lucia didn't have anything to do with her plan. But she was traveling with them, and if bigger trouble waited, she needed to know.

Danny sighed and turned his gaze towards the streetlights.

"It's what keeps *me* up at night. Don't know if you really want to share in the misery."

"Look, if some big bad monster is hiding under the bed, I'd rather be prepared to face it."

"I don't know that you can, blades or not. Besides, it's probably not my place," he hedged.

"Topher is my ride. Not my babysitter and not my guardian. I'm my own person and I need to have the information to make my own decisions. Whatever this is that made you opt out of Topher's merry little band of runaways, I need to know. I need to know what I've gotten myself into."

Ivy held her breath, watching Danny mull over her words, attention turned inward as if holding an argument with himself. When he sighed, leaning over to dangle hands between his knees, she knew she had him.

"We call it the Soul Eater."

Topher's theories regarding what made a person likely to Resurrect involved quick, brutal deaths, often from freak accidents. Their idea was that death had to be so unexpected the body simply rejected it, thanks to some black hole tachyon nonsense that Ivy was sure she would never understand.

Knowing this helped them narrow their search once Topher's algorithm spit out potential geographical areas. Though, since said geographical areas were usually the size of a major city or larger, Ivy wasn't quite sure how useful it really was. So far, all of its suggestions had been dead ends. If you asked her, the morbid work of checking obituaries and scanning news from March 21 would get them closer to their next Resurrected sighting. It could be brutal, searching out who had died in violent ways, even when Ivy had seen her fair share of bloodshed in her prior life. And such work didn't make it any easier to ignore Danny's revelation.

Three days into their D.C. stint, Ivy directed them to a morgue outside of the city limits on the Maryland side. They waited in the hot air for the place to shut for the day so she could break them in and hunt for clues on one Phil Harris, who'd died on just the right date via gunshot.

"So," Ivy said as they waited out of sight behind a copse of trees. Sweat dripped down her back as she tied up her hair with false nonchalance. "What the fuck is a Soul Eater?"

Lucia and Topher whipped around so fast it was comical. Ivy grinned at their confusion, watching their silent conversation as they accused each other of letting the secret slide without the other's knowledge. It was a relief really, to have proof they'd been hiding things from her all along.

"Look, you need to level with me," she pressed. "Why do the Resurrected move around so much? What's so dangerous that we can't stay in one place for more than a few weeks? That no one seems interested in fighting back?"

Topher sighed and Ivy swallowed her glee, seeing their defeat. Danny had given her a name and very little else. She'd be damned if she let this slide.

"It's not that we can't stay anywhere," Topher began. "But when a few of us link up like this and stay in one area for a while it tends to leave a...signature."

"Like this Law of Attraction you keep talking about?"

"Yeah...but it also attracts something else."

Ivy nodded. "The Soul Eater. Another one of us?"

"We don't know," Lucia said in a small voice. "It showed up when we did, like another fluke in the universe. We think, somehow, it came from the same anomaly that brought us back. But it's not human. We don't even know its name. Some folks call it the Shadow. Others the Devourer. We call it the Soul Eater."

"And does it actually eat souls?"

"We don't know what it does exactly," Topher admitted. "But it does more than just kill. It's like it steals its victims' whole essence. And it only targets the Resurrected."

They met Ivy's eyes for the first time the entire conversation and a chill ran down her spine. Topher was *never* this serious. "That's why we're doing all of this. We're trying to help as many Resurrected as we can. Bring them into a network of aid before the Soul Eater gets to them."

Ivy held their gaze for a moment, processing the insanity of their words, swallowing a painful knot of panic. Then stated the obvious.

"Fucking yikes."

The statement hid the tightness in her chest, the way her heart raced, screaming for her to run. Far from whatever the fuck nightmare she'd stumbled on. Hunting Lenox was bad enough, but now she had to worry about a monster trailing after her?

"We didn't want to tell you because we didn't want to worry you," Lucia said. "Adjusting after Resurrection is hard enough without knowing that some nightmare is hunting us all down."

"So instead I've just been walking around with a target on my back without even knowing it was there. Does that sound safe to you?"

Neither of them answered. Ivy wanted to soak in her own vindication of catching them out, but somehow the sense of betrayal was worse.

Ivy looked at the morgue. If she could break in on her own, surely Lucia and Topher could figure it out for themselves.

"Fuck this shit. I thought Danny was pulling my leg, but this is *not* what I signed up for."

With Lenox, information had been a weapon. The sharing or hiding of it manipulated Ivy into whatever course of action he wanted. She wasn't about to put up with that bullshit again, not with her second life on the line.

"Ivy, we have to find the others before the Soul Eater can. Before it can destroy all the Resurrected," Topher appealed.

"Sure. And good fucking luck with that. I'd rather *not* get my soul sucked out dementor-style, thank you very much."

She left without a backward glance, making her way back to a busy enough road where she was able to pick up a taxi back to the apartment.

Danny was out, much to her relief. She stuffed her things into her duffle bag and left before anyone could return and try to talk her out of it.

She double checked the stack of cash she'd kept hidden all this time, all in different compartments of her bag. Still there, not a dollar missing. Not even from the obvious pockets. She wasn't used to spending this much time with people who weren't out to slit her throat, literally or figuratively. If she thought about it too long, it made her gut clench. Just a bit. Just enough that she could chalk it up to indigestion.

Don't you dare give anyone a second chance, Iv, Lenox had always said. *You do that? That's as good as showing someone where to gut you.* And he'd certainly followed through with *that* bit of advice.

Topher and Lucia had their own agenda, and if they'd been hiding the Soul Eater, chances were they had other secrets. So she'd handle the Soul Eater on her own. It was working for Danny, wasn't it?

She heaved the bag onto her shoulder and left. No looking back. No notes. No hints.

It was time to start over. Again.

13

DINA

Dina might not have control over her powers, but she *was* turning into an excellent pickpocket.

At first, she only tried when the waters would sweep her away, timing her attempts for the least repercussions possible. But now, stealing had become second nature.

She deleted her call history and placed the "borrowed" cell phone beneath a park bench, telling herself it would be easy enough for someone to track it down with an app to appease her guilt. "Thou shalt not steal" and all that.

If the owner of the phone got it back, did it still count? And if it was the only way she could get in contact with Zev so she could have a roof over her head, would the Big Guy forgive her? Despite coming back from the dead (definitely not kosher), she found she still cared. Besides, she didn't *actively* want to screw anyone over.

When she'd called Zev from the phone, he'd once again chided her for not going to the library. And then she had pointed out that D.C. was designed by someone on an acid trip and she didn't know her way *to* the library. And that had been that.

It was a shame she hadn't landed in a more affordable city than D.C., but Zev had waved off her guilt and booked her a room on 14th near Dupont Circle for two nights (a room he then had to provide her directions to). She wasn't sure she'd last that long, but he'd wanted to leave her a cushion. It was unfamiliar, having an older brother looking out for her again. Unfamiliar, but oh so welcome.

By the time she made it to the apartment someone was renting out as an AirBnB (Dina wasn't sure how legal that was, but she wasn't going to question it), there were already a couple of packages waiting for her at the front desk. Dina tried to ignore the curious look she got from the desk clerk as she picked up the key under the pretense of housesitting. When she got up to the room, she dumped all the packages onto the minimalistic, gray couch and opened the cardboard to find a low-end smartphone, as well as a dry bag, power converter, protein bars, leave in conditioner for "extra dry hair", and a mini first aid kit. Truly a treasure trove.

The apartment was cheaply made. Dina could hear the people above walking around and the slightest breeze whistled between the glass. But the sheets were clean and the air conditioning was a balm after returning to east coast humidity once more.

Dina flopped onto the bed with its worn bedspring and soaked it all in.

"How the fuck did you manage that so fast?" Dina asked once the phone had charged enough for her to call Zev.

"There's this great thing called ride-share deliveries, D. Come and join the 21st century."

"Well, thank you."

"Don't thank me yet. First we're gonna have to get my credit card connected to your phone."

It took a while and some insults hurled back and forth, but they managed.

"Don't go too crazy. I'm not made out of money, and neither is Ben."

"So no strippers. Got it."

He snorted. "Not unless we're invited."

"Well, thank you both."

"That's what family's for."

The words churned in Dina's gut.

"Sorry," he murmured, obviously thinking about their parents, the same way Dina was. He cleared his throat. "Anyway, I've been trying to do my research on hydrology and ocean currents. Do you have any idea what part of the water cycle you're getting picked up in? Like, are you only dragged along when it's raining?"

"No, the weather doesn't seem to matter so much as the nearest water source."

"Hmm. Well, there isn't much between D.C. and a different continent. Bermuda obviously. Do you ever make shorter jumps? Like would you wind up in the Chesapeake again?"

"So far, no. It's just...random."

"Well, I'll keep looking."

Dina blew out a frustrated sigh. "I keep trying to direct it. Push it to take me to Sacramento, but it's like trying to move a mountain."

If she could find a reliable, consistent way to get to Zev, even if she had to endure whole orbits in between, he could actually help her. Provide shelter until the current took her away again. If she could just resurface in that one place, again and again, even that would be better than this unpredictability.

She let herself imagine it for a moment, curling up on the couch together, watching old episodes of Teen Titans, launching popcorn at each other like they were kids again, even if it only lasted for hours or days. A dream.

She'd shrunk somehow, in those years after Zev left. Shrunk until she became someone her parents would never reject. Until she didn't recognize herself. That kid who used to nerd out over a fantasy novel, who used to run screaming between the trees of their suburban backyard while she pretended they were some creature from Zev's latest anime. That kid had grown into a mild-mannered adult who didn't even have real friends. And one day, that mild-mannered adult had come home to an empty apartment in an empty life and imagined taking a sledgehammer to everything she owned just to feel something again.

Instead, she'd decided to come out to her parents, to break free of the cage she'd locked with her own two hands, only to find herself in this strange limbo. Living by the terms of the water itself.

"We'll figure it out," Zev was saying now. "There's gotta be a way to control it. Maybe it just takes time."

"It's been *months*, Z."

It was his time to sigh. "I know, I know. We'll just have to keep trying."

"Yeah," she grumbled.

"In the meantime, D.C.'s Pride Parade is today. We're clearly not going to work this out in the next few hours. You should get out there."

"I dunno," Dina mumbled.

She'd never been "out". Not even in her personal life away from her parents. Even without their prying eyes, it felt like a dirty secret, something to be whispered in dark corners and swept under rugs. She could be happy for the people who had the courage, but she could never make the jump herself, to meet the outstretched hands waiting to welcome her into a world of glitter and rainbows. Being closeted had ruined more than one of her relationships, and she'd never blamed the girls who'd broken it off.

So she didn't feel especially prideful. Going to the parade would only make her even more aware of how much she didn't fit in.

"Come on, D. It'd be good for you. Be normal for a minute or two before you go back to being one of the weirder X-men."

"Zev—"

"For me?"

She groaned. He wasn't playing fair. And Zev always complained about Jewish guilt. But then she remembered that cage she still hadn't quite escaped. She'd died in a car crash and come back anyway. Maybe it really was time to start living. Break all the locks and chains and live life by her own rules for once.

"Fiiiiiine."

"And maybe treat yourself to some new clothes while you're at it? Get something with sequins."

"It's your wallet," she warned.

"I'll consider it worth it if it gets your ass out to Pride."

In the end, Dina did treat herself to new clothes. Nothing with too much glitter, and she kept the bomber jacket. But it was nice to have something new. Well, new to her. She'd stuck to thrift stores for her new outfit, not wanting to blow through Zev and Ben's savings. But D.C. had enough to pick from and she'd landed on green, linen overalls with deep pockets and a black tank top, eager to have something versatile, but better suited for the heat. She tied the jacket around her waist, regretting bringing it from her room, but she hated parting with her few belongings. If she predicted her next episode wrong, she didn't want to be left without the necessities once more.

Once her outfit was settled, it was simple enough to follow the crowds.

At first, it was overwhelming to be surrounded by so many people, many of whom were clearly comfortable in their own skin with rainbows plastered on flags and shirts and bags like badges of honor. Like armor instead of shame.

She couldn't help her nerves, not after years of hiding in the dark, of fearing a hate crime at her doorstep. But as she delved further into the throng, something loosened in her. She was surrounded yes, but surrounded by people like her. Caught in a current she could happily surrender to.

Zev was right, she thought with a laugh. She needed a day to be normal. To *feel* normal. In a way she hadn't for years and years. So she let the masses pull her along, until she encountered a metal barrier along the parade route and found a spot that wasn't already taken. She pulled out of the current of sequins and chants and laughter, and set up shop in the shade, leaning on the metal and watching the people walk by as they waited for the parade to begin.

For a heartbeat, she wondered what would happen if she ran into someone she knew. Enough Marylanders came to D.C. for it to happen. Then again, if she was spotted, they'd probably have more pressing questions. Like how she was still alive.

It's a big enough city and a big enough parade. You won't see anyone you know, she reassured herself, taking a deep breath and focusing on people-watching.

Another figure peeled away from the crowd and took a nearby spot, resting their elbows on the guard rail. Heat radiated through Dina's chest, a light pressure on her skin, like someone had sat a cooling ember there. She'd felt that before...back in—

Dina glanced over. Did a double take. Of all the people it *was* someone she recognized.

Hazel eyes and dark hair. Posture straight and confident, as if the world could burn and she wouldn't stop twice to think about the ashes. It was her alright.

The woman from Portland.

14

DINA

The other woman must have felt Dina watching because she looked over, surprise lighting up her face as their eyes made contact. She immediately came closer and took the spot to Dina's right.

Dina could do nothing but stare until she gave herself a good mental kick.

Then said eloquently, "Uh...hey."

She immediately considered throwing herself back into the crowd to be trampled and put out of her misery.

But the other woman just smirked, like it was a private joke. "Hey yourself."

Dina couldn't breathe. It was like being underwater again, the pressure crushing down on her chest. Only this time, she didn't mind being swept away.

This close, she could make out the thin scar cutting through the woman's upper lip, and another just below her hairline. The hint of blonde roots growing out beneath pitch black hair. A sharp undercut that came up to the tips of her heavily pierced ears. A smattering of freckles across her nose. She wore all black again, though this time a tank top and jean shorts. The expanse of skin on display was well muscled, like a boxer, more scars slashing fine, white lines here and there on her arms and legs.

"What brings you to D.C., Bathroom Girl?" the woman asked, lip twitching up to the side.

Dina blinked, made herself look away so she wouldn't look like an absolute nut job. Then she grimaced, processing the question.

"Please tell me that's not how you've been thinking of me."

"Do you *want* me to be thinking of you?"

Yes. Because I've been thinking of you.

Their previous interaction had lasted all of about five minutes. Yet Dina hadn't been able to get this woman out of her head.

"My name's Dina," she said, instead of answering.

"Dina." The woman seemed to taste her name the way you would a fine wine. "I'm Ivy," she said. Her smile could have cut Dina's heart out, and she would have thanked her for the honor.

"I-I can't believe you're here," Dina said before she could stop herself. "I mean, it's so..."

"Random?" Ivy provided. Dina's own incredulity was reflected in her face. "Yeah. You're kinda the last person I would have expected to bump into here. I mean, how insane is this?"

Dina nodded. "Insane. For sure."

All these people, all these festivities, and somehow it was Ivy who'd found a spot by her side.

They watched each other for a moment too long, and both turned away. Did Dina imagine the other woman's flush? Her own had to be from the heat, right?

She tried to focus on the crowds lining either side of the street. And then blurted out, "I've never been to Pride before."

She didn't look over. Didn't want to see the shock or judgment or whatever Ivy surely had written on her face in the wake of such an admission.

"Then you're in for a treat," Ivy said.

When Dina braved a look, the woman was smiling at her, not even the smallest ounce of pity on her face.

"Seriously? You're not gonna make fun of me for going to my first pride at the late age of twenty-six?"

Ivy scoffed. "That's not late. I met someone at a parade who hadn't come out to himself until he was like...I dunno, fifty. You come out when you come out. And now you're old enough to experience the parade in all its glory."

"Oh yeah?"

"Yeah. Much easier to get into all the good gay bars when you don't have to have a fake ID."

Dina laughed. "Is that your plan for Pride? Parade and then queer bar crawl?"

Ivy smirked. "Not much of a crawl when there's only two lesbian bars in the city and they're thirty minutes apart."

"So we'll have time to sober up and start all over is what you're saying."

"Knew you were a smart one," Ivy grinned.

Someone drunkenly stumbled into Dina, pushing her off balance. Ivy's hand shot out, righting her with a protective pressure on Dina's lower back.

Dina grimaced internally. She was so sweaty. But Ivy didn't seem to mind, keeping her hand there for a moment longer than necessary. Then she spied something over the top of Dina's head.

"I'll be right back. Save my spot?"

Dina nodded, tongue-tied. The second Ivy's back was turned, she checked her hair. Better than before she'd used about a quart of conditioner on it. It would suffice.

She hadn't flirted with anyone in ages. This was flirting, wasn't it? She was so rusty she wasn't sure she could tell the difference between a friendly gesture and something more. But she waited with her stomach tying itself in knots over a woman with a Cheshire Cat smile and a glint of something cunning in her eyes.

Fuck I'm in trouble.

When Ivy returned, she was swathed in rainbows. Rainbow flags, rainbow stickers, rainbow fans.

"It's a bit 'Corporate America does Pride', but since neither of us have much gear on..."

Ivy draped a flag around Dina's shoulders like a cloak. And for the first time it was a joy. Not a target painted on her back.

The other woman tied a lesbian flag around her own waist as a belt and then pulled something out of her pocket. "Got these too. Want some?"

Dina practically squealed at the sight of the adhesive gemstones. "Yes!"

Ivy laughed, the sound gravelly and warm. Dina wanted to bottle it up to carry in her pocket when she was inevitably carried away on the next wave.

No. Just be here. Focus on this moment, she told herself.

She was going to enjoy her first Pride. Universe be damned.

She closed her eyes and allowed Ivy to adorn her with sticky, rainbow gemstones, reveling in the touch of another human being. Of this *specific* human being. A woman she barely knew, but left pinpricks of heat across her skin with every touch.

Maybe, she mused, it was the excitement of Pride catching up to her, of being out, *really* out for the first time in her life.

Whatever the reason, she had to bite back her disappointment when Ivy withdrew. But then the woman handed her the sheet of gems.

"My turn," she said.

Dina mimicked the pattern she'd felt Ivy using, placing matching rainbows above her brows. Ivy didn't close her eyes though, and Dina's kept darting to the hazel, heart thudding like a tsunami beneath her ribs.

When she finished, she absentmindedly pressed a finger to the scar at Ivy's hairline.

The other woman flinched, but didn't move back.

"Sorry," Dina said, pulling away, warm with embarrassment. She really had been away from normal society too long.

Ivy took her hand and placed it back along the scar. "Don't be."

Dina wanted to ask, but if Ivy wanted to tell her about the scar's origin, she would. And if she didn't, she'd keep her curiosity under wraps. Instead, she let her fingers trace the raised skin.

God, she wanted to kiss her.

But she'd just met this woman. Well, sort of. Did the first time really count? Was she that starved for attention?

Yet this moment felt fragile as walking on ice. If she didn't hurry, she'd fall through and be lost in the dark depths.

A cheer went through the crowd and Dina jolted back, clearing her throat and turning away as music swelled around them. The parade had arrived.

Dina tried to focus on the first floats, telling herself the heat in her cheeks was from the D.C. summer, not her own heart leaping into her throat and stomach by turns. That the prickling of her skin was from the sun, not her hyperawareness of the woman next to her.

She'd nearly done it. Kissed a total stranger, out in public. Did Ivy know how close she'd been? How much she still wanted to? That she was imagining the taste of her lips even now? And Dina had touched her scar. Like some sort of idiot. This woman had to think she was completely nuts.

But when she dared a glance towards Ivy, the other woman held her gaze, grinning wickedly. Dina felt herself mimicking the expression with a laugh, relaxing back against the rail to watch the floats go by. Maybe she *was* completely nuts. But at least Ivy didn't seem to mind.

The parade itself was less exciting than Dina expected, corporation floats mixed in with other queer organizations. She yelled the loudest when the JCC group walked by with a trans Star of David in the middle of their rainbow flag. But the best part of the whole thing was that Ivy pressed close to her side despite the heat, watching Dina watch the parade.

By the time the last float shuffled by, Dina was sunburnt and drenched in sweat, but deliriously happy. At home in her own skin for the first time...maybe ever.

"And now?" she asked Ivy, surprised by her own assumption that they would continue the day together.

Ivy didn't hesitate.

"I saw a block party advertised, but if you ask me, we should head to one of the bars before the line gets too absurd. You down for that?"

"Down for anything," Dina said, meaning it.

Ivy laughed and slipped her hand into Dina's pulling her along with the metro crowd. And that easy gesture, the comfort of Ivy's strong grip, kept her heart racing the whole way.

On another day, Dina would have been overwhelmed by the crowds. Irritated by so many hot, sweaty bodies pressed next to hers. On another day, she would have worried about being caught by a neighbor. A friend of a friend of a friend who would have reported seeing Dina Adler hand in hand with a woman who looked like she belonged in a motorcycle gang.

Not today.

Somewhere along their ride to the Northwest side of the city, someone walked into the metro blasting Cher from their phone. The entire car, minus a few overwhelmed tourists, joined in. And the whole ride, Ivy stayed close, holding Dina steady as they swayed with the movement of the train, singing along, scratchy and off-key.

Eventually, Ivy nodded towards the doors.

"I think this is it."

They exited from the heat of bodies, back to the marginally cooler heat of a D.C. summer. Ivy checked her phone now and again to make sure they were on the right path.

"Have you been to this place before?" Dina asked.

She'd never really gone out in D.C. Happy hour with her friends had always meant meeting up at one of the chain restaurants at the nearby strip mall, all of them too lazy to drive into the city.

"Nah," Ivy said. "But I heard a few people talking about it and it sounded like a good time." She shot Dina a smile. "Up for an adventure?"

Dina laughed. A freer sound than she'd ever imagined emerging from her mouth. "Something tells me your whole life is an adventure."

Ivy grinned, and Dina wondered if she misread the sadness there.

"Wouldn't be any fun otherwise."

The other woman turned away before Dina could prod further. And she wasn't quite sure how to express what she was feeling without sounding creepy. That she could take more than smirks and laughter. That she wanted to hear all of it. How Ivy got her scars. What had spurred that flash of pain.

Then again, it was Pride. No one wanted a stranger digging into their past on a normal day, let alone one that was supposed to be celebratory. She let the question slide away, let herself be pulled over to Sapphics Anonymous, the singular lesbian bar on this side of the city. There was already a line out the door to the downstairs area (the top floor was a gay bar, apparently), but she and Ivy passed the time with ease, people-watching and cheering on other party goers.

And then they were in. Despite the sun still high in the sky, the place was packed, the room dark, like it was midnight rather than 8 pm.

"Can I buy you a drink?" Ivy asked over the din, angling them to the bar where a Black woman with long, red braids poured drinks with all the talent of an acrobat.

"Oh, you don't have to," Dina said thinking about Zev's borrowed money. She wasn't sure she could return the favor without heaps of guilt about how she was spending his hard-earned cash.

As if reading her thoughts, Ivy said, "No strings, promise. I just have money burning a hole in my pocket and want to buy a pretty girl a drink at a gay bar on Pride."

Dina laughed, cheeks pleasantly warm. "Far be it from me to stand in your way then."

This elicited another laugh, and Ivy leaned into the bar to shout their order.

"Let's look around," Ivy said once they both had drinks in hand. A tequila sunrise for Dina, old fashioned for Ivy. She'd have to remember that.

The bar had several floors, including a dedicated dance floor and a patio rooftop with a photo booth at the other end.

Dina dragged Ivy to the photo booth for a laugh. Knowing it was cheesy. Knowing she didn't care. Knowing she'd keep that strip of photos in her dry bag even if most of the pictures made it clear they hadn't been quite ready for the flash.

Then she steered Ivy down to the dance floor.

"You wanted to buy a pretty girl a drink, and I want to dance with a pretty girl."

Ivy laughed in her ear. "I live to please."

It was awkward at first, dancing with someone new while surrounded by strangers in one of the gayest places Dina had ever been. But then the crowd was shouting along to Shania Twain, and Dina went from feeling smothered to embraced. Sweat clung to her skin and the heat of other bodies wrapped around her, but so did Ivy, hand pressed against her waist, one leg between hers, face inching closer each time they swayed.

And Dina couldn't look away. Drowning in hazel and eager for the plunge. And God those lips. That scar. What would it be like to press her lips to the corner of Ivy's mouth?

"You can kiss me. If you want," Ivy said, breath whispering across Dina's skin. A smirk played across her face.

Dina's eyes flicked up to meet Ivy's again, like she'd been caught. She supposed she had.

"You're a bit cocky, huh?" she said, laughing despite her nerves.

"Part of my charm," Ivy replied, mouth widening once more into a grin.

Dina chuckled, fingers tracing the side of Ivy's face like she had earlier at the parade, falling to the other scar through the woman's lip.

She'd never kissed a woman in public like this. It felt daring somehow, though she'd already seen plenty of queer couples making out since she'd stepped out of her rented room. But for her, it was rebellious as a cigarette beneath the bleachers at school. She'd always hurried by those kids on her way to track.

But that was a part of her old life. She'd been across the world and back. Had become a part of the water, and it a part of her. And at any moment, that same water could drag her away.

She was no longer the Dina Adler who had fallen from the Bay Bridge. And this Dina Adler could kiss a stranger, a woman, during Pride, out in the world for all to see.

And she did.

Ivy gasped, as if despite everything, she wasn't ready for Dina to make the final leap. But once their lips met, the world fell quiet around them, waves breaking against the secret cove they formed.

Someone whooped nearby, and Dina pulled the flag from her shoulders to cover the both of them in a shield of rainbow, skin warm as Ivy pulled her closer. Her hands had come to either side of Dina's waist, leaning into Dina's touch as she threaded fingers through Ivy's hair and deepened the heart-pounding kiss. Their lips met again and again. Dina couldn't breathe. But she didn't need to.

Ivy tasted like mint gum and shelter. And Dina wanted more. As much as she could get. Ravenous after years of starving herself. Like she was stealing scant breaths before the dive underwater. Greedy for each and every one, aware that this would all shatter when the waves came crashing down.

They kissed and danced and kissed again. Until the spaces between each kiss became torture. Until Dina gathered courage with every inch of her on fire from tangling with Ivy.

"Do you want to get out of here?" she shouted in Ivy's ear, immediately heating up at the words. It sounded too much like something from a movie. Or something you said before a one-night stand. And she didn't know what she wanted from Ivy, but it wasn't that.

"Lead the way, Supernova," Ivy returned.

"Supernova?"

"I know someone who's obsessed with astronomy. Says it's the explosion of a star. That feels like you today."

Dina grinned. She did feel like an explosion. Bursting at the seams. Unable to contain this new version of herself. One that didn't hide in shadowy corners hoping no one would realize she was about as straight as Lombard Street.

"Hmm, beats 'Bathroom Girl'."

Ivy chuckled, sweat dripping down the sides of her temple and let Dina lead her into the night air, still sticky and humid, but refreshing after the press of so many bodies.

The whole walk to the apartment, Dina waited for Ivy to change her mind. Decide this was too much too fast. Let go of her hand and leave her alone again.

But the other woman held tight, occasionally bringing their clasped hands to her lips as they spoke in soft voices about city lights and what being queer meant to them. When Dina shared a story about a crush she'd had at Hebrew school, Ivy didn't ask her about Kosher salt or how she could be religious, queer, and believe in science all at once. And when Ivy spoke in calm tones about the fight she'd gotten in the first time someone caught her kissing a girl, Dina didn't ask if that was the story behind her scars. They let the words roll between them like a river undammed, never interfering with their flow, allowing for shelter from the current when it was needed.

When they entered the lobby and the desk clerk passed the two women a glance, Dina's first instinct was to drop Ivy's hand. Pretend this wasn't exactly what it was. She swallowed hard, held tight, and kept walking.

When the silver doors of the elevator shut them in, Ivy asked, "Still not used to being out?"

Dina shook her head. "No. Sorry, I'm not ashamed of you or—"

Ivy squeezed her hand and leaned back against the elevator, pulling her in after her.

"It's okay. I get it. I never felt like I could tell anyone about my relationships before."

Dina tried to read the other woman's expression. To unbury the meaning of those words.

"And now?" she asked instead.

"Now..." the other woman shook her head, eyes distant. Like she was lost among the rapids of her own mind.

"You don't have to answer that," Dina said, placing fingers gently against Ivy's lips.

The other woman kissed them, then stood up straight when the elevator rang open.

It only occurred to Dina to be nervous again when she let Ivy into the apartment and the door shut with a soft whoosh behind them. The lights were off, orange streetlamps illuminating the room from between the curtains and leaving corners of shadows untouched.

Ivy stepped close, pressing Dina back into the tiny entryway, leaning in, like she too was relying on the other woman for breath.

Dina's whole body tingled as Ivy pressed a soft kiss to her mouth, her cheek, her neck.

Everything in her burned, fire pooling in her core, between her legs. But—

"I can't believe you want to kiss me right now," she blurted out.

Ivy laughed. "Have you seen yourself, Dina? Of course I want to kiss you."

Dina snorted. "I meant...Ivy, I'm *so* gross right now."

The other woman chuckled, falling against her, head nestled in the crook of Dina's neck.

"Yeah, me too honestly."

Dina fought against the lump in her throat. "Shower?"

"Shower," Ivy agreed. "Do you want to go first?"

Dina hesitated, trying to read the other woman in the dark.

"Or..." Ivy began when Dina failed to find words to answer.

"Or," Dina said with a nod. She gently pushed Ivy away and headed to the bathroom, turning on the faucet. She waited for it to reach the right temperature, the flow of water another reminder of how ephemeral this moment was. If she was going to pick a time to be brave, now was that moment.

Ivy crowded into the room with her, her sheer presence filling the space. Like Dina stood near a bonfire, soaking in its glow. Like dancing across knives for the thrill of it.

Dina reached up to undo the buttons of her overalls, but Ivy stopped her.

"I want to do that," she murmured. "If that's alright."

Dina nodded, and the other woman slid callused hands up her ribcage, undoing the overalls, pulling the shirt over Dina's head to reveal the plainest underwear Dina had ever worn in front of a partner.

But the other woman didn't seem to care, eyes roaming over Dina's body like she couldn't believe her own luck.

"Your turn," Dina said, gently tugging the hem of Ivy's tank top.

There was a brief hesitation. A moment where Ivy stilled like a rabbit caught in a fox's gaze. Then she nodded and let Dina lift the shirt away.

Ivy's skin was puckered with scars. Most small, many old and jagged. One by her pelvis that looked suspiciously like it had come from a bullet.

Ivy closed her eyes when Dina traced them with her fingers.

"I can feel you wanting to ask," Ivy whispered.

"I won't if you don't want to tell me," she returned, kissing the point where Ivy's jaw met her neck, fingers moving to unbutton her shorts.

"Not today," Ivy breathed.

She nodded, and kept her hands moving. She liked the way Ivy said it. Like there would be a tomorrow.

The shorts slid to the floor, followed by black panties and bra and Dina's own undergarments. She nearly slipped and cracked her head open as she stepped backward into the shower.

Ivy saved her just in time and Dina hoped the other woman would let her drown under the shower head.

"Definitely thought that would be a lot sexier," she muttered.

"Yeah, shower sex for a first time is a hell of a move."

Dina backed into the fall of water, sighing as the sweat washed from her skin. "We could—"

"Nope," Ivy said, following her in. "We're already here. I feel disgusting, and you're hogging the water."

Despite the promise of Ivy's fingers trailing her wet skin, despite the heat building in her core, the two of them washed, using soap that smelled foreign and familiar, belonging to no one and everyone the way generic soaps did.

Only when they were both clean did Ivy's hands roam again, as if she'd been waiting for the right moment, to make sure Dina was cared for before fanning the flames high once more.

And when she did, when she slid her hand between Dina's legs, ecstasy. She closed her eyes, with a gasp, clutching Ivy to keep upright, utterly lost in the delicate touch of those fingers. Right where she wanted, where she needed them. Dina was like one of the fireworks someone had lit outside, a thousand pieces bursting apart before falling to earth again as Ivy let the pleasure build and build and build. And explode.

"Fuck," she said, when she could speak again. She still clung to Ivy for dear life. The other woman only laughed.

Laughed until Dina kissed the sound from her lips. Until she circled Ivy's rosebud nipple with her thumb.

Ivy pitched forward and turned off the faucet, pulling Dina with her as she stumbled out of the shower and towards the bed.

They were both soaked, but Dina didn't care. The only thing that mattered was her tongue on Ivy's damp skin, the other woman's gasp as she danced her fingers down between Ivy's legs, found the warm heat of her and explored, until she too lay cursing and panting and shaking.

And after, long long after, they lay face to face, unafraid as they watched each other in comfortable silence, hands tracing here and there, kisses exchanged and errant hairs brushed from eyes. And in that quiet shelter, Dina thought she was living for the first time in either of her lives. And that she wanted to keep living.

What would Ivy say if she told her the truth? This strange woman who felt familiar as the air you smell only in your hometown.

My name is Dina Adler. On March 21st, I died. But for some reason, I didn't stay dead. And now I'm not sure if I was even living before now.

Aloud, all she said was, "I've never had a day like this."

She whispered the words, holding Ivy's gaze even though it felt like a secret. Something she ought to duck her head and hide from.

"I haven't either," Ivy said with equal quiet, equal seriousness. "Would you like to have a day like this with me tomorrow?"

The woman immediately bit her lip, as if she couldn't believe she'd asked. The expression tugged at the scar.

"I would," Dina answered truthfully. And as they lay awake, whispering in hushed voices, she prayed and prayed for the crashing of waves to stay far away.

15

IVY

When the first beam of sunlight reached greedy fingers into the room, Ivy jolted up, breathing hard, bone dagger already in fist.

But she wasn't at the manor house with its suffocating walls of crimson and fragile web of "shelter". No one was coming to rat her out or slip another blade between her ribs. She was in an apartment, lying in clean sheets, next to a woman whose hair haloed around her head like waves flowing across sand. Whose skin tasted like honey and whose smile cut through all the chinks in Ivy's armor.

And thank God she was a sound sleeper.

Ivy dragged in a deep breath, sheathed the dagger within herself once more, and tried to lie back down and enjoy a normal morning after. One where she didn't have anyone from the crew waiting for her to slip up, eager to use anyone she expressed interest in as leverage. One where Lenox wasn't about to call with a job that needed doing now, yes now.

Oh, you *have something important? More important than your own hide once I get my hands on you? Get your ass back here, Ivy.*

The "or else" never needed saying.

But Lenox wasn't going to call. She could just lie down and have the awkward conversation about how sober they'd both been (pretty sober, she thought), if the other woman would stand by all she'd said last night (was that too much to hope for?), how quickly Dina wanted her to leave (maybe not at all?).

Dina. Supernova. Three times was a charm, but what about two? And she'd known. Somehow she'd just *known* she would turn her head and find Dina staring right back. Surely…

No, Ivy chided herself. *You're not into that woo woo shit. Things like this don't happen because of magic. If the universe gave a shit, you wouldn't have ended up dead.*

Then again, maybe her second life was proof that the universe *did* give a shit.

Dina muttered something unintelligible and rolled towards Ivy, wincing in her sleep.

Last night's rules might no longer apply, but Ivy couldn't stop herself from brushing the hair out of Dina's face, away from dark brows and the straight line of her nose.

"Alright?" she murmured, not quite sure the other woman was awake.

Dina mumbled something, eyes squeezed tight, as if in pain.

"Got any Ibuprofen?"

Dina shook her head, which Ivy assumed to be a no, until the other woman said, "Not a hangover."

Ivy had half a second more to take her in, run her fingers along Dina's temple, through those tendrils of hair.

Then Dina was springing out of bed, wandering around the place, clearly looking for scattered clothing.

"Shit. Shit. Shit. Shit," she was saying on loop, bursting into the bathroom.

"Not the most promising start," Ivy said to no one in particular, hand still half lifted towards the now empty bed.

Dina sprinted back in, mostly clothed with her overalls buttoned on just the one side.

"I have to go, I'm so sorry, I have to go," she said, darting around the room until she found a wallet, her phone, and what looked like a mini first aid kit. The most shocking thing was not that Ivy was experiencing a true one-night stand, but that said one-night stand was now stuffing all her things into a dry bag, clipping it to herself, and shrugging into a bomber jacket that was way too warm for a D.C. summer.

"Look, this is your place. You can kick me out if you want," Ivy said, feigning nonchalance as she went in search of her own clothes.

Fuck having this *conversation naked.*

Dina seemed to realize she was there for the first time all morning. Really see her the same way she had the night before. "Ivy, I'm sorry. I don't *want* to go, but I don't have a choice."

"Look, you can just tell me you were looking for a good time. It was Pride. I know how it goes."

Ivy yanked on her tank top. By the time she'd gotten the fabric over her eyes and had her head through the neck of the garment, Dina was in front of her, hands pressed to the sides of Ivy's face.

"Ivy, I mean it. I'm sorry. I-I—"

She was looking around with frantic, darting eyes. Like a fish on the line or an animal with its leg in a trap. Real fear soaked through those brown eyes. Fear and sadness.

Ivy grabbed Dina's hands before she could slip away.

"Dina, are you alright? Do you need help?"

She laughed, but it wasn't a joyful sound, marred as it was by the threat of tears.

"Fuck, I don't even know my own phone number. Can you give me yours?"

"Um—"

"If you want to, that is. But you have to be quick. You can say no."

Dina was trembling. So Ivy found a marker in one of the drawers and scribbled her number on Dina's proffered forearm.

When she finished, she reached for Dina's shaking hands, trying to steady them with her own. "Hey, talk to me. Whatever it is, let me help."

Help how, she wasn't sure. With daggers if she needed to. Even if the act of pulling them from her own flesh might scare the other woman away for good.

"I really, truly wish you could," Dina said, almost gasping for breath now. "Look, maybe you should go before I...before things get weird."

You don't even know the half of it.

"I can take weird, Dina."

"This isn't normal weird."

"Is there such a thing?"

Ivy was rewarded with a laugh that sounded slightly more genuine. Like one of the ones she'd heard last night.

"In the grand scheme of things, yes." Dina squeezed her eyes shut. "I can't—" she gasped.

And then it was like the woman's body was shaking apart, the pieces of it losing substance like ink dropped into water. Like watching one of those bath bombs fizzle into nothing. The brown hair became streams of water, the soft flesh mist. Dina shook apart in front of Ivy, and there was nothing she could do but watch with her mouth hanging open, hands clinging uselessly to the disappearing form. And as they faded into the ether, Dina's eyes held a deep sorrow, like the woman had truly fractured apart.

And then she was gone, not even the smallest raindrop left in her wake. Only the faint scent of a riverbed.

Ivy stood staring for long moments. Mouth slack, hands empty. Even when she finally retreated back into the busy streets of the city, she couldn't make her mind focus on anything else.

She'd finally done what Topher and Lucia had brought her on to do.

She'd found a Resurrected.

In the Water

*D**roplets becoming rivulets becoming streams becoming oceans.*

Pieces pulled apart, together, woven then shredded.

She's in the rain, in the crowds. The cry of a tern. The crash of a wave.

Everywhere. Nowhere.

There was a girl. With scars on her knuckles and cracked mirrors behind her eyes.

This is not her. But she remembers this woman, clings to hazel eyes and sharp teeth. To soft skin and hard edges. A girl sharp as a blade, ready to cut.

Dina. Her name is Dina. Not this brass knuckle girl, but her. Dina Adler.

She died. She resurfaced. She keeps dying. She keeps resurfacing. Reborn the way a phoenix rises from ash. And now, she flows across ocean beds and cracks in the Earth's crust. She brushes against islands and the forgotten places of the world, its deepest secrets exposed. And these she clings to as well, the strange creatures of the water, bones of sunken ships, currents gone astray.

The water takes her and she lets it. She fought at first. To hold onto a girl in a dim-lit room, who covered her in jewels and made her glow. But there is no fighting an ocean of might. The rivers that carve stones into canyons.

And so the water takes her, only the smallest corner of her consciousness able to track the pieces of her mind that have exploded apart and will reform once more on a distant shore.

16

Ivy

I vy kept checking her phone. First every minute or so, convinced Dina would call or text and let her know what the fuck happened. Then, after the first day passed without a word, she restricted it to every five minutes. Three days later, she permitted herself a look once an hour.

Nothing.

The woman had to be another Resurrected, right? What other explanation was there? Ivy didn't think she could handle other supernatural beings. The idea of a Soul Eater out in the world was bad enough. And that feeling again. Like...magnets. Just how Lucia had described it. Gravity pulling them together before they even locked eyes.

So. A Resurrected who had power over water. Maybe. The other woman had been far too frantic to claim power over anything. More like water had power over her. And if Dina had no control, was she being ghosted? Or was the other woman in trouble?

Ivy shook her head. She'd just met her. Sort of. It was a one-night stand plus a dash of the supernatural for flavor. Apparently, a normal one-night stand was too much to ask for. The fucking universe and its fucked up sense of humor.

Her fingers hovered over the keyboard. Maybe she should tell Topher.

No. You're done with those two. Deal with your own shit, Ivy.

She pocketed her phone. It was time to focus. Because it turned out Rita's list was finally good for something after all.

It wasn't Lenox's new hideout. It wasn't even a key to the hideout. But it was a dive bar in Southeast with a floor that Ivy stuck to and a harried looking white man serving drinks.

She'd come a few times now, breaking her own rules about not becoming a regular anywhere. But even though Michael's Tavern looked nothing like an actual tavern, she'd made a point of coming every night since Pride and ordering an old fashioned, sitting at the bar and making small talk with the other customers while watching the balding bartender out of the corner of her eye.

Ivy took her usual seat at the bar, ordered her drink, and opened her phone, making a show of texting imaginary friends, keeping her face bored even though her stomach clenched at the lack of messages or calls.

Where are you, Supernova?

Her drink arrived with a solid clunk, but the bartender kept his hand around the glass, looking her up and down. Taking in the scars she was sure.

"I don't want trouble," he said under his breath.

"I'm not here to bring any," Ivy replied, pocketing her phone with her expression schooled.

Here we go.

She hadn't been sure at first. Rita's notes on D.C. had told her to look for Andy, the bartender at this place. Only Ivy was pretty sure he didn't go by that name anymore given how wide the man's eyes had gone when she'd signed her receipt, "Hello Andy" a few minutes prior.

"Kid, I've been out of the game for a decade. Really don't have the energy for you to pull me back in."

He kept his voice low. Over the din of customers, no one was going to catch anything.

Ivy shrugged out of her leather jacket, holding her hands palms up when the man flinched. "I just want information. That's all. Not here to pull anyone into anything. Lenox won't ever know I talked to you."

"Jesus, kid. *That's* who you're after?"

Ivy leaned forward. "Who did you think I was here for?"

The man gulped and made a show of wiping down the bar. "None of my business who you're after. Like I said, I'm out of the game now."

Ivy took a sip of her drink, making a disbelieving noise in the back of her throat. "Bet you've still got a toe in the door. We all do."

He sighed. "If you've gotten out, take my advice and *keep* out."

An echo of Rita's words. She wasn't much for following good advice though.

When the man went to take the towel away, presumably to busy himself with another task, she grabbed his hand. Like they were having an intimate conversation. Like she was a lonely girl at a bar confiding in her bartender. But with the other hand, she pulled free a bone dagger and kept the sharp edge of it against the inside of his arm, ready to slice it open if he didn't give her an answer she liked.

"Who's here?" she asked, voice quiet. As if she didn't really care. As if her heart wasn't hammering in her chest.

The man had gone white as a sheet, even under the dim lights of the bar. He was breathing hard, sweating. Then his face hardened.

"Fuck. This." At first Ivy thought it meant an attack. Maybe he'd pressed a button for the police under the bar.

Instead, he leaned forward, mouth against her ear.

"Heard Lenox's heir is recruiting. Parading around U Street like he's the next Tony Soprano and the sun shines out of his own ass. You both can slit each other's throats for all I care. Just leave me the fuck out of it."

Ivy's grasp went limp and Andy stepped away, glaring.

"Now, get the fuck out of my bar and don't come back unless you want a bullet through your useless excuse for a brain."

She nodded. Fair was fair. Sheathed her knife in her skin, ignoring the way Andy's expression went from shocked and angry to downright horrified. Good.

Once she'd grabbed her jacket and slung it over one shoulder, she dug in her pocket for cash and left a generous tip, then strolled out whistling between her teeth.

It wasn't Lenox, but it was leaps and bounds more to go on than she'd had before. She was just a metro ride away from having whoever the new heir was at the end of her knife.

Wouldn't that put a spring in her step?

The section of U Street Ivy found herself on had more "For Lease" signs than actual shops. She had a sneaking suspicion that at least one storefront would soon be opening as a dispensary or another innocuous business that would cover for Lenox's other dealings.

She spent a solid two hours casing the main corridor, walking like she knew these streets. Like she was home. Her skin itched to pull on the jacket and its hood, but that would be even more conspicuous in the heat of the night. She kept her hair down, partially obscuring her face, and her wits about her. No way she would be the first one caught out.

A crowd of tipsy college-aged kids walked by, cackling like hyenas, ignoring the unhoused person who asked them for spare change. On the other side of the street, another group was blasting music from speakers outside the 7-Eleven. For a Tuesday night, it was lively enough.

Ivy took in the passerby, ignoring the weight of the phone in her pocket, wondering who Lenox would have chosen to replace her as heir.

And then a group of men spilled out of an Irish pub, more scenery along the popular street.

Ivy froze for half a beat when she spied the man in the middle of the group. Long, dirty-blonde hair and pale skin. Beady black eyes that were imprinted on her soul. A silhouette like a tank. He laughed over all his companions, the sound tracing knives down her spine, chipping at her ribs.

Jason.

She ducked into a pizza place at random, ordering a slice even though her stomach was twisting far too much to allow something as mundane as food. It felt like a million years later that the server handed her the greasy slice on a paper plate. But Jason and his groupies were loud enough, slow enough, that Ivy tracked their pace without glancing behind her once.

It wouldn't do to go bursting out of the shop after them, no matter how tempting it was. So she strolled back outside, the fatty cheese and stretchy dough smelling like vomit as her gut churned with anticipation.

And just her luck, they were still in sight. Moving like a wolf pack after prey. Lenox was recruiting alright. And as usual, Jason was the one getting his hands dirty.

She followed at a safe distance, giving her uneaten slice to the unhoused man she'd passed earlier. The knowledge that Jason was the new heir hummed in her veins, and she reflected on all those years they'd worked together. Never willingly, never without growls. But Lenox would order Jason to come along on jobs as extra incentive for targets to cooperate. Just look at the guy. She could still feel the kick to the stomach, the arm at her throat, all before he'd plunged the dagger in her.

The brick of shopfronts threatened to collapse around her.

No. Jason's an idiot. And you know what to do with idiots.

After all, she herself was a weapon. Jason was big, brutish, strong. But he wasn't clever. Lenox must have learned his lesson from choosing Ivy as his heir. He'd wanted her for more than his proclaimed attachment as a horror movie version of a father figure. Ivy might not be smart the way Topher and Lucia were, but she was cunning, and she was resourceful. Two things Lenox believed made a good leader.

It made sense Lenox would pick Jason next. The guy wasn't intelligent enough to make plans of his own. He'd follow orders, even after Lenox's eventual demise. Keep the business running. Jason was an idiot alright, but he was a useful one. And this time, there was no Pete to whisper in his ear that life could be more than playing "kill or be killed".

She breathed in deep, and kept stalking.

Eventually, the group broke off in twos and threes, slapping each other on the back in good-natured, overly machismo goodbyes.

And then Jason was on his own, strutting east with the confidence of a man who assumes he's far too large for anyone to consider jumping.

He'll bleed all the same, Ivy thought, biting back a smile.

She followed him to Shaw, an area that stank of gentrification, like so much of the city. As she walked, planning all the ways she'd like to dismember the man in front of her, an image floated into her head. Dina, asleep in the bed, face pressed into the pillow as if gravity alone wasn't strong enough to keep her in place, hair fanning around her like some ethereal creature of the deep.

What would she think if she knew what Ivy was doing now?

It hadn't been an hour.

Ivy pulled her phone out anyway.

Dropped it with a clatter, along with her jacket, when an arm came around her neck, choking the air from her lungs.

She scratched at the muscled arm, tearing away flesh, but gaining no freedom. Panic turned her into a wild beast before she remembered everything Lenox had taught her. Before she remembered her own strength.

She threw her body weight low, twisted around so her head slipped through the hold and punched her captor in the nuts.

Tried to anyway. He grabbed her wrist, and this too she broke free of, controlling the limbs that wanted to flail out in terror.

It took her a few missed punches to get a good look at her assailant in the dark alley he'd managed to drag her into. But she'd know that silhouette anywhere.

Fucking Jason.

She'd been too confident. When had she even lost sight of him?

Well. Lesson learned.

She clocked him on the side of the head and he stepped back, cursing.

"You're supposed to be fucking dead," he said, glaring and holding his face.

"Surprise, you little fucker."

"How?" he spat. Despite the curses, he'd turned a shade of green. Like he'd seen a ghost. In a way, he had.

"Sheer dumb luck. Where's Lenox?" She kept her fists raised, ready to deliver another blow. No need to reveal all her tricks yet.

"As if I'd tell you. Think you can weasel your way back into the gang after what you pulled?"

Ivy laughed, long and hard and cruel. Jason had always been a moron. Gullible enough to believe Lenox was a god. The way she used to. She knew better now.

"One more chance."

Jason stood straight, sizing her up. Hands clenching in neat fists.

But he didn't know what she'd become. She wasn't the same Ivy who'd gone into that shallow grave. She let the heat pool in her veins.

Jason stepped forward, more agile than she remembered. Or maybe she was out of practice. She ought to have seen the hay-maker coming. Dodged it with ease.

It landed against her chin with a crack before she could free her daggers from her skin. She tasted blood, white flashed when her head hit the— Her stomach roiled when she tried to right herself, world spinning around her.

Jason didn't let her go far. He kicked her in the stomach, making her dry heave.

"You should have stayed dead."

She scrabbled along the asphalt, fighting to make space, to kick out at his shins. Tried again to call her daggers despite her panic. But then he was on her. And that knife. That awful knife was in his hand.

A sickening squelch as he buried it in her ribs for a second time. Panicked gulps for air as she relived her death, a thick layer over this new one. Jason's satisfied grunt as he held her down and waited for her to die. Again.

And Ivy waited too. For the familiar blackness to drag her under. For the heat to fade from her body and her mind to go quiet once and for all.

But she kept breathing. Kept living.

Jason stared down at her in wonder. Made a choking sound as someone's hand grasped the back of his neck. As his veins turned a dark, vivid green.

What the—

She didn't pause to finish the thought. Jason's grip had gone slack on the knife. Her left arm went hot as she finally unsheathed a bone dagger. And struck hard and deep.

A gasp like surprise as Jason's eyes went wide and blank in an instant. As blood poured from the wound and down Ivy's hand, onto her own chest, sticky and warm as it exited his body.

And Jason fell, a dead weight landing on top of her. Pain a starburst through her torso as his body pressed the blade deeper into her chest.

Ivy lay panting for a second, mind whirring to understand what had just happened, still waiting for death to wash over her again.

Then Jason's body was moving. A woman's voice grunted. Ivy finally had the wherewithal to help whoever it was roll the dead body off her.

She yanked Jason's dagger free before she could think about the awful sensation of the metal slipping between her ribs yet again. Jumped to her feet, head swimming, wielding Jason's dagger along with her own as she took in her unexpected companion.

Lucia merely stared at her, arms crossed.

"Did-did you follow me here?" Ivy asked, mouth hinging open as she stared.

Lucia rolled her eyes and whispered to herself. Ivy caught the word 'Díos' somewhere in the stream of curses.

Louder, Lucia said, "No, you self-centered idiot. But maybe I should have, seeing how much trouble you manage to get into on your own. Sheer dumb luck, I was close enough for the Law of Attraction to pull me in your direction."

Ivy's eyes darted to the green tinge of Jason's skin. Fuck. So *that* was how Lucia's powers worked.

She swallowed hard to mask her surprise.

"I had it under control."

Lucia rubbed her temple. "I don't know why Topher even bothers. Fuck you too, Ivy. Have a nice life. Maybe think about hiding a murder weapon before you go onto the next disaster, hmm?"

Without another word, the woman turned on her heel and stomped back out of the alley.

Good. Ivy didn't need her meddling. Though with how the woman had handled Jason, paired with her lack of shock to find herself standing over a dead body...

She shook her head. Immediately regretted the motion when the world started spinning again.

Now that her shock had worn off, there was more to attend to. Ivy didn't want to look, but she had to. She pulled up her tank top and examined her torso, wondering how much she could trust Topher and their claim that she was now immune to the thing that had killed her.

Nothing. Not even a scar.

A breath of relief. Then she assessed the body at her feet, face down and limp. Without the sound of gunshots, it would take the cops a while to find him here. And she'd be long gone before that happened.

She swallowed back the nausea and searched Jason's body. Found a wallet and keys, a phone she unlocked with Jason's thumbprint. She'd pull what she could from it and then toss the thing before it could be tracked.

No missed messages from Lenox yet. That gave her some time. She didn't worry about DNA on him. She was dead. A ghost. And that was if the police bothered to investigate the murder of someone who was on Washington and California watchlists among others.

Her dropped jacket and phone came last. The screen was cracked, just like her head felt.

It was harder to read the interface now, but at least it turned on.

She'd have to work fast, no matter how the world swam around her or how her vision darkened at the edges.

She left Jason lying in the alley. No remorse for one of the men who'd left her in the dirt.

She ran blood-drenched hands through her hair. And got to work.

17

Ivy

A familiar living room swam into view as Ivy rolled over and vomited into a conveniently placed trash can.

"Topher, maybe this would be a good time to break the 'no hospital' rule," a man's voice said.

She tried to make sense of the words. It sounded like a conversation that was being repeated without much hope.

"Topher?" she rasped when her stomach was empty.

They were kneeling beside her where she was laid up on Danny's couch. They handed her a glass of water, which she drank gratefully.

"No hospitals," she managed when she'd drained the glass dry and struggled to a sitting position. "I've had concussions before. I'll be fine."

Danny threw up his hands and fled the room, looking irritated.

"I don't know what's more reassuring. That statement, or all the blood on your hands," Topher said, voice absent of its usual joviality.

"How'd I get here?" Ivy muttered. There were flashes. A cracked phone, an arm around her neck. She pressed the bruise along her jaw, felt the cavity where a tooth was missing.

Shit. Jason.

This was why she tried to *avoid* close-range fights. She wasn't a scrawny kid anymore, but if it was between her and someone like

Jason, getting into a fistfight was always more trouble than it was worth. It was why Lenox had started teaching her how to throw knives and shoot a gun when she was like...ten. Another cheery childhood memory.

Ivy took in her hands. Topher wasn't wrong, they were covered in dried blood. Pretty fucking gross.

"Luz saw you hobbling down 14th. How you made it that far without a cop stopping you, I have no idea."

Jagged edges of memories clicked into place. The green veins spreading across Jason's face. Lucia stomping away.

Now, the woman leaned against the wall with her arms crossed, as if she couldn't care less about the state of Ivy's head.

"You just happened to find me? Again?"

Lucia shrugged. "Resurrected Law of Attraction, remember? Don't think about it too hard. Actually, maybe try not to think about anything. Shouldn't be hard for you."

"Low blow for the concussed woman," Ivy grunted.

"Think you deserve it."

"A bit," Ivy conceded.

She couldn't remember Lucia finding her again later. She'd gone to Jason's apartment and then...

The rest was a blur. Lucia must have followed her after helping her take down Jason, despite her assertions that she was washing her hands of Ivy's mess. Ivy's stomach flopped. Probably the concussion. She sure as hell didn't know what to do with the idea that she'd been rescued. By someone who didn't even *like* her.

"Uh..."

"You're welcome," Lucia said before stalking out of the apartment.

"Shit." Ivy dropped her head in her hands for a scant second before remembering the blood.

She looked up, taking in the apartment, now empty except for her and Topher. She didn't blame Lucia or Danny for leaving. She'd have to clean up, and clean up good.

"Did anyone see me come in here? Is Danny—"

"We kept you covered. And hacked the security cameras. Cleaned anything that connected you and Danny."

"Thought you two weren't hackers," she mumbled.

"Not for work, but doesn't mean we're not capable."

That was good. Bad enough if she got caught. She wasn't about to bring Danny down with her. She didn't mind dragging in Andy or anyone who knew the rules of life between gangs. But Danny was a bystander. A kind one. She wasn't about to drag him into this. Not when he'd opened his home to them. Not when being Black meant guilty before proven innocent even in the best of circumstances. One of her former contacts, Puck, had drilled that into her when they still worked together.

"You're sure he's good?"

"Surprised you care, but yes. I'm sure."

"And Lucia just like...*found* me?"

"Like she said, Law of Attraction."

"How come I never attract *other* Resurrected," Ivy grumbled.

She hadn't really expected an answer, but Topher gave one anyway. "The Resurrected all seem to be kind of orbiting each other. Unless we make an effort to run into someone else's orbit, like me and Luz are trying to do now, we often find ourselves running into the same Resurrected over and over. Like...I dunno, binary stars."

"Does everything have to have a space metaphor?" Ivy groaned.

"We're dealing with black holes and resurrections, so yes."

They went silent, and Ivy went from trying to process Topher's bullshit theories to trying to process the fact that they were still here, keeping an eye out for her.

And then they had to make things worse by saying, "I'm sorry we didn't tell you about the Soul Eater sooner."

She blinked at them, unsure she'd ever received a sincere apology before. Another beat of silence.

"Uh...so..." she began and trailed off with eloquence.

"Now, do you want to tell me about the blood?" Topher asked. Their face gave nothing away.

"I mean, no. Not really."

Topher sighed. "Lucia said there was a big guy trying to stab you when she found you. Was it self defense?"

"Partially."

They stared at each other for a long time before Topher nodded. "You should shower. You look like a horror movie on prom night. I'll check on you if you're not out in fifteen, okay?"

Ivy worked her mouth for a minute, during which nothing came out.

Finally, she managed, "That's it?"

"That's it," Topher said with a nod.

"Dude, for all you know, I murdered someone."

In fact, she had. Had Lucia told them?

"You came back clutching those," they said, pointing to a folder of notes on the coffee table.

Ivy lurched forward. The paper was covered in dried bits of blood, crumpled to hell, but still, she knew what they were. Every detail she'd gotten from Jason's phone before she'd dumped it. Anything she could find after she'd broken into his apartment. Receipts, hidden notebooks, anything even slightly suspicious. Much of it was coded in a way she'd never decipher in her current state. But with time...

"How'd you end up with a dagger in your heart?" Topher asked quietly.

She kept her eyes on the folder, even as she turned over the thousand tiny steps that had led to that moment. It wasn't so much that she'd broken with Lenox over one incident or another, but each time she'd carried out an order, brought yet another person sobbing and begging to answer to Lenox's wrath, it was another paper cut between her fingers. And she'd gotten tired of bleeding out through paper cuts. She'd wanted something more. Pete had told her she *could* want something more. And she'd gotten them both killed for the wanting.

But how was she to tell Topher any of that?

"How'd you go from data analyst to human torch?" she asked instead.

"Electrical fire."

"Huh. Not the sob story I was expecting."

They shrugged. "I had a good life, Ivy. A decent job, family who gave a shit, nerdy friends to geek out with. One night, I went to sleep and woke up with the house burning down around me. I died, and I lost that life. Watched everyone I knew mourn me while I figured out how *not* to burn down everything I touched because I'd suddenly become a walking bonfire. That enough of a sob story?"

Topher spoke with a calm detachment, like they'd put it all behind them. Maybe they had.

No one wants to feel like a ghost in their own life.

She swallowed hard, wondering what she'd prefer: her own blood-soaked history, or a past that was worth missing. Twin blades, each carving the same wounds.

Topher inclined their chin towards her. "And you? Is yours a sob story?"

Ivy chewed her lip. She didn't owe Topher much of anything. But she owed them at least a crumb.

"I was trying to get out of my old life. I got stabbed instead. That's all there is to it."

"And the person who produced all that blood? They related to that?"

Ivy breathed in once through her nose. Out through her mouth.

"Yeah."

Topher nodded. "Then we're good. I'm looking out for Resurrected. You count. Not everyone has a story, but not everyone had it easy. You have someone to blame. All I have is cursing my bad luck. But Ivy, I have one thing I'd like to say."

Of course they did.

"Which is?" she asked, steeling herself.

"These people took your first life. Don't let them take your second."

The words hung like concern Ivy wasn't ready to accept. Instead she staggered to her feet.

"So where to next?"

Topher raised a brow. "Thought you were done tagging along."

Ivy shrugged. "Need to stay on the move for now."

Topher nodded. "London. We leave tomorrow."

Far from the scene of her crime, and another big city for her to explore for signs of Lenox. If the fucker had fled the country altogether, England wouldn't be a bad place to search.

"Great."

She began hobbling towards the shower and paused.

"Hey, Topher?"

"Yeah?"

"I found one."

They stilled, as if listening with their whole body.

"A Resurrected. I think."

"Where are they now?"

Ivy shrugged. "They got away. And I got busy."

Something kept her from saying more. From speaking aloud just *how* she'd come across one of the Resurrected. How Dina had swum before her very eyes and disappeared into oblivion. How, even now, she itched to check her phone for a text. A call. Signs that her own binary star had come over the horizon.

"Next time," Ivy said, keeping her tone casual.

"Yeah," Topher said. "Next time."

Ivy turned from them, scratching at the dried blood under her nails. Thoughts moving to her next steps. And to a girl who smelled of sea salt and rivers.

18

DINA

Dina stared at her phone as she walked to the beach in Dakar. It had taken her a while to work out where she was, especially since she didn't speak more than a dozen words of French. As the only white person around, she'd narrowed it down a bit before realizing that Zev had the foresight to pay for an international data plan.

God bless GPS and God bless her brother. She'd have to make it up to him some day.

She found an empty rock to sit on and kept staring at her phone, turning the screen on and off.

Zev knew she was alive. She'd been able to find a store that took PayWave, so she was fed. But she was by the ocean, so she didn't have long.

She'd already plugged Ivy's number into her phone, the marker on her skin mostly intact after her swim to shore. But it had been days since she'd literally ghosted the other woman. What had she been thinking in the meantime? Maybe she'd been hungover and had chalked it up to alcohol. Even if that wasn't the case, Dina had no idea how she would explain herself.

But she wanted a familiar voice. *This* familiar voice. A voice from a hushed room and glittery dance floors. Who'd made her second life feel like truly living.

She turned the phone over to the photo booth pictures she'd stuck behind the clear case. Wondered if doing so made her an absolute lunatic. Took a deep breath. Then pressed the contact, and held the phone to her ear.

Ivy didn't make her wait long.

"Hello?" breathed a rough voice.

Dina's heart clenched in her chest and she put her free hand to it automatically, feeling it thrum away against her palm. She almost let out a sob. It was so ridiculous a reaction she had to laugh.

"That you, Supernova?"

"That nickname feels more appropriate now," Dina said, smiling.

There was a breath of relief on the other end. Then, "Shit. *Shit*. I can't believe you actually called."

"I would have sooner but it's um...complicated."

"More or less complicated than turning into mist and disappearing like Houdini come again?"

"I wasn't sure you'd uh...remember."

"A bit hard to forget, Dina."

"Didn't know if you'd chalk it up to alcohol."

"Unless we were drinking absinthe, I can't imagine any drink giving me a trip like that. Besides, I was pretty sober."

"Right. Yeah, I didn't know, given how the day went down."

"You're stalling."

"And you're rude to call me out on it," Dina said with a breathy laugh. Now that it had come to it, the words wouldn't connect to her tongue. Was this what they meant when they said "tongue-tied"? Being so lost for words that your mouth would rather devour itself, twist inside out, than say what was on your mind?

"It's hard to say when I can't see your face," she said at last.

"We could FaceTime."

Dina shook her head, even though Ivy couldn't see. "I'd chew through my brother's data."

"Didn't mention you had a brother."

"It wasn't exactly on my mind when we…"

"Yeah?"

"Yeah."

A pause on the other line. Dina wondered how long Ivy would give her before hanging up. Deciding a girl who turned into raindrops and water currents wasn't worth her time.

"Look, I can explain," she burst out as the line crackled with static. God, maybe they *should* FaceTime. Not having the feedback of Ivy's expression was torture. "But I don't think you'll believe me," she added lamely.

More silence.

Then, emerging from the phone's speaker like a lifeline: "What if I told you something first. We can do an exchange."

"Okay," Dina said, voice small as she tucked her knees to her chin.

It was like telling Zev all over again, but worse somehow. She'd almost known he'd believe her. Eventually. Maybe because they'd both kept the same secret from their parents. Maybe because she'd had faith that a sibling bond would keep them tied together even now. Ivy was a hot woman she'd met twice and slept with once. The fact she'd even picked up was its own miracle.

She heard the deep inhale of breath as Ivy prepared herself on the other end. Dina thought of all those scars, wondered again who, or what, had left them. But what Ivy said instead made the earth fall out from under her.

"Before I met you, I died. Someone put me in the ground, and someone else dug me back up. I shouldn't be alive, but I am. And I came back different."

My name is Dina Adler. On March 21ˢᵗ, I died.

Dina clutched her mouth, staring at the golden sand without seeing it, pressing the phone so close she thought she might absorb it into her skin and keep Ivy there in her head.

"Dina?" Ivy asked, wary.

"I died, Ivy," she whispered. "I died and I came back different."

She sobbed, a strangled, gasping sound that made the beach goers turn and stare harder than they already had been. A woman approached and asked her something in French. An offer of help maybe. She tried to signal as best she could that she was fine, and the woman retreated, looking skeptical.

"Who was that?" Ivy asked.

"I don't know," Dina sniffed.

"Where are you? It sounds like a beach?"

"I'm in Dakar."

"Uh...you're where now?"

"Senegal. Western Africa."

Ivy let out a low whistle. "Is that how your powers work? You travel through water or something?"

Dina rocked forward, wishing Ivy were there so she could grab her arms, hold onto her and all her answers. "You have powers too?"

"Yeah. Different from yours though."

"Do you know how..." she fumbled over the words, willing them into the right configuration. "Do you know how to make them stop?"

Hesitation. "You can't control it...can you?"

"No," Dina whispered. She hated how it came out. Like a frightened child lost in the dark. But that's how she felt. Her whole life had once had order and rhythm and now there was none.

"Dina, I'm sorry. I don't know."

She nodded and swiped uselessly at the tears, trying to cut off the sobs with her arm until it was slick with mucus.

"Hey," Ivy said. "Hey, I'm here."

But she wasn't. And Dina was on a beach where she didn't speak the language and didn't know a soul. Surrounded by people and devastatingly alone. For fuck's sake, she should be enjoying the fact that she'd finally gotten so see the tiniest piece of the African continent. But she was tired and hungry and all she wanted was a familiar face.

Ivy wasn't there. But she stayed on the phone as Dina tried to hide her sobs from the mic.

Eventually, she walked to the shoreline and used the salt water to scrub her snotty arm. Its tug was getting stronger by the second. She ought to put the phone in the dry bag and find somewhere private for her little disappearing act.

"I don't have much longer," Dina said as she walked up the steps, away from the beach and through the crowded market, each stall lined with freshly caught fish or vivid fabrics of pinks and greens and blues.

"'Til you disappear again?"

"Yeah."

"Where will you go next?"

"I don't know. Somewhere further east. But I don't seem to get a choice in the matter. Just wherever the water takes me next."

"That sounds…"

"Horrible? Terrifying? Maddening?"

"All of the above. I'm sorry, I don't know much about all of this, Dina. My powers are different."

"Different how?"

"I uh…well I'm kind of like a one-woman utility knife. I can pull blades out of my body."

Dina laughed without mirth. "That sounds much more useful."

"Not with this," Ivy said, echoing the defeat Dina felt.

"There are more of us, you know," Dina said. "I saw someone when I was in Chicago."

"Yeah, I know. I've uh…met some, too."

Dina froze for half a step, then made herself walk on until she'd left the market behind. "And they have powers like ours?"

"Yes and no. Seems to depend on how we died."

The cool rush of the Chesapeake washed over Dina's skin all over again, dripped into her lungs. She shivered.

"I guess that makes sense. How did—No, sorry. That seems...rude."

Ivy chuckled but didn't answer the aborted question. "You said you didn't have long. How do you know when you're going to uh..."

"Go under?" She blew out a sigh. "It's like I can feel the water pulling at me. When the pull gets stronger I get these headaches, and it's like there's this buzzing in my skull."

"Sounds fun."

"*Sooo* fun."

"And when you're out of the water? How long do you have?"

"Sometimes hours, like now. Sometimes days. I had a week when I was in the Great Lakes. I get more time by slow-moving water."

"Got it. Well...want me to stay on until you go?"

Something tight and sharp in Dina's chest loosened. Like Ivy had used one of the knives she spoke of to pry loose a splinter. No, a stake, right in the center of her chest.

"I...yeah. I'd like that. Tell me...Tell me about D.C. What am I missing?"

"Probably overpaid politicians ruining the planet. But I'm not there. I'm in London."

"So you don't live in D.C.? Or I guess I met you in Portland."

"I don't really live anywhere right now. I kind of bounce around."

"Can relate."

Ivy snorted. "Got a good sense of humor given the circumstances."

"I'm Jewish. Give me an atrocity and I'll hand back a joke."

Ivy laughed. "Wait, am I allowed to laugh at that?"

"Yeah, it was hilarious. Anyway, tell me about London."

She turned down a street at random. An empty stretch of white plaster. Walked until she found a quiet alcove and leaned against the curve of the wall.

"Well, the traffic is shit, or 'shite' as the Brits say. And the people are obnoxious. I mean, polite. But it's overkill if you ask me. Big Ben is cool I guess."

"Anyone ever tell you you should write a travel guide?"

"You know, maybe I will. The curry slaps, at least."

"Ah, yes. One of the perks of colonization. The food."

Ivy snorted. "But yeah, been fun hearing them say 'mind the gap' and listening to people complain about getting sunburnt on a cloudy day."

"What are you doing there anyway?"

"Oh, I'm meeting the Queen."

"That sounds challenging, given that she's dead."

"I'm secretly an excellent necromancer."

"Shit, what if she's like us? What did you call it?"

"The Resurrected. And I don't think it happens when you die from old age, far as I can tell."

"The Resurrected? Sounds like a pretentious superhero gang made up by a ten-year-old."

"That's what I said!"

"Who came up with that anyway?"

Ivy paused, and Dina had the sensation of stumbling on a crack in the sidewalk. Wondered what bruise she'd pressed on.

Eventually, Ivy sighed. "One of the people I'm traveling with calls us that. Topher. They can be a bit of a know-it-all."

Dina swallowed something hard and painful. "So you're traveling with others?"

"Yeah. They're...we're kind of looking for people like us. It's weird. A bit too X-men for my taste."

"So that's why you were in D.C.? Looking for more of us?"

"Yeah. But I don't think you were the person I was supposed to be looking for."

Dina rubbed at the pain in her chest.

Ivy cursed. "Not what I meant—I mean—I wasn't looking for you, but I'm glad I found you, Dina."

The words were far too intimate for someone she'd just met. For a woman a thousand miles away and speaking to her through a phone. But she didn't take them back, and Dina latched onto the treasure of them.

The buzzing grew louder.

"I need to put my phone away before I go under," Dina said with a wince. "It's going to happen any minute now."

"Will you call me again when you resurface? Maybe...maybe we'll end up in the same place again?"

Dina hadn't had much luck since that day on the bridge. She doubted that would change any time soon. All the same, she could at least answer one question. "I'll call. Promise. Goodbye, Ivy."

"Talk to you soon, Supernova. Safe travels."

Dina hung up and tucked the phone away, huddling into herself despite the heat. As if she could hold every word of that conversation to her chest and allow them to buoy her to safety. To keep her steady even when she next resurfaced, alone and disoriented.

Ivy didn't know how to stop the powers from manifesting. Neither had that boy with the lightning. But there were others still. She could go on her own mission to find them.

A power for a death.

Who by water? And who by fire?

How many ways could someone die and come back to this plane of existence? One of them must have answers for her.

She tilted her head back against the wall, breathing in the sea breeze and squeezing hands into fists to ready herself for the journey. The world was going dark around her. The heavy air pressed against her neck.

Wait.

That hadn't happened before. Not since—

A lone figure strode down the empty street. Footfall silent, black coat cutting sharply into the white-washed surroundings. Empty eyes locked onto Dina where she stood.

The Void advanced, gait casual, face blank.

Dina's only panicked thought was that she'd spent far too much breath joking with Ivy and not enough asking the important questions.

Like if she too had seen a creature like this. A monster who ate up the light and shadow as it walked.

She shrank against the wall, heart racing, skin dissolving into droplets, mind fragmenting until all that remained was an animalistic fear.

And as she drifted into the water, the Void froze. Smiled. As if it had all the time in the world. Because it would devour her soon enough.

19

IVY

Recovering from a concussion, jet lag, and missing a girl who had disappeared to god-knows-where meant Ivy had let the matter rest too long. So she didn't give a shit about bringing it up in a cafe in Edinburgh while Lucia and Topher worked their day jobs. She'd avoided the return to coding bootcamp this long in favor of searching for the Resurrected and odds-and-ends service jobs to replenish her wallet. Now, it was time to shatter some glass.

She leaned back in her metal chair, tipping it onto the back two legs. "So. Tell me more about the Soul Eater."

Lucia's head shot up from her screen and she whipped it around. As if anyone could even hear her above the din of the cafe. As if anyone had any idea what they were talking about.

"What?" Ivy asked with a smirk. "Thought I was just gonna drop it?"

Lucia gave an irritated sigh and returned to her work. "This is on you, Toph. I wanted to tell her on day one."

Things between them had been...better since the unsolicited rescue in D.C. But Ivy was almost grateful the other woman was as sardonic as ever.

"Traitor," Topher grumbled before glancing back at Ivy. "Aren't you busy playing spymaster or something?" they asked, pointing their chin at the closed notebook next to her laptop. She'd taken to keeping the folder of notes she'd stolen from Jason's place taped to the back of a rather ugly painting of fruit. But she'd copied some of the contents into a pocket-sized notebook, slowly working her way through the different codes Lenox had once taught her, hoping she'd manage to break his new one. So far, she hadn't managed to make sense of the seemingly useless phrases.

The narrow way is how the light gets in.

Three in flight, two by foot.

Lines upon lines of the like. And Ivy hadn't a clue what it all meant.

"I need a break. And answers," she added for good measure.

Topher checked the bustling cafe and leaned in close. Ivy bit her lip to hide a grin as she watched them give in.

"We don't know its actual name. We call it that because of what it does to the Resurrected."

"And what even is this thing? You said it's not like us?"

Topher shook their head. "Not even remotely. It's like an afterimage almost. Like...okay, so when astronomers observe black holes, they can't see the black hole itself. They see all the matter that's sucked into it. Stars and gasses and stuff. So really, they only see a shadow of the black hole." They paused and swallowed. "This thing feels the same, looks the same almost. It looks like a person, but without all the edges drawn in. As far as we can tell, it didn't exist before the first wave of Resurrected came back. We think it's the shadow of our resurrection."

The words should have been ridiculous, but somehow they still made Ivy shudder. "So this thing hunts us down and kills us?"

Topher shook their head. "It's worse than that. It's like it...steals our additional life. The corpses it leaves behind are...wrong."

"Sounds spooky."

"It's not a joke, Ivy," Topher said, catching her gaze. "This is serious. It's why we keep looking for more of us. To help them out. Give them a head start before the Soul Eater finds them."

"And do you hide this from the others you find, too? Help them figure out their powers and then release them into the wild? Tell them to run without telling them what they're up against?"

"In the past, we told the Resurrected when we found them. It hasn't always gone well."

"No shit. But like...dude, your method makes no sense to me. Bounce around the world and then set the Resurrected loose? Why not gather us all? Really lean into the superhero shit."

"First," Lucia said, finally chiming in, "how would we move that many people around with us while we look for more Resurrected?"

"Duh. Send out scouts."

She nodded. "Okay. So we send out scouts and bring all the Resurrected to one place. Great. Now we're like a beacon for the Soul Eater. It knows exactly where to find us and devour us in one go."

"Come on. What the fuck is this thing that you can't take it down with a half dozen of us? Maybe even less. Surely with all the different powers we have—"

"No one who has been in a fight with the Soul Eater has made it out, Ivy. No one," Topher emphasized quietly. "Luz and I have only seen it once, and I really hope we never see it again. The only way we got away was running for our lives. So yes, we find the others. We give them the best connections and skills we can. And then we tell them to run and don't stop running."

Lucia nodded grimly. "Remember the Resurrected Law of Attraction? Well, it works with the Soul Eater too. It would be drawn to us and we'd be sitting ducks, trying to fight it off as it sucks out our souls one by one."

"And me? You didn't tell me to run. You didn't tell me any of this."

"Ivy, you're the cagiest, most bullheaded person I've ever had the pleasure to meet," Topher said with a sigh. "I didn't want to tell you before you got oriented. Had a stable foundation."

"Like fucking coding bootcamp."

"Yes. Like fucking coding bootcamp." A pause. Then, "So, any more questions?"

"Yeah. How's that algorithm of yours going? I mean, seems like you're the linchpin in this whole operation, right? We can search obituaries all the live-long day but doesn't seem like we're having much luck."

Topher sighed. "It's running, but pinning down the Resurrected to a location more than a region or even a country is...difficult. The UK seems likely, but someone could have Resurrected anywhere from London to Inverness. During the first wave of Resurrections, we only found each other through the Law of Attraction. It took years to build out our network and intersect with more of the Resurrected." Their brows furrowed in an uncharacteristic expression of frustration. "Having the model was supposed to make the process go faster this time. And I keep updating it when we strike out, but without more datapoints of newer Resurrected, it's hard to get it to be more accurate than it is."

They cleaned their glasses on their shirt, which somehow resulted in more smudges. "What about you, Luz? How's your search going?"

"Hard to find anyone in Scotland who died of anything other than old age or disease honestly. And none of them died on the right date. We were probably better off in London, Toph. Although..." Lucia's eyes darted further down the webpage she was reading. "This girl might be a good candidate. Some sort of freak accident at the factory she was working at. Got trampled by the cattle they were gonna slaughter."

"Uh...morbid as fuck, thanks." Ivy pushed away her half eaten tattie scone.

"There's a bus that goes out there it looks like," Lucia said, shooting Ivy a pointed look. "Wanna check it out? Call us if you find anything?"

Ivy shoved herself up from the table. "Yeah, yeah. Get rid of the nosy bitch so you can concentrate. I know."

"It's quieter when you're out searching," Lucia admitted, eyes back to her screen. "I'll let you know if we see anything else promising."

"Gee, thanks."

"If you don't like the search gig, you could always tell us more about the other Resurrected you thought you found," Topher suggested.

Ivy shrugged. She wasn't quite sure why she kept Dina to herself. Maybe these two could help her. But she'd only managed to get intel about the Soul Eater through brute force. Not to mention that for all their bravado, Lucia and Topher were clearly still bumbling their way through the dark. Somehow, despite such a short time together, Ivy felt protective of the other woman. So until she trusted Topher and Lucia, she wasn't about to share Dina with them. And given her track record, trust might not come for a very long time, if ever.

"Nothing more to tell. Got away before I could get a good look."

"Then we'll follow the lead we have here."

Ivy gave them a mock salute and donned her jacket.

Outside, it was raining *sideways*. And people thought Scotland was eerie and beautiful. If you asked Ivy, it was just wet.

At least the buses were decent. She shook off and settled into a seat as the gray world passed by in a series of old stone walls and rain jackets. Crowds of people tightening their hoods to keep dry in the downpour.

The city soon retreated, giving way to highway and cropland, and by the time Ivy got off the bus, she was just about the only passenger left.

She checked her cracked phone again, and turned towards the cemetery, shoulders hunched against the fine mist that had replaced the rain.

A little plot of worn-down headstones lay a short walk down a dirt (or mud, really) road. The newest plot was an easy find. Ivy wondered if it was nice to have been buried in an actual cemetery, rather than a hidden pocket of a forest.

You're just as dead either way, she thought to comfort herself.

It wasn't long before a groundskeeper came her way. Just as she'd made out the date on the tombstone. March 21 of that year.

"Oi, what are ye doing here?" the old man asked, features completely obscured by a neon yellow rain jacket.

"Just touring," Ivy said, tone bright. "We don't have graveyards this old where I'm from."

Not technically true if you counted pre-colonial graveyards. But the Scots and the Brits loved the reminder of how young and dull the US was.

"Ah, yes, we get that from time to time. Ye out on a ghost hunt or something? We get groups here and there."

"No ghost hunt." *Well, not really.* "Just exploring."

"Well, I'm afraid I'll have to send ye on yer way. Sweet lass up the way died earlier this year. Aisling McIntosh. Someone disturbed her grave not long after, so we're not as keen on having strangers visit anymore."

Ivy nodded, feigning sympathy. Her skin buzzed with the excitement of a lead. "Understood. Sorry to hear people don't have any respect for the dead anymore. I'll be on my way."

The man waved at her and tromped through the ground to a nearby house.

His dismissal didn't matter though. For the first time, she had real evidence that another Resurrected had popped up from this town. Next stop would be the woman's old haunts.

Ivy started with the Aisling's parents' home. According to the obituary Lucia had texted her, the woman had spent her whole life in the same village she'd grown up in. Ivy wondered if she'd chosen that life or gotten stuck the way she had.

Through the window, an older couple sat at the kitchen table, heads bent together, silent as statues.

She moved on.

The options in town were limited. A pub, a fish and chips takeout, a bookstore already closed for the day, a corner shop, and the post office (also closed). In her old life, Ivy had almost *enjoyed* the chase of rooting people out from their hiding places, the way scattered clues came together to become a trail, how fake names resolved into hidden identities, the small victory of catching her prey unawares. Then again, the heat of the chase was always immediately smothered when Lenox extracted everything he wanted from her trophies to the tune of snapped bones and beaten flesh.

Still, searching for the dead was somehow even more depressing. Had Aisling tried and failed to go back to her life? Had she fled? Ivy tried to imagine what she might have done if Topher and Luz hadn't found her, but all her thoughts were drenched in blood.

Her last stop was the factory where Aisling had died. It seemed to be the main industry for the town outside of farming. Ivy supposed the cattle had to go somewhere in the end.

The door was already ajar despite the empty quiet that hung over the place, and when Ivy peeked inside, the lights were low, the machinery all switched off. She was grateful not to hear any desperate mooing from inside. She didn't want any pitiful-looking cows convincing her to become a vegetarian.

Ivy let herself in, ears pricked, walking the empty rows of meat hooks and other implements whose uses Ivy shivered to think about. Unlike the horror movie she'd imagined, the place was pristine.

Her boots echoed, too loud for her liking on the concrete floor as she kept an eye out for anything odd.

Anything odd, it turned out, meant a woman standing just outside the building when Ivy gave it up for a lost cause. She stood near a corral, stock still, gaze on the muddy center of the pen. Standing in the mist without a raincoat to cover the clothes that had seen far better days. A pale, pink dress that once would have been fine, now torn and stained.

Ivy stepped forward, her chest going warm, just like when she saw Dina. Topher's stupid Law of Attraction might have some weight after all.

Another step, this time far less careful. She cursed when her boots squelched in the mud.

The woman whipped around, brown eyes wide with panic, bulging large in her gaunt, pale face. With the rain, Ivy couldn't distinguish the woman's real hair color, something dark and muddied, plastered to her skull.

Ivy held up her hands to signal that it was safe.

"Are you Aisling?" she asked.

The woman nodded, round-eyed and slack-mouthed.

"My name is Ivy. I'm betting you're pretty confused right now, but I can help."

Aisling stepped back into the fence of the corral. No. *Through* the fence. As if the metal wasn't even there.

Well, that's interesting.

She thought about Danny and his powers. How a car crash could manifest as something different. The stampede must have played a part in Aisling's abilities. She'd have to ask Topher. Probably something to do with force and gravity or some science shit.

"Please, I'm not here to hurt you. I want to help."

The woman swallowed. "I saw my name. It was carved into a gravestone." She stared down at empty hands. "It took so long to get out of that box. And my parents...they said I was a ghost. But I don't *feel* like a ghost. Even if I..." she trailed off, looking at the fence she had walked through like it was no more substantial than the air around them.

Ivy watched her, wondering what to say. She'd never been good at this sort of thing. She ought to text Topher and Luz. Have them step in with their camp counselor voices.

But she knew a flight risk when she saw one. She'd have to calm Aisling down first if she wanted any chance of getting her to come back with her.

"I know you've been through a lot, Aisling. Look, I've been through something similar. I have friends who can help. We can explain everything. Can you come with me? We'll get you some clean clothes, and food, and get you situated, okay?"

It sounded like a lie leaving her mouth. Explain everything? Hardly. She was still trying to wrap her own head around it.

Aisling blinked, seeming to take Ivy in for the first time. Lord, she must have been hiding somewhere out here for months, her own parents telling her she was a ghost. Must have done a number on her mental state from the look of it.

Eventually, she nodded. Took a step towards Ivy, back through the fence.

She was only a pace or two away when Ivy felt the pressure on the nape of her neck. Aisling's eyes went wide again, staring at something over Ivy's shoulder.

Ivy didn't hesitate. She slotted a knife free and held it firm, backing towards Aisling with her ears pricked for danger. ut the woman flinched away, horrified gaze glued to Ivy's dagger.

Ivy didn't have time for that. The shadowy world of mist was coalescing in the dark corners of the building. Gained substance until it formed a figure. Someone draped in darkness, resolving into pale skin and buzzed blonde hair.

And empty eyes.

Ivy sucked in a breath. Topher and Lucia had given the Soul Eater an apt name.

"Abominations," the thing said, as if in greeting. Its voice brushed like spider legs across Ivy's skin.

"Get behind me," she said, low and commanding.

Aisling whipped her head between her and the Soul Eater. Some people had never been in a life-threatening situation before and it showed. Ivy for one wasn't going to wait around for more information. Safety first, questions later.

Aisling was of a different mindset.

"What's going on? I don't understand."

"Aisling, you need to come with me. Right now," Ivy growled, goosebumps pricking her flesh. This thing, whatever it was, had the shape of a man. But the world around him—it—whatever—it was like the light bent towards the thing, dimmed in its presence. The edges of its body were warped. Wrong.

And Aisling was just staring at the damned thing, eyes huge and mostly whites.

"Goddamnit, stop staring and start running!"

Ivy lunged and grabbed the other woman's forearm. Tugged so hard the woman was forced forward. They took two steps together, Ivy ready to spring through the sucking mud, when something wrenched Aisling out of her grasp, setting her off balance and tumbling to the rain-soaked ground.

It was fast. A lightning strike rather than the swarm of shadows Ivy had imagined. The thing was just suddenly there. Like one of those flip books, where the image changes from one page to the next, a glitch almost, quick enough that the discerning eye won't catch it.

And it had Aisling by the throat.

The woman thrashed, went misty as she tried to shift out of its grip, the way she'd walked through that fence with such ease.

But the Soul Eater had her. Kept her solid. And fuck. It was leaking into her. Pouring itself, its whole shadowy essence, into the woman. Black lines where her veins should have been. White nothing where there had been iris and pupil.

Ivy had never been a hero. It was always about saving your own skin in Lenox's world.

But this was worse than watching someone come to the wrong end of a knife or walk into a deal gone sour.

She stumbled forward and yanked hard on Aisling's arms, grappled for her waist, tugged and pulled on the woman's limp frame.

And yelped when a piece of oblivion, or shadow, or whatever the fuck, jumped from Aisling's body to her own.

"Fuck this."

She lunged forward and thrust a dagger right into the Soul Eater's vacant, depthless eye.

It didn't even flinch.

Another piece of darkness came lurching towards Ivy and she let go, stumbling backwards, windmilling her arms so she didn't go down.

The Soul Eater's attention was all for the woman it sucked dry, bone dagger still jutting from its eye. And it would come for her next.

Ivy wasn't a hero. And Aisling was dead or worse.

She ran. Ran until her lungs burned and she was thoroughly lost in the small town streets. Ran until she could hear nothing but her own wheezing and pounding heart. She only slowed long enough to dig out her phone. Tapped Topher's name, and pressed the phone to her ear.

"Hey, did you—"

"We have to go," Ivy interrupted in a single gasp, all the words running together.

"What—"

"It's here!"

She didn't have to say more than that. From the other end of the line came: "Fuck. FUCK!"

There was the sound of shuffling. Bags zipped up.

"Can you get back to us? I'll get us on the next flight out. We may be okay in the city. Enough regular humans to distract it."

Ivy was running out of steam. Every time she looked over her shoulder, the coast was clear. But that didn't mean the Soul Eater wasn't hiding in the nearest shadow, or however it operated.

She was forced to catch her breath at the first bus stop she saw. And for the first time, the universe seemed to care about her continued existence since a bus was fast approaching, lights shining through the mist like a chariot of angels. She wasn't sure where it was going, but hopefully all roads led to Edinburgh.

"There's a bus. I can get back," she finally managed.

"Okay, stay on the line with me, okay?"

Ivy let out a semi-hysterical laugh and the bus driver gave her a look like she was deranged.

"What are you gonna do, Toph? Crawl through the phone and beat up what appears to be a living black hole?"

"Look, yeah, I don't know. But I'd rather stay on with you than twiddle my thumbs praying you make it back in one piece."

Now Ivy could hear the sounds of the city through the speaker. They and Lucia must be headed back to the flat to pack. It was strange to have someone care. Someone Ivy hadn't even been particularly nice to. Once, it might have been a liability. An opening in her armor.

But now?

Now there was a comfort in it. In having the breathing of another person on the line to see her on her way.

She wasn't entirely sure what to do with it as she tilted her head onto the glass of the window to cool off from her wild dash.

"Hey, Toph?" she asked when her breath returned to a marginally normal rhythm.

"Yeah?"

"For once, I don't disagree with the name you picked."

The Soul Eater. Ivy hoped she never saw the damned thing again.

20

DINA

"Cairo, huh?"

"Looks that way."

"How are the pyramids?"

"Wouldn't know. Haven't made it quite that far yet."

"You're gonna go though, right?"

"I dunno. Feels weird to *ooh* and *ah* at something my ancestors supposedly built when they were slaves. Though historians debate on that one."

"Yeah, fair."

Dina didn't question these conversations anymore. The ease of them. Like she and Ivy had known each other for years, sending texts, calling and FaceTiming at regular intervals. "Regular" being whenever Dina was above water. And in those calls, Dina found herself sharing more than she'd ever shared with another person. The hope and fear that one day she'd be able to tell her parents she was alive. The way she'd always felt so removed from her groups of so-called friends. Like she was a stranger to the people she'd known for years. Her guilt at barely even missing them. She told Ivy everything.

Everything except her encounters with the Void. She didn't want to worry her with a monster that may or may not be a product of her own exhaustion. Sometimes she was so sure it was real. Other times it felt like a nightmare, something burned away in the light of day. That boy with the lightning had seen it too, but even *he* didn't feel real to Dina most days. Another shadow being that belonged to the twilight hours.

God grant me the serenity to get a decent night's sleep so I can stop questioning my own sanity, she grumbled to herself.

"Do you have time to walk around?" Ivy asked, interrupting her dark thoughts.

Dina closed her eyes, feeling for the Nile's gentle tug northward.

"A bit, yeah. I'm just sort of wandering to be honest. I did go by the Pharaonic Village, but I didn't want to spend Zev's money on too many tourist attractions."

Charging the phone had been a bit tricky this time around, even with the adapter. Eventually, she'd found a hotel with a large tourist population and snuck into a room as the cleaners were leaving.

Zev would tell her to use his money to book herself a room, but most places still required an ID to check in. Besides, if she could save him some cash and still charge her phone, what was the harm of borrowing an unused room for a bit?

"You gonna take the bus anywhere further out?"

"Nah. Sometimes I don't get the timing quite right and I'd rather not disappear on a bus full of commuters or tourists. It's easier on the street, even if I do stick out now that I'm not in the city center."

"Tell me what you're seeing."

This had become a common exchange for them: any time Dina called, Ivy was in a different city. Often a place she'd never been herself. The time before last, when she'd called from somewhere in Morocco, Ivy had been in Copenhagen. That phone call had been different from the others. Ivy had been quiet and distant. Less the brash charmer and more a reserved woman who couldn't seem to find the right words to send across the line.

"Talk to me," Ivy had said, voice murmured like a prayer. So Dina had. She told her all about the rolling, green hills, covered in scrub, how the water looked unreal against the brown of the shore, how she'd seen a pomegranate outside of a store for the first time in her life and her surprise to find the tree from which it grew.

And Ivy had listened until it was time for Dina to go. Just before they'd hung up, she simply whispered, "Thanks, Supernova."

This time, Ivy's voice had life once more, color bleeding back into a black-and-white film. Dina wanted to ask what had drained all that color and texture before, but now seemed too late to bring it up. And the last thing she wanted to do with this precious time was poke at old hurts.

Dina walked the streets of Cairo and described the colors, the shops and vendors and the strange looks she got as she made her way south, against the flow of the Nile.

"What about you? Tell me about Stockholm."

"Well, it's painfully clean for starters. Sometimes I'm afraid to even *look* at a building for fear of leaving a smudge. But then I *want* to put my handprints all over the glass. Just out of spite."

Dina laughed. Imagined Ivy's sly smile on the other end.

"But the people are nice. Like, weirdly nice. It's definitely the most boring place I've ever been. But not sure that's a bad thing. Maybe the whole Socialism thing isn't so bad."

"I hear good things. Must be nice to have universal healthcare."

"Seriously. Did you know that during the winter people leave their babies out in their strollers to take naps outside?"

"Seriously?"

"Seriously. Imagine living somewhere that safe. It's weird. Though, like...is that okay for those babies do you think?"

"Seems to be working for them so far."

"Still, Dina, it gets really fucking cold. I mean it's only August and it feels like an east coast fall. How are those babies okay?"

Dina laughed. "Look, what I know about babies could fit inside a thimble."

She turned the corner, smiling.

And froze when she recognized someone walking towards her. The boy with lightning at his fingertips. And in the clear light of day, afternoon sun high overhead, certainty flooded through her warm chest.

He's real.

And if he was real, what did that mean for the Void?

"Shit," Dina muttered, taking a step back, as if that might stop him from noticing her. "I have to go. I'll call you back."

"You okay?"

"Yeah." She hung up before she could say more. She'd been spotted.

The boy's eyes flew wide. He didn't hesitate. Just turned and ran.

"Fuck!"

Dina went careening after him, damp, secondhand shoes leaving blisters in the heat.

"Wait!" she cried.

She hadn't caught up to another Resurrected since she'd seen Ivy, and her heart pounded faster than the chase required. He hadn't had answers for her the last time, but he must know something, or even someone. Someone that could help her.

Please, I just want it to stop.

They hurtled down the streets of Cairo, people darting out of their way, exclaiming about the two foreigners wreaking havoc in an otherwise calm part of the city.

The boy was fast.

Dina was faster. And when he turned into a dead end, she knew she had him.

"Wait—please!" she gasped. "Please, I need help. I have questions."

The boy's eyes darted left to right. "We can't be together."

"Jesus, you're like a decade younger than me and I don't play for your team," Dina grumbled.

"No, I mean here. We can't be in the same space together. You'll draw it out."

"It?"

The boy never stopped darting his head around. "The Shadow."

The Void.

Dina swallowed, Cairo's heat condensing into a cold sweat down her back.

"What do you mean we'll draw it out?"

"It's looking for us. The ones who came back. Trying to snuff us out. Put too many of us together and it comes like a moth to a flame. I'm sorry. I can't help you."

"But I saw you controlling lightning. Controlling nature. Please, I don't know how to control it. I need help. Need—"

"I can't help you," the boy said, shaking his head like a spooked horse. "We're all on our own. I'm sorry."

"No. You're not." She stepped into the boy's space. Screw all these threads and mysteries. She needed answers and she was tired of waiting for them to show up. "You're not sorry at all. But you're going to help me. I won't let you leave until you tell me how you control it."

The boy backed up, nearly against the stone wall, looking over Dina's shoulder.

"How do you think you'll manage that?"

Dina grabbed the boy then. She'd never had a violent streak. Even punching that driver months ago had sent adrenaline coursing through her like a tempest. In her previous life, she wasn't sure how well she would have managed it.

Her second life had turned her desperation into a weapon, her hands into claws, and she dug into the boy's arms, slamming him hard into the stone.

And for the first time, she had his full attention.

"I just need to figure out how to control it," she urged. "How to stop it."

The boy shook his head. "It's like telling someone how to breathe. You just do it. And you should be worried about other things. Laying low. That's the only advice I'll give you. And if you meet any others like us, run the other way."

Hazel eyes and hair dyed black as night. Sly smiles and callused fingers. No, Dina wasn't going to run. Not from her.

She gripped tighter and the boy winced. "So that's your only solution? You see other people who could use your help and you run?"

"Yeah," he said, mouth grim. "I do."

And then Dina's hands were burning. A shock went through her body and she cried out, stumbled back. Like she'd touched a live wire. But worse somehow. Sparks shot out of her fingertips and she crumpled to the ground, rolling like she was on fire. Knowing in some small corner of her mind, somewhere far from the white flashes of pain, it was electricity burning through her body.

By the time the pain stopped, mere seconds or hours later, Dina was panting and shaking, her heart in her throat as she checked herself over. Beyond a few scrapes, she was still in one piece. Her head rang with aftershocks, but she could stand and look around the alley once more. She rounded on the boy, mind whirring. Thinking of how to get him to cooperate.

But he was long gone.

21

IVY

It had been three weeks since Dina had called. Three weeks since she'd told her everything was okay and abruptly hung up. And then seemingly fell off the face of the Earth. By now, Ivy had worn through the soles of her boots trying to walk off her mounting anxiety.

Topher and Lucia had both taken it upon themselves to check on Ivy and try to pry the source of her agitation loose. But she kept mum as they bounced from country to country, and even now in New Zealand. No matter the vice tightening around her chest. No matter the way it felt like someone was piercing her through over and over again.

She'd keep her alternating fear and despondent rejection to herself.

It hadn't exactly been a few fruitless weeks. They'd even managed to find another Resurrected in Kiev. Though when they'd knocked on his family's door, their offer of help was met with a terse "thanks very much but my family's taken the whole coming back from the dead thing quite well so you can fuck right off." Or at least that appeared to be the rough translation.

Their current stop in Queenstown was less about following up on leads and more about taking a break. Their frantic run from the Soul Eater had left all of them snappish and brooding. Topher hoped this far corner of the world might be safer for longer. Give them time to regroup before they resumed the search.

Safer sure, but Ivy was further from finding Lenox than ever before. If Rita was sending any help her way, she doubted they'd find her here. Without hope for any new contacts, she was still trying to sort through the notes she'd stolen from Jason's apartment. But she doubted Lenox had become a Kiwi for his next move.

And where the hell was Dina?

Ivy had nightmares every night now. The Soul Eater emerging from a nest of shadows with a woman in its grip. At first, its victim was Aisling, staring at Ivy as the creature sucked the life out of her.

Now, all she could see was Dina. Dina with black veins and blank eyes.

Call me, dammit. Even if it's to say goodbye.

Ivy cursed herself under her breath and marched through the narrow streets until she reached the edge of Lake Wakatipu. This late at night, the buskers were gone, as were the tourists. The sky reflected off the black water and Ivy was alone with her blacker thoughts.

She should be thinking about Lenox. Strategizing and tracking down leads, even from the edge of the world. She had internet and a folder full of notes, after all.

Instead, she couldn't stop thinking about Dina. The fright in her eyes as the water washed her away.

Ivy took the steps down to the barely-there beach, zipping up her jacket. It wasn't quite summer yet in the Southern Hemisphere, the chill still thick in the evening air. The calm lapping of the lake water soothed Ivy a touch as her Docs crunched over the pebbles. It was a relief to have the beach to herself.

She unsheathed a dagger and rolled her shoulders, ready to move into her now nightly practice routine. Couldn't let traveling with the likes of Topher and Lucia make her soft.

And quickly disappeared the blade when she took in a shape at the far end of the beach. A woman sitting at the lake's edge.

Damnit.

She half turned away, but then...

Warmth in her chest. Brown hair, wet clothes, the familiar tilt of a chin.

Dina sat, huddled into herself, watching the mirror of water with distant eyes.

Ivy's heart gave a painful thud. She took a step closer. Another, sure at any moment the mirage would disappear. And what would that say about her? That she'd gone weak enough to hallucinate a girl made of water and soft smiles?

But Dina stayed where she was, staring into the middle distance, not even moving until Ivy took off her jacket and placed it around the other woman's shoulders.

Dina startled so hard the jacket immediately slipped off one shoulder. She watched with an open mouth as Ivy adjusted it and sat beside her on the stony beach.

"Hey there, Supernova," she murmured.

Dina pitched forward. Stopped herself as if she couldn't quite believe Ivy was real. The same way Ivy felt now, as if the woman before her would dissolve into raindrops at any second. She reached through the remaining distance with a trembling hand, blew out a sigh that was nearly a sob when her cold hand met with Ivy's cheek. The same sigh of relief that loosened Ivy's own chest.

"Are you really here?" Dina asked, before swallowing with an audible click. Her voice was harsher than Ivy remembered, as if she didn't remember how to use it.

Ivy held the cool hand to her cheek, pressed her forehead to Dina's. "Are you?"

Dina nodded against her, and Ivy wondered at the feelings swirled all together in her chest. The sense of homecoming juxtaposed with the strangeness of it all. They'd only met twice before now. Had all those texts and long phone calls added up to the same thing on both ends of the line? The overwhelming tug and ache of it all?

She thought the answer might be yes from how Dina wrapped her arms around Ivy and burrowed her head in her neck. How she sighed when Ivy held her tight, not caring that the lake water was seeping from Dina's clothes into her own.

"I missed you. Is that alright?" Dina murmured against Ivy's neck, warm breath making her shiver.

"I did, too, so yes."

They sat like that for long moments, until their breaths and heartbeats floated together as one.

"Why didn't you call?" Ivy asked, eyes squeezed shut, afraid of the words the second they left her mouth, afraid of the answer she'd receive.

Dina pulled away and fished around inside her dry bag, pulling out her phone.

The screen was cracked to hell.

"It's um...well it's bricked."

"Yeah, I can see that. What happened?"

In the dim light of the distant streetlamps, Ivy couldn't see any hurts, but that didn't mean much. She tilted Dina's chin back towards her, running her fingers across her cheek to assure herself the woman was in one piece.

"I ran into another Resurrected. Tried to get some answers. He wasn't too happy about being found. I think his powers channel electricity, or lightning. He fried my phone when I got into a scuffle with him and getting a replacement has been...difficult."

The last knot of tension untied itself from between Ivy's ribs. Dina's phone had died. The Soul Eater hadn't gotten to her, nor had she decided that someone like Ivy wasn't worth her time. Just a technical issue. Ivy could have laughed.

"How long do you have?" she asked, barely daring to hope.

Dina turned her head to the water, frowning in thought. Ivy loved the way her brows furrowed together as she concentrated.

And when Dina said, "A week. I think." Ivy nearly kissed her then and there.

But they needed to take care of a few matters first.

"Okay. Plenty of time to get you sorted out then."

She took Dina in, really saw her. The sharp angles of her face, the hollows under her eyes exacerbated by the shadows.

"You hungry?"

Dina laughed. "Starving."

Ivy stood and helped her up. "Come on then. You're gonna love the meat pies."

Ivy didn't question it when Dina kept hold of her hand, when the other woman walked close, as if the next gust of wind might separate them.

"Erm, could I actually borrow your phone?" Dina asked as they approached the pie shop. "I haven't been able to call Zev either, obviously. I'm sure he's worried."

"Yeah, sure. Want me to grab us dinner while you chat?" she asked, hooking a thumb over her shoulder.

Dina's stomach let out an enormous rumble and Ivy raised a brow.

"Taking that as a 'yes'."

Dina laughed softly, a sound Ivy wished she might catch in a jar and hold to her chest to keep her warm on nights like these.

"Yes, please."

Ivy handed the other woman her phone, trying not to worry about her opening up the notes app, nor about how letting her out of her sight again so soon felt like putting her hand over a mouse trap and hoping it wouldn't snap.

Thankfully, Dina remained visible through the shop window as Ivy ordered (nothing with pork, please). Ivy watched her, the crinkle of her eyes, the way her shoulders loosened as she spoke with her brother.

They were still talking when Ivy came out, hot pies bundled in a paper bag.

"Yes, Zev, a friend. I'm capable of making them, believe it or not."

Ivy could just barely hear the other end of the conversation, grateful that Dina made no move to hide it.

"Are we talking a friend, or a Friend with a capital 'F'?" asked a male voice.

Dina went red. "Oh, shut up."

"Hey, get some."

Dina hid her face in her free hand, which was categorically adorable. "You don't have to do all the annoying brother shit, you know."

"Making up for lost time, D. Go have fun. GET A NEW PHONE."

"She will," Ivy said into the mouthpiece.

Dina hung up before Zev could do more than cackle over the ear piece.

"Don't add fuel to the fire," Dina grumbled, handing Ivy back her phone.

"Aww, but it's fun to see you blush."

Dina rolled her eyes, turning even redder, and pulled Ivy's jacket tighter around her.

"Shit," Ivy blurted out.

"What?"

"I'm an idiot. You must be freezing."

In her excitement, Ivy had somehow managed to forget all about the cold.

"I'm fine," Dina said, shivering.

"Uh huh."

Ivy grabbed Dina's hand. "Come on, my place isn't far."

It was a steady incline to the room Ivy was renting partway up Queenstown Hill. On the bright side, it meant Dina stopped shivering. On the downside, Ivy's legs were burning, still unused to the climb.

They were both breathing hard when Ivy let them into the sparsely decorated apartment with its pale blue walls. The kitchenette, bed and sofa were all in the same room, but it was everything Ivy needed and more. And best of all, it was her own private space, since Lucia had suggested everyone getting some time on their own might relieve a bit of tension.

"Here, I'll put these in the oven. Shower's over there. I'll get you something dry to wear."

Dina didn't argue. But she did start peeling off her shirt before she even got to the bathroom. So it was going to be like that then? It was Ivy's turn to blush.

While the shower ran, Ivy put some clothes on the toilet lid (pointedly not looking into the shower like an absolute creep) and texted the group chat.

Doing my own thing tonight. If anyone's dead lmk

Debbie Downer (Luz)

K

Professor T

Does that mean you're getting laid?

Debbie Downer (Luz)

Toph, leave it

Professor T

What? Someone ought to get some since it ain't gonna be us

Wait, are you two NOT boning?

Debbie Downer (Luz)

IVY WTF

Professor T

Bit hard to do when one of you is AroAce (hint, it's me)

Damn you really saw alphabet mafia and said "yes"

Professor T

Gotta catch 'em all

Fucking neeeeeeerd

Debbie Downer (Luz)

I hate you both

Homophobic but alright

Debbie Downer (Luz)

I'M BISEXUAL

I hear internalized homophobia's a thing

Ivy chuckled and turned off the screen. Startled when Dina sat across the table from her, as if she'd been caught doing...she wasn't sure what. Something.

She didn't have long to think about the reaction. Not when Dina was wearing the towel Ivy had given her and nothing else.

"Friends of yours?"

Ivy shrugged. "More like acquaintances I can't shake."

Dina opened her mouth to ask something, then closed it again when her stomach rumbled.

"I gotchu."

Ivy retrieved the pies from the oven, ripping open the paper bag and settling the food in the middle of the table. Belatedly, she stood back up again to grab plates. Maybe she didn't need to eat like a feral animal all the time.

They devoured the food quietly, and stood to wash the scant few dishes. The whole time, Ivy remained keenly aware of how little Dina was wearing. She'd pictured this moment so many times, and in her head, she was chivalrous, offering Dina care and space and whatever she needed. Patient. And Dina was making that virtue less and less realistic.

"Can I ask you something?" Dina murmured, leaning against the counter.

"Hmm?" Ivy asked, dragging her eyes up from Dina's bare shoulders. The curve of her neck.

"A while ago, when we talked you seemed...did something happen?"

It was a blade to her skin. A bucket of ice water. Ivy closed her eyes. There'd been a call, weeks ago now. Dina's voice on the line a glowing beacon in an otherwise black world. The nightmares since. Dreams that roused her from sleep, swallowing Dina's name before she could scream it aloud.

"Yeah, but I don't want to talk about it."

In the past, Dina had let such statements go. Allowed Ivy to shutter herself in when they spoke on the phone, tactfully switching topics to something easier.

This time, she said, "Can you anyway?"

Ivy stared out the little window that looked out onto a sleeping Queenstown, trying to take in the streetlamps instead of the surrounding darkness and the shadows it might be hiding. She swallowed bile, the warm food threatening to come back up as she remembered Aisling's lifeless form, held in midair, drained of substance by the Soul Eater. How wrong it looked. Not the typical emptiness of death, but a void. An absence beyond the ending of a life.

She blinked hard when she felt the warmth of a hand on hers. Steadied herself in Dina's brown eyes. Tried not to think too hard about what that meant, that she could anchor herself so easily with another person's gaze.

"Dina, I've seen things that I'm not sure a person should ever see. And I know we've been talking for a while now, but I haven't shared a lot about myself. Things that...maybe you wouldn't want to stick around for."

"Like what?" Dina pressed.

"Like the blood on my hands," Ivy whispered.

To her relief, Dina didn't budge.

So Ivy continued, too close to the edge to pull back. "I think we've led very different lives, Dina. And mine hasn't been very...peaceful.

I've seen people get hurt. Killed. I've—" she cut off abruptly, looking away, words choking in her own throat.

Found others. "All that is to say, I saw something a few weeks ago that scared the shit out of me. Scared me worse than anything I've ever seen. I saw..." she swallowed and tried again. "We call him the Soul Eater."

Dina's grip tightened. She nodded, encouraging Ivy to go on.

"It goes after people like us. I saw it get this girl I was supposed to help and..." she shook her head. "It was awful."

Silence filled the room. And then:

"I've been calling it The Void."

Ivy sucked in a breath, head whipping up again to meet Dina's hard gaze. "You've seen it too?"

Dina nodded, mouth tightened to a grim line. "I was half-convinced I'd imagined it. But I've seen it twice now, and the first time, it attacked. Before the water took me away."

"Dina, if you see that thing again, you run. Fast and far as you can."

"Don't need to tell me twice," she said with false levity. "I'm sorry you had to see that."

No one had ever apologized to Ivy about any of the horrible things she'd witnessed in her lifetime. And it was now the second apology she'd received. So even though it wasn't even remotely Dina's fault, the words comforted her somehow.

"So you've all seen it too?" Dina asked.

"Yeah. And there's no way of stopping it. Other than running."

Dina sighed. "At least I have that one down."

"I hate to say it, but might be for the best."

"You and the others you keep talking about. Do you have plans to take it down?"

Ivy sighed and pushed her free hand through her hair. Her undercut was growing out again and it was starting to irritate her. "We don't know how. So we're running too."

Dina nodded, thumb running back and forth across Ivy's knuckles. They stood together, the silence not quite comfortable, but not awkward either.

"Anyway, can we uh...talk about something else a bit less catastrophe-focused?"

Dina smiled and stepped closer, taking her hand from Ivy's and putting it on her hip instead. Her other hand toyed with the collar of Ivy's shirt.

"Like what?"

"Like the fact that you've been prancing around in a towel and driving me nuts all evening."

Dina rolled her eyes. "I'd hardly call it prancing—"

Ivy closed the distance between them before she could finish the thought, satisfied by the small gasp that emerged from Dina's mouth.

No more dark words and darker thoughts. This was what Ivy had held out hope for for weeks. To know the flesh-and-blood woman on the other end of the phone line once more. This strange girl she couldn't get out of her head. And maybe, she wouldn't have to.

Ivy pulled off her shirt and tossed it to the floor while Dina worked frantically at the button of her jeans, both of them breathing the same erratic breaths, hearts pounding through chests, fingers caressing every inch of bare skin.

For weeks, Ivy had wondered what this was. What it meant. Had tried to convince herself it was a one-night stand gone awry. That Dina only kept calling because it was convenient to. And so she had tempered her emotions, caged them deep between her ribs. Tried so damn hard to keep that flawless armor in place.

But now that she was here, kissing Ivy's neck, undressing her like she was something precious, that cage loosened to let that pent up longing free. The want and loneliness. The heartache of missing a girl with rain in her hair and mist in her breath. Now, with Dina here, Ivy couldn't pretend any more.

Kissing her was like drowning. Air sucked out of lungs, the world gone quiet around them. Ivy's mind itself silent without the constant whir of thoughts.

They didn't stumble into bed so much as dance. A step at a time. Lips on shoulders by the table, hands tracing breasts against the wall, the slow descent into a sea of blankets.

When Ivy slid her hand between Dina's legs, the other woman tilted her head back, eyes closed, clinging to Ivy with one hand and the bedframe with the other. Ivy loved watching her like this. Like she was storm and anchor both. And the way Dina said her name sent heat pouring through her core, made her eager to see just how far she could take the other woman.

"God, you're beautiful," she whispered in Dina's ear. Because she could. Because she saw no reason not to.

And when Dina came, legs clamping tight around her hand, Ivy held her as she shook, heart pounding like a wild animal. Because she had done that. Because Dina had let her.

And if the time apart had been a hell all on its own, a purgatory of constantly questioning what all this meant, how real any of it was, the coming together was a sense of peace Ivy had never felt before.

More than the ecstasy of it. More than the feel of Dina's tongue on her clit. In Dina's arms, she let herself uncoil in a way that had once been impossible. Not entirely. Not without leaving bits of armor intact. But with Dina, she didn't need to be a dagger of a girl. A human blade. She could just be Ivy.

And in these moments, in phone calls separated by oceans, or here together in the dark, that was enough.

22

DINA

The bed was cool when Dina woke. She groped around, blinking in the darkness of another unfamiliar room. Another unfamiliar bed. But this one at least ought to hold a familiar woman.

Ivy sat on the floor, crossed legged and hunched, looking out the glass door of the balcony. She'd pulled on an oversized t-shirt, that somehow made her look smaller, curled up as she was around herself.

Dina pulled up the duvet and joined her, draping the blanket so it covered them both.

"Where are you?" Dina whispered. The question Ivy always asked her when she called.

Ivy shook her head, wide-eyed. Staring. "I'm not sure."

Dina leaned her head on Ivy's shoulder, wishing she could draw her back.

"Is *it* there, wherever you are? The Soul Eater?"

"No," Ivy murmured. She pressed a hand to her chest, right below her breast.

Dina wondered if she was aware of the motion.

"How does a woman become a blade?" Dina asked.

For several minutes, she held her breath, assuming Ivy wouldn't answer. That she would wake from the grip of her thoughts and brush the question away, like cleaning rust from metal.

But then her lips parted.

"They bury a knife in her back. And the other in her heart."

Ivy said the words to a dark world, more to the emptiness than to Dina.

Dina's nightmares were filled with shadows and faces lined with disappointment. Shut doors and raised voices. A thing with the face of a man reaching down her throat and stealing every last breath. Raging waters and a cracked windshield.

If Ivy's were filled with blades in the dark, then at least she could try to be a shield.

She wrapped the blanket tighter around the both of them and pulled Ivy close.

They sat together, staring at the darkness the whole night long.

If weeks without Ivy had been like swimming through a storm, holding onto the smallest fragment of rope for dear life, days by her side were the peaceful shores in between.

Queenstown was full of more tourists than locals, so Ivy took it upon herself to rent a motorcycle and take them south to Alexandria, to the Caitlins, to Inverness.

It was strange to be by water that didn't call to her, as if the piece she'd left behind when she resurfaced was contained within the banks of the lake.

She prayed it would stay put.

When they saw seals and Ivy jumped because one ran in their direction before veering off back towards the water, Dina thought she'd prefer to die here, rather than in the Chesapeake Bay. Because she'd never seen a seal before. And she'd never ridden on the back of a motorcycle. And for God's sake, she'd never been to New Zealand.

She'd never been able to take the time. And now, she couldn't fathom why she'd put balancing other people's finances ahead of taking a vacation. Her parents' expectations above her own self-acceptance.

She'd held too much fear bottled up inside her during her first life. And she was still afraid, here in her second. She lived in terror that at any moment, the Void would peel away from the nearest shadow and lunge for her and Ivy.

But for the first time since she died and managed not to stay dead, she was taking in the world without the crushing weight of water filling her chest. She had a roof over her head and food in her stomach and a woman by her side who smiled out the side of her mouth and cackled like a crow and looked at Dina like she'd put the stars in the sky herself.

And so when they were sitting on top of Roy's Peak, breathing hard from the hike, but taking in the sunshine world at their feet, Dina felt guilty about bringing the whole thing up.

"So you're sure there's no way to fight it?"

She didn't need to explain herself. Ivy stilled beside her, eyes traveling far from the landscape before them. She shook her head.

"I don't know. I've seen what it can do. And I've seen it take a dagger straight through the eye and not flinch."

Dina grimaced, curling her knees to her chest despite how sweaty she was.

"Sorry. I should have a filter," Ivy said, placing a hand on Dina's knee. So much more comfortable than even a few days ago when every touch was hesitant, awaiting permission.

"No. I'd rather know what to expect. Do you think it's like us? Someone that came back from the dead? Maybe there's reasoning with it?"

"I don't know. I mean...look, I tend to reason with my fists. But even if I didn't, that thing called us 'Abominations'. I don't think it's interested in diplomacy."

Dina nodded. "That's what it said to me, too. So it's trying to wipe us all out?"

Ivy shrugged. "That's our best guess."

"And it feeds on souls. What if we starved it out then?"

"Honestly, I have no idea. But Dina, promise me. If you see that thing, you get the fuck out of there."

Dina nodded and Ivy's shoulders loosened.

"By the way, these other Resurrected you keep referring to. How do you know them?"

From the way Ivy straightened, Dina knew she'd stepped on something Ivy wasn't ready to share. Still, the more Resurrected she found, the more possibility there was for fixing her situation. For finding a way to Zev, to a life beyond this scattered existence. She couldn't spare the other woman's feelings this time.

"I...they're acquaintances. That's all."

"Seems like more than that, Ivy."

No reply.

So Dina turned away. "Ivy, I need help. I can't keep going like this. It's not...it isn't—"

"Never in the whole time I've known those two have they said it was possible to get rid of our powers. Not once."

Dina flinched. Blinked hard against burning eyes. Then a hand at her chin, tilting her back towards Ivy.

"If there were a way to help you, I would find it and lay it at your feet," Ivy told her. "But these other Resurrected...I don't trust them. Not with you. Not yet. They've kept things from me in the past, and I don't know what else they're hiding."

"Does that mean you trust me?"

Ivy tilted her forehead to hers. "I'm starting to. Terrifying as that is."

Dina sighed. "I just want to stop running all the time. I miss having a home. Or if not a home, at least roots. If there's a way to stop all of this, my powers, the Soul Eater, shouldn't we try?"

"I'm tired of trying," came the exhausted reply.

Dina kissed her cheek. "I know. But that wasn't a 'no'."

"No, it wasn't. Look, what if I try to pry out any more information the other Resurrected we find have to offer and then pass it onto you? Topher and Luz they're…They mean well, but so do plenty of people with their own agendas. And I still don't fully understand what theirs is. I don't like the idea of you getting dragged into that mess."

Dina pulled back. "I can take care of myself, Ivy. How do you think I've made it this long bouncing around the world like a ping pong ball?"

"I know, I know, I just—" she cut herself off and stood, eyes distant once more, the beautiful hills and valleys a foreign plane to her.

Whatever it was in Ivy's past they kept dancing around, Dina had brushed too close once more.

Dina stood and wrapped her arms around Ivy's middle, feeling the bellow of her stomach as she breathed hard, seeing something Dina couldn't touch.

"I won't break, Ivy. I'm too strong for that."

How else was she still going when the world kept falling out from under her feet? When she'd lived in fear of being who she really was for over a decade? When the opportunity to show her parents who she'd become was still beyond her reach? When she was coming to the conclusion that maybe that was alright, so long as she put her second life to use?

"I know," Ivy whispered. She didn't say anything more, but after a while, she relaxed into Dina's embrace. They stood like that until Dina could no longer avoid the inevitable. Until the buzzing in her head was undeniable.

"Come on. We should get back. It'll be time soon," she said.

Ivy whirled, stricken, hands coming to either side of Dina's face, as if she could keep her there. How Dina wished she could.

"Now?"

Dina shook her head. "A few hours. But maybe we should get off the mountainside so I don't give any tourists a heart attack."

Ivy swallowed, and it broke Dina's heart to watch her pull herself together, to mask the pain in her eyes. The look lingered in Dina's head the whole hike back down, with Ivy holding her hand despite the impracticality of it. Ivy deserved so much more than Dina could give between raindrops and serendipitous reunions.

So when they were back in Ivy's temporary apartment, sorting through the limited belongings Dina would take along in her dry bag, Dina forced herself to make an offer.

"I don't have to call next time. If you don't want me to."

"What?" Ivy asked, eyes going wide.

"I mean," Dina looked at her feet. "Until I can get my situation sorted, I'm going to keep on this way. Popping up somewhere I don't know every few days, not sure how to get to you. *If* I can get to you. This time was sheer luck and I don't know..." she trailed off, throat constricting. She could wind up anywhere. The chances of finding Ivy again...

"We've made it happen three times now, right?" Ivy pointed out. "And we keep finding others like us, like we're all drawn to each other. Topher calls it the 'Resurrected Law of Attraction'. So we'll find each other again. I'll find *you* again."

She took Dina's hand and squeezed. "I'll find you anywhere. I promise."

Dina swallowed. "But do you want to keep doing this? Do you—"

Ivy kissed her. Soft at first, then hard and bruising, driving the point home.

"Yes, Supernova," she said when they came up for air. "I want to keep doing this."

Dina sighed and wrapped her arms around Ivy, feeling every inch of her connected to the other woman. Breathing her in, reveling in these last moments.

Ivy held her the whole time. Until Dina began to shake apart. And even then, she stayed until there was nothing for her to hold onto.

And following Dina into the rush of water, replacing all the shadows and nightmares, were the words, "I'll find you again, Supernova."

23

Ivy

Time became a warped series of peaks and valleys for Ivy. The constant movement from city to city. The never-ending quest of finding more Resurrected without being found themselves, the lack of leads in her own search for Lenox's new hideout.

All broken up by the meteor showers that were her moments with Dina. Phone calls drenched in disappointment when they realized they were on different continents. Sparks lighting the night sky that was the drudgery of life when Dina called and they found themselves in reach once more. Fireworks when they came together and a plunge into darkness when they were torn apart.

And through it all, the secrets piled up. She'd kept Topher, Lucia, and Dina away from each other so far, but that was becoming a logistical nightmare. And she kept catching Topher sneaking glances at her laptop whenever she had a moment's peace to examine Jason's notes.

All that, along with all the bullshit she never told anyone anyway.

Ivy checked her phone again, wondering when and where Dina would land this time. Hoping it was somewhere close to São Paulo.

Nothing.

She stood and stretched, lining up for another cappuccino. She was really going to need it to keep staring at a computer screen the way Lucia and Topher were happy to for the rest of the day.

As she approached the register, the cashier said something to her in rapid Portuguese.

"Uh...desculpe?" she tried.

The woman rolled her eyes, clearly annoyed. Then in heavily accented English said, "Someone left this for you."

Dina?

No, that didn't make sense. Dina would have called or texted. And she certainly wouldn't have left a phone number on a napkin with no sign that it was her who'd left it.

Ivy quickly shoved the napkin in her pocket, ordered her drink even though her pulse was now racing fast enough that the caffeine would probably put her in cardiac arrest.

Back at the table, she typed the number into her phone, having memorized it from a quick glance. And texted:

> Who the fuck is this?

The unknown number replied immediately.

Unknown

> 4:50 pm Praça da Paz

Unknown

> Ditch your friends

Ivy considered the text far longer than she realized since Lucia tried to sneak a peek.

"That the girl you keep sneaking off with?"

Ivy pocketed the phone, heart clenching at the thought of Dina. Maybe one day she *would* trust Lucia and Topher with her. But she still couldn't quite let the Soul Eater ordeal go.

So instead, all she said was, "Judgy."

Luz shrugged. "No judgment, just curious. Girl must be loaded to keep meeting you all over the world."

"Yeah, you gonna ditch us for a sugar momma?" Topher teased.

"You wish," Ivy said, rolling her eyes.

"That I had a sugar momma instead of a job? Daily," Lucia said, eyeing one of the baristas a bit wistfully.

"Not the direction I'd be looking if you want to marry rich," Ivy pointed out.

"Look, my last partner was pre-Resurrection, let me drool over the hot barista." She said it as a joke, but there was something sad in her eyes as she spoke.

Every once in a while, Lucia let details like that drop, puzzle pieces, that if one slotted together would form the image of a full life. The mention of an older brother, a joke her tía had told her once. Hints and clues. But enough that Ivy knew better than to press on old wounds.

"Fine, fine. Drool away. Just maybe think about actually approaching her? The puppy dog eyes are worse than an ASPCA commercial."

Lucia glared and bent her head back towards her computer. Ivy relaxed. The anger was far better than the ache she wished she hadn't seen.

"You're one to talk, Iv. How many times have you checked your phone in the past five minutes?"

Ivy snorted. "Enough to know it's time for me to clear out." She stood and packed her things.

"Hey, we're only teasing. We won't pry if you don't want," Topher offered.

"You are disgustingly understanding sometimes, Toph," Ivy said, pulling on her backpack.

"Yeah, I get that a lot."

"Besides, I'm just tired of looking at a screen. Gonna take a walk and then chill at the place. See you there later?"

"Yeah, alright," Topher said.

Lucia shot her a look with a raised brow, but neither asked any more questions. It was the main thing Ivy appreciated about the two of them. It made things easier.

She waited to pull out her phone 'til she was far down the street. No additional texts.

She debated the stupidity of playing right into the unknown texter's strategy. But she knew, deep in her gut, this was related to Lenox. And she'd spent enough time feeling like a pawn in someone else's chess game.

> Friends ditched. Protocol?

She told herself she wouldn't go if there wasn't some assurance of safety. Then again, surely no one was expecting her to come armed to the gills in her own skin.

Unknown

> The usual. Assuming the name Rita Baxter means anything to you.

Ivy grinned. So Rita was good for something after all. It'd taken her long enough.

> Got it.

She navigated her way to the busy park: it crawled with picnics, tiny children and their parents, couples kissing on the grass. Crowded enough for safety, but the people would be too distracted to notice two strangers meeting up. Ivy had to give it to the unknown contact. It was an ideal location.

She spotted them sitting against a tree. Someone with tawny skin and black braids woven tight to their head. Their outfit was nondescript. A plain, dark gray tee over jeans. They were engrossed in the book they had close to their face. Looked like something Dina would enjoy, given the dragons on the cover.

Don't get distracted.

She turned her attention to the white kerchief sticking out of the person's jacket pocket. A signal from her old life that this was a parley of sorts. In theory, no harm would come to her.

Ivy sat on the other side of the tree after catching a quick peek to confirm who it was beneath the sunglasses.

"You should stop painting your nails, Puck. It's a dead giveaway."

Puck tucked the kerchief back into their pocket, keeping the book up to their nose.

"Speaking of dead, how come you're not?" Puck asked, accent holding just a touch of Brazilian Portuguese. Ivy wondered what had brought them home. If Rita had sent them all the way here. Back to a place where they were deadnamed and misgendered on a regular basis. She'd never considered Puck a friend. More like a landmark in her life. Maybe she'd have to reconsider given the effort they'd made to find her. Though in Puck's line of work, they could easily be here on other business. Handling negotiations between warring mobs and the like.

"Too spicy for death. It spat me back out."

"Hmm."

"Don't sound too surprised," Ivy commented.

Puck sat for a moment and Ivy could feel them considering their next words.

"I've heard you're not the only one death couldn't keep a hold of."

That *did* surprise her. "Who? A friend of ours?"

If Puck had met another Resurrected, the Soul Eater, if they knew a danger coming their way...

"Friend is not the word I'd use. And I don't have anything concrete. Just rumor. But keep an eye out, will ya?"

"Aw, you do care."

"You were generally the least unlikeable person in Lenox's gang that I had the displeasure of working with. If you take that as a compliment, that says more about you than it does me."

Ivy snorted. "Fair. So what've you got for me?"

Puck pulled off one of their bracelets. One of those slap bracelets that were popular in the early 2000s, or something like it.

"There's a USB on that with details about Lenox's latest movements. Seems he's settled somewhere around London."

London. Fuck, she'd been so close and hadn't even known.

The narrow way is how the light gets in.

Three in flight, two by foot.

Some of Jason's notes must have pointed a way there, but she still hadn't cracked it.

Ivy snapped the bracelet onto her wrist. "This is all a bit MI6 already. Where in London?"

"Hey, I'm supposed to be the neutral party here. You've already seen first-hand what happens when someone gets in Lenox's way," Puck said by way of answering. "Also heard through the rumor mill that someone offed his new heir. You hear anything about that?"

"You know how the rumor mill runs."

"So yes," Puck sighed. "Ivy, look...whatever happened, however you got back, you got out. It's your life, but if you ask me, you're better off just enjoying the freedom of having escaped for good."

Ivy leaned her head back, tree bark grating against her skull. The canopy of leaves dissolved into shadows and a pale figure waiting around every corner. A sucking, hungry thing. And behind it, grinned Lenox.

The blades of grass beneath her fingers cut like a knife between the ribs.

"If this is freedom, it sure as hell doesn't feel it," she whispered. Until the nightmares stopped, until she'd wiped Lenox from the face of the Earth, there was no true freedom. Not in her first life, and not in her second.

Puck said nothing. Simply stood and walked away, book tucked beneath their arm, job finished.

Ivy peeked around the side of the tree and smiled at the chocolate bar that had been left like an offering. Dark with sea salt. Her favorite, and one of the only personal things she'd ever told Puck. She tore into it immediately and considered her new jewelry.

Once she'd confirmed that Topher and Luz were still hard at work, she retreated to their rooms. Plugging in the USB felt like that step before you jumped off a cliff, knowing sharp rocks would meet you at the bottom.

Well, Ivy was always one for the plunge. Better to get it over with fast.

The drive contained nothing but a single word document.

"*Mince Pies. Bread and Honey,*" Ivy muttered to herself.

It was just a list of food, mixed in with random phrases like "well and hail" and "hey diddle diddle".

Another fucking code.

"We are *not* smart enough for this spy shit," she muttered, grinding her teeth as she tried to make sense of the numbers and ingredients.

At least she had a location now. London. And it seemed Lenox had set up shop permanently. Topher and Lucia had proposed Cape Town next, followed by Delhi, both achingly far from the UK. And there were weeks' worth of leads to track down in São Paulo. Even if it was like looking for a needle in a needlestack.

She still held out hope that Dina would resurface somewhere nearby. Last they'd spoken, she'd popped up on the coast of Washington. Another turn around the globe. Both of them running and orbiting so fast it made Ivy dizzy. But she'd hold on for the ride as long as she could.

The door opened, dashing apart Ivy's attempts to untangle her competing focuses. Topher's eyes immediately darted to Ivy's wrist where she'd just snapped the USB bracelet back in place. She'd been quick to close the laptop, but not quick enough. Though her screen held nothing but a few nonsense lists, she didn't want them getting any ideas.

"Any luck?" she asked.

Luz grunted and went to her room, presumably to flop face first onto the bed, as was usually her ritual at the end of a long day. So that was a "no".

"How was your date?" Topher asked, the question somehow empty of the usual teasing tone.

But they couldn't know. She'd been careful as always. No one had followed her.

"Fine. Maybe we'll have better luck with the search tomorrow," she offered. She'd have to redouble her efforts to actually *look* for obituaries and the like. Put in effort to get Topher off her case.

"Maybe," Topher agreed.

"Well at least there's still no sign of Soul Sucker. You want a drink?" Ivy asked, moving for the beers in the fridge.

"Sure."

As Ivy passed, Topher tapped her wrist with a light touch. Gentle. But Ivy flinched away nonetheless.

Topher regarded her calmly, hands at their sides.

"I know you think Luz and I are only with you out of professional interest or necessity, but I need you to know that we care, Ivy. If you're going through something, something that has to do with how you ended up in that grave, well...I just want you to know you can tell us."

Ivy brushed past them and pulled out the six pack. Now she *really* needed a drink.

"The nice thing about a past life is that it's dead and buried, right?"

"Is it?" Topher asked, brow raised. "Someone probably thinks the same about you."

"And hopefully, for all our sakes, they keep thinking it."

Ivy popped the top off the beer and took a swig before opening another for Topher and handing it over.

They accepted it without taking a drink, considering it like they'd never seen a beer before.

"I know you're gonna hate this, but we're worried about you."

They weren't wrong. Ivy's skin prickled, irritated.

"Because if I leave you'll be one man down? I haven't been pulling my weight and you know it. So I doubt you'll miss my sorry ass."

Topher made a frustrated sound in the back of their throat. "Can you pretend for two seconds that this is more than a business relationship?"

Ivy shook her head. "It's easier this way."

"For us? Or for you?"

Ivy chugged the rest of her bottle, regretting it immediately from the way it sat in her stomach.

"For all of us," she called over her shoulder, walking back into the night.

As she walked the empty streets, searching for a quiet place to practice with her knives, she tried to erase those words from her head. The notion that Topher and Luz wouldn't dump her the second she stopped proving her use. Not that she'd been an effective Resurrected hunter. Since she'd started with them, she'd helped find three. One was worse than dead, the other had told them to fuck off, and the third was a secret. Not a great track record.

But much as the two of them nudged her to keep looking, they never got frustrated with how often she came home empty-handed. And if they really cared...and if she admitted she did in return, how was she ever going to extricate herself to finish her business with Lenox? Bad enough that she was thinking of Dina when she ought to be focused on the hunt.

Ivy breathed in deep, plucking out splinters of thoughts. Cups of tea Lucia always had waiting for her when she came home from a failed search. Jokes passed back and forth to make the difficult days and constant travel smooth out. A girl who belonged to the water, who she hoped, in the deepest, most secretive corners of her heart, also belonged to her.

She pulled them out, one by one. Because she couldn't sort through Puck's information like this, nor go after Lenox with a dagger at the ready. Not with a head full of splinters. And if some remained wedged in, well, there was still time. She'd use her knives if she had to. Pull them out one by one. Til she was empty and clean.

24

DINA

Ivy had told Dina once about the Resurrected Law of Attraction. A strange sort of gravity that kept them colliding into each other, even as they racketed around the globe.

There must have been something missing in her explanation though. She never ran into new Resurrected. And yet she kept finding Ivy over and over, against all odds.

She thought about that piece of gravity to comfort herself when it felt like existing was too great a task. She simply had to hold on. Wait for her orbit to bring her back into Ivy's arms.

Now, walking down the streets of what looked to be a town somewhere in the southern US (Louisiana was her bet), that so-called Law carried even more weight.

Within five minutes of resurfacing, just as Dina's phone had turned on and was starting to receive a data signal, she'd spotted the boy again. The one who called lightning to his fingertips.

How nice it must have been to have powers that helped you fight. Dina, still drenched, with no hope of drying in the humidity, would have to make do with her wits.

The water kept bringing her back to this boy. She had to hope it was for a reason.

She was panting hard, walking fast and trying to keep up with his hurried pace, while staying far enough behind for him not to catch wise. It helped that she'd resurfaced at night. But after a while, she wondered if he'd even notice, hellbent as he was on getting wherever he was going.

He slowed a hair when he checked his phone, then darted down an alley.

Dina cursed and sped up, praying it was a dead end. But when she approached and peered around the corner, she realized she needn't have worried.

The boy had slowed, nearly to a stop, and was now crouching down beside another man.

Dina crept closer, body low, footsteps silent as she hid behind a dumpster, trying to ignore the awful stench.

"I can't keep doing this, Yousef, I can't," came a quiet voice, aching with defeat. The man sitting with his back against the wall of the alley was curled in on himself, arms clutched around his middle as if covering a wound.

"Alec, you have to get up," came the boy—Yousef's—firm reply. "I can't stay long, you know that. But I got your text, and I won't have it. You get up now, and you keep running."

"I can't," the man murmured. "I'm so tired. Don't you ever get tired of running?"

"Not tired enough to stop."

"I'm done, Yousef. I'm just done." Alec leaned his head back against the brick. This far away Dina couldn't make out his features, but it looked as though he'd closed his eyes.

Yousef shook the man's shoulders. "No, you're not. Come on, Alec. Get up."

The figure at his feet didn't answer. After a moment, in which Yousef watched the hunched man in silence, he stood. Hesitated for a breath. Then walked away towards the mouth of the alley. Towards Dina.

She put herself in his path so quickly his eyes went wide with shock. Lightning shot up his arms and she flinched despite herself. But the boy simply stood there sparking, electricity contained to his own body, for which Dina was eternally grateful. She really didn't want to replace her phone again.

Yousef scowled at her. "You."

"Why won't you help him?" she asked, with a pointed look at the figure in the alley.

Yousef shook his head. The lightning tamped down slightly, arcing between his fingertips.

"I've helped him as much as I can. The only thing we can do now is keep running. If he won't run, then the best I can do is stay away, and hope that *thing* doesn't come for him. So I'm leaving."

"Is that all you ever do when someone needs help? Run?"

She returned his answering glare with equal heat. For herself. For the man on the ground who clearly needed help. Anger licked through her veins like the caress of fire.

"It's how we stay alive. I've seen too many of us die by trying to stick together. Before, we could do it. Work together a bit. But now..." he shook his head. "Things have been different since more of us came back. If you were smart, if you really wanted to help Alec, you'd turn tail now. Run the other way the second you saw another one of us. We stand a better chance on our own. Too many of us together and it's worse than blood in shark-infested water."

Dina shook her head, eyes on Alec. "I highly doubt that man over there stands a better chance if you just abandon him."

Yousef huffed out an annoyed breath. "Believe it or not, he does. Now kindly fuck off or I'll make you."

The lightning rose again. The hair on her arms stood on end from the static.

So she kindly fucked off and moved aside, watching Yousef walk with purpose away from the alley to disappear once more.

Ass.

She stepped forward to kneel by Alec.

"Hey," she murmured. "How can I help? What can I do?"

The man considered her, head hung, eyes black. A boy really, like Yousef. Just bigger. Tan skin and a pimply face. A mop of messy blonde hair.

"Yousef is right," he said miserably. "There's only one thing to do, and it's run. But I'm so fucking tired of running."

"What did he mean by 'before'? What was different?"

"He was talking about this second wave. You and the other new souls. You've seen the Shadow, I take it?"

The Shadow. The Void. The Soul Eater.

She nodded.

"Before, it was easier to outrun. You could stay somewhere for months without seeing it. And even then it was more like a warning. A ghost you could ignore. It only lashed out on the odd occasion. Still terrible. Still horrifying. But most of us were lucky enough to outrun the thing. We were even able to stay in groups if we stayed on the move."

"And now?"

Alec shook his head, carding fingers through his messy hair.

"Now, our luck seems to be running out. It's getting systematic almost. Making a concerted effort to wipe us all out. You should listen to Yousef. When too many of us are together, it attracts that thing. It's not safe."

"Well, there's only two of us here. And I've spent time with other Resurrected before and haven't seen it with them. Most times when I see it, I'm alone."

"That's the problem. It's hard to predict. Sometimes it's fine, and you lull yourself into this sense of security that you're safe and then—"

he cut himself off, head shooting up, staring in horror at the entryway to the alley, just as a familiar weight prickled the back of Dina's neck.

It was as if the street lamps had been blown out, all the light gone from the world. Consumed by the pale figure shrouded in blacker than black.

The Void had come to feast.

If you see that thing, you run, Dina.

She'd promised.

But Alec was still on the ground.

Dina tugged at his arm, trying to get him to his feet. "Come on, we have to go." She could barely hear the words over the pounding of her own heart.

The Void advanced, slow, footsteps sure. As if time would bend to fit its will. As if it knew there was no escape.

Trying to get Alec up was like lifting a corpse. His arm was limp in her grasp, his eyes far away.

"It's over," he whispered. "This is what happens when we find each other."

The Void kept coming.

Dina dropped Alec's arm and took a step away from him, heart racing until her breath was shaky and thin, her limbs a trembling mess.

"Abominations," the thing hissed.

"Come on," Dina said, taking another step back, eyes darting around for an escape route. No windows and no backdoors. Nothing to climb either. A dead end had never been more aptly named.

"Get up," she urged.

They were well and truly trapped. But she wasn't going to accept death lying down.

Alec had other ideas, staring at the Void with resigned eyes. Something like relief softening his features.

"I smelled your blight," the Void said. "And I will exterminate it."

Dina shook her head. Another step. Away from Alec. Away from the mouth of the alley.

Could she run past it? If she was fast enough—

She didn't see the thing move. It just did. One second it was leering at them. The next it had Alec by the throat, lifting him up as though he weighed nothing.

The boy's eyes flew open. He thrashed like a puppet on strings. And *now* he fought. His skin turned bright red, the heat shining off him like a sun, waves of steam, like a pot boiling over.

And the Void ignored him.

It shot its hand down the man's throat, reaching in until it was buried to the shoulder, shadows of nothing leaking like droplets from its form. Dina watched in horror as the Void so neatly accomplished what it had tried to do to her.

Before, she had escaped because the waters had taken her, but this time they were days away.

Come on, she begged them. *Be useful for once!*

She felt the water at the edge of her consciousness, a hungry beast biding its time.

Better the beast she knew.

Alec writhed against the Void, smacking against the concrete.

Please, she begged, *work with me!*

A whining sound emerged from Alec's body. The Void swelled, more corporeal than the shadows had suggested all those months ago, when it had first come for her.

A black tendril caught her ankle, and she yelped at the cold, kicking herself free, backing further into the alley. She smothered her own panic. Focused all her attention on the memory of crashing waves, the fall of a raindrop into a puddle. The pieces of her that broke apart and came together again in the lakes and rivers and currents of the world. The water all around her, even now.

And then, an answering call, buzzing in her head. She nearly sobbed, feeling the oncoming storm, approaching to sweep her away.

Take me. I'm giving myself to you. I won't fight. Just take me away.

Alec's body fell limp to the ground. Eyes wide and lifeless, the color drained like she'd stepped into an old movie.

The Void approached. "You next, abomination. I will end you all. And when I have righted the wrongs of this universe, I will rest at last."

"I am no abomination," Dina whispered, taking another step back. "And you will not end me."

The last crash of the wave. The inhale before the plunge as the water split her apart with relief.

She disappeared in a tumble of images. The rage on the Void's face. The way it leapt for her and failed to make contact. The crooked smile of a girl with daggers beneath her skin.

Ivy!

The name was heavy in her mouth when she resurfaced. She swam to shore, uncaring where she'd landed. A pond? A lake? It didn't matter if it was a puddle. She didn't even care how long she'd been under this time. All she could see was the Void, grasping for her, as if it had followed her through the water somehow.

But when she dragged herself up through the reeds, she was mercifully alone, lungs heaving, heart ready to burst through her chest.

She'd brought that thing to Alec. It was her fault. Yousef had tried to warn her. All this time, he'd told her to stay away, and she'd ignored him.

If you really wanted to help Alec, you'd turn tail now. Run the other way the second you saw another one of us.

She should have listened. And maybe Alec would be just as dead, but at least she wouldn't have brought that *thing* right to him.

Dina put her face in her hands, as if to blot out the memory of Alec's writhing body. The awful sound he'd made. But when she closed her eyes, it wasn't Alec's body draining of life.

It was Ivy's. And the image was worse than someone reaching into her chest and crushing her heart.

She retrieved her phone from the dry bag, not even bothering to check the GPS. Pulled up the long thread between her and Ivy.

When too many of us are together, it attracts that thing. It's not safe.

Ivy was already on the run. Without Dina around to attract the Void, she'd have a better chance of keeping far from its long reach. One less Resurrected to draw its attention.

If Dina gave her the choice, she knew Ivy would take the risk. Say it didn't matter if Dina's presence brought a terrible monster to her doorstep. It would be just like her to spit in the face of danger, careless of her own safety. Dina couldn't let her take that chance.

But her hands shook with every letter.

I don't want to do this anymore. It's too much. I won't call next time. It's over. If you see me again, stay away.

Pressed send.

And screamed at the empty shore until her throat was on fire and her aching heart was empty. Nothing but water.

25

DINA

"Dina, talk to me," someone was saying.

"Huh?"

"Are you even listening?" Zev sighed, rolling his eyes on her phone's screen.

She'd booked an AirBnB just outside of Columbia, South Carolina when she popped up on the edge of Cary's Lake. There were still a couple days before she went under again. She should be grateful that her jumps since landing in Louisiana had been pretty close together from a geographical standpoint, but the anticipation she once might have felt had been replaced with apathy. A deep, empty hollow in her gut.

There would be no jettisoning around the world, wondering each time she resurfaced if Ivy was in reach. The endless wandering was without reprieve once more. No more phone calls to light the way. No more warm embraces at the end of a long journey. And the dwindling hope that she would one day get to Zev wasn't enough to keep her aloft anymore.

God, what *if* she saw Ivy again? What if the force that kept drawing them together had them stumbling into each other once more? She'd have to see first-hand the damage she'd left in her wake. And then run the other way.

Just the idea of locking eyes with Ivy, strangers once more, meeting in a crowded street made Dina want to scream.

And she'd picked this. This agony, this grief, over losing Ivy to the Void.

She was such a coward. Ivy was probably cursing her. Another name on the list of people who'd let her down. Who hadn't carried the shield long enough to protect her.

But when Dina closed her eyes, all she could see was Alec, thrashing in the Void's grip. Ivy, dead-eyed and limp as it tossed her to the ground. The thought made her chest hurt, eyes prick. She swallowed something hard and painful.

"Hey. You okay?" Zev asked, brows bunching together with concern.

She blinked hard, taking in the green walls of the rented apartment. The frog decorations on every open surface. The clock on the wall that told her cheerily to "hop to it". How she dreamed of smashing it to bits.

"Yeah," she said. Or tried. The word came out watery and garbled. She cleared her throat. "It's nothing. Just tired. What were you saying?"

Zev looked like he wanted to argue but bit his tongue.

"Well, you said that time in Louisiana was easier, right? You asked the water to take you away early, and it seemed to follow your instructions?"

She tapped a finger on the lacquer of the kitchen table. "I wouldn't call them instructions. It was more like I pleaded with it."

She still hadn't told Zev about the Void. Every time they spoke, it stayed there on the tip of her tongue. But he was worried enough.

"And you said the next time you came up was less disorienting, right?"

"Yeah."

"Okay, so maybe we've been thinking about this all wrong. You've been looking for a way to control your powers. To stop moving. But maybe you can move *with* the water."

"Meaning..."

"Like, let the water take you away before you get those terrible headaches. Maybe it can be like a partnership that way. You could bargain with it almost. Navigate it better."

Dina sighed. "That feels like giving up."

"Accepting something isn't the same as giving up."

She rolled her eyes and leaned back in the wooden chair.

"I hate when you get philosophical on me."

"Look, D. You died, right? Ever think that maybe you need to work through the stages of grief for your own life?"

Pulling her knees to her chin, Dina stared anywhere but him. "Have Mom and Dad worked through them?"

It had been nearly a year now. How much did you recover from the loss of a child in a year? How much had *she* recovered from losing her life?

"They're..." Zev trailed off.

"Shit. Sorry. That was dumb." Dina could have kicked herself. They probably weren't even talking.

"I spoke to them the other day," Zev said, eyes going distant. "They're coming here in a month. They want to meet Ben."

Dina grabbed at the phone, pulling it closer. "Wait, they what?"

"I know, I know." Zev ran a hand through his thick hair, leaving it in disarray. "I'm freaking the fuck out. But also...I dunno. It means a lot. I didn't think...I never even let myself picture it, them coming to meet him."

Dina had never been able to picture it either, introducing a partner to her parents. They hadn't even liked the *boys* she'd brought home, back in high school when she still thought she could fake her way straight.

"I think...I think we should tell them soon, D," Zev pressed. "I think they could hear it and take it now."

She laughed. A bitter sound. "Which part? The fact that I've got the dumbest superpowers on Earth, or that I'm gayer than the Tony Awards?"

Zev didn't laugh, which was annoying since Dina thought it was a good joke.

"All of it," he said.

She opened her mouth to argue, but he cut her off.

"I'm not saying today. I'm not saying tomorrow. But I think they deserve to know you're alive. And they deserve to know the real you. I won't make you do it, but just think about it. Okay?"

He was kind enough to ignore the tear that escaped her eye. The one she hastily brushed away.

"Okay," she muttered after a while.

He nodded. "So back to my first point. I think you should try it again. Go to the lake *before* the water forces your hand. See if that changes anything. If it gives you leverage."

"Fine," Dina grumbled. "I'll try."

"Love the enthusiasm."

"You know it," she muttered.

"You wanna tell me what else is going on? Anything up with that situationship you refuse to talk about?"

Dina's lips went tight. She dug her nails into the table so it wouldn't hurt. So she could pretend the mere thought of Ivy didn't feel like the water ripping the air from her lungs. Pretend she didn't wake at night reaching across the bed for her, knowing the sheets would be empty.

"It's over," she finally managed. "It's over and it's my fault."

"If it's your fault, doesn't that mean you can fix it?"

Dina shook her head. "Not this, Zev. Anyway, maybe I should try your suggestion sooner rather than later, yeah? See if I can figure out how to navigate myself."

"Not buying it, but I'll let you off the hook this time. Let me know when you resurface, okay?"

"Will do. Love ya."

"Love ya too, Gremlin."

Dina snorted and hung up. Zev hadn't called her that in years. The mirth lasted half a second before she glanced back at the phone screen.

Nothing.

She ought to be grateful Ivy hadn't tried to talk her out of it. That she hadn't received any calls or messages to peel the wounds apart, to carve out her heart through a series of texts that ended in words she was familiar with. Words telling her to fuck off.

But what if Ivy was relieved? She was free from the chaos of Dina's life after all. Maybe she was whistling to herself as she walked down the street, content that a strange girl who traveled through raindrops wasn't her chain anymore.

It wasn't fair, not when she'd called it off through a terse text and no explanation. But in a secret corner of Dina's heart, one she'd pushed aside to gather dust, she'd hoped Ivy would fight her. Fight *for* her.

But the silence meant she'd given up. And somehow that hurt worse than the absence.

Dina allowed herself another moment to curl into herself. To stifle the choking sobs. To ache for the familiar scent of mint gum and the soft caress of callused fingers. To imagine familiar arms, holding her up as the world crashed down around her. And then stood and gathered her things.

She could have booked a cab to the lake, but walking helped clear her mind, burn off the anxious hum in her veins. Going to the water like this, willingly giving herself over, felt wrong somehow. And yet...

The humming in her veins wasn't just her own heart reverberating in her skin. It was the call of ocean tides, the caress of a stream meandering through the forest.

Okay, she thought. *Okay. Let's work together.*

Ducking away from the lane, Dina made her way through the trees, down to the lake's edge. The brown water was tinged gray against the cloudy sky.

You better be right about this, Zev.

The water crested the rocks, lapping quietly. Daring her to take one step forward into its embrace.

She caught herself breathing hard and laughed. This wasn't any more terrifying than when the water forced her hand, was it? At least this time she was going on her own terms.

"I'm early," she said, as if the water might hear her. "Hope you'll take that into consideration."

No response, except a noticeable quietude to her mind. As if the water was…waiting.

She stepped into the lake, the coolness quickly overtopping her boots and soaking the hem of her pants. The ripples pulled her along as she moved forward, water coming to her knees, her hips, her chest.

Dina could feel the call all around her, like bells echoing inside her head. The water seemed eager, but pleased.

You took my life. Time you gave me something in return.

She took one more look at the heavy clouds above. Imagined the call of a crow was the laugh of a girl with knives beneath her skin. Breathed in until her chest ached.

And dove.

26

IVY

For the millionth time, Ivy considered throwing her phone into the street, allowing fate to take over and decide if a passing car would crush it out of existence and Dina's words with it.

But she needed her phone if she was going to make her next move. And the lack of a screen wouldn't give her the blank start she craved.

She hadn't replied to the text. What was the point? Dina had decided Ivy wasn't worth the effort the second she thought she could make a good try at a real relationship. How original.

Ivy's head was full of fire and smoke and if she peered too deep into it, she might allow herself to see the alcove of hurt, still unmarred by the inferno of anger, the sharp pain that pierced as deep as the blade that had taken her life. Worse in some ways. At least the blade had been quick. This was...

Well, anyway, she let the fires burn. And instead of staring at her phone, wishing it would ring, she kept working on the clues Puck had left for her.

Hey diddle diddle. Bees and Honey. Mince Pies.

What the fuck is this supposed to mean, Puck?

A knock came to her door and she closed her laptop.

Lucia poked her head in. "You nearly ready?"

"Yeah, just putting this away. Was checking some potential Jo-burg leads."

Luz raised a brow. "Going for student of the year all of a sudden?"

Ivy shrugged. "Just keeping you on your toes."

The other woman rolled her eyes, but her lips twitched up in a smile. "Well, fine. I'll get you a gold sticker at our next stop. But if we don't leave soon, we'll miss our flight."

Ivy smirked and stashed the laptop into her backpack. "You and Toph are too anxious. There's no need to get to the airport three hours early."

"Until the one time airport security is being more of a bitch than usual for no reason."

Ivy sighed and pulled on her pack and duffle bag.

"Come on then. Let's go."

The universe is held within the steady stream of the current. Her universe is the ebb and flow of tides. The push and pull of gravity from a faraway sphere. The pulsing heartbeat of clouds and the inhale-exhale of raindrops.

She reaches for something to clutch. Water in cupped palms.

But the current. The current is the leviathan that circles the world. It will not be tamed.

They got through security and found their gate hours ahead of schedule, just as Ivy predicted. It was all for the best though. Topher held their Cape Town tickets. A flight that would board in an hour and a half.

Her own flight was far sooner.

She'd told the others to go ahead when she "found a rock in her boot". Held back far enough that she could check her bags to London without Lucia or Topher overhearing. And all the international flights left from the same terminal. Less time for anyone to try and stop her.

She let the fires in her head burn bright, consume any lingering guilt. Shouldered her backpack with an air of nonchalance and said, "Gonna go pee. I'll see you back here?"

Lucia barely looked up from her phone as she nodded. Topher was staring out the window at the incoming planes.

Ivy turned away without another word and headed for her gate.

Streams weave together to become rivers.

She cannot move against the current, but currents don't flow one way. When the waters urges her this way, she tries another, flexing her consciousness. One droplet here, another there. Until she is a cloud, a torrent, a waterfall. Motion unending and yet not without control. The water has taken her, but now she lets it.

I am yours, and you are mine, *she thinks.* I won't fight you, if you don't hurt me.

And this time, the water listens.

"Now boarding passengers in Group 2."

Ivy was Group 6, but the staff at the gates rarely gave a shit. And the sooner she was on the plane, the better. She stepped into the line.

"Ivy, you sure you want to do this?" asked a calm voice behind her.

Ivy whipped around, cursing as she faced Topher and Lucia. The first had the look of a disappointed parent, at least what Ivy imagined they might look like. The latter had her arms crossed, glaring.

"This is idiotic, even for you," Luz said.

"Appreciate the vote of confidence and *so* glad my intelligence is still in question."

"What she means," Topher said, holding her gaze, "is we're worried you're about to do something—"

"Dumb?"

"Dangerous."

"Because I might reveal all your intel? To who? Who wants to believe people came back from the dead as walking weapons?" She whispered the last bit. They were still in an airport after all. "You said it yourself, no one has noticed people are back from the grave, and I'm the last person they'd believe if I *did* want to share with the world."

"That's not it," they replied. "It's dangerous because you might get hurt and we won't be there to help this time. Not if you don't let us."

Ivy scoffed. "You offering to come with?"

If they offered, could she really say no to the extra, quite literal, firepower?

"Not without knowing what your plan is," Lucia said. "But you could still come with us. We could talk about all this. I know you keep calling us camp counselors, but Topher and I have done a lot of work in the past four, now almost five years to move on from our previous lives. You could do the same. We could help."

"The only way I'm going to move on is if I see Lenox in the ground," Ivy whispered.

"So you're going to go through with it then?" Lucia asked, shaking her head. "Take another life?"

"As if my hands were ever clean," Ivy said with a shrug, turning away from whatever was on Topher's face. The clear hope that she could change.

But the blood had soaked into her skin over the years. She was a girl with daggers in her flesh. No point in being anything but a weapon. With Dina she'd thought—

"You could start over," Lucia insisted. "You've been given a second life. A clean slate. Come with us."

"And spend the rest of my life running from a psychopathic black hole of a creature? Keep finding other Resurrected so I can tell them to do the same?"

"It's a *life*, Ivy," Topher murmured.

Ivy shook her head. They were announcing the last boarding call for her flight.

"But it's not *my* life. You're right, Luz. I've been given a second chance. I'm gonna use it."

Without another word, she hurried to the gate and scanned her boarding pass, a numb resolve guiding every footstep. She didn't turn back as she walked through, not even with Topher and Lucia's stricken gazes on her back the whole while.

Elation. The swooping joy that is the fall from a precipice into the embrace of a river.

The thrilling crash of waves against the shore. But up here there are obstacles. Unfamiliar patterns. Sensations she might recognize if she had a body. Here there is only the change in tempo and strange movements, interruptions in her flow. And she wonders where she has gone.

Ivy found her seat and settled in for the long flight to Heathrow. She'd have to lay low for a bit when she got there. No rendezvous with anyone she might find from her old life. No reaching out to Puck. For all she knew, this could all be an elaborate trap. Just as her first death had been. She'd underestimated Lenox then.

Not this time.

This time, she would be the one digging a grave.

She turned off her phone before she was told to put it in Airplane Mode. No one was going to be calling anyway. Not Topher, not Lucia. Not Dina. She was on her own.

She settled into the rigid seatback and told herself she preferred it that way.

This isn't the way the water meant to take her. Not where she wanted go and now she is—

Why is the water so strange? Why does it settle and stand still? Brush against surfaces she does not recognize?

Where am I?

Ivy. Ivy. I wish you were—

I wish I was —

Where?

Where am I?

27

DINA

Wrongness seeped into Dina's consciousness before she and the water separated once more. Before she could fully return to herself. And once she did—

She screamed. Tried to. Because she was still in the water. Water that was ice cold. Freeze-your-bones cold. Crystal clear blue and biting.

She struck out with clumsy limbs and waterlogged boots, reaching for the surface where she *should* have come up. Turned upside down, feeling for the edges of water to point her upwards. To breath. To air.

They'd been working together, hadn't they? She'd thought she'd finally mastered this connection but—

No time to dwell on that. Her lungs burned and she'd already wasted a lungful of air on a useless scream. Couldn't feel her fingers or toes. Water that burned until it didn't.

Kicking useless legs. Flailing useless arms.

And contact. With the surface. But not.

A wall of ice against her fists. And all around her, endless expanses of it.

Dina struck with the flat of her palm, then with fists and boots. She couldn't build enough force.

Trapped in a world of ice and snowmelt. Air a universe away.

Take me away! You did it before! Take me away! she screamed as she beat her hands bloody. Clawing towards safety. Where was such a thing in this second life of hers?

Please! Work with me! I thought we were together in this!

Her thoughts were sluggish. Chest on fire. Aching for a breath, one last scream into the nothingness of water.

And it came against her will. Sucking in sea water, burning her lungs out. Back in the bay, engulfed by brine and screaming to herself *don't breathe don't breathe don't breathe.*

A buzzing in her head as the edges of her vision went black. The broken windshield, the plunge from the bridge.

Her last scream was a wasted thing. Returned with nothing but a darkening world of ice.

28

IVY

I vy's second trip to London was far less inspiring. She wondered if everyone who had the opportunity to travel eventually
felt this way. That all the cities of the world were strange mirrors
of each other. As if, when you got so many people together in
one place, things began to look the same. She couldn't tell if that
thought was depressing or comforting. Maybe it just meant she
was an uncultured heathen.

Or maybe she'd spent too long sitting in the rented apartment,
scrolling back and forth over the map of London and its outlying
towns. Because Puck's stupid list was starting to make sense.

It was Cockney rhyming slang. Some of it anyway. She'd only
sussed that out by happenstance. Some tour group passing by
as their local guide explained the term. A number of phrases on
Puck's list followed the pattern of it, but when it came to the
actual meaning, they didn't fall under any list of common rhymes.

And she still needed to figure out how it fit into the notes she
had from Jason.

The narrow way is how the light gets in.
Three in flight, two by foot.
Hey diddle diddle.

Ivy smacked her forehead with her fist a few times. She'd been at this so long the English language had lost all meaning, letters blurring together on the screen until they became nonsense.

Except.

Hey diddle diddle.

Cockney rhyming slang for fiddle. Where had she seen...

She zoomed into Fiddler's Brook. It crossed through a village up north.

She switched to street view, moving along until she found a wall with graffiti on the side. Most of it words and random phrases about the Prime Minister. She wasn't even sure if these pictures had been taken recently.

But one of the better murals stuck out. Three vultures circling over a couple of deer.

Three in flight, two by foot.

Ivy pinned the location and scrolled through the street view, taking in mural after mural as the wall stretched on, leading away from the village center and towards an isolated warehouse. About half of the graffitied images connected with something Jason or Puck had written.

"Fuuuuuuck," she whispered even though she was in an apartment with no one around the hear her.

Lenox's new center of operations was here alright. And she was only a train ride away.

She tied her hair back with shaking hands, just for something to do to calm the spasming of her heart.

Okay, think this through. No sense bursting in tonight. Not while you have the advantage.

A deep, steadying breath. That failed. God, she needed some target practice. And a drink.

Ivy slammed the laptop closed and grabbed her jacket, stalking out the door without a backward glance. No one to warn about her plans.

No one to check in with. No one stopping her from plunging head-first into danger. Once it would have been freeing. Now it was disorienting.

If Dina could see her now...

No. Don't, she schooled herself as she headed to the park she'd been frequenting for practice sessions with her knives.

She didn't have time to think about Dina. To be distracted by a woman that didn't even *want* her. Maybe she ought to triple that post-target-practice drink.

Ivy was nearly there when she caught a figure down the street fiddling with something beside a car. They kept darting glances up here and there, so she stuck to the shadows and froze. She knew a carjacking when she saw one, and if it was someone associated with Lenox, that would be her cover blown.

The person was struggling. Maybe they were new to this line of work. They stepped back and held their palm flat, took another look around, and closed their eyes.

Ivy stifled a gasp, finally aware that the heat in her chest was more than the tension she'd been holding all day. The figure held a piece of metal. And before her eyes, it was warping shapes. Melting together almost and then solidifying once more. To become a key.

The person—on closer inspection, it appeared to be a woman with brown skin and thick waves of black hair—slotted the key into the lock and turned. The door clicked open and she grinned.

Ivy hesitated. Then slunk closer. The woman didn't seem to hear her coming as she slid into the driver's seat. Ivy increased her pace. If the Resurrected drove away, she'd never find her again.

"Hey!" she shouted.

The woman didn't even pause. Just closed the door and turned the car on.

So Ivy ran up to the driver's side window and banged hard. The woman finally realized she was there and startled away from the wheel.

Ivy moved quickly. Rolled up her sleeve and pulled out a knife. Showed off her power to the awestruck woman, and then sheathed it once more.

The woman stared, mouth hinged open. And then, to Ivy's relief, cracked the window.

"Hey," Ivy panted, only now wondering what the hell she was doing. She didn't work for Topher and Luz anymore. She should let the other Resurrected be. Worry about her own problems.

But this close, Ivy tracked the harried gaze and hollowed eyes. Signs of sleepless nights. Of someone else on the run. Well, just because she wasn't looking for Topher and Luz's counseling didn't mean someone else couldn't use it.

"Are you on your own?" she asked.

The woman closed her mouth and motioned towards her ear. Oh. That's why she hadn't heard Ivy approach.

"Sorry, I don't speak sign language," Ivy said like an idiot.

But the woman seemed to read some of what she said, because she rolled her eyes and rolled the window all the way down. Then she pulled out her phone and pointed to it.

"Right. Duh."

Ivy copied her and typed out:

> My name is Ivy. I have powers too. And I
> know more folks who came back from the
> dead. Have you found others?

The woman read the text, eyes widening, and shook her head. She stared at Ivy like she'd grown an extra limb.

Ignoring the look, Ivy kept typing.

> I have a couple friends who have a network
> of Resurrected. That's what we call people
> with powers. I can put you in touch.

Now, the woman scrunched her brows together. Then typed something in her own phone and showed it to Ivy.

Kala. Can I trust you and your friends?

Oof. Ivy bit her lip, wondering the same thing. Shook her head and typed.

I think so. It's better than being on your own anyway. Are you on your own?

Kala's facial expression was answer enough. She seemed to stare far away. Then typed something else.

Have you seen the monster? The one with shadowed eyes?

Ivy nodded emphatically.

Yes. And if you see it again, run. But Topher and Luz can help you find places to stay. Make things easier. If you want.

She let the woman think it over. Let out a sigh of relief when she nodded to herself and handed Ivy her phone. She quickly typed out the two phone numbers. Didn't bother adding hers. She wasn't much help to anyone really.

Best get out of here before someone comes looking for your car.

Kala rolled her eyes as if to say she would have been out of here already if it hadn't been for Ivy. She pocketed her phone, rolled up the window, and peeled off down the dark street, leaving Ivy to stare after the fading tail lights.

Well, that was anticlimactic.

Why did she only ever find Resurrected when it was least convenient for her?

Ivy sighed. At least Topher and Lucia were finally getting what they wanted. Assuming Kala ever texted them.

It's better than being on your own.

Did she really mean that?

Ivy realized she was still staring after the long-departed car and continued on, wondering when she'd started trusting Topher and Luz enough to give another Resurrected their contact information.

Well, maybe Kala would be more grateful for their interference.

Ivy checked the park for any stray teens out for a late-night make-out session before heading to her usual tree. Tucked away enough that no one would notice a few notches in the bark. Even if they did, most people would blame kids, not a woman with a vendetta and the supernatural power to back it up.

Ivy loosed a new dagger, breathing deep to clear away her interaction with Kala, along with the whirlwind of conflicting longings. There was only one she needed to focus on. And that was Lenox's blood on her knife.

Come and get me, kid, she imagined him laughing. *We can rip each other to shreds and see who bleeds out first.*

As Ivy threw dagger after dagger at her makeshift target, even the satisfaction of a perfect shot couldn't dull the pressure of the knife peeling away her ribs, cutting straight into her heart.

Enough, she grumbled to herself.

She knew where Lenox was. She had one Resurrected off her conscience and two others blocked on her phone. No one and nothing to hold her back. No anchors. No chains. It was time to end this dance. Show Lenox she was far worse than any ghost he could ever imagine.

Tomorrow, she told herself, tasting blood and fire and the burn of rage as she loosed another dagger. *This ends tomorrow.*

29

DINA

Dina coughed into the mud. Just like when she'd heaved into the sand on Little Hunting Island that first time, months and months ago now.

But there was no kind man with his dog to tow her to shore.

Move dammit. Move!

She lay, half submerged still, the water lapping up to her waist, so cold it hurt. No ice this time, but her breath still fogged in the air, and the chill would kill her all the same if she lay there long enough. She sobbed, half her mind stuck under the ice, the rest of her unable to will her body into action.

You have to move, Dina. You didn't come back from the dead to freeze to death.

But her limbs were glued to the muddy shore. She couldn't even lift her head. Just lay there, hollow and shivering.

Footsteps. Pressure on her neck. A boot at her stomach, kicking her over onto her back.

How?

The Void grinned down at her, skin so pale it glowed against the cloudy sky.

"The girl in the water," it said. "Just my luck that I keep finding you."

Dina's mind stumbled, frozen still. Unable to fathom how the Void could be here, when she didn't even know where "here" was.

It watched her for a moment, seeming satisfied she couldn't escape.

"It's a shame, girl in the water. What's more natural than the tides following the pattern of gravity? And yet you, you horrible thing. You're as far from natural as has ever been."

Dina pushed all her conscience back to the water, screamed for its attention.

We were working together, dammit! Help me!

She beat her consciousness against that ever-present tug. Directed every scrap of focus towards the familiar crash of waves. And maybe Zev was right. For all her failure to direct the water to where she wanted it to take her, she could feel it. Listening. She could barely move. But she could fade.

"No!" the Void hissed as her limbs began to shiver apart.

It grabbed her throat with one hand, pried her mouth open with the other. That awful touch, so cold it broke through the numbness of the ice.

Terror injected one more burst of energy through her veins, stuck as she was between flesh and blood and mist. She scrabbled at the grip, tears streaming down her cheeks, choking on the nothingness the Void was stuffing down her throat. Gagging as she scratched and clawed and *yanked*. Not with her hands this time. But with her mind.

A wave crashed over them both, swept them apart, the Void lost in a whir of water as she was pulled back into the depths.

The splashing of footsteps running towards her as she pushed through the mud, half crawling, half swimming.

And finally. *Finally*, the water was listening. Speaking almost, as her body cascaded apart into droplets. And to her it seemed to say:

We won't let it have you. Not today.

30

IVY

I vy walked along the Thames the following morning, contemplating her plan. To use the British term, it was still a bit rubbish.

She knew where the hideout was. Knew the general set-up. But the list of unknowns was truly monumental.

Had the schedule of jobs changed? Had the crew? How much had killing Jason disrupted Lenox's hierarchy?

Ivy had never been one for elaborate plans. Maybe if she'd brought Topher, they could have helped her with that part. Maybe if Pete were still alive, he'd be able to navigate her towards something less risky.

In either case, she'd never know. But her body was a weapon. At the very least, she might as well throw it at something.

I'm ending this Lenox, you colossal fuckwad.

Good luck with that, he chided in her head.

Distracted, she nearly walked into the person in front of her on the sidewalk. Idiot had come to a dead stop. She was ready to chew them out when she noticed the man gawking at something in the water.

"Who in their right mind," asked the woman at his side, "is swimming in the Thames? Jesus."

Ivy scooted around the Londoner to get a look. Someone was indeed swimming in the Thames, kicking through the murky water with frantic, tired movements.

And even in those brief flashes of limbs and hair above the surface, even without her chest radiating a familiar heat, Ivy knew who it was.

She was vaulting over the rail and shucking off her jacket before she could catch up to her own thoughts. The reminder that Dina had called it off. Wanted nothing more to do with her. She ignored the gawking onlookers, scrambled down the bank, kicking off her boots, and plunged into the cool embrace of the Thames. She cut through the water with ease, grabbing Dina around the chest as the other woman's limbs began to fail, dragging the both of them back to shore.

They flopped onto the rocky beach. Beside her, Dina was breathing hard. This close Ivy could see a worrying blue tint to the other woman's skin. The darkness of her veins. Nearly black like—

Like Aisling. Fuck.

Dina opened her eyes slowly, and then locked onto Ivy like she was flotsam in a raging sea.

Ivy quickly helped Dina out of her jacket, replacing it with her own. She got the woman to a sitting position and tugged her shoes back on.

"Can you walk? My place is close, okay?"

Dina nodded, the motion slow.

Behind her someone shouted, "She alright?"

"Yeah!" Ivy lied. "Just a thrill-seeking friend! I've got her!"

The crowd moved on, as if relieved not to have to help. Some folks still stared, but no one stopped them as Ivy helped Dina to her feet, taking as much of her weight as she could. Hopefully, no one would call the police.

The other woman was cold as ice. For half a second, Ivy considered breaking all her rules. Catching a cab to a hospital. But avoiding medical institutions was a precaution deep in her bones, reinforced by Topher and Lucia's hesitancy to use them. Who knew what questions they would ask, which they could answer. If the Soul Eater would come while Dina was attached to a hospital bed.

So when she hailed a cab, ignoring the driver's immediate look of regret, she told it to go back to hers, clutching Dina tight as they huddled and dripped all over the back seat. The whole ride crept by at a snail's pace. And Ivy gritted her teeth, hoping with every fiber within that she was making the right choice.

When the cab finally pulled up to the apartment complex, Ivy helped Dina out, and the two of them squelched up the stairs.

"We're almost there, okay?"

Two floors up. Ivy swore as she dropped the key in her haste to open the lock. Jammed it in with shaking hands, hauling them both inside and immediately stripping Dina down. She was blue all over, blackened veins stark against too pale skin, gazing around with eyes that didn't focus on anything. She wasn't even shaking now. Ivy didn't know much about medicine but that couldn't be good.

She sprinted for a blanket and wrapped it around the naked woman, chafing her arms for a second before fetching a towel while simultaneously scrabbling around for her phone, dialing on speaker phone.

"Pick up pick up pick up pick—"

"Ivy? You alright?" Topher asked.

"How do you treat hypothermia? And if you don't know, I need you to do some Googling. And fast."

To their credit, Topher didn't ask.

"You got them somewhere warm?"

"Yeah and took off the wet clothes. I've got her under a blanket."

She grabbed the phone and led the despondent Dina over to the couch.

"Okay, well it says to warm the person slowly, 'trunk first'. So try to get her torso warm. Are you anywhere where they use hot water bottles by chance?"

"Never thought I'd thank the Brits for anything," Ivy muttered, leaving Dina behind to throw on the electric kettle and dig in the kitchen drawers for the hot water bottle she'd all but ignored.

"And while you're boiling water, try to get her to drink something warm, like tea. No caffeine though."

"Got it. What else?"

"Body heat. Hoping this is someone you're comfortable with?"

"Yeah, we'll be fine."

"Saving commentary for later."

"Figured as much."

"Toph..." she started. Swallowed the lump in her throat. Tried again. "Topher, I think it attacked her."

Silence from the other end. Then: "And she got away?"

"Yeah. Her veins are all black and—have you seen anything like that before? Do you think she'll be okay?"

Topher's sigh crackled through the speaker. "Can't say I've ever seen anyone get away from that thing once it's gotten ahold of them. And 'escaped from a soul-eating monster' isn't exactly a textbook medical condition. I think all you can do is treat the hypothermia and hope it helps with the rest. Keep checking her pulse and all that."

"Yeah. Yeah, okay."

The kettle went off and Ivy filled the bottle, along with a mug of mint tea she'd found in the cabinet.

"Hey, Ivy?"

"Yeah?" she asked, only half listening as she brought everything over to Dina, whose eyes kept fluttering towards closed.

"Glad you're still alive."

"Glad you picked up."

With her eyes on Dina, she made a decision.

"I'll call tomorrow, alright?"

"Yeah. Let me know if you need more help and how she's doing, okay?"

"Yeah. Thanks."

She hung up and blew on the tea before holding the mug up to Dina's lips. "Gotta go slow, okay?"

If Dina acknowledged the words, she made no sign of it. Regardless, Ivy managed to get her to take a few sips and settled the hot water bottle and its wool cover into the nest of blankets, flush against Dina's stomach. She removed her own wet clothes with little ceremony.

It was a bit awkward, getting herself into the blanket burrito she'd made for Dina, but after a moment's struggle, they lay skin to skin, with Ivy leaning back against the arm of the couch and Dina cradled between her arms and legs.

Ivy didn't think about the sensation of Dina's familiar touch, nor the way she smelled of sea salt and summer rain. She wouldn't let herself. Not even as she buried her head in Dina's shoulder and closed her eyes, listening to the other woman's pulse, willing it to remain steady. Willing the dark tint of her veins to go blue again. Because in the end, it didn't matter that Dina had walked away like everyone else. Decided Ivy wasn't worth the bother.

She wondered if she was pathetic for it. No second chances. That had been Lenox's rule. And here she was, pointing out all the soft bits of her for someone to pierce through.

But as Dina shivered and leaned into her like a river flowing down-stream, she didn't particularly care.

It felt like an eternity before the shivering subsided again. Before Dina turned her head and sighed, grasping the arm Ivy had wrapped around her middle.

"Ivy," she whispered. And the way she said it was supplication.

It wrenched the blades and weapons out of Ivy's hands.

"Hey there, Supernova."

Dina nuzzled Ivy's shoulder. "Missed hearing that."

"Missed saying it," Ivy confessed, voice low, as if the wrong words would send Dina straight out of her arms once more.

They sat there in a silence that ached. And then Dina began to shudder.

Ivy shot up, angling for a better look.

"Dina? Are you—"

But Dina was crying. Big, fat sobs that shook through her whole body, a look of panic etched into the wide eyes, as if she still wasn't really seeing her surroundings, but something else.

That fucking thing.

Ivy pulled her closer, letting Dina sob with her head turned into Ivy's shoulder.

"Hey, I've got you. I've got you."

She pressed her lips to the back of Dina's head, saying it over and over again. Telling her she was safe now, even if she wasn't sure that was true. Holding her until the trembling eased and Dina's veins were blessedly blue once more.

A long while later, once Dina's breath had evened out again, Ivy finally asked, "What happened?"

She reached up to test the towel around Dina's hair. Still damp, but at least it was warmer.

Dina's head lolled back against her, and she stared up at the ceiling. Or nothing. Her eyes were red and her face splotchy.

"I thought I'd figured it out," she said at last, voice hoarse. "My power, if that's what you want to call it. Not to...control it. But I was there this time. Conscious almost. I could see where I was going. It was like...like seeing several tunnels. You can only go forward. You have to pick one. But at least you can choose. But I got something wrong this time. I resurfaced, and all I could see was ice."

Ivy cursed.

"How long were you stuck there?"

Dina hesitated.

Then whispered, "I don't know. Long enough that I should have drowned. Maybe I did."

Ivy tensed against the instinct to pull Dina tighter. Even though she knew firsthand that the Resurrected couldn't be killed the same way twice. Had experienced the immunity herself. And yet all she could picture was Dina, stuck below the ice, alone and terrified.

"And then it came for me."

"The Soul Eater," Ivy said, confirming what she already knew.

"Yeah."

"How did you get away?"

"The water," Dina murmured. "I think it was finally listening. The waves pulled me away before it could finish the job."

They lapsed into silence once more. What else could Ivy say? That she'd protect her? Kick that thing's ass? Yeah right.

Instead, she asked, "How long before you get pulled away again?"

If it was soon, Dina wouldn't have recovered enough to make another swim to shore. Drowning wouldn't kill her, but Ivy was learning there were a myriad of ways to die.

It took Dina a few moments to answer, and Ivy wondered if the other woman had fallen asleep.

Then: "A few days. I think. And...I think I can negotiate for more."

"Negotiate?" Ivy asked, trying to temper her relief.

"Something like that. I let the water take me away sooner than it was supposed to a couple times, and since then it's been more...flexible I suppose. Seems like it wants to keep me alive."

Ivy wasn't sure what to make of that, but at least they had a little time to get Dina back on her feet.

"Okay, well you're staying here tonight. And then, if you're feeling better, we can get you set up somewhere else."

Dina stiffened. "I don't know if it's safe for me to be here. For either of us. Too many of us together will only attract the Void's attention. Maybe I should—"

"Sending you out on your own after you just nearly froze to death hardly constitutes as safe, Dina. I'll take my chances."

Dina struggled to a sitting position, fixing Ivy in a hard stare. "I don't want it coming for you because I'm here. I might be able to get away again, hide in the water. But that thing is like a walking black hole. If it shows up—"

"*If*, Dina. If. It doesn't always come. I've been traveling around with two other Resurrected for ages now and we've been okay so long as we keep moving. And you and I have met up how many times without seeing that thing? I'll risk it."

"But more of us together draws it out. It's safer for you if—"

"I said I'll risk it."

Dina's face turned miserable.

Well, being hunted by a creature called the Soul Eater, nearly freezing to death, and now being cared for by someone she'd dumped was hardly anyone's cup of tea.

"I thought I was protecting you," Dina murmured. "And here I am, putting you in danger anyway."

She took off the towel and scrunched her hair, looking any- where but at Ivy.

Until Ivy, whose heart had stuttered in her chest, turned Dina's chin to face her.

"What do you mean by that?" She kept her voice calm, despite the way her heart was now thundering away.

Dina tilted her forehead to Ivy's. Placed palms that were finally warm to either side of her neck, thumbs rubbing up and down.

"I'm sorry, Ivy. I'm so, so sorry. I saw it get one of us, and it was because *I* was there. We drew it out. Too many of us together...I didn't know that would happen. And that boy...he died. Or-or I don't know. And if the same thing happened to you, I—"

Ivy pressed a finger to Dina's lips, cutting off the frantic rush of words. Because she barely dared to hope, to give into such a terrible thing.

But Dina kept speaking around her, hand grasping Ivy's and holding it to her chest. "I'm so, so sorry. I didn't want to do it. I didn't want to say that to you or hurt you. Never in a million years. I thought if I stayed away, I could keep you safe. Safer anyway. I still don't think I should stay. I still don't want to endanger you. But God, I missed you."

The last came out in a breath, as if it were a relief to say. Her eyes had gone glassy and her bottom lip trembled. Then she was wrapping herself around Ivy, pressing close.

"I missed you so much. Every day hurt so much."

Ivy hesitated, barely breathing. If she stayed still as a statue, maybe she could hold onto this dream of Dina back in her arms.

When she finally gained the courage to return the embrace, the dream stayed put.

So she crushed the woman against her, mouth to her shoulder as she said, "Don't ever do that again. Promise me, Dina."

Dina nodded. "I promise."

Her face was wet against Ivy's neck. But she was here. Here and warm and safe. Safe as either of them could be with the Soul Eater on the loose. And she was in Ivy's arms again. At last.

Ivy couldn't remember a time someone had tried to protect her like that. Her whole life had been a game of gaining Lenox's transient affection. Everyone looking out for themselves. No attachments. No weaknesses.

If Dina meant what she said, what must that have been like? To cut off all attachments to keep someone safe. Ivy *could* imagine. She'd just never imagined someone doing that for *her*.

Dina sat up again, brushing tears away to look at Ivy once more. "I wouldn't have left you, Ivy. Not for anything. Not unless it meant keeping you safe. Do you understand?"

Ivy nodded mutely, unsure what to say. How to react. If this was all real and she could keep hold of the woman before her, or if she would dissolve like mist if she clung too tight.

"Do you believe me?"

Ivy sighed, considering a spot by Dina's shoulders. Steeled herself before meeting the other woman's gaze again. "I'll try."

Dina nodded, disappointment etching lines in her face. "That's fair. Do you want some space? I know this isn't—"

Ivy sighed and pulled Dina to her chest.

"Come here, Supernova. If I wanted space, I would have stuck your ass in a sauna and called it a day."

Dina laughed, the sound warm but welcome.

"You're too much of a softy to do that."

"A softy? I don't think anyone has ever called me that in either of my lives."

"Hmm. Does that make me special?"

"You turn into water and travel the world via currents. How much more special do you need to be?"

"When you put it like that, less special might be nice."

"Nah. Normal is boring."

"Hmm," came the tired reply.

Ivy shifted them so they lay horizontal on the couch. Face to face, tucked into a cocoon of blankets.

"Go to sleep, Supernova," Ivy whispered. From the silence that greeted her, it seemed the instructions were unnecessary. So Ivy held her very own supernova tight and kept her warm, begging the universe not to bring the water crashing down again too soon.

31

DINA

Dina woke to warm sheets and the ghost of familiar scents. It took her a moment to remember where exactly she was. A foreign apartment in a district of London Ivy had called "Bermondsey". The bed beside her was empty, and the nightstand held a note. One that took her a minute to decipher given the messy handwriting.

Breakfast in the fridge. Kettle is full for tea. You need to drink some. Put Topher's name in your phone for emergencies. Back soon. —I

She considered just staying in bed til Ivy came back. The other woman had bandaged her scratched up hands at some point and she was finally aware of the way they stung. Though it was the only pain, a bone-deep weariness still dragged her down. All she wanted was to nest in the pile of duvets and blankets for the next century.

But she *was* hungry. And thirsty besides. She could at least drag herself out of bed to remedy that.

Dina texted Ivy to let her know she was awake and pulled on a hoodie and sweatpants. She'd never get used to constantly borrowing clothes and beds. Then again, it wasn't so bad borrowing Ivy's.

Despite the initial desire to roll her eyes at being babied, Dina did as instructed. She was sitting at the kitchen table, stuffing reheated potatoes and scrambled eggs into her mouth when her phone rang with a video call.

Topher.

As she answered the call, Dina wondered what had changed so drastically that Ivy had decided to trust them and put them in touch.

The screen lit up while she chewed on rubbery eggs, revealing a white person with a septum piercing and scraggly brown beard.

"You must be Dina," Topher said with a warm smile. "I'm Topher. They/them. Ivy's been using 'she/her' pronouns for you. Is that right?"

"Yeah," Dina said. She couldn't remember the last time she'd been in conversation with someone who introduced their pronouns like it was natural. It was nice.

"How are you feeling? I got some of the story from Ivy, but—"

"But that girl is locked up tighter than my abuela's bowels," grumbled a voice off-screen.

"That's Lucia. She/her. And uh...she's not wrong."

Dina chuckled. "I'm aware."

"I'm assuming you're the person she's been sneaking off with for the past few months?"

"Well, I sure hope so," Dina said.

Topher grinned. "Hard to say. Rinse and repeat the abuela's bowels comment. But pretty sure you're her. Anyway, how are you doing?"

"Drinking tea as instructed," Dina said, demonstrating.

"Good. Any lingering numbness or slowness? Mentally or physically?"

"Are you the person Ivy called last night? Are you a doctor?"

"God no. That would've been waaaay too stereotypical with a last name like Levitz."

"Ah, part of the tribe then?"

They grinned wider.

"You betcha. Hey, shabbat shalom. But anyway, I Googled around until I found something that didn't say you were going to die from cancer and did my best."

"Well, I'm still here, so I think you and Ivy did alright. But no, Doc, I'm doing fine. Just tired."

"Makes sense. Ivy said you might not be able to stay in one place for long, but didn't elaborate."

"Shocking," the person off-screen—Lucia—said with dripping sarcasm.

Topher ignored her. "Think you'll be back on your feet before you're off again?"

Dina felt the edges of her awareness. The faint buzzing. This close to the river, it ought to be louder. Perhaps the water had taken pity on her.

"I think I'll be okay."

As she spoke, the door opened and Ivy came in, stomping her boots on the doormat and shaking the rain off her jacket. She caught Dina's gaze and froze, immediately wary.

Dina placed the call on hold with a "one sec".

"Hey," Ivy said, still standing in the doorway.

"Hey."

She wondered if Ivy knew that seeing her again felt like that first breath of air when the water released her and she became herself again. Like she'd been drowning for weeks and had finally broken the surface.

"Is that Topher and Luz?" Ivy asked.

"Yeah," she said, the word somewhat mangled by her heart jumping up to her throat.

Ivy managed to get her boots and jacket off, and approached the table, dumping a bag of outdoor gear onto it. Dina spied an emergency blanket and ice pick, among other items, both small enough to fit into her dry bag.

"How-um-how are you feeling?" Ivy asked.

Dina wanted to take Ivy's hand and press it to the side of her neck, to her lips. But she didn't dare. Not when Ivy was behaving like one wrong word would send her scrambling for the door. Not when being in the same room was a risk all its own. A risk Ivy said she'd take.

Dina would have to find a way to make peace with that.

"I'm alright. Tired, but alright. Thank you for the food."

Ivy shrugged, stuffing hands into pockets. "Sorry I'm a shit cook."

"Sorry I'm a shit girlfr—er date."

"Were you going to say 'girlfriend'?" Ivy asked, face unreadable.

"It was a slip of the tongue. Sorry, that's not fair to you after everything."

"Did you want to say it though?"

Dina turned away, chest throbbing as she nodded. "But that wasn't the right moment. Not after that text I sent. And I know we still need to talk, but I didn't want to hurt you and I—"

She stopped when a soft hand came to the back of her head. The press of lips to her forehead.

Ivy pulled up a chair beside her, throwing an arm around the back of the one Dina sat in.

"That sounds like a long conversation. Best see what these two chuckleheads are up to before then."

Dina looked away, trying to hide the warmth in her cheeks. Un-paused the call just in time to catch Topher saying, "How long do we give it before we assume they forgot about us and just went off to fuck somewhere?"

"Real nice, Toph," Ivy said, rolling her eyes.

Dina's face went hot, and if she wasn't holding the phone, she would have hid her head in her hands.

"Hey, Ivy. Good to see you in one piece."

Ivy grunted.

"Any sign of our friend on your end?" Topher asked.

Dina shivered and Ivy shot her a glance, surreptitiously moving her arm to Dina's waist, probably thinking she was cold. Dina wished that were the reason.

"None here," Ivy said, returning her gaze to the phone. "You?"

"Nothing," they said with obvious relief. "How's the side project?"

At first, Dina thought it was a euphemism, but beside her, Ivy tensed, and though she didn't look her way, Dina felt the woman's attention on her.

"On hiatus," she said at last, every word measured to the letter.

Topher made a sound that Dina took to be something between pleased and noncommittal. She would definitely be pestering Ivy about that later then.

"Anyway, I've been looking into more resources for you, Dina. There are some safe houses littered around that we've stayed at in the past. I okayed it with some others and sent you a map with them bookmarked. Though I was hoping you could tell me a bit more about your powers and why you're moving around even more than the rest of us from the sound of it."

Dina exchanged a glance with Ivy and the other woman nodded.

That was good enough for her.

"I have a connection to water. I travel through it. Resurface every few days in a different place. It's been unpredictable. When I'm let out in fast moving water, I only resurface for a couple of hours, sometimes only minutes. By lakes or ponds, I have days. So I've been moving around the world since I came back to life without much say in the matter. 'Til recently."

Ivy shot her a look, but Topher's mind was already whirring.

"I work a lot with algorithms. I bet if you tell me about where and when you've resurfaced to date, I could help predict where you're going next. Might take a bit. I'd need to factor in weather patterns and ocean currents it seems. But it might help. Make it easier for you to get to safety."

"That would be great," she agreed. "But also, I think I can direct it a bit now...sort of."

This time, Ivy's whole head turned. She hadn't fully explained it last night. So Dina spoke directly to her. "It's not perfect. I think that's how I wound up under the ice. Lately, I've been able to push back against the water. I got it right once, wound up close to where I wanted to go. By accident really. But this time, I pushed too hard. It was like we both lost control or something."

"You make it sound like it's alive," Ivy commented.

"It's water," Lucia jumped in, having appeared by Topher's shoulder. "Of course it's alive."

Dina nodded. "That time, when I pushed, it was like it wasn't ready for it. But the time before that, and coming here, to London, to you really, it was more like...like I could see all the currents. All the options. See where they were trying to take me and pick the one that felt right."

"You said this wasn't the first time. Could you do it again?" Topher asked.

Dina shrugged. "I think so. But I still wouldn't say I'm in total control. It's like...instead of steering, I'm nudging."

"And when you nudged too hard..."

This time, Dina did shiver from the cold. The memory of it. Ivy rubbed her back.

"Got it, well maybe I can provide better directions. Options, so you know more of what to expect. Can you tell me where you've been so far?"

Dina bit her lip, glancing at Ivy. Still thinking of Ivy's previous distrust. But all this time she'd been seeking out other Resurrected for answers. Well, here they were, glowing in bright neon, screaming her name. So she dove in.

It took a while to recollect all the stops she'd made across the globe. Ivy helped her here and there with pinning down specific dates, referring back to their trail of text messages, coordinating where they could meet. A trail of words wrapping around the world, full orbits colliding over and over.

"Good. Thanks, Dina. I'll do my best to get something before you go next."

She nodded, her chest loosening just a hitch. She'd convinced herself she was alone. Part of her was still trapped in that car, sinking into the briny depths of the Chesapeake. But she had Zev and Ivy, and now Topher and Lucia. Like the sun breaking through to point the way to the surface.

As Topher started rattling off information about predictive modeling and a myriad of topics Dina could barely follow, Ivy's gaze turned distant. She frowned and clenched her jaw. Dina wanted to curl her fingers under her chin, smooth her fingers down the frown lines to soften such a hard look. But she wasn't yet sure if that touch would be welcome.

Topher was trying to explain the basics of machine learning (Dina wasn't sure she'd really asked and was nodding along without the slightest understanding) when Ivy cut them off.

"When did the Soul Eater first appear?"

Topher's entire demeanor changed. Shifted from nerdy enthusiasm to an expression like a locked door. It might have been a non sequitur, if not for the way the Void nagged at Dina's attention, never far away. She imagined for the others it was much the same.

"It's been around as long as we have," Lucia provided, dark eyes serious. "As far as we can tell, it arrived when the first wave of Resurrected emerged."

"And it keeps coming after us. Calling us 'abominations'. Like it's trying to rectify something."

"Like our existence," Lucia muttered.

"Nature doesn't like things tampering with it," Topher said.

Lucia nodded. "And tampering with life and death is a huge imbalance. We've always assumed that's how it came about. Like a ghost to mark our new lives."

"Or an afterbirth," Topher provided.

"Gross," Ivy grimaced.

Lucia ignored them both. "And it got stronger when the second wave happened."

"And it's getting stronger still," Dina murmured. She wasn't sure if Topher and Lucia heard her, but their side of the call went silent, both sets of eyes, one slightly obscured by smudged glasses, focused on her.

"The first time I saw it, it was like...it didn't have a solid form yet. Like the lines around it were blurred. But the last time I saw it, it was..." she trailed off, unable to find words to describe the awful feeling of being around that thing. Like it was going to pull her apart, atom by atom. The terror of emerging from the water, half frozen, only to have it attack when she could barely even move.

"Dina..." Topher said carefully. "How many times have you seen the Soul Eater?"

"Four."

The others absorbed this.

"Shit," Lucia said at last.

"I take it that's abnormal," Dina ventured, feeling ill.

Topher mussed their curls. "Lucia and I have only ever seen it once, and same for Ivy. There are others that have had multiple encounters and gotten away. But according to the network of Resurrected, it's being spotted more frequently. And the fact that you've seen it that many times, even on the move is...concerning to say the least."

A weighty silence settled on the four of them.

Then Ivy jumped in, lobbing the words with all the eloquence of dropping a bomb.

"We need to stop running from it. We need to take it out."

Lucia made an irritated noise. "No. That's suicide and I'm not going to listen to talk of suicide and martyrdom, Ivy. Not today. Not any day. We're not just going to lay down our lives and—"

"That's not what I'm saying. I'm saying we need to eliminate it."

"Ivy," Topher said with shocking calm. "It's a walking black hole. How do you propose taking it down?"

"I dunno, Carl Sagan. You're the scientist."

"Computer scientist. That hardly counts. Also, how do you know who Carl Sagan is?"

Ivy rolled her eyes. "Because you talk about him the way normal people talk about celebrities. And you're deflecting. There *has* to be a way to take it down. We can't keep running forever. If Dina's right, sooner or later, it will get so powerful, running won't even be an option."

Or we won't want *to run,* Dina thought, remembering Alec, squeezing her eyes shut for a moment, as if that might shut out the memory of his body, worse than lifeless on the ground.

"I agree," she found herself saying. No more nightmares about the Void pulling her out of the water, of it walking over Ivy's drained body. Ever since she'd come back from the dead, she'd learned to fight. For herself. For her powers. Maybe Lucia was right. Maybe it was suicide. But better to go out fighting, taking control into her hands, than being torn out of this life against her will once more.

Ivy met her gaze again, mouth twitching up at the corner. And Dina stared back, resolute. Terrified, but sure.

Lucia's sigh crackled through the speaker. "But if we approach it, we're defenseless."

"It'd be easier with more of us," Ivy said calmly.

Dina wondered how long she'd been considering this. Perhaps since they'd first broached the topic up on that mountainside.

"We've never seen what would happen if we all came together," Ivy continued. "With all of us, maybe we could find a way to contain it."

Topher considered. Typed something into their computer and hummed to themself.

"If we assume the Soul Eater is also related to the black hole anomaly, and based on the way it operates..."

"Maybe it really *is* a walking black hole," Dina finished. "What if it abides by the same rules?"

Ivy had explained Topher's anomaly theory to her. Another subject she'd have to trust them on, given her lack of astronomy knowledge. But she'd seen the way light bent around the Soul Eater. Like it was consuming it. Not darkness, but the absence, the devouring of light. It made sense. Not that it made this idea any easier.

"Well, according to about five seconds of Googling, the only way to destroy a black hole is to starve it. If that applies to the Soul Eater and we find a way to cage it somehow..."

"It wouldn't have its favorite meal. It would waste away to nothing. And with all of us in one place, it won't be able to resist," Ivy said, nodding.

"In theory," Topher said, not sounding convinced. But not denying the option.

"How would we get a bunch of Resurrected together though?" Dina asked. "It's been so hard to track them down."

"Topher has a lot of contacts from the first wave of Resurrections. More than the ones they sent you that map of. We could use your whisper network, Toph," Ivy said.

She held Dina's gaze for the next thought. "I know what I'm suggesting. I know it's a lot of guesswork. But we're already getting hurt. Others are already being killed. Worse. Running isn't working anymore. I think we need to face it head on, but I can't make the decision for anyone else. We don't need to do this."

She was talking to all three of them, but Dina heard the unspoken message sent her way.

You could keep running. Let us do the fighting. Stay in the water. Stay safe.

Well, the water wasn't safe either. And Dina would rather drown again than let Ivy stand alone against that *thing*. If Ivy was fighting, so was she.

"I'm in," she said.

Ivy nodded and returned her attention to the phone where Lucia and Topher were having a silent conversation of their own.

Eventually, Topher sighed.

"Alright. But we need time to figure this out. Do some actual research and talk to the others. I don't want us rushing in, guns blazing, and getting us all killed."

Ivy shrugged and grinned. One of those blade-thin ones that made Dina's blood rush.

"Eh, we'll probably still die anyway. So let's at least add some fireworks to the show."

32

Ivy

Planning had never been Ivy's strength. Working for Lenox, she'd take instructions and turn them into actions. It was the whole reason finding him had taken so damn long. She only had a location now thanks to Puck. And even now that she *had* a location, her plan to stick a knife in his eye wasn't exactly going off without a hitch. Ivy never thought anything would knock her revenge against Lenox down from being her top priority. That was before yesterday, when she'd had to revive a freezing and catatonic Dina.

So, as Topher, Lucia, and Dina talked strategy, she did her best to follow the suggested logistics and still missed about half the details. There were references to cities around the world, to people Topher and Luz had never mentioned before. Talk of science and research that Ivy *really* couldn't follow. But Topher thought one of their contacts would know more.

They all agreed to chat again before Dina went under. In the meantime, Topher would send Dina contact information for any Resurrected who agreed to take her in if she showed up in their neighborhood, or would at least arrange a place for her to stay.

The idea of Dina safe made Ivy's chest loosen. Simultaneously, guilt turned in her gut. If she had trusted Topher sooner, had believed they truly meant well, even if they'd kept secrets of their own, would things have been better for Dina? Would she have even ended up under the ice? Would she have cut Ivy off in an effort to keep her safe?

They hung up, and the silence that followed the call carried weight, tension filling the vacuum. A quietude louder than the unsaid words between them. Some of them easier than others.

Ivy started with those. "How are you feeling?"

Dina bit her lip, staring resolutely at the table. "Alright. Still tired. Not like....I need to go to sleep. Just...tired. More than I can put into words."

"You nearly froze to death and had to fight off that *thing* again, so I feel like that's to be expected. But uh...not a doctor. You talk to Zev?"

She shook her head. "Not yet. He has enough to worry about. I'll check in soon though. It's been a while since I called."

"Hmm."

Ivy couldn't think of anything more eloquent to say, so she lapsed into silence again.

"What's the side project Topher mentioned?" Dina asked.

Damn Topher to Hell and back.

Ivy kept her voice neutral as she answered, "It's nothing. I was debating about reaching out to someone from my first life."

"I know how that is," Dina muttered, unfazed.

"Oh?" Ivy prodded to hide the guilt curdling in her stomach.

She sighed. "Zev wants to tell our parents I'm alive. And I'm still not sure."

"Hmm." Dina didn't talk about her parents much. But neither did she. "Are you not sure because you don't think they'll believe you? Or because you don't want to tell them?"

Dina went distant for a moment, biting her lip.

"I want to tell them," she said at last. "But I'm scared. And I can't decide if I'm more afraid to tell them I'm alive or to tell them I'm a lesbian."

Ivy nodded. She'd never had a chance to come out on her own terms. Had been outed by the first person who caught her kissing a girl at the bar. Even if she'd been given the chance, she doubted she would have seized it.

"You know...you don't have to tell them. If you don't want to."

Dina shook her head. "I don't know. But this person from your life, are they a friend? Family?"

Ivy couldn't help snorting.

When Dina raised her brow she tried to backtrack.

"Just someone who owes me a debt. Topher thinks I shouldn't collect. And...maybe they're right. Maybe some things should stay buried."

It was the second time she'd considered the possibility. The first had come while watching Dina sleep the night before, monitoring her every heartbeat to make sure she'd really staved off the hypothermia. She'd watched every rise and dip of Dina's steady breathing and thought to herself, *This is enough. This could be enough.*

But this time, the idea of burying her vendetta felt less like a dream and more like a plan. After all, she was dead as far as Lenox knew. She could just...walk away. Easy as closing a door.

But could she lock that same door and leave it closed? Forever?

Silence washed over them, more awkward than ever.

"Do you want me to go?" Dina whispered.

Ivy removed her hand from Dina's back and placed it in her lap, creating distance. A shield if she needed to pick one up.

"Do you want to go?" she found herself asking.

Dina shook her head, emphatic, even with her gaze on the table. "No. No, I really don't. Only I thought you might still be angry or want space or...I don't know. I thought...yeah."

Ivy took a breath. And a gamble. "Well, you did say 'girlfriend' earlier. Don't have a ton of experience in that department, but I hear girlfriends tend to talk things out."

Dina nodded and finally looked at Ivy. "I'd really like to do that. Talk it out. If you're game."

"I'm game. So long as you want to be here."

Dina grabbed Ivy's hands in both of hers, forcing her to meet her wild gaze. "I do, Ivy. I promise. I'm so sorry for making you doubt that."

Ivy held her gaze, and finally rocked her head against Dina's, breathing in the same air and reveling in the sharing of it. "It's alright. I understand."

"Thank you," Dina whispered. "When I woke up, I still wasn't sure if this was a good idea. Me being here, I mean. Not us," she added when Ivy flinched. "But if you're ready to fight, then so can I."

"I'm sorry too, you know," Ivy said. "For not telling you about Topher and Luz sooner. This whole time I've wondered if they were using me somehow. That's all I've ever known, really. And I've let people use me to stay alive. But I'd burn down the world before I ever let them use *you*. It never occurred to me that they would just help because they could. If I'd trusted them sooner..."

The words fell away, choked off by regret, twisted with guilt, and tangled with the shocking revelation that not everyone in the universe was a manipulative piece of shit.

Dina shook her head and put hands to either side of Ivy's face. "It's alright. We're both alright."

She said it as if trying to convince herself. And Ivy clung to the words, wondering if they might allow her the courage to tell Dina the other bit. Why she was really in London. How she'd gotten the scars that Dina touched with gentle hands every time they were together. The knives and guns and blood.

You tell anyone about us, you die. You're a good kid, Ivy, but that won't stop me from putting a bullet between your eyes.

How old had she been when Lenox had said that to her? She couldn't remember. All the threats, all the cajoling and scheming jumbled together. One giant dumpster fire of a past. For the first time, instead of wishing Lenox dead, instead of craving his life in her hands, squashing him from existence, she wished for something even more selfish. That her death and reawakening had really given her a clean slate. One without the trauma of that first life.

If she'd met Topher and Lucia without that baggage. If she'd met *Dina* without that baggage, what would her life look like now?

"You make me wish I were a different person," Ivy confessed, whispering the words as if it would keep them secret still. "A better person."

Dina slid into Ivy's lap, still holding her gaze, tilting Ivy's chin so she couldn't look away. "You're so strong, Ivy. You make me wish I was stronger. I want to be a fighter for you. I would never wish you different. Not a hair on your head. Not a single scar."

She kissed Ivy's forehead and wrapped her arms around her, curling into her. Like Ivy was *her* shield. Her air.

Ivy wasn't a shield though. She was the exposed sharpness of a blade, full of so many secrets she wasn't sure anymore which were safe, and which ones still had bite.

The words were on the tip of her tongue.

You asked how a woman becomes a blade. You sharpen her bit by bit, til none of the softness remains. And then you spill her blood anyway. He spilled my blood. And I don't know if I'll ever be free until I've spilt his.

But she could try. She could just...walk away.

If she told Dina, would she still sit there? Still tell Ivy she wanted her just the way she was, sharp edges and all? The thought scared her even more than the idea of facing the Soul Eater. She'd rather fight a monster than risk losing Dina again.

She wondered once more about closing that door. Wasn't one monster enough? Everyone kept telling her she'd gotten out. That she should stay out. Maybe they were right. And with Dina right here, warm against her chest, somehow the killing of a man who didn't even know she was alive felt so feeble.

Lenox. If I let you go, will you do the same?

She didn't know. But she would try. For Dina and herself.

I'm ending it, Lenox. You're not worth losing this.

The conviction had weight to it, like something to be screamed from a rooftop, decried to the world. But a secret still. The calm feeling of acceptance, of release, of letting her side of this stupid tug-of-war fall loose was for her alone.

So she held her tongue and her love, and tried to erase any thought that wasn't the warmth and comfort of being together again. At last.

33

DINA

Dina squeezed Ivy's hand, feeling every callus, every contour of it against her own. They'd found a secluded section of the Thames for Dina to go under, cloudy sky reflecting in the water as shades of gray and brown. She still hadn't sorted out all the limitations of her powers, but it seemed the water was more conducive to listening if she did the same.

"It's going to be okay," Ivy said against the cool breeze.

Dina wasn't sure if the words were for herself or Ivy, but she was grateful for them anyway. It felt less like a lie when someone else said it.

"Yeah."

The buzzing in her head wasn't quite as loud as the times she'd been dragged under against her will, but that was the point.

"You feel good about where you're aiming?"

Dina nodded. "Antwerp ought to be a straight shot. Even if I wind up close, I'll take that as a success. Topher thinks somewhere in Western Europe is a good bet, so we'll see how well their algorithm is working."

"Well, hope you like chocolate."

Dina snorted. "Assuming I get a chance to try some." She glanced at Ivy. "You sure you don't mind being in touch with Zev for me?"

Ivy shrugged. "I don't mind. And as someone who worries when a certain someone disappears into the water, it might be nice to form a little support group."

She smiled. "And what will you call this little support group?"

Ivy returned the expression and squeezed Dina's hand tight. "Dina Lovers Anonymous. DLA for short."

Dina's heart thudded hard in her chest. It was the closest either of them had come to saying the thing itself. Though by now, Dina wondered if it needed saying.

"So long as you have snacks in my honor."

"Only the best chocolate-covered pretzels and hamentaschen to pay you homage."

"Well, now I'm going to be jealous that I can't join."

Ivy kissed Dina's temple. "I'll save some for you, alright?"

"Yeah."

Ivy kept her mouth there. Turned her head into Dina's to nuzzle her. "Gonna miss you, Supernova."

She'd never adapt to this. Leaving Ivy behind when nothing in her was remotely ready to do so. Saying goodbye without knowing under what conditions, what alignment of stars they would meet again. But if Dina got this right, perhaps the parting wouldn't be nearly so awful.

Ivy had wanted to fly to Belgium to meet her, assuming she made it. But Dina convinced her to save her money and stay in London in case she ended up far off base. With Heathrow so close at hand, perhaps Ivy would have an easier time getting to Dina wherever she landed, even if not where she intended.

"I think it's time," Dina whispered, each word tasting of river water and salt.

"Want me to go?" Ivy asked, not budging, breathing deep in a way that mirrored Dina's own attempts to keep Ivy bottled inside of her. A secret message all her own to carry across the waves.

"No," she answered.

Ivy lifted their clasped hands to her lips and kept them there as Dina began to fade and the weight of muscle, skin, bone dissolved into steady streams of water entering the Thames. Until that soft touch was the only thing that remained. Until that too was gone.

The rocking is gentle and the current speaks. Whispers into those places where the city has brushed too close to the waters. Where the riverbed is made of trash and sewage instead of silt and rock.

And then.

Oh.

The freedom of open water.

Here she can breathe. Or something like it. And there is joy around her, etched into each drop that makes up the channel.

It takes a long time—if time were relevant in this space—to orient herself. But she remembers this sensation. The wholeness of belonging to something beyond the understanding of the human mind.

The water tugs at her, but this time it is a question. A suggestion. The presentation of a tapestry, from which she might pull a thread. Some threads are too tangled to reach and snagging one will spell disaster. But there are others, and the waters guide her consciousness towards them.

The human part of her tries to formulate the image of a map, a place she marked on it. But she must give up. For the dimensionality of this liminal space is entirely wrong for such a thing. So she feels at the threads of water. Holds the tapestry to her consciousness.

There, she and the water sigh.

The thread pulls. The current pulses. A girl made of water whispers against the shore, crashes into the rock face, feels her way up and up and up the river from mouth to body. Expels herself onto a new shore.

Dina lay among the tall grasses and stared at the sky, body shuddering with gasping breaths as it remembered how to be a body. Sometimes when she resurfaced, it felt like a dream within a dream. Like she was trying to force herself to wake from her own paralysis, until finally, her consciousness clicked into place.

But eventually, she could heave full breaths into her lungs, force herself into a seated position and take in her surroundings.

She'd swum ashore across the way from a city of stone and peaked roofs. Vaguely Dutch in appearance, but perhaps that was wishful thinking.

Dina pulled out her phone with shaking fingers, nearly dropping it in the mud as she turned it on and waited for the GPS to pinpoint her location.

The gray dot wandered for a moment. Then lit up bright blue.

Right at the edge of Antwerp.

Her sob was almost a laugh, and she clasped a hand over her mouth, hardly daring to believe the screen.

Ivy, I did it, she thought.

She'd have to call and tell her the good news. If she could keep this up, it would change everything. The entirety of her existence in this strange second life.

She turned and got to her knees, thinking to walk up the bank and find a safe place to dry off.

But when she looked up, she found a familiar figure looking down at her, shock written over his features. Heat prickled through her chest, reaching her through the cold of her damp clothes.

She'd washed ashore just in time to land right at Yousef's feet.

34

Ivy

I vy's phone remained silent. It was to be expected with Dina only a couple hours gone. Still, a part of her had hoped that if Dina could control her powers somehow, she would be able to resurface again more quickly. That even if she were miles away, she could at least have her voice coming through the phone again. The absence of it gnawed. Not entirely unpleasant. Somehow the missing of someone, a supernova of a girl who'd burst her second life apart in the most delicious way, hurt like chocolate after long hours without food. Bitter and biting and sweet all at once.

But she'd rather have the chocolate without the pain. Would rather have the days and weeks and months that often kept them separated dwindle to nothing. And instead of time apart, they'd have days and weeks and months together.

The waiting was the only thing keeping her mind off of Lenox. Off her discarded plans and this new normal. A life whose sole purpose was something more than revenge.

Besides, if she got herself killed, what would happen to Dina the next time she had trouble? If she woke up under the ice once more? She had Topher and Luz and Zev, who'd sent Ivy a polite introductory text. But who would be there when Dina washed ashore, shivering and alone? The memory of Dina's blue lips and vacant stare had kept her up at night, though she'd tried to hide those nightmares when Dina was sleeping in her arms. Until Dina called again, she'd be stuck in this endless loop of fretting and hoping. She couldn't go after Lenox now.

I'm letting it go, Lenox. I'm letting you live, so I get my own shot at it.

It was more than he deserved. And less than she wanted. It would have to do.

"Ivy? Ivyyyyyy."

From the tone, Topher had been calling her name for a while now. She focused back on the video call on her laptop.

"Uh, yeah?"

"You didn't catch a word of what we just said, did you?" Lucia asked, frowning.

Danny was also on the line. The first time Ivy had seen him since they'd left D.C. If he was miffed by her lack of attention, he hid it.

"You're gonna reach out to your little whisper network, spread the word, and arrange a time and place. What else do I need to pay attention to?"

Lucia rolled her eyes.

"A lot actually. Topher had an idea for how to cage this thing."

Ivy perked up at that. "All the black hole research paid off?"

"You say as if you contributed," Lucia grumbled.

Topher rubbed the back of their neck. "Not exactly. This solution is a bit more uh...woo woo than astronomy."

"So we align our chakras and do some white people magic shit?"

Lucia smacked her forehead and muttered to herself in rapid Spanish. Probably asking Díos why she'd been saddled with this absolute wrecking ball of a human. Topher smirked. Danny ignored them all. In fact, Ivy was pretty sure he was doodling off-screen.

"Before you keep interrupting to make a sarcastic comment, we're going to need your daggers," Topher said. "And we'll need to keep some of them."

"Ummmm, why?"

"Topher has a theory that we can use the physical manifestations of our powers to create a cage," Danny finally said, holding up the page he'd been scribbling on. It depicted a net thrown over a black shadow. Around it, arrows were pointing inward.

"You can produce daggers. Another Resurrected works with stone, and I also know of a couple metalworkers. That woman you found, Kala, says she can forge materials into new forms. She can construct a cage from those physical manifestations, pieces of us rather than the souls it wants. I use my powers to keep it locked in place. And we think these pieces of us, pieces that come from what should be human bodies, will react with the Soul Eater. Keep it contained. Then we let gravity do the rest."

Ivy hadn't known Kala had reached out. She was surprised to find herself relieved by the knowledge.

"So you'll crush it?"

Danny shrugged. "In theory, I'll force it to starve itself out more quickly than if we left it in place and just waited. And we want to do this quickly."

"So we get it into this cage by...what, asking nicely?"

"We'll have to lure it out," Topher said. "That'll be the most dangerous part, of course. Getting us all together and caging that thing before it can get to us."

"That sounds..." Ivy bit her lip, fumbling for the right word.

"You look like you're going to say 'idiotic'," Topher commented.

Ivy sighed. "There are so many ways for this to go wrong."

"You're the one who wanted to go after it," Lucia pointed out. "Got a better idea?"

Ivy stayed silent. Lucia knew she didn't, but it was petty of her to point it out.

"It's not masterful," the other woman pressed, "but it could be our best shot of eliminating this thing before it tracks all of us down and eats us one by one."

Ivy shuddered, brought back to one of her many nightmares. God, she needed to stop collecting them like shiny pebbles.

"Alright, so you need my daggers. I suppose that means we're in for a reunion."

"Joy," Luz said.

Ivy smirked. "Aww, I knew I was growing on you."

"Yeah, like a fungus," Luz shot back, but she was biting back a grin.

As they spoke, Ivy's phone lit up. She immediately grabbed it, anxious to see Dina's name lighting up the screen. Most of the other people she knew were on the video call.

Instead, she had an anonymous text that read:

Unknown

Miss me?

Ivy had no time to process the words before the window in the living room burst into shards and the world went up in flames.

She leaped under the table before the blast had entirely finished. Her ears rang, but she wasn't on fire. She couldn't say the same for the rest of the apartment.

The sprinkler system engaged in time for another Molotov cocktail to crash into the room.

Ivy curled up, hands over ears, eyes squeezed tight, the blast buffeting against her in a wave of heat.

The world went silent beyond the ringing of her ears. She could just make out Topher frantically calling her name before the laptop died under a barrage of water.

Get to the door, she instructed herself. *Get out.*

She crawled, phone in her back pocket. Snatched up her jacket and wallet and went tumbling out of the apartment in a smokey, coughing heap. Her neighbors were streaming down the hallway, the rush of terrified and confused voices muffled by the lingering effects of the blast.

Ivy joined the masses of terrified residents, blending in and trying to hide the fact that it was her sublet that had been targeted.

Her phone buzzed in her pocket. Another anonymous text, this time with two photos.

One of her and Dina, holding hands by the Thames, just before Dina had gone under.

The other was Puck, glaring around a gag and blackened eye.

Unknown

Stop the trail. Send evidence that you've gone VERY far away, or they'll pay for the fact that you didn't stay dead

Out on the streets now, Ivy looked around, trying to find her tail. But with the crowd of confused residents and onslaught of firetrucks and ambulances, it was impossible to pin down anyone suspicious amidst the chaos.

She slunk away from the throng, down the street. Walking fast without making it look like she was running from the scene of a crime. Missed three of Topher's calls before she picked up, still looking around and willing her head to stop ringing like a goddamned bell.

"Thank God," Topher breathed. Ivy could barely hear them, but enough came through to piece it together. "I assume you're alive then?"

"Still working through all nine of my lives. Reunion's going to need a rain check though."

No way the Lenox she knew would simply let her go about her life in peace, not now that he knew she was alive. And no way he'd just let Puck walk away from all this unscathed. If she let the man live, she'd forever be looking over her shoulder, waiting for a bullet through the skull, waiting for the target on her back to switch to Dina's. Lenox may not have put a nail in her coffin, but he'd sure put one in his own.

That calm again, sweeping through her body like a drug. But this time it wasn't because she was letting go. It was because the decision burrowed deep in her chest fit so well.

I'm ending this.

"Ivy, don't do it. Whatever it is you're thinking, it's not worth it."

Ivy didn't have time to explain exactly how "worth it" it was.

"When Dina resurfaces, tell her…" Ivy swallowed. She wasn't being fair. None of this was fair. But she was going to *make* it fair.

She tried again. "Just look after her, dammit."

"Ivy—"

She hung up. Bought the next ticket leaving from Heathrow and sent a screenshot to the unknown number, ignoring Topher's incoming calls. Then she dropped her phone on the concrete and smashed it with her boot for good measure.

Topher and Lucia would keep an eye on Dina. She'd have to trust that. Have to just live with the agony of remorse that Dina would never know what Ivy had planned this whole time. Who Ivy really was deep in her heart. Not a "softy" at all. Just a messed up girl who couldn't let go. But she wouldn't be leaving any loose ends behind. No more indecision.

She hailed a cab and directed it to Heathrow, still unable to pin down a tail, but assuming they were watching. She also assumed her cab made it to Heathrow in one piece.

By the time it did, she was long gone.

35

Ivy

Navigating the outskirts of London would have been difficult without her phone once upon a time. But Ivy had practice. In the days before Dina had melted back into her life, when she'd felt sharp enough to cut the next person who had the bad luck of speaking to her, she'd walked the streets over and over. Memorized the relevant train and bus patterns. Learned the underground like unraveling one of Lenox's codes. It was probably how she'd gotten caught. She couldn't think about that now though.

She found the crowds of rush hour and used them as cover the whole train ride to Harlow, quaint towns passing in a blur, until she reached the warehouse. A white-washed building abutting a forest, now familiar graffiti marring the wall running along the front.

Three in flight, two by foot.

She walked right past the vultures and deer, down to a break in the concrete wall. The narrow way Jason had written about. As she crept through the opening, she used a dagger to cut slits along the insides of her jacket sleeves, only vaguely mourning the ruined garment. She wasn't about to let a little fabric impede her daggers from shooting loose, but the thick material might still provide a modicum of protection.

There were security cameras covering just about every angle of the rundown warehouse. Except one.

She fit into it like a glove. Found a broken window. Retrieved a dagger to peel away the bits of glass, and then crawled inside, belly over the frame.

She landed in a crouch behind a pile of boxes. Drugs. Weapons. Both. She wasn't sure, and she didn't care.

What mattered was the soft murmur of voices coming from the other side of the large, open room, echoing across the concrete floor.

"But has she gotten on the plane yet?"

The voice shot through her. Hard eyes watching as someone else did his bidding. As Jason locked his arm against her neck and buried a blade in her heart. A callused palm on the back of her neck as she demonstrated a new trick from throwing a knife. A smile that never quite reached the eyes. The swirl of want as she tried to stir pride in that face, blended with the guilt of what she'd done to earn it. The slow years of that longing giving way to rage and new dreams. Dreams of freedom and a life she'd carved out for herself, rather than the one Lenox had dumped her into.

And after all these months imagining his voice, remembering how it had felt to be under his thumb, nothing compared to hearing the real thing once again. Like sandpaper stripping away her skin.

"No one's seen her yet," someone answered.

Lenox made a noise like a grunt. "I want more eyes on the perimeter. I don't trust your security cameras. She's a sneaky little bitch."

You have no idea.

Footsteps faded away. More than she'd like. She'd hoped Lenox would send more people out to chase her decoy. So much for that.

As she strained her ears, someone coughed.

"Shut up," Lenox said. "Got no one to blame but yourself. Should know better by now, Puck. You're supposed to be a neutral party. Plain and simple. Now look what you've gotten yourself into."

The soft thud of his feet echoed around the warehouse as he left. The scent of a cigarette trailed in his wake.

Ivy waited until her knees ached from kneeling behind the crates, then slowly eased forward.

Puck was tied to one of the steel columns holding up the ceiling, head lolled back, eyes distant as they stared at nothing.

Ivy approached from behind, hand over their already gagged mouth before they could startle and give her away.

"It's me," she hissed, using one of her daggers to cut Puck's binds. First the gag, then the zip ties cutting into their wrists.

Puck started to groan before stifling the sound with clear effort. They turned their head towards Ivy and mouthed, "You shouldn't be here."

Their eyes were still clouded. Probably from a knock on the head.

No time to argue with that. Ivy slid the daggers back into her flesh, ignoring Puck's wide-eyed stare, wrapped an arm around their waist and hauled them up.

"How many goons?" she whispered in Puck's ear.

"Twenty. I think. But—"

"What the—"

Ivy didn't wait to see who had stumbled on them. Simply released Puck, hoping they'd stay upright, and launched herself at them. The man's eyes went wide. He hesitated just a breath too long. Ivy used her opening to close the scant space between them and plunge a dagger between his ribs. There was a strangled gasp, the warm cascade of blood, then a thud as he hit the ground and stayed there, eyes staring vacantly at the ceiling.

No one Ivy recognized.

"Come on," Ivy hissed, yanking the dagger free and pulling Puck back up from the column they were leaning on.

They shuffled towards the open window, moving far too slowly for Ivy's liking. But now they were behind the crates.

Footsteps at their back. Someone cursed. Ivy swore she could feel the weight of a gun in someone else's hands.

She dropped Puck with little ceremony once more, snatching up the scrap of paper she'd stuffed into her bra before coming here. The one with Topher's number. She shoved it into Puck's pocket, and after a second's hesitation, wrapped their hand around her still-bloody bone dagger. She could make more.

She motioned to the window, and mouthed, "Get out. I'll cover you."

Puck stared at the dagger, clearly wondering how hard they'd hit their head. Then they looked back at her, eyebrows raised, as if to ask "what about you?". They were clutching a crate for support. God, Ivy hoped they could hold it together long enough to get out in one piece.

"I'll be fine," she returned, shaping the words without sound. "Go!"

Puck looked like they wanted to say more. But Ivy didn't have time for this. She turned her attention back to the room, satisfied by the awkward shuffling behind her. Just in time for someone new to round the corner and spot her. Someone familiar this time. A white woman named Cleo. She'd been at the bottom of Lenox's ranks when she'd left. Probably still was if she was being used for security.

Cleo had a gun cocked, but Ivy still had the element of surprise. The woman's pale face drained of blood as she took in the heir Lenox had murdered. And before she could shake off the shock, Ivy whipped another dagger free. Threw it at Cleo, who dodged so that it caught her at the shoulder instead of the neck.

Cleo cried out and the gun exploded as she went down, the shot missing Ivy by miles, but smashing through one of the crates with such gusto there was no way the rest of the crew hadn't heard it.

Shit. This was why Ivy hadn't gone for a gun sooner. She stepped on Cleo's hand, ignoring the pained grunts as she picked up the weapon up for herself. She wasn't sure she had a limit on the number of daggers she could produce. Hadn't yet found out. But today might be the day, and she wasn't about to let that stop her when she was this close to putting Lenox in the ground once and for all.

She held the gun steady as the bottom floor of the warehouse began to swarm with Lenox's crew. Familiar faces and new.

She never hesitated. She'd learned from that fight with Jason. And Lenox had raised her to be a weapon. Becoming a Resurrected had only honed the blade. She fired the gun. Ducked back behind the crates, shooting as best she could without the time she needed to aim properly. Somehow managing to leave shouts of dismay and pain, the smell of blood, as she fired the handgun until it was empty. And then it was back to the daggers. They flew from her hands, driven by her bloodlust, and she swore it was her will behind those blades, directing them into flesh. She left a riot of chaos as she darted in and out of crates and shelves.

But not enough. There were far too many of them, and her aim was only so good.

Something flew by her ear and blood trickled down the side of her face. She dashed out and released a flurry of daggers, the flesh of her arms unsheathing from wrist to shoulder, bone blades hurtling towards her enemies. Each new dagger pried out of her like yanking off fingernails. Ivy growled with the effort; but even that wouldn't stop her.

Fury burned through her skin. Heat flooded her veins, the now familiar power spreading through her body. And this time, as she reached for more daggers, one emerged from the back of her forearm. It tore through the remaining leather, but stayed connected to her skin, a shield of bone protruding from her right arm.

Just in time to catch the bullet that would have blown out her shoulder.

She cried out as the shield burst apart. As bone shards followed the bullet into the meat of her shoulder. But the pain was a far-off thing.

There was only the searing rage, the sharp point of a dagger between her ribs, stealing the life she'd clawed and scraped for. She kept going.

Gunshots exploded. Bodies hit the ground.

And into Ivy's reign of terror, one word rang out.

"Enough!"

The room froze. Ivy couldn't help herself. She snuck a look over the top of a crate. Watched Lenox step forward, hands by his side, head high, as if Ivy hadn't just dropped half a dozen of his people.

"So you've finally come home," he said, looking directly at her hiding spot. "Quite the entrance, Ivy."

Her wounded shoulder was beginning to ache above the numbness of adrenaline. The blood loss would get to her before long. Even now it would be slowing her down. But seeing Lenox again, hearing his voice saying her name, was enough to make her forget everything.

He was just as tall as she remembered. Thick and commanding, even if his freshly cut hair had gone more salt than pepper. Once, it had been muscle that gave him such a figure. But he'd gone soft around the middle without working at the front lines. Not soft enough though. He'd have armor on that she couldn't see. A bullet-proof vest almost certainly. Or some trap she'd missed. That was his way.

Knowing that didn't stop her from standing straight and stepping into the light to face him.

She dropped the empty gun with a clatter onto the floor. There was no hiding she was out. Anyone working for Lenox would have been counting shots. But he didn't know about the other tricks she had up her sleeves. How the daggers had come from nothing, from her, even when no one else could see them.

"I assume you're to blame for me losing yet another heir?" Lenox asked mildly.

As if Jason, too, hadn't already been replaced.

Ivy said nothing, simply counted the people still standing. Another half dozen in sight. Definitely more out of sight. Still, she'd done some damage and she took satisfaction in it.

"We placed bets, you know. About whether you'd run off with your tail between your legs or pull something as idiotic as coming back for your friend. 'An acquaintance', to use your words. Must be a hell of an acquaintance for you to risk showing your face again."

Lenox rolled his beefy shoulders.

"My bet was on the first. After all, you broke my heart trying to leave like that. I hated putting you down. Such a waste. A shame really. But you're here now. Immortal as a god and bleeding like an ordinary human. I've heard stories. None of them are as reliable as I'd like. So tell me: How *did* you crawl your way out of your grave?"

"Sheer spite," Ivy offered, rolling her wrists.

Lenox snorted. "Come on, Iv, I know you better than that. Tell me what you're hiding, and I'll let you out of here in one piece as thanks."

Ivy had her tells, even if she tried to mask them. But so did Lenox. He wasn't letting her out of here by his good mercy.

"Leave the goon squad behind and I'll tell you how I unburied myself," she goaded.

Behind Lenox, hands tightened on weapons. Shoulders stiffened. She hadn't taken down nearly enough of them.

Lenox merely grinned. And just as she'd hoped, he stepped closer. Too blinded by his own ego to know better.

Her heart thudded in her throat as he approached, footsteps echoing on the concrete. That old cocktail of emotions rose up, threatening to crash down on her. The admiration. The desire for some sense of pride, even now. The fear and loathing. Well, she only needed one of those right now.

Closer, she willed. *Come on, you prick.*

With every step, she examined him. The loose, confident walk. The apparent lack of weapons. The bulk of what was definitely a bullet-proof vest beneath his shirt.

Fine. So she wouldn't carve out his heart. But the man still had a head to lose. What the rest of the crew did after she made her move would be a problem for later.

Closer. Closer. He stopped, just out of arm's reach, wearing that same grin that made Ivy want to knock all his teeth out.

"Come on, Iv. You've never been one for dramatics."

The dagger flew from her body without an ounce of hesitation. No fine speeches. No pause of regret. Just a carefully aimed weapon made of her own flesh and bone, her will itself carrying it spiraling towards the man who'd raised her to be a walking blade. Until she'd taught herself to want more.

Her pulse raced in that narrow half second, eager for the spatter of blood as the knife found Lenox's jugular. As his followers advanced and recovered from their shock enough to fire their weapons on her. For one to catch her in the chest. For another shallow, forgotten grave.

I'm so sorry. Dina, she thought as the dagger wound through the air.

And clattered to the ground as it crashed harmlessly into a rusted metal shield that hadn't been there mere seconds before.

Ivy jolted back.

"The fuck?"

Familiar heat burst through her chest.

No.

Metal wrapped around her ankles in the blink of an eye. She toppled to the ground, flinging daggers without aim so they caught no one. Crashing into the concrete, a jolt of pain shooting through her injured shoulder. She thrashed to a seated position in time for more metal to come flying up and around her mouth, her wrists, pushing her to the ground so she was pinned, cheek to the concrete.

All she could do was stare as Lenox loomed over her. Joined by another figure with impassive, blue eyes and a shaved head. The rage searing in her blood did nothing but burn her from the inside out.

Lenox knelt down to better meet her glare. The scent of cigarettes and sweat wafting off of him.

"So you came back from the dead. Big woop. You're still nothing special. And you're not the only one who has some new tricks."

He stood again and the Resurrected turned his gaze to Lenox. Pale face nearly blank, as if waiting for instruction. A look she recognized. One she'd once had.

Her breath came fast through her nose, her brain tracing every corner, every option, and finding nothing.

A silent conversation passed between Lenox and his new golden child. And then that goddamned smirk before the Resurrected kicked her in the head.

Everything went black.

36

Dina

D ina's mind was an ocean away, trying to catch up as Yousef stared, wide-eyed at her. Any second now, everything would snap back into focus. He would run, or attack, or both.

And because half her consciousness was still in the water, because she'd managed it once before, she did it without thinking. The bank of the river overflowed without the slightest breeze, colliding into her and Yousef. It swelled around her, embracing her like an old friend, not quite ready to let go. The closest to home she'd ever felt outside of Ivy's arms. And as the water rushed up, it swept her right into Yousef.

They crashed together, the smallest yelp escaping his lips before the water engulfed him and their bodies went swirling up the riverbank. Until Dina had his arms pinned to his sides, both of them drenched and slick with mud.

"Don't attack," she said frantically as she knelt over him. He'd electrocute the shit out of her if he did with all the water. "Please don't attack! I just want to talk."

"How the fuck—" he thrashed, but didn't shock her. A good sign. "Let me go or I'll scorch you! Don't be an idiot!"

"Listen to me," she growled. "We have a plan for it! The Shadow. The Void. Whatever. And if you ever want to stop running, you'll stop fighting me and fucking *listen*."

She wasn't sure it would work, but the frantic flailing stopped. The boy went limp under her. Cautiously, she released his arms. Then retreated to kneel across from him. She swiped mud from her eyes and the two of them stared at each other as the now calm water floated by.

"How did you do that?" the boy hissed, sitting up and testing his limbs for injury.

Dina swallowed.

"I don't know," she answered truthfully. "But I'm pretty sure I could do it again if you try to hurt me."

The water almost seemed to be listening. Waiting for suggestions. A calm hand on her back, offering support rather than pushing her over the edge.

"Fine," Yousef grumbled. "Tell me your plan quickly. Then I'm out of here."

"We're going to capture it. Starve it out until we've taken its power away. So it can't hurt us anymore."

The boy blinked.

"You can't be serious. *That's* your plan?"

"Look, it's not just me. There's a bunch of others like us who are working on this. We're still getting all the details arranged, but it's going to take all of us to pin it down for good. I've run into this thing enough times to see it's getting stronger. It's not a shadow anymore. Can't you feel it?"

The boy said nothing, but his eyes hardened. Dina took that for agreement. She knew it was about all she would get.

"If we don't fight this thing, running won't be an option. It won't stop until we're all worse than dead. Please. Just trust me. Please. For Alec."

Yousef blinked hard and looked away.

"And when is this grand scheme of yours going down?" the boy asked, eyes darting around every second or so, watching the shadows the same way Dina did herself.

"Once we've reached enough of us, we'll pick a time and place that's far enough away from civilization for us to unleash our various powers. Probably somewhere close to water so I can get there. We'll gather all at once. Draw it out and cage it until we can drain it for good."

Silence. Then Yousef held out his hand.

"You got a phone?"

Dina sighed with relief and retrieved her phone, which was miraculously mud-free. Mostly. She handed it to Yousef, who plugged in his contact information and tossed the phone back.

"Your nickname is 'Sunny'?" Dina asked, frowning.

"Allah's joke or my parents. You decide. Anyway, I'm out."

Dina rose and trudged up the bank after him.

"So you'll help?" she shouted at his retreating form.

He didn't answer. But he'd given her his number. That was something.

Dina sank into the mud, trying to remember the usual business of orienting herself. According to her phone, she'd only spent three days in the water, cutting her usual travel time in half.

She shot Zev a quick text before calling Ivy, eager to share both the good news and her encounter with Yousef, AKA Sunny.

The phone went straight to voicemail.

She tried again. No response. Maybe her phone had run out of battery.

She stood and made her own slippery way up the bank, wondering if she should call Zev. But damn, did she want to hear Ivy's voice.

So she called Topher.

Who picked up immediately.

"Dina? You alright?"

"Yeah. Made it to Antwerp. It's better than I'd ever hoped. Still some kinks to work out, but I'll take it for now."

She started walking down the sidewalk towards the city lights.

"Good. That's really good to hear."

Dina waited for more, but they said nothing. The wet clothes chafed, somehow feeling colder as she waited for something. Anything.

"Did Ivy get to you?" she finally prompted. "I know she was excited to see you, though I doubt she'd say it."

More silence. Dina checked to make sure the call hadn't dropped. When she saw it was still connected, a cold shiver trailed down her spine.

"Topher?"

"Dina, I'm so sorry. I don't know where Ivy is. She's been offline for the past two days."

Two days. Almost since Dina had willingly gone back to the water. Traveled east and away. All those sleepless nights. The dreams that woke Ivy with screams and shaking limbs. Which of those nightmares had risen from the past to catch her in its grip?

"Dina?"

She left herself for a moment. Unable to feel the phone in her hand, let alone make sense of the voice on the line.

"Do you have any idea where she would have gone?" she asked through numb lips.

"Luz and I got back to London early this morning. We're hoping she's still here."

They went quiet again. Then asked, as if already regretting the question: "How much has she told you about her past?"

Dina bit her lip. She'd never pushed Ivy all that much to talk about it. From what she'd gathered, she didn't have parents. And something had happened to her in the years in between losing them and the day she came back from the dead. Maybe she should have pressed harder. Maybe she could have helped the wounds stitch together, healing through pain.

"Not enough. You?"

Topher sighed. "All I know is that when I met her, we were digging her out of a shallow grave in the middle of the woods. Someone stabbed her. Someone she knew. As far as I can tell, she's been trying to track them down ever since."

Guilt coiled in Dina's gut, slick and acidic. That whole time, she'd been so focused on her own problems. How had she not noticed? Had Ivy been quieter? More distant? Has she been too distracted to notice?

"And you think she tracked them down to London?"

"Yes, but we haven't found any sign of her. She's too damn good at covering her tracks."

Dina swallowed and turned back to the river. The water moved slowly. Ever eastward. By the time she caught a plane to London, it would only drag her back under.

"Okay," Dina said, more to herself than Topher. "Okay, let me know the second you hear anything."

"I really don't like the way you said that. What are you thinking, Dina?"

"That I'm going to meet you in London the long way and hope I get there in time."

"Look, Luz and I can handle this. We'll find her and call the second we do. Just take care of yourself. You don't both need to be idiots."

"Why do you think we've worked out this long? Besides, I never said I was doing anything stupid. Just trust me. I've found her before. I'll find her now."

"Just don't get yourself killed in the process," Topher muttered. "You sapphic maniacs are gonna be the death of me, I swear."

"You'll have to get used to it. I'll talk to you soon."

She hung up and stuffed the phone back into the dry bag, slipping and sliding back down the bank, feeling that thread of connection and grabbing on with the weight of her consciousness.

Come on. You've taken me away from her enough. This time, take me to her.

The water made no reply, except to crest the riverbank and brush her ankles. A call almost, to join its embrace. She'd have to take that for an answer.

Without another glance at the Antwerp skyline, Dina stepped forward until the water rose to her knees, her waist, her chin. Then she ducked her head under and waited for the sweet release of water to take her away.

37

DINA

Dina had never traveled so quickly with the water before. Moments blended together, occasionally coalescing in foreign towns and shorelines. Forest lakes and mountain streams.

And finally, a familiar, misty shore.

The edge of a skyline she recognized, if not the one she raced towards with all her being.

Portland.

Dina hauled herself onto the dock, flopping down on the wood, exhausted and uncaring that she didn't fit in with the occasional people walking along the river at this time of night.

She was trying to work with the water, rather than fighting to wrest control. It had allowed her to travel this far in a day instead of weeks. But every moment ticked by like a death knell.

She had to keep going. Had to dive back into the water, no matter how her limbs protested. How her mind struggled to remember what it was like to be a human girl and not an ocean current.

Dina groaned and sat up. Tried to anyway. The attempt failed, cresting and falling like a half-formed wave.

Her eyes closed against her own accord.

Snapped back open when someone lightly kicked her side.

"You're not dead, are you?" a voice asked from above.

Dina looked up to find an unfamiliar white woman looking down at her. She smelled of cigarettes, and even in the low light, her bottle blonde hair seemed to glow.

"I'm fine," Dina mumbled. "Just need a minute."

"Bit late in the season for a night swim. And I'm skeptical of the water quality. You're better off in a swimming pool like a normal person."

"Thanks, I'll keep that in mind."

Dina waited for the woman to move on. Instead, she squatted beside Dina and pulled out a cigarette, lighting it with deft fingers. She blew the smoke out the side of her mouth.

"Your name is Dina, right?"

She squinted up at the woman. Maybe she wasn't a stranger after all. But who did she know in Portland? She'd met Ivy here, sure, but no one else. And no matter how she tried, her tired brain couldn't seem to place her.

"Ivy told me to keep an eye out for you if you ever popped up in my city."

At the familiar name, Dina shot up, exhaustion forgotten.

"Is she alright? Did she call?"

The woman shrugged. "Haven't heard from her in days."

Dina deflated, hope shriveled.

The stranger didn't seem to notice. "I was surprised she trusted me enough to tell me about you. But maybe she figured her mother wouldn't be heartless enough to turn her girlfriend away."

"But Ivy doesn't have...I mean she told me she didn't know—"

"Oh, she knows. Name's Rita by the way. And don't get me wrong. I was a shit mother. Never really wanted to be one. Having a kid was a nuisance." She took another drag from the cigarette. "Probably my fault she ended up the way she did. Though Lenox is owed his fair share of the blame for raising her like that."

Dina's head was spinning. Rita talked like she hadn't just dumped Dina in halfway through a story with no introduction.

"Is Lenox...Who is he? Her father?"

Rita laughed so hard, she began to cough. When the laughter and choking coughs subsided, she wiped tears from her eyes.

"Oh, *that's* a good one. I was stupid back then, but not *that* stupid. Dunno who the father was. But he was a looker. They all were."

Dina wanted to throttle the woman. If she'd had more strength, she might have.

"Look, Ivy is in trouble. I haven't heard from her and I think she's going after this man. Lenox. Do you have any idea if she's alright? If she found him?"

Rita shook her head, looking out over the water.

"Your guess is as good as mine. Last time I saw her, she had a knife to my throat trying to figure out where Lenox was. And last I *heard* from her it was a few days ago when she told me to keep a look out for a girl who might pop up somewhere along the river."

"Did he...did Lenox try to kill her? I mean a year ago."

Rita turned further away so Dina couldn't read her expression.

"They told me they *did* kill her. But seems my daughter's got a knack for wriggling her way out of impossible situations. Wish she'd learn from my mistakes and use her luck better." She eyed Dina up and down. "At least you won't get her pregnant."

Dina flushed. Then stood, edging back towards the water.

"Thanks, but I need to go now."

Rita stood too. "What. You gonna swim all the way there?"

"Something like that," Dina muttered.

Rita rifled through her pockets, pulling out cigarettes and then something else.

"Here, you look like you need to eat. Well, you look like a zombie, truth be told. But if you're not gonna come back with me and get some rest like you ought to, at least have a granola bar."

Dina took the food and guzzled it down with little grace.

"Thanks," she said, wiping the crumbs from her lips and preparing for the next dive. It wasn't enough to really refuel her, but it would help.

Rita watched her, expression still unreadable. "I may have been a shit mother, but I'm glad Ivy found someone. She deserves better than the cards she drew."

The other woman waited, as if Dina might say it was alright. That she was absolved of all guilt. Maybe she was. That wasn't for Dina to decide.

"Ivy deserves the world," she murmured, praying she'd be alive to see it.

Without another glance, she dove off the pier, rushing ever onward. Towards London. Towards Ivy.

38

IVY

S omeone groaned in the dark, right in Ivy's ear.

Or was that her? Her limbs all tingled like they'd fallen asleep. Something bit into her wrists, wrenched her arms back into a painful position. And from the way it throbbed, her left shoulder was likely fucked.

She wasn't sure how long she'd been strapped to this particular chair. Memories flashed like a demented strobe light. Had it been hours? Days? Someone had shoved food into her mouth at some point. Water too. But she couldn't remember when exactly that had been.

"Fuck."

"You're not what I expected," a voice said in the darkness.

"Well, I don't give a fuck, buddy," Ivy muttered.

She blinked to clear her vision, found herself sitting in a dim room with a pounding head. Or maybe that was her brain beating against her skull.

"And Lenox thinks *I'm* the idiot," the stranger muttered.

Ivy squinted in the gloom, making out the figure leaning against a pile of crates across from her. It was hard to tell, but given the unfamiliar voice, she figured this was the Resurrected Lenox had taken on to replace her and Jason. Really an upgrade if she was being honest.

After all, he'd managed to cage her and bind her to the chair she found herself in, not far from where she'd found Puck.

"What'd he promise you?" Ivy asked.

A shadowy shrug. "What'd he promise you? And why wasn't that enough?"

Ivy had a million answers to that question. *He promised me a life and a home, but that life was someone else's and the home was full of poison.*

But those were her own secrets.

"He'll only hold onto you until you stop proving your use, you know," Ivy said. "Heir or not, that remains true for everyone he touches."

"I know. That's why I've decided to be useful."

"You're one of us though. Why settle to be some mobster's right-hand man when you could be more?"

"Is that what you wanted? To be more?"

"More than Lenox would ever allow, yeah."

The Resurrected considered her. Or seemed to. Light haloed behind him, silhouetting his tall, lanky figure. He walked closer, flicked a switch.

Ivy hissed as light flared into life above. Squeezed her eyes shut, head throbbing.

"Maybe I don't need to be more. So long as I protect my own hide."

"And you think Lenox will do that? You'd be safer with others like us. We're gathering and—"

"Oh, I know what happens when we gather. Found out the hard way."

"We have a plan," she insisted.

The man approached, crouching in front of her so they were eye-to-eye, pale features bright under the fluorescents.

"There's no escaping that monster. Not if you're relying on others like us." Those blue eyes were flat as they took her in. The look of someone who'd given up. Who'd made the most of their miserable life and accepted the morsels they'd scavenged.

She tried anyway. "It's better than working with that shithead, trust me."

If she could keep him talking, keep him distracted. The metal bound her tight. But she was used to being a weapon. And a good weapon was versatile.

"So you say," the Resurrected replied. "But I'll take my chances."

Ivy laughed. "Then you're even more of a fool than I ever was."

She spat in the Resurrected's face. The cuffs chafed as she wrenched her wrist. A minuscule, painful twist of her hand. All she needed to pull the smallest of daggers free from her flesh.

"You're no better than him," she growled as he wiped away the spit, looking disgusted.

He inched away. Just as she'd hoped.

She kept her movements minuscule as she worked. She'd never used a dagger so small. Small enough to find the edges where the metal came together. To wedge into the cracks and pry it open.

Almost. Almost.

"The only fool I see here is you," he was saying. "But Lenox seems to think you're a useful one. I couldn't tell him how I got my powers, and he's not willing to die and try his own luck. But you've met others. You have answers that he and I both want. And he could have a use for a girl made of daggers. When he comes down here again, you'll be given a choice. One you'd be smart to take if you don't want to end up in a new grave. And this time, we'll make sure you stay dead."

Ivy shrugged to disguise the way she slid the dagger into the gap. She cut herself in the process. But she didn't wince. That would give it all away.

It's just pain. You've felt it before.

"And what kind of offer could Lenox possibly make to convince me *not* to rip his throat out?" she asked, channeling that calm tone Topher was always using.

"Same as me. Protection from a shadow. All you need to do is to run the occasional job. Which conveniently keeps you on the move and your soul still in your body."

She laughed. "Lenox can't protect either of us from that thing."

She wedged the dagger further, blood dripping from her wrist. Damn, the metal was tough.

The Resurrected caught the movement. Leaned closer to check.

Close enough for Ivy to headbutt him and send him reeling back.

For a second, she thought she'd blacked out. But then the world sharpened, albeit painfully. Her arms screamed as she finally pried the metal free. Her limbs were just shy of numb, the joints on fire. From both the shoulder wound and being trapped at such an odd angle.

But there was no time to address any of that. The other Resurrected was righting himself and holding out his hands.

She willed the needle-like blade to grow to the size of a kitchen knife. Adjusted her grip on the hilt. Then shoved the knife into the man's neck before he could form a metal shield. Blood flowed warm down her hands, spurted in her face as the life left his eyes. Maybe she should have felt a sense of kinship towards him. Topher would certainly be angry with her for killing one of the people they'd been looking for all this time. But Topher probably hadn't ever considered what poorly adjusted people, desperate people, would do with their powers. Would do for some semblance of safety.

She pulled the dagger free and let the man fall boneless to the floor, feeling nothing but relief.

And pain.

Only then did she allow one grunt, shaking more feeling back into her limbs. She prodded her wounded shoulder. Someone had dressed it. Pulled out the splinters of her bone shield, along with the bullet.

Proof that the man hadn't been bullshitting about Lenox wanting to make a deal. So much for not giving anyone a second chance. Nice of him, she supposed.

She tested the bad arm. The damage from her impromptu shield bursting apart hadn't done her any favors, but without it, the gunshot wound would have put her out of commission completely. Despite the pain, she still had her grip, still had a decent range of motion.

Good enough.

She loosed another dagger, groaning from the effort. She hadn't run out yet, but too many at once had strained her.

Just a little further.

Time to bring Lenox's world crashing down around him.

The first few floors were easy, Lenox's crew too confident to keep their eyes peeled for a murderous rampage to come stalking down the halls. Simple enough to sneak up from behind the twisting corners of the warehouse and knock someone out.

Until someone caught her. They shouted out a warning and shot before she'd made it around the corner. The bullet missed Ivy's temple by a hair as she ducked back out of the way, grinding her teeth with frustration.

She groaned as she called on her powers. Creating the bone shields came naturally this time. She grinned, wiping the sweat from her forehead, and burst forward.

Another gunshot. Her righthand shield shattered as it deflected the bullet. In the same instant, she threw a dagger with her left hand, grunting from the pain tearing through her shoulder. The shot went wide.

No!

And the blade corrected, guided by that one thought. The knife found flesh, taking the guard down. She barely stopped to catch her breath.

Between her throbbing head and shoulder and the new spike of adrenaline, the rest of the walk up the metal stairs into each floor of the warehouse passed in a strange blur. Whatever goods Lenox was trading in these days, the crates made good cover as she took down his crew. People she recognized from another life. Strangers. All of them caring for nothing but their own hides.

Many of them had watched a monster raise a little girl into his own reflection. Until she herself smashed the mirror apart to become something more. Something better. Good? No. Kind? No. But more than Lenox or the world ever thought she'd become.

By the time she made it to the top floor, she'd gotten ahold of a gun somehow. Shouts came from down the hallway. No more hiding her rampage by knocking people out or taking them down quietly.

The guards up here were far better prepared. Bullets ricocheted off plaster and steel beams before she even summited the final step and rounded the corner. One grazed her ear before she darted back out of the way.

She leaned against the wall, cursing and breathing hard. She'd glimpsed an office at the end of the hall, but there were too many people between her and the damned door. Not enough of her. She'd be dead on the ground before she even crossed the hallway.

She flinched when a piercing scream filled the air. Lights flashed from the fire alarm. Water, dark and tasting of copper and old pipes, poured down on her, and she caught a whiff of smoke from somewhere far below. Ivy wasn't sure who or what to thank, but she wasn't about to pass up a stroke of luck.

While Lenox's guards yelled back and forth about what the fuck was happening, she left her hiding place, taking one man in the eye and catching another in the shoulder, launching herself down with him as he fell, punching him out before he could make another stand.

Someone pierced her through the gut with a knife of their own, and even as the wound healed, she went down, screaming, the world gone white. Knives flew out of her, wrenched from her flesh, from her arms, her legs, her back. More than she'd ever produced in one go. They tore through her clothes and through every guard keeping her from Lenox.

Smoke began to rise from the lower floors, the water in the pipes unable to quench the raging inferno coming from below. Ivy ignored the heat, the signs that perhaps she wasn't nearly as alone as she suspected, the smoke curling at her feet as she righted herself. She tore down the hallway like she'd become one with the flames. Kicked through the door, and flung a knife ahead of her, catching Lenox at the corner of his ear before he could even draw a weapon.

For a moment, they stood there. Just...staring. Ivy's lungs heaving like bellows. Lenox calm as a pond on a still day.

And then that stupid fucking grin.

"You got rusty."

"That was a warning," she said, biting a groan as she unsheathed a new blade. The sharp edge begged for blood.

"I was wrong before, Ivy. You've earned your place back at my side. Earned your place as my heir."

"Do you not see how this is going to play out, old man?"

Lenox's gaze darted behind her, taking in the smoke and flames, then back to the demon that had crawled all the way back from hell to draw his blood.

Distantly, a loud crash reverberated through the warehouse. The building shook slightly. What happened when all those weapons and their ammo caught, Ivy wondered.

"Come on, Ivy. Let's be reasonable adults here."

"Didn't take you for either, Lenox," Ivy said, wagging her knife at him, keeping her grip tight on the gun in her left hand.

A trickle of sweat beaded down Lenox's face. He was growing remarkably pale. "If the ground floors are on fire, this whole place will blow, and us with it. You know that right?"

"I do," Ivy admitted. She'd gone cold all the way through. Couldn't even feel her wounded shoulder anymore. She'd known for some time now that if she met Lenox again, she probably wouldn't come out alive. That a second death would likely stick. But she felt that dagger through her chest, every waking moment, chipping her ribs, piercing her heart. It was only fair if he felt the same.

Lenox made a great show of holding up his hands to show he was harmless. "Come on, Ivy," he pleaded.

She laughed. Did he really think her that much of an idiot? That desperate for affection that she would still accept his crumbs? She might have, once upon a time. Before she met a person who could summon fire at will but refused to use their powers for harm. A woman with a gaze as poisonous as her skin and yet looked at Ivy with affectionate annoyance. And a supernova of a girl. A woman who disappeared into water and found her way back. To her.

She'd been starving for years. Crumbs would no longer suffice.

Still, she let him approach and put a hand on her good shoulder.

"Come on, Ivy. You and me against the world. Like old times."

She held his gaze. Dropped the gun with a clatter. Lenox smiled as she held up her right hand to show that she was putting that weapon away too, absorbing it back into her flesh.

And used her left to plunge a new dagger up through Lenox's chin and into his skull. He made a shocked, choking sound. The way his Resurrected had, eyes wide, last of his strength scrabbling to find purchase on Ivy. Blood splashed hot and viscous over her hand, down her arm.

And then he was dead. Sliding to the ground, the way she must have when he ordered Jason to put a knife through her heart.

The roaring flames were getting closer. Wood cracked below. Metal screamed. Something exploded and the floor shook again.

But Ivy stood motionless, dagger drenched in blood, making sure the man who killed her was dead. And that he stayed that way.

39

DINA

When Dina caught sight of Big Ben in the distance, she almost broke down all over again. But there was no time.

She turned on her phone, grateful for that tiny bar of battery, still kicking. Paced along the Thames, waiting for her service to pick up her new location and transfer her to the UK network.

The second it did, she called Topher.

They picked up before the first ring even finished. "Thank fuck. Please tell me you're somewhere that's obsessed with fish and chips."

"I'm by the Thames. Sharing my location but my battery may die."

"Okay. We're coming now. Don't move. We know where she went."

Dina stifled a sob. "Is she—do you know if she—"

"I'm sorry, Dina. I don't have anything more than that. I just know where she is. We were on our way there and can swing by you in five. Hang tight. Need anything?"

"No, just get as here fast as you can."

Topher hadn't lied about being close, but those five minutes were as long as that slow descent into the Chesapeake.

A blue hatchback pulled up alongside her, and Lucia waved through the window. Dina slid in, squelching across the leather and Topher sped off again before she even had her seatbelt on.

Lucia sat in the back with her and held out a hand, which Dina squeezed tight. In the passenger seat, sat someone Dina didn't recognize. They raised a brow at her drenched hair and clothes, but kept their mouth shut in a thin line. Dina wondered if she was the strangest thing they'd seen today.

"Dina, this is Puck, they/them, one of Ivy's friends," Topher introduced.

Puck snorted. "Don't know if she'd agree with that—turn left here—but appreciate the vote of confidence."

Dina didn't have time to think about the fact that Ivy had never mentioned Puck before. Or that Puck looked like they'd been hit by a truck.

"Where are we going? Have you heard from her?"

"A warehouse north of the city," Puck said. "Lenox has been using it to set up shop. Ivy got me out and I came back for these two. She seemed to think they might be helpful, despite their lack of familiarity with firearms."

Puck met Dina's gaze through the rearview mirror, one of their eyes swollen shut, the other narrowing. "How about you? Know your way around a gun? Got any stashed up your sleeves?"

Dina shook her head and Puck shrugged. "Cool. Then we're fucked."

Just how much firepower is it going to take to get Ivy out of there? she wanted to ask.

But she figured if she had to ask, she wouldn't like the answer.

"So," Puck said. "Any of you got a plan? I've got a gun—yep, take a right here—but kinda hoping we can do something better than a pitiful shoot-out that will likely get all of us killed."

"I'm the plan," Topher said, sounding calmer than they had any right to.

"The fuck is that supposed to mean?" Puck asked, voicing Dina's own concerns.

"It means you shouldn't need any firearms at all. I'll set up a distraction, and the rest of you can work on getting Ivy out of there before the whole place goes down."

"Before—you know what, maybe I don't want to know."

"Probably for the best," Topher said sagely. From the back seat, Dina could make out the stiff set of their shoulders as they drove.

She looked over at Lucia and mouthed, "What the fuck?"

Lucia's expression was grim. "You haven't managed to get control of your powers much more, have you?" she asked, quietly enough that only Dina would hear.

She fumbled for a moment. The truth was that she *had*. But if Lucia was asking if she'd be useful in a fight...she shook her head.

Lucia nodded. "Just be smart then."

The rest of the drive passed in tense silence, broken by Puck's clipped instructions and the occasional cursing as they hit traffic on their way north. The entirety of the city and the surrounding rolling hills passed unseen beyond Dina's eyes.

Ivy. What have you gotten yourself into?

They parked by a nondescript bit of forest.

"Why are we—"

"Any closer and Lenox's patrols will shoot out our tires before we can say 'cheerio'," Puck answered.

Topher turned off the car and they all got out, following Puck as they moved silently through the woods.

The walk through the trees was unnervingly calm. So at odds with Dina's racing heartbeat. The trickling seconds that told her each moment was another lost opportunity to retrieve Ivy in one piece.

It wasn't until they reached the edge of the woods that she heard gunshots.

"Shit," Puck hissed. "Never patient enough, that girl. Your time to shine, Topher."

The Resurrected stepped forward without even hesitating. And with each step, fire crept down their arms and pooled into their hands. And then they *were* the flames. A great inferno vaguely shaped like a person.

"What in the absolute *fuck*?" Puck whispered by Dina's side.

A guard stepped away from the building, eyes wide with surprise, focused on the gunshots going off behind him. Then he spotted Topher.

"Hey, stop—"

But it was his turn to stop as Topher unleashed a ball of fire, catching him at the leg.

The guard screamed, dropping to the ground to put out the flame.

Topher kept walking forward, shooting another fireball at the man's arm when he reached for his gun. And like an avenging angel, the sweet person Dina had only met over video chats and phone calls stepped up to the warehouse, and sent fire raging through a broken window.

"Come on," they shouted over their shoulder at a stunned Puck and Dina.

Their voice rang out like a wildfire. Lucia was already striding forward.

"Get Ivy out of there before the building comes down!" Topher urged.

"This was your plan?" Puck griped, pushing forward, gun at the ready, kicking their way through the door Lucia was trying to open.

Dina agreed with the sentiment. But she steeled herself as she followed the two of them into a wall of smoke and screams.

"We'll split up," Puck yelled over the chaos. The sounds of wooden crates starting to catch. "Lucia and I can take this floor and work up. You run straight to the top and work down. And don't get shot!"

It was easier said than done as Dina raced up the clanking metal stairs to the top floor of the warehouse. Most of the people Dina passed were too distracted by the flames to pay her much notice as they made their escape. But a few stray bullets came her way.

Dina had never been in a gunfight. She zig-zagged up the stairs, the way she'd read about in books, ignoring her own exhaustion from racing across the world to get back here. Cold fear narrowed her vision to the next step. Something nicked her arm, but she got to the top floor without taking a bullet anywhere worse.

As she rounded the corner to the final landing, she crouched, breathing hard, ready to find more guards waiting for her. But the hallway was already empty. If you didn't count the bone knives littered across the floor. Or the bodies.

Dina's eyes skimmed over them, trying to ignore the shapes of the recently deceased. None of them were Ivy. She'd think about the rest later when she had Ivy safe.

The door at the end of the hallway was ajar, and when Dina peeked around the corner, it seemed empty.

She took a breath, made herself pick up the gun lying just beyond a dead person's reach, and slid into the room, gun aimed ahead of her. God, she hoped the safety was off. She knew that was important, but she'd never even held a gun before.

One lone figure stood in the room.

The anticipation of being met by a stray bullet fled. She staggered with relief. Because it was Ivy. Upright and whole.

Dina threw the gun aside. "Thank God."

Ivy didn't move. Not even when she approached, trying not to vomit at the sight of the dead body at Ivy's feet. The body Ivy couldn't seem to tear her gaze from.

This close, Dina could make out the damage. Blood soaking the sleeve of Ivy's jacket. A bruise swelling across her cheek. But if the woman was in pain, there was no sign of it on her blank face.

Dina inched closer, moving as slow as she could, even though the fires below were climbing ever higher with each passing breath.

When she touched Ivy's shoulder, the woman whipped around, eyes in the wide stare of an animal caught in a trap. Something sharp pressed into Dina's throat. She didn't dare breathe as Ivy kept the bone knife there, panting.

It was like the other woman had gone somewhere far away again. That realm of nightmares where Dina couldn't reach her. Looking at her without seeing.

Slowly, the way she would approach a scared cat, Dina raised her hand. Clasped it around Ivy's, her hand over the grip of the knife.

"Ivy," she whispered.

Ivy blinked. Once. Twice. Leaned away and disappeared the dagger.

"Supernova," she breathed.

Dina could have sobbed. But there was no time.

"We have to go, Ivy. Now."

Ivy glanced behind her at the body on the floor. "I can't. I have to make sure."

Dina tilted Ivy's face back to hers. Away from Lenox. "He's dead, Ivy. And we will be too if we don't get out of here. Topher's set the building on fire."

It was like talking to a sleepwalker. "Topher's here?"

Dina swallowed, flicking an eye at the door. "Yes. We're all here. Please. Will you come with me?"

Another glance at the body. Then much to Dina's relief, Ivy took Dina's hand and followed her back down the hallway.

The place was filled with flames now. But Topher must have had better control of their powers than they'd let on, for a gap opened through the wall of fire, guiding them down the stairs.

Puck and Lucia met them halfway, covered in ash.

"Fucking hell," Puck said. "We need to get out of here ten minutes ago."

They raced back down the stairs, the flames licking their ankles as they fled.

The sweet relief as they burst through the door, back into the open air.

Ivy's footsteps dragged as they escaped, but Dina kept a firm grip, hauling her along until they reached the safety of the forest.

Behind them, Dina heard movement. She turned in a panic, only to find Topher joining them, looking human once more. Mouth set in a firm line and not a flame in sight.

At the forest's edge, Ivy froze. Her hazel eyes reflected the fire as she watched the building go down with an almost feverish expression.

"We should get a move on," Puck said. "This place is remote, but the police will come eventually. That smoke will be visible for miles."

Ivy glanced at Topher. "How long does it take?"

Dina thought she meant the fire, but Topher understood better.

They sighed. "Ivy, there hasn't been another anomaly. No one who died today is coming back."

Ivy held their gaze, long and hard. "Swear it."

"I swear," Topher said.

Dina wasn't sure what they would do if Ivy insisted on staying. Puck was right. Police would be headed this way any minute. And even though Ivy appeared not to notice, Dina tracked the distinct trickle of blood escaping her leather jacket sleeve.

Dina loosened her hand from Ivy's grip and grazed her fingers against the gaping fabric.

"Let me take a look at that."

Ivy watched her, gaze unfocused. "I can't leave. Not 'til I'm sure."

Puck let out an exasperated sigh as Dina took inventory of the torn fabric of Ivy's jacket and jeans, none of them revealing more wounds beyond the bleeding shoulder. The gashes in the leather and denim had the shredded appearance of a knife rocketing loose. Ivy the dagger, tearing herself apart to free herself from her past.

"You stabbed him, right?" Puck insisted. "How the fuck would he come back from that?"

"*I* came back," Ivy said, never taking her eyes off Dina.

Topher put a hand on Puck's shoulder. "I'll explain everything later. But Ivy, we can't stay here. Please. You're just going to have to trust me."

Ivy wasn't looking at them though. Like she needed Dina's confirmation as well. And maybe Dina didn't know much about black holes or tachyon particles. But Topher had burnt that warehouse to the ground just to get Ivy out. That was enough for her.

"He's not coming back, Ivy."

Ivy looked over her shoulder, back at the disaster zone they'd left behind. Ash and smoke swirled around the remains of the warehouse, clustering around the fire to form ghosts and ghouls. But nothing more emerged.

When she spoke, her voice came out small and lost. "Okay."

Dina swallowed the sigh of relief, and gently tugged Ivy towards the car. And as Dina settled in next to her in the backseat, helping Lucia tend to the scrapes and cuts and the partially bandaged shoulder, Ivy held her gaze, a sleepwalker still.

But each time Dina repeated those four words, she relaxed just a fraction more. And so the whole ride back, Dina told her a truth Ivy might not ever fully believe.

"He's not coming back."

40

Ivy

S tanding under the showerhead with Dina, Ivy wished other circumstances had brought them here. Like that night, months ago now, when Dina had brought her back to a quiet room in D.C. and everything changed. A supernova had come over the horizon and Ivy was happy just to bask in the heat of the explosion. If she wished hard enough, maybe they could go back there.

But the universe was a heartless fucker, so instead, they were both too tired for anything more than washing off the thick layer of grime they'd accumulated upon escaping the warehouse. And then they needed to join the planning session with Topher and Luz.

Because Ivy had killed one monster, but another lay in wait.

A heartless fucker, indeed.

At least she wasn't in danger of bleeding out from her shoulder wounds. She'd been stitched up rather neatly before she went and tore everything open again during her reign of terror. Lucia had grumbled the whole time she sat sewing Ivy back together at the flat she and Topher were renting. When she deemed Ivy "unlikely to hemorrhage and die on the spot", she'd shocked the shit out of her by squeezing her hand and holding it tight for a moment before storming off into the next room. For Luz, that was practically a declaration of love.

Now, Ivy and Dina were on their own in the apartment Topher had arranged ahead of time, the damn optimist. They hadn't spoken since Topher had dropped them off. Simply shucked off the clothes that reeked of blood and smoke and stepped into the shower as if they'd already agreed on it.

Dina massaged some soap into Ivy's back, avoiding her bad shoulder. Even with painkillers, the injury ached now that her body had stopped pumping out adrenaline like a fire hydrant. Ivy found herself chewing up her lip, biting back gasps of pain when she tried to use her left arm too much. Even though she still had a decent range of motion, it was going to take months to fully recover.

Still, her muscles relaxed under Dina's familiar touch. She'd never expected to have that. Never expected to have someone she cared for so deeply. That she loved.

When Dina reached her good shoulder, she grabbed her hand and clung on, silent still. But Dina was patient as water carving through a canyon as she pieced together her words.

"The scars aren't all from him, you know," she said at last.

"But you got them under his care...if you can even call it that."

"Yeah," Ivy whispered.

"Are you regretting it?" There was no judgment in the question.

Ivy shook her head. "It's not that. It's just...I've only ever known a world with him in it."

It should have been a relief. A weight off her shoulders. Satisfaction. Something other than the hollowed out feeling in her chest that made her wonder if it was all a dream. Like she'd come back as a ghost, not a flesh and blood woman.

If Dina hadn't been there, would she have let the flames take her?

"Yeah," Dina said, as if she understood. Maybe she did.

Ivy turned to meet her gaze. The other woman still had purplish bruises under her eyes, even if she looked less like a wraith since Lucia had practically force-fed her some energy bars on the drive over. Ivy wondered if she'd ever know what she'd done to deserve someone racing across the entire globe for her. And others who'd risked their necks and their morals to save her from herself, much as she'd resented it at first. Even *Puck* had come back for her. She certainly hadn't deserved that.

She motioned Dina to switch places with her under the shower, helping Dina lather some deep conditioner into the waves of her hair.

There was nothing but the sound of the tap running.

Then: "I met Rita."

Ivy froze with her good hand still tangled in Dina's hair. "Oh?"

"If I hadn't been looking for you, I would have thrown her into the Columbia River. Still tempted."

Not the reaction Ivy had expected. She snorted, and moved Dina back under the water, facing her this time.

"She does have that effect on people."

"I hate her," Dina whispered. "I hate her for leaving you with him."

Ivy shrugged, immediately regretting it when her shoulder gave a sharp complaint. She'd given up on that hate a long time ago. She'd only had enough room for Lenox.

"She was a shit mother. But honestly? I don't think of her unless I have to. Did she help you at least?"

Dina shrugged, wringing out her hair.

"Yes. But I still hate her."

Ivy pressed a kiss to Dina's forehead. "You're allowed. I don't mind. But you don't have to just for me."

Dina shook her head, looking at the shower tiles. "She was irritating outside of that, don't you worry."

Ivy chuckled. "At least I inherited her good looks instead of her personality."

Dina glanced at her and Ivy's wiggling eyebrows elicited a small laugh. Then she bit her lip, leaning back into the water with closed eyes, holding back, Ivy realized.

"You can ask," Ivy murmured. "If you want."

She could handle it now, she thought. Now that Dina had gone through who-knew-what-Hell to get to her.

Dina wiped the water from her eyes, meeting Ivy's gaze again. "You lived with him most of your life, didn't you?"

Ivy nodded slowly. "Yes. Lenox. He...raised me, I guess is a nice way of putting it. I don't really remember what life was like before that. Before Rita stopped trying. I used to run small jobs for him. The kind of things no one would look twice at a kid for pulling. Pickpocketing, taking pictures of targets. The jobs got bigger as I got older, became more useful. There was a time when that was all I wanted. To be useful to him. To earn his praise. Until I wanted more. And when I tried to leave, he caught onto my plan and...well..."

She didn't mention Pete. Somehow, after all this time, it was still a hurt too deep.

Dina placed a hand to Ivy's chest, just below her breast. Right where the dagger had gone through. As if she knew just where.

"I'm not a good person," Ivy murmured. "Maybe I could lay all the blame on him, but my hands are stained either way. And I can't do anything about that. And I won't apologize either. I'm glad he's dead, Dina."

Dina shook her head. "I'm not asking you to apologize for any of it."

"You're not going to tell me I should have forgiven him? The whole lot of them?"

"They killed you, Ivy," Dina said, holding her gaze without a flinch. "And if they'd done it again, *I* would have been the one bringing the building down."

Ah. There. There was the relief Ivy had been waiting for. It hadn't come from escaping Lenox's long shadow, but from the way this woman saw her. The way she and Topher and Luz, even Puck, showed her they were still here, by her side.

"There's forgiveness, but there's also justice," Dina continued. "I won't judge you for achieving the latter."

She took Ivy's hand, the one she'd used to drive a knife into Lenox's skull. The one she'd used to exact revenge on Jason. She curled her fingers around that vicious hand and brought it to her lips, pressing the softest of kisses on her scabbed-over knuckles.

Ivy leaned her head on Dina's shoulder, realizing at last just how tired she was. Allowing herself to feel that exhaustion in every inch of her body, the aching pain of her shoulder. She wasn't sure when she started crying. God, she couldn't remember the last time she cried. But she sobbed under the fall of water, mouth pressed to Dina's warm neck, sobbed until she was well and truly empty. And Dina held her the whole time.

The spray of the shower washed away every tear. Ivy found herself wishing it would do the same for her past. Wash it clean so she could start over, unblemished by Lenox and his twisting words. But when the water ran cold and the memory of him stayed put, she supposed she'd make do with the stains.

In companionable silence, they dried off and redressed Ivy's wound. Caught a cab to where Lucia and Topher were staying.

When they walked in, the two Resurrected were sitting at a dining room table with Puck. And Kala.

Ivy raised an eyebrow at the woman, who spared her a glance and not much more.

"Dina, this is Kala. She/Her," Topher said, motioning to the stranger as they took the open chairs at the table.

Kala nodded towards Dina in greeting.

"She's a Resurrected," Topher added unnecessarily.

Ivy glanced at Puck, who shrugged. "Topher filled me in."

Topher cut in as Ivy was opening her mouth to ask exactly what that meant. "We'll have to be quick. There's too many of us here and we're not ready to fight this thing today. Once we're set, we'll have to scatter and then regroup when we've made contact with the rest of our network of Resurrected. Kala suggested somewhere in the Mediterranean with an abandoned airstrip, so we'll reconvene there when we're ready to put the plan into effect. Ivy, are you still on board to provide the materials we need?"

As they spoke, Lucia typed furiously on her phone.

"You're our smithy then?" Ivy asked, retrieving a dagger from her flesh. It was easy again, now that she'd rested.

Kala wrote something on a sheet of paper on the table.

Still deaf, idiot

Right. *That* was why Lucia was glued to her phone. She was transcribing the conversation.

"Guess I've got some homework then," Ivy said, shaping the words with more care.

Yep. Time to catch up, bitch.

Cool. Another snarky Resurrected.

Ivy held eye contact with Kala and placed the dagger into her open palms.

The woman turned the dagger over. And as her brows knit together, it changed. Subtly, but noticeable. The edge smoothed, the straight lines of it curved. Then the bone became putty in Kala's hands, the same way she'd formed that key to hijack the car.

"Woah," Dina said.

Kala returned the dagger to its original shape and handed it back to Ivy. Signed something excitedly, and then took up the paper again and wrote out:

I can work with that. How many can you make?

Ivy shrugged. Grabbed the paper from her and wrote:

As many as you need

Kala frowned at her terrible handwriting, made worse by writing with her non-dominant hand when her left shoulder proved too painful. So Dina took the paper and rewrote Ivy's note as something more legible. She was really going to have to work on that.

Kala nodded, pointed at Ivy, and then tilted her head to the door, clearly ready to get a move on.

Ivy turned to Dina.

"How long do you have?"

Dina's brows bunched together. "Not long. I'm surprised I've lasted this long. But sometimes the water seems to give me more time if I choose to go with it. And I've been traveling with it for a bit now."

Ivy swallowed, thinking about what that must have been like, rushing across the globe, trying to get back to her. She hadn't thought that...well, she hadn't thought really.

"I'll go when Dina's ready. We'll start packing."

Kala frowned at the transcription Lucia typed for her. Eventually she rolled her eyes and nodded. Scribbled down an address and phone number. Then stood and left. Fair enough, she supposed. The Soul Eater wasn't putting anyone in a stellar mood.

Dina shot her a worried glance, and Ivy tried to give her a reassuring smile. It felt more like a grimace.

"You sure you're up for this Ivy?" Topher asked. "If you need more time—"

"I'll be ready," she squeezed Dina's hand. "Let's throw this asshole back into the abyss where it belongs."

41

DINA

The River Thames crawled by, beckoning Dina to dive in and let it wash her away to a foreign shore. The buzz of a headache threatened in the corner of her mind. Not yet forcing her hand but letting her know she couldn't stall much longer. None of them could.

"You're clear on the plan?" Ivy asked for the hundredth time.

It would have been frustrating if Dina couldn't hear the anxiety lying under the surface of the question. The worry of what would happen if this all went to shit. Which it likely would.

Dina leaned back into Ivy, who stood behind her, good arm around her waist, mouth against Dina's neck.

"Yes, I'm clear."

Ivy nodded, pressing her forehead to Dina's shoulder. "I hate this," she murmured.

Dina wasn't sure what she meant. The fact that even after tearing Ivy free from a burning building and a haunting past, they still had a Soul Eater to battle, or that they'd barely had a moment of peace between the exhaustion and meticulous planning. Or that she was leaving. Again. Perhaps it was all of it. Dina could certainly get behind that.

Ivy squeezed her tighter, breathing deep.

"I wish we could just stay here. I wish...I want you to stay."

"What? Here in Bermondsey? I can think of better places," Dina tried to quip. It fell flat.

"Anywhere you are, Supernova. That's fine by me." Ivy took a breath. "What if you tried...what if you fought it? Gave it something that wasn't all of you?"

Dina closed her eyes, then turned and tilted Ivy's face to hers.

"I've tried, Ivy. I think...this is just how I am now."

"I know," Ivy said with a sigh. "I know. I just—I want—" She pressed her forehead to Dina's. "When you're gone, it's like the world is flat. Like it's not even real. You make the world real to me, Dina."

Dina swallowed. And asked, because that was only fair. "Is this enough, though? I can't offer you more, Ivy. I want to, and I can't. Is it enough?"

Ivy kissed her hard, set Dina's heart racing so that she needn't choke on her own tears.

"Always," Ivy whispered against her lips, both of them breathing hard. "You're enough. This is enough. Always."

Part of her wanted to push back. To tell her that she could have so much more.

Ivy deserves the world.

But when she looked at Dina, it was like *she* was her world. Dina would have to believe her.

"When the world goes flat, when I'm away, will you be alright? If things are..." She took a breath. "Please. I don't want to resurface like that ever again. Finding out you're in trouble somewhere I can't reach."

Ivy nodded, brushing the tears from the corners of Dina's eyes. "My business with that part of my life is done. I promise."

"Even with Puck around?"

"Trust me, they're even more tired of that old life than I am. Well, maybe not. But the point is that we're both done with it. And they're the closest thing I have to a friend from that time."

Dina nodded. What she wouldn't give for some vestige of her old life. To see Zev in person, instead of through a phone screen. "Alright. Just be careful with them. And Kala. And all of it."

"You too, Supernova," Ivy whispered.

"You know," Dina said. "Zev and I have been talking. When we get through this, I think I'm going to tell my parents everything."

"Yeah?" Ivy asked brushing hair behind her ear.

"Yeah."

"Well, I can be there when you do. If you like."

Dina smiled, and the warmth in her chest had nothing to do with the Law of Attraction. "Yeah. You know, I'm glad I met you in my second life."

"Oh?"

"My first one was far too boring."

Ivy chuckled. "Mine wasn't boring enough. And my second seems to be shaping up just as well. Maybe in our third, we can just be bored together."

"That sounds oddly comforting."

The buzzing grew. And Dina didn't want to leave like that, fighting every step of the way.

"It's time, Ivy."

"Alright," Ivy breathed, leaning away until the only thing connecting them was the fingers interwoven like streams of a river coming together to form a delta. An ocean.

There would be more of this, Dina told herself. This last fight, and she could go back to understanding her own powers. Find out if there was a way to keep them from dragging her from Ivy's side. Or at least understand how to overcome the distance.

In the past, Dina had clung to every droplet of time with Ivy, dissolving like mist before she let herself be torn away.

It felt different this way. Being safeguarded back to the water, released knowing there would be an embrace waiting for her on the other side.

Ivy brought their clasped hands to her lips, then handed Dina off to the hungry river.

"See you soon, Supernova," she murmured.

Dina smiled. Let her eyes roam Ivy's face one last time, soaking in each detail.

And became the water itself.

On a rocky strand, cradling a river that flowed beneath a quiet forest canopy, Dina emerged to find a figure watching her.

She'd been swimming to shore on instinct, reaching for the boulders along the water's edge, pulling herself up onto the rocks. She froze when she took in her companion. It watched her with fathomless eyes. A hawk who knew its prey was well within reach. And she'd been too focused on the swim to notice that familiar pressure at the nape of her neck.

The Void had gained and lost since their last meeting. Once, it had been like smoke and shadow made into the shape of a person. Now, the pale skin was opaque. Dina could make out fine hairs on its hands, the way veins formed small ridges beneath the skin. Beyond the dark eyes that consumed and consumed, never sating its endless hunger, it looked almost human.

She stayed like that, half submerged in the river flow, keeping part of her mind connected to the water, ready to flee. But it only observed her.

"You reek," it told her. "You reek of wrong. You turn nature against its course. You and the others should not walk this world."

Dina hesitated, heart racing, shuddering body begging her to flee. But when it didn't move, she swallowed and said, "It seems to me nature chose us. Gave us a second chance. Why do you get to decide that's wrong?"

The thing wrinkled its nose. "It wasn't so bad when it happened the last time. I could ignore the stench of the blight. Now, there is no peace from it. There is no comfort in oblivion. I do this to right the world."

"What allows you to decide what makes the world right?" Dina growled. "You think you're the first to try it? You think you're better? You're not different. Just leave us be."

"Or you will take me down? I know you gather. I can *feel* it. You mock the universe itself. And I will consume you all until nothing remains but the memory of your footsteps. As it should be."

Cold seeped into Dina's bones. Cold that had nothing to do with the water all around her. How? How could it possibly know of their plan?

Aloud, she asked, "How do you keep finding *me*?"

It grinned. "Water and gravity. One pulls towards the other, does it not?"

Dina shivered. The idea that the water was somehow tugging her towards this thing made her skin crawl.

But the Void didn't seem to care. "I will make right the anomalies of the universe. Stitch together the cracks in its fabric. I will use the disease of you to inoculate this world."

"And what about you?" she countered. "You kill us all, and then what? You can hardly call yourself natural. If we are a disease, then what are you?"

The Void cocked its head. "What is more natural than a void seeking to fill itself and never having its appetite assuaged? Than a star consuming itself and everything around it for an eternity? Until the universe itself is nothing but dust? No, abomination. I will continue, and keep watch, and keep this world intact."

It launched itself towards her, moving between one blink and the next. Suddenly in front of her face.

The water screamed in her head, moving without hesitation, without her even needing to ask, shoving the thing back and away. Not enough to knock it down—it held its ground, unaffected by the onslaught of waves—but enough for Dina to dive beyond its grasp, swim down and down and down, not daring to look back, letting the water take her again.

She dissolved, became the rushing current.

Take me to them, she asked of the water.

The Void's hunger pressed into her, a shadow at her back as she fell away into the river. And she could only pray it would spit her back out before the Soul Eater could devour them all.

42

IVY

Watching Kala break down and reform material that had come from Ivy's own body was one of the strangest things she'd ever witnessed. Coming back from the dead still ranked as #1.

The woman worked silently in the small Nicosia apartment she'd driven them to after they landed in Cyprus. She had very little interest in Ivy, other than what she could provide for the net, and that was fine with her. She'd only picked up enough ISL to convey and understand the basics (she was getting better at finger spelling, though it was a bitch with her bum shoulder). Kala also used a speech-to-text app when the conversation didn't involve life-threatening circumstances (the app liked correcting "Soul Eater" to "solitaire"). But even if she could communicate well with Kala, she was far too in her head for small talk with strangers.

Having Dina there to catch her after the whole business with Lenox had been like receiving a torch to light the night. Now, without her, she felt as though she was waiting for the gray dawn to approach. Knowing it would come. Wishing it was already here.

There was a hollowness in her chest. Not regret, but still not quite relief. She found herself checking every escape, every street corner. Even though Lenox had gone down in the flames. Even though she'd watched to make sure he didn't rise from the ashes. She'd have to get used to the extra paranoia. At least for a while.

Kala motioned for another dagger. Ivy drew one from her flesh, biting her lip, and sweating with the effort. She'd lost count of how many she'd produced by now. So far, there'd been no limit to how many she could pull forth, other than her own exhaustion from the effort. This dagger came, but sluggishly. As if her body were unwilling to part with more of herself.

She handed the piece to Kala, drained. Like she'd run a marathon. Not that she'd ever tried to torture herself with something like sports or long-distance running. Nightmare.

Kala broke the piece down and reformed it to fit her desired shape. Apparently, she'd been an engineer in her previous life. Had died in an accident she wouldn't elaborate on. Fair enough, since Ivy didn't go about sharing all the gory details of her murder.

Once satisfied, Kala nodded and made a shooing motion towards Ivy. So they were done for the day.

Ivy sighed with relief and stood, slowly so Kala wouldn't catch her legs shaking. The other woman didn't need to know how weak she felt, how much her shoulder still radiated pain. Ivy could only count on one hand the people she trusted. Up from no one to three. And a half. Maybe she and Puck would fully trust each other some day. Kala wasn't yet anywhere near being added to the list.

Ivy retreated to the balcony and pulled out her phone. Kala had a different sign when she wanted Ivy to leave the apartment so another Resurrected could come in and deliver their own supplies (stone, wood, and stranger items like feathers and tendons). Ivy had gathered that there were about five of them on the island at any given point in time, though she knew some had come just the once, and then fled back to the continent so as not to fully draw the Shadow Eater out. Today, it didn't seem like anyone else was coming. She'd camp out here to give Kala her space and return if the woman needed more supplies.

She FaceTimed Topher, examining the tops of whitewashed buildings beyond the edges of her phone, the glimmer of the Mediterranean in the distance, until the dark screen lit up with their face.

"Hey, how's it on your end?" Topher asked. "Still ready to go the day after tomorrow?"

Ivy nodded. "Yeah, Kala says she's nearly done."

"I'll send the word out then. Day after tomorrow at the abandoned airstrip. 10 am your time."

"Wow, not the crack of dawn for extra drama?"

Topher shrugged. "Think we have enough drama as is. And there will be flights and boats coming in from all directions. Need to give people enough time to get there."

Ivy sighed. "And hope no one gets offed on their way here."

Topher frowned, face absent of their usual forced good humor. It made Ivy more anxious. She needed camp counselor Topher in this moment. But even they had their limits.

"Any word from Dina?" they asked.

Ivy shook her head. "No. We may have to start without her."

"You sound hopeful for that scenario."

Ivy glanced away from the screen. They needed all the Resurrected they could get, but the thought of Dina facing that thing again twisted her insides. "Can you blame me?"

"Not even a little. Still, the more of us we can get, the better."

"I hate this plan. For the record."

Topher opened their mouth but Ivy cut them off. "I didn't say I didn't start all this. And I didn't say I had a better one. But I'm still allowed to hate it."

They sighed. "If it makes you feel any better, I hate it too. But I've been running from this thing for nearly five years now. The idea of being able to stand still? Put down roots and build a life? Not gonna lie, Iv, that sounds like the dream."

Ivy bit her tongue so she wouldn't comment on how useless dreams were. So she wouldn't say her own aloud.

"You're good with the location?" she asked instead.

The abandoned airstrip Kala had scoped out would give them enough space to manage the fallout. And maybe escape if necessary.

"Yeah. It'll be fine, Ivy."

"You're a terrible liar."

"And a worse arsonist, but here we are."

Ivy swallowed. They really should have had this conversation in person. "Topher, I—"

"You don't have to say anything. That wasn't a dig."

"I know." And she did, much to her own surprise. "But I've never had anyone come back for me the way you four did. The way you and Luz have done more than once now. Thank you."

"God, I hope you were recording that," Lucia said from somewhere behind Topher.

Ivy snorted. "Hey, we get through this in one piece and I'll say it in person."

Luz appeared over Topher's shoulder. "Well, I was gonna half-ass the whole plan before, but now I guess I've got to whole-ass it."

"That's the spirit," Ivy grinned.

"Alright, we'd better finish packing. See you across the pond," Topher said.

"See ya," Ivy replied, grateful they hadn't said anything about seeing each other on "the other side". If this all went to shit, they'd be finding out if their second deaths were more permanent than the first.

The sea breeze blew through the abandoned airstrip, tendrils of salty air toying with the loose strands falling out of Ivy's bun as she shuffled from foot to foot. Rusted out planes littered the cracked asphalt. Grasses poked through the tarmac here and there, the scrubby trees keeping to the far edges of the open field. In the distance, far down the runway, Ivy could make out the disintegrating letters advertising the "Nicosia International Airport".

Ugh. This place gave her the creeps.

Beside her, Kala had closed her eyes, fingers on the horrific net she'd woven of bone knives and pieces of people who just wanted to live. It pooled around her feet, heavy as chainmail, a strange, luminescent white. The other woman's brow was scrunched in concentration. Ivy suspected she was praying. She wondered if picking a deity at random to appeal to would help at this point. Probably not. They were utterly fucked if this plan didn't work. No backups, except to run, hard and fast, and hope some of them lived to run another day. They were betting on a bunch of calculated guesses.

Fuck, this was a bad idea.

Heat licked through Ivy's chest. She whipped around as the hole she'd cut in the chain link fence spat out three distant figures. Topher, Lucia, and Danny had arrived just in time. Ivy tapped Kala, who opened her eyes and nodded a greeting to the others.

On their heels, a dozen more Resurrected streamed onto the airstrip. Then another dozen. More and more until there were maybe fifty of them. And those were just the ones who'd shown. Who knew how many more were still in hiding, undiscovered. Finding group solidarity wasn't something Ivy was familiar with. Not when everyone on Lenox's crew had been eager to climb to the top by any means necessary. Maybe if they made it through this, she could rethink that strategy. There was something oddly hopeful about finding so many people that shared something secret and powerful with her.

As the group gathered, they arranged themselves in patterns, grouping in clusters of fives or so. Topher must have strategized the setup, given how they were motioning the groups to their places.

"What're they doing?" Ivy asked Danny as Topher motioned them both to join Kala towards the front.

"Folks that have powers with a large range are going to the back. People without combat powers are staying in the middle to help pick up anyone who gets taken down. And folks like us with close-range or mid-range powers are at the front."

"Huh. Seems like everyone synchronized their watches at least," Ivy commented when Topher joined their group.

A young man stepped close to Topher, dark eyes darting.

"The girl with the water powers here?" he asked.

"You the kid with lightning?" Ivy replied before Topher could say anything.

He swallowed. "Uh, yeah. Yousef. You can call me Sunny."

Ivy looked him up and down. He was at that age where scrawniness was giving way to lean muscle and broad shoulders. Still a baby, really.

"You fried my girlfriend's phone," she said, hands in pockets.

He rubbed the back of his neck. "Seemed necessary at the time. She here? Pretty shitty to drag me into this and not show herself."

"She's on her way," Topher said before Ivy could snap at him. "Her power is more complicated."

"If you say so," Sunny said with a shrug and stepped back towards his group.

Teenagers.

Once everyone took their places, the waiting settled in, tense and heavy. No one else was speaking. Most were staring with the wide-eyed expression of someone taking a test for a language they'd never studied. Others had a fierce determination lining their brows. And the rest appeared resigned to their fate.

"Any sign from Dina?" Lucia asked.

Ivy was about to shake her head when her phone began buzzing in her pocket.

She picked up and breathed, "Dina?"

"Ivy, it knows."

"What?" Ivy asked, even though she didn't need the words repeated to understand their meaning.

Blood rushed from her face. She clenched the phone tight to stop her hands from shaking.

"It found me," came the frantic reply. "I don't know how it figured it out, but it knows what we're planning to do. I'm in the car with Puck like we planned. They're taking me to you now, but it's got to be a trap. You all have to get out of there or—"

Ivy didn't hear the rest. Between one blink and the next, a pool of shadows opened up before them. The darkness of space coalescing into a void where there had once been only empty air and the occasional tufts of grass growing through the abandoned airstrip.

The void grew limbs, a trick of the light. Light swallowed whole by something monstrous, by a thing that snatched up souls and devoured them like they'd never mattered. A blackhole feasting on planets and galaxies. It took the shape of a human, far more solid than when last Ivy had seen it. No transparent flesh now.

The Soul Eater had consumed its fill and came to them hungry as ever. And more powerful than Ivy could have ever imagined.

43

"It's here," Ivy whispered before the line went dead.

Dina cursed. She was still soaked from the water of the Mediterranean, shivering despite the bright shine of the sun. She could barely hear above the drum of her heart.

"We need to go faster," she told Puck. "It's already there."

"Going as fast as I can, Waterworks," came the grim response. Their hands tightened on the wheel of the rental car as they tore through quiet streets.

Dina would have to reprimand them for the terrible nickname later. She was far too busy chewing her fingernails, clutching the seat.

Hold on, Ivy. I'm coming. I'm coming.

The Soul Eater stepped forward, hunger written in the edges of its jaw. In the way its tongue licked across its lips, gray and desiccated, like that of a corpse. Fathomless eyes eager. Movements graceful. As if it had all the time in the world to feast on them.

It knows, Dina had said.

It knew what it would find here. It had come anyway. It knew it would win.

Puck whipped around another corner, tires screeching as they wound down back roads and kept an eye out for cops, threading the needle between speed and asking to be deported. Trees and rocks flew by in a rush of greens and reds and browns.

Dina saw none of it. Felt only the racing car, the leather seat she dug her nails into. Her mind swam between the crash from the bridge and every new place she'd emerged since. The way her first death had swallowed her whole and spat her out as something new. The way the Void might be devouring Ivy even now. And this time, death would keep them all.

A blast of fire as Topher ignited and threw a column of flames from their chest like the wrath of a god. It hit the Soul Eater straight on.

It didn't even flinch. Just kept walking with carefree strides.

"Abominations," it hissed. "I will sleep in satisfaction at last. How I *hunger*."

The last word growled through the air like thunder.

Topher released a fireball, and this time the others that had frozen on the Soul Eater's arrival took their cue. From around Ivy, all the forces of nature converged on the Soul Eater. It opened its mouth wide and Ivy threw a dagger with her off hand, cursing when it fell short. Course corrected, and this time, pushed her will into the bone blade, willing it to fly true into the whirlwind of lighting and fire and wind. A perfect shot, aimed right for the thing's head.

But a useless shot in the end.

The Soul Eater unhinged its jaw, wider than any viper, teeth and gum and bones splitting apart to form a maw, impossibly wide. Wide enough to swallow every attack whole.

She didn't wait for the car to stop as Puck pulled up next to the row of cars already parked just outside of the airstrip. Almost tripped and fell on her face. Windmilled her arms to right herself and kept going. The waves still loud in her ears, matching the wind bellowing through the open landscape.

It seemed as though she ran towards an explosion, her whole body screaming that she was going the wrong way. That she needed shelter and fast.

But Ivy was out there, at the front of the battle she'd been too late to stop. She barely even paused at the chain link fence, ignoring the scrape of exposed metal tearing into her cheek. Even as she pushed through the crowd of Resurrected, shoving horrified people aside while their attacks landed without impact, she saw nothing but the Soul Eater's glee. It took another step towards Ivy.

"I will consume you until the universe forgets your existence," it crowed.

"The fuck we do now?" someone shouted.

"The fucking net!" Ivy screamed, wondering why Kala hadn't already thrown it. Forgetting she couldn't hear her.

The woman stood like a statue, mouth agape, watching the Soul Eater lick its lips with a horrified gaze.

Ivy grabbed her arm. Hard.

The woman flinched, but burst into action. Lifting the net in tandem with Ivy.

"Again!" Topher shouted, releasing another blast of fire. "Danny, now!"

Kala and Ivy hoisted up the net, the movement wrenching at her bad shoulder. She pushed the throbbing pain into a small corner of her mind as they threw the net up with matching grunts of effort. It flew and spun and beside them, Danny was holding out his hands, ready to alter the gravity around them. The world grew lighter.

The net grazed the Soul Eater's head.

And came down hard as Danny tightened his hands into fists. Ivy stumbled forward, along with the Resurrected around her. The world gained weight. Gravity pulling them towards the asphalt. Yanking the net tight around the Soul Eater.

But before they could pull it taut, the creature oozed through the opening like an oil slick.

It roared, wide mouth leering as it stepped forward.

Ivy pulled her daggers to her, recreating the shields she'd made along her forearms. Futile protection if that thing got ahold of her. The ache in her shoulder was growing into an angry roar by the second, but she didn't dare stop to check the wound. If the Soul Eater got to them, bleeding out would be the least of her concerns.

Someone darted to her side. And then the world began to shake.

Ivy lurched as the asphalt tore free from the ground, wrapping the Soul Eater in a dark cocoon. Another Resurrected ran forward, and as she raised her hands, a wellspring of dirt irrupted, pummeling the Soul Eater with all the force of a firehose. And then it was Sunny at the front, calling lightning down from the sky to lash at the Soul Eater again and again.

More of the Resurrected darted forward, forming a circle around the shadow that had haunted their afterlives, hurtling all manner of attacks at the thing. When Aisling had died by its hand, even her strange phasing hadn't been enough to escape. But the Soul Eater had become a solid thing. A real thing. More a man than a shadow at last. And the people it had hunted were done with being prey.

One woman was sobbing as air sucked towards her, like she was stealing the oxygen from around the Soul Eater. Another person screamed, guttural and desperate, flinging metal shards from their fingers. A crowd of the weary and fearful, who had gathered enough courage for a final stand. And Ivy stood beside them, hurling pieces of herself in the form of blades at a creature of nightmares. No matter the pain, no matter the exhaustion. She cried aloud as she carved herself apart to keep attacking.

But the Soul Eater wasn't done yet. The attacks kept it contained for a few scant breaths. And then it tore free of its asphalt tomb, and advanced towards the closest Resurrected. Someone screamed as it grabbed him by the throat. Sunny blasted the thing with another rod of lightning while another Resurrected tugged on the captured man's arm. But it held fast, drained him in seconds, and stepped forward for more, its mouth open wide to swallow anything they hurled its way. Grabbed the next Resurrected in its path. Ravaged their soul and lurched forward with starvation dark in its eyes.

Ivy stepped back and searched for the net. Kala and Danny were already running that way and she sprinted to catch up. The three of them grasped it again. Flung it with all their might. And as they hurled it into the air, as gravity itself shifted around them, this time, when the net made contact it stayed put.

The Soul Eater grunted, too busy swallowing their futile attacks to dodge. And just as Danny clenched his fist, yanking gravity down so the net held tight, Ivy spotted an opening. Hadn't Lenox taught her how to find just the right one?

She hurled another dagger, directed by her consciousness, into the hunched form of the Soul Eater as the net closed and dragged it to the ground.

And the scream that tore from it was worth all the terror in that moment. The Soul Eater had become solid at last.

It felt like being dragged along with the current. No matter how she shouted, she was moving too slow. Could only watch as Ivy and Kala threw the net over the Soul Eater a second time.

She gasped when it landed and stayed put. She hadn't really believed Topher's plan would work. Not until she saw the proof of it. She didn't stop running though.

Ivy was pulling the net taut, even as Danny weighed it down. Others dashed forward to help. And finally. Finally, she reached Ivy's side.

She couldn't even spare her a glance as Ivy grunted to Topher, "And now?"

The Soul Eater glared up at them, all the hate of a star avenging its death by swallowing the light around it.

"We have to keep it in place until we can starve it out. We need to get it back to the cars and cage it up in the storage container Luz and I found by the port."

They looked grim. This would be the tricky bit. A part of the plan Dina was sure no one had believed they would see come to fruition.

There were pieces of rope in the net that allowed them to draw it tighter and keep it that way. It looked like sinew. Dina didn't want to think too hard on where that had come from.

Topher pulled, the movement tossing the Soul Eater onto its back, where it hissed and growled. Bits of darkness peeled away from it, testing the gaps in the nets, searching for a way to disappear.

But the Void had eaten too well. It couldn't phase itself free.

It's had too much at once, *Dina thought.* It's becoming more real as it feeds. But if we starve it out, does it become—

The realization hit her just as a flurry of darkness spilled from the Void's form. As the thing lost its solid form.

The Void's arm became vapor in the air for a split second. Long enough to reach through the net.

And grab Topher by the throat.

The moment the Soul Eater made contact with Topher, the net went loose.

Ivy screamed, hurling herself towards the two grappling figures. Satisfied when her dagger sliced into the Soul Eater's flesh.

It screamed, bleeding oblivion. Stuck, for the moment, as something in between real and ephemeral. Darkness swirled at their feet, crawled up Ivy's ankles as she dragged Topher away from the thing's clawing hands. Leached heat and life anywhere it touched. Others jumped in to help. Dina and Luz got their hands under Topher's armpits and got them the rest of the way free. Every move too frantic, too slow to keep the net in place. It opened an inch. No more. An inch too much.

The hand, colder than death, grabbed Ivy's ankle and pulled her to the ground, asphalt tearing up her skin. It crawled up the length of her with impossible speed. Clutched at her mouth. Her throat. Fingers lengthening as they dove into her screaming mouth to tear her from existence.

Ivy went down hard in the puddle of darkness pouring from the Void's wound. The Resurrected were falling over each other, reeling away from the consuming shadows. Screaming as tendrils reached towards mouths and throats, spreading like cracks in the universe.

And Dina was running straight into a black hole. Grabbing it by the neck as it howled. And she was howling with it, hands burning from the awful cold, her body hurled back into those horrible moments before the darkness had closed in. Before the water had taken her and given her this strange new life. Worse than the drowning ice. Than the terror of waking miles from home without knowing how she'd gotten there.

Ivy's muffled gags were worse than any of it.

She clawed and scraped. Heard Topher screaming senselessly. Far off it sounded. But then heat brushed her cheek. Another blast of fire. Enough.

The Void flinched, grip loosened. And then released Ivy, threw her hard to the ground. Stood with Dina still clinging to its back. A tangle of limbs and a net of bone and metal and sinew.

The darkness puddled around Ivy's limp form. Then Topher was there, pulling Ivy out of the way.

Good.

Someone else screamed for her to get out of there.

When it feeds all at once, it becomes real. It becomes like us. It becomes vulnerable.

It wasn't a black hole at all, but some strange other thing that had risen from death when she and others like her had breathed once more. A shadow of their creation, but one that could be forced to follow their rules. If they could stuff it full, force it to become solid once more...

She let go. Let her body fall to the ground. Waited for the Void to turn and face her. Fathomless eyes and hungry mouth. It opened wide and shot towards her.

"Dina!"

The scream, close to Ivy's ear, sent her shooting back to her feet, ignoring her massive bruise of a body. Sent her running, hobbling towards the dark pools flowing forth from the Soul Eater's wound. Though others were writhing on the ground, screaming with pain where those pieces of darkness made contact. Though it bit at her legs, clawed at her skin through boots and jeans.

The Soul Eater held Dina aloft with one hand. Reached down her throat with the other.

The memory of Aisling, the nightmare of it all made real once more.

But not Dina. It couldn't have Dina.

As she ran, Dina shot her a look of panic, that even now held a spark of intelligence. Even now, when her soul was being ripped from her body.

She curled her fist. Made the smallest motion with her hand, keeping wide eyes on Ivy all the while.

Ivy produced a long, long dagger and hurtled forward.

She let the Void have its fill. And in her ears, her head, her lungs, the ocean sang. Waves crashed. Particles of the water flowed through her veins, feeding into the Void.

Take it. Just try to take it all. I fucking dare you.

She was more than a human girl. A woman brought back from the dead by an anomaly in the universe. She was the water itself. The clouds in the sky and the raindrops feeding a thirsty earth. And when the earth had its fill, she would roll off the drenched soil and find the ocean once more.

Whatever the Void was, itself an anomaly of the universe, it would never starve out of existence. But they could feed it to bursting.

And so Dina fed it the might of the sea. Gave and gave until she couldn't feel the world around her anymore. Until consciousness streamed away. The essence of her being sucked into the Void's own gravity.

Until a sharp bone knife skewered the Void. Pierced deep enough for Dina to feel the very tip against her own chest, just barely breaking the skin.

And the world screamed into nothing.

Emptiness took over Dina's eyes. The way it had Aisling's. The way it meant to take all of them.

Something poured down Ivy's hand, gripped around the knife deeply rooted in the Soul Eater's back.

Cold. Cold. And growing warmer.

But she couldn't tear her eyes away from Dina's, wide to nearly white. Not even as the scent of ozone and emptiness turned to the sickening cloy of blood and the Soul Eater shuddered. Not even when the cold creeping up her legs disappeared.

Only when the thing released Dina, who fell rag doll limp to the ground, did she let go of the knife. In time to watch as the darkness oozing from the Soul Eater's body consumed Dina's form.

She reached forward into the murk, diving after Dina. The woman who'd been open enough to cry in front of her by the bathroom sink one night. Who'd taken her to a borrowed apartment and changed everything.

But as she dashed forward, the dark pools of oblivion receded. As if they had never been. Leaving nothing but asphalt and a dead body at her feet.

The Soul Eater bled out. Real blood. Human blood. It stared at the sky with eyes blank and blue. A body. Pale skin and splayed out limbs. No more a nightmare walking. Just some dead thing that would trouble them no more.

And perhaps that was the irony of it all. Perhaps it wasn't the Resurrected who had tipped the balance of nature, but the Soul Eater itself.

But Ivy didn't care about the balance of the universe. About the sounds of sobbing and relief coming from all around her.

For its final act, the Soul Eater had consumed Dina whole. Down to the last drop.

44

IVY

A round her, the Resurrected got to their feet. Many groaning. Some struggling with the help of others. Some not moving at all.

Ivy stayed where she was, staring at the empty ground beside the Soul Eater's body, a numb disbelief taking hold.

What am I going to tell Zev?

She'd never thought she'd actually have to make that call. To have any sort of conversation with him in which Dina wasn't there too. In her wildest fantasies, maybe she'd even imagined what that would be like. To take a breath after all this was over. Do the things normal girlfriends did. Introduce each other to their family and friends. Go on normal-ass dates. Get bored and watch TV together. Argue over who had skipped ahead on episodes while the other was at work.

Normal experiences. Normal conversations. Not a phone call with someone she'd never met to tell him his sister...to tell him Dina...that she was—

Ivy started when someone grasped her uninjured shoulder. Whipped around, dagger ready. Ripped from her flesh like a splinter caught on the edges of her skin.

As she held it to Topher's throat, her skin gaped open where the dagger had emerged. Slower to heal than ever before. Muscle and bone exposed to the world. She hardly cared.

Topher took it all in stride. A somber expression on their face.

"I'm going to keep watch over the body. Me and Luz and a few others. And then we'll burn the remains. Puck is here. If you'd rather..." they swallowed hard, eyes trailing to the blank asphalt. Where Dina had been devoured by a void.

Ivy couldn't find the words to respond. Simply turned away. Hollowed out.

All those pieces of bone, pieces of her still stuck in the Soul Eater's bloated body. For the first time, she felt the absence of their weight. As if she'd carved herself out with a dull knife, stripped herself of bone and marrow and flesh.

That's what it felt like, watching Dina disappear and knowing she wouldn't reemerge on some distant shore.

"Ivy?" Lucia murmured.

Ivy ignored her and took a step closer to the Soul Eater's body. The others had given it a wide berth, already disappearing, some with the bodies of their friends, temporary alliance dissolving as if still in disbelief that they were truly safe.

But Ivy wasn't going to leave the thing's side. Not 'til they were sure.

She approached and found the long dagger, still stuck through the thing's back.

Wrenched it out. Blade sucking clean from flesh and blood.

Stabbed it back in.

Over and over and over. Until she was dripping sweat and bleeding from her reopened wound, and a cry rose around her, and fuck that was her voice, but fuck she didn't care.

No one stopped her. Maybe some were pleased. But eventually there was no more blood to spill. No more strength in her body.

So she stabbed the dagger in and left it there. Stood and stepped away. Drew up the net and placed it over the body like a shroud. Then joined the others to keep watch over yet another dead body.

A week went by with groups of Resurrected ferrying food and trash. Taking turns so others could shower or use a proper toilet and sleep in a real bed. A week of smelling the rotting flesh until they were all numb to it. Until Topher lit up like the sunset, drawing the heat towards their palms.

"I think we call it," they said.

"You're sure?" Sunny asked.

If Ivy had any room for feeling anything, she might have been surprised that he'd stayed. He kept his eyes on the unmoving body, now beyond disgusting, covered in flies and worse.

"No one's ever taken this long to come back. And no one has decomposed like this between their death and Resurrection. I'm sure. It's time."

They looked around until everyone in the group nodded. Everyone but Ivy, who couldn't seem to muster the strength. Topher took her silence as agreement.

The fire spread through them, haloing around as they became that strange fire creature once more. And hurled the flames at the body.

Once the skin caught, the smell was horrific. Ivy gagged, surprised almost that something had reached her in the hollowed-out state she'd occupied since the fight.

The Resurrected stood around the body, each face gaunt and skeletal in the flames. All of them grim as they made sure every bit of flesh caught. Until the fire burnt out and there was nothing but ash. Fires didn't burn that hot. Ivy knew that. But Topher was a living torch. Perhaps the rules didn't apply to them.

They came to Ivy's side, careful not to touch her. Spoke softly without looking at her. "Puck is back. They found a place for us to stay since Kala's headed back to Delhi."

When Ivy said nothing, they motioned towards the edge of the airstrip with a tilt of their chin. Something like concern written in the lines of their face, as if they worried she wouldn't follow. But Ivy kicked at the pile of ash and let Topher lead her, Lucia, and Danny to the car.

As they approached the sedan, so normal in appearance compared to what they'd just faced, Ivy let the others crowd in first. The clouds above were moving quickly, threatening rain.

And as she ducked her head into the car, a droplet fell on her cheek, running down the skin like a caress.

45

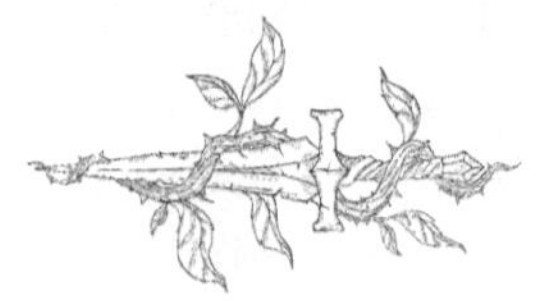

IVY

Two months later

The lake sounded through the mist, assuring her it was really there, gently lapping against the shore. More than a figment of Ivy's imagination. The fog hung so thick, it became a wall of white in front of her.

Somewhere off to the side, Zev stood nearby. Further away, Topher, Lucia, and Danny waited with his partner, Ben. And Ivy felt a fool for dragging them all out here.

It had been two months since their fight with the Soul Eater. Two months in which the Resurrected started putting down roots, coming out of hiding. Danny had even convinced Topher and Lucia to move to D.C. more permanently. The Resurrected were recalibrating, giving this second life a real chance. Most of them anyway.

Ivy still couldn't seem to settle. She'd thought about visiting Zev when he offered. Just after she'd called to deliver the news that his sister was dead. Really dead this time. She'd left out the gruesome details. The way the Soul Eater dragged its victims off to a fate worse than death. Bad enough that she had to live with those nightmares. Waking from them, sweating and screaming and finding a cold, empty bed beside her.

"Sorry," she said into the quiet.

She and Zev texted every day now. He still felt like a stranger, but he'd begun checking in with her, not seeming to mind the fact that she'd struggled to write back at first. And then it had been...nice to have someone on the other end of the phone again. He never asked if she was okay and she returned the favor. But still, it was another person who seemed to care that she was alive, even if they gained nothing other than her dubious company as thanks.

"Nothing to be sorry for," Zev said, scuffing the gravel with his shoe.

The mist was beginning to thin enough that she could observe him sidelong. His eyes were trained straight ahead. The way hers had been all night. But now, with the sun fighting its way through the fog, she doubted those words.

"She'd be happy to know we did this," Zev said. "Even if..." he trailed off.

Even if the voice in my head is nothing but the rain pounding on the roof. Even if it's just the waves on the shore and nothing more. Even if Topher's so-called Law of Attraction isn't holding up anymore.

Still, she'd had to try. And no one had yet called her crazy for it, though they were well within their rights.

Topher had been the one to pick the spot. Based on the last place they'd seen Dina. The place she'd died. They were working on the assumption that she wasn't in control anymore. Assuming she...

Don't hope. Don't you dare hope.

But they were all standing here out of hope. Any chance she'd had of keeping her heart safe beneath its armor had fled. Perhaps that armor had been destroyed since the beginning. Since she'd stumbled across a strange girl. And then stumbled across her again and again.

And the rain. The rain seemed to sing her name. It couldn't be for nothing. It couldn't just be idle fancy. A wish. Ivy was too smart to make wishes.

"How long do we give it?" Ivy asked.

She would have waited there until the world turned to stone and her with it. But she didn't need to pull the others into the orbit of her foolishness.

Zev crossed his arms and didn't answer, seeming to settle into his stance even more. They watched the white world take on shape and color. Resolve into water that was near glass in its stillness.

Clear water. Nothing but the scurrying of small fish to mar its peace.

Ivy had waited the whole night through. Yet when her eyes revealed what she already knew to be true, it was a gut punch. Her heart dropped to her toes.

It took me a second life to learn how to live, Dina. But I don't know how I'm supposed to do that without you.

She didn't cry. She hadn't since Dina died. And if she woke up with the pillows soaked through, she ignored the salt-stained fabric. But she gave into the knife-sharp ache in her chest. The imagined grip around her throat.

Zev nodded beside her. "We tried. Maybe we got it wrong. Maybe…"

"Maybe she isn't coming back," Ivy choked out. She wouldn't let Dina's brother waste his life searching every stream and puddle on the minuscule chance that Dina was alive. He had a partner. A life. And perhaps she had a friend. But she'd already spent her first life. She could afford to waste another.

"She wouldn't want you to give up everything to look for her," Ivy murmured.

Zev swallowed. "And you? What would she want for you?"

A safe home. Blankets to curl under together. A warm meal and friends that no longer came as a shock.

Ivy shook her head. "Doesn't matter. Everyone's bound to be freezing and you can't afford to lose your job standing around a random lake in the middle of nowhere."

"She'd get in touch, wouldn't she? She figured it out before."

Ivy nodded. It was part of her fear. Her hope. That one day she might get a call from an unknown number. Whisper "Supernova" into the receiver and be met by Dina's laughter. The absence of it was an emptiness that devoured.

But the rain sounds like you, Ivy thought, taking one last look at the lake.

She gently touched Zev's elbow. "I think we should head back."

Zev looked at her for a steady moment before nodding, shoulders slumped, dejected.

Ben stepped forward, wrapping him up in his arms. Topher and Lucia watched, waiting to see if Ivy would allow the same. At the slight shake of her head, they kept their hands down by their sides.

So the five of them headed towards the trail back to the car. Back to face a world without a shadow haunting every step.

The water's stillness soothes. Heals fractures. Brings all the scattered pieces of itself together once more.

Ivy froze, cold awareness climbing up her spine. Heat bursting through her chest like the explosion of a star. Like a supernova.

It trickles from the tops of mountains. Through the leaf litter and moist soil. Spills across rocks. A steady drip drip drip *into the smooth water.*

"Ivy?"

Blood rushed in her ears, the pounding of it like a knock at the door. Like rain pounding on the roof. Like a storm blowing in.

The water holds memories of hurt it cannot feel itself. It takes her away. Grants her rest. Time. Water has so much time. What does it care how long it takes for a stream to find the ocean? For clouds to burst and form rain and quench the thirsty land.

She ran, tripping on stones and twigs, sprinting full tilt towards the shore.

And as the droplets fall and mingle, so too do the fragments of her. Drop by drop. To once again form a body, limbs, hair. A girl who died and came back different.

Cold water splashed up Ivy's legs, the crashing of it exploding around the quiet lakeside. It climbed to her waist, freezing as she pushed forward, dove under the water with eyes wide open.

She is the water. The water is her. And when she ended, the water continued. And it brought her with it. So she puts the pieces of herself together, remembers what it was like to have warm blood and a beating heart. To have a body.

A body around which arms have wrapped. They pull her to the surface. Where it is warm. Where the embrace feels like home. Like a girl who became a weapon for another man. Who died and became a blade for herself.

The arms pull her upward. To shore. To desperate kisses, sobs and laughter.

And when her head breaches the surface, she takes a breath.

Acknowledgments

I have had the utmost fortune over my writing career to be surrounded by a truly incredible network of support. People who saw me struggling in the query trenches and reminded me that "You wrote a book! You wrote another book! That's still worth celebrating!" It can be difficult to acknowledge the milestones of publishing, even when you're holding the book in your hands. So my profound thanks to:

My writing coven (Danielle and Katie), who were my first ever beta readers and have read just about every word I've written since 2020. Your insight has been so critical for making these books so much more than "no plot, only vibes". And to Tiera and Taylor, my other amazing beta readers. Thank you for asking questions I didn't want to answer. The Soul Eater is a better antagonist for it. And thank you for all the unhinged comments, which had me giggling throughout the revision process.

I am so grateful to my Pitch Wars community for their support. We've all been on one giant emotional rollercoaster together, and I would have hopped off by now if I wasn't riding alongside all of you. I would especially like to thank Valo, whose advice I always hate, but is (almost) always the right advice. I also want to thank Lillian and Chrissy, who held my hand throughout the process of self-publishing my first book. And so much love to Alistair, Jamison, Sul, Janet, Loro, The Latest Hyperfixation group chat, and so many more of our PW class!

To my editor, Corey, you are a champion and your encouragement has kept me afloat throughout the writing of this book! I hope this acknowledgements section isn't missing too many commas because I'm not sending it to you to edit. Thank you for loving me and for helping me make this book a better product. And of course for feeding me.

Youness, my cover designer, thank you for your hard work on this art. Since the day you sent the final version, I have not been able to stop staring! Thank you for being such a breeze to work with!

Thank you to my high school astronomy teacher, Mr. Rosenfeld. I don't think this is what you had in mind when you were encouraging me to go into astrophysics, and I honestly hope you never find this book, but at least I haven't stopped thinking about astronomy, right?

To the Scrump for the Crump group chat: Thank you for answering all my non sequiturs like, "Does someone want to read an explanation on how black holes could be bringing people back from the dead with super powers and tell me if it's believable?"

To the friends who have been waiting to hold one of my books in their hands. And to Anna, Lu, Rachel, and Ashley who kept me company while I was in the final stages of revisions and desperately needed other people to remind me that eating a solid dinner is a worthy pursuit. Seriously, if you have ever fed me in the last few months, THANK YOU!

And to my family for your love and support. Especially to my parents who spent years worrying about if I would ever make a living studying birds and tromping around the woods but never tried to stop me. Thank you for all the encouragement, notebooks, and fun pens over the years. I've been putting them to good use!

ABOUT THE AUTHOR

Avrah C. Baren (she/they) is a SciFi/Fantasy writer based in the DMV, where she lives with a neurotic tuxedo cat. She is an alum of the Pitch Wars Class of 2021 and a graduate of the Futurescapes 2023 Writers' Workshop. She holds a B.S. in Environmental Science, an M.S. in Wildlife Science, and is working on a PhD in Geographic Information Systems. They spend their days researching mangroves and landcover change, and continue to nurse a passion for avian ecology. They love writing fantastical tales with Jewish-coded and explicitly Jewish characters that explore our connections with nature and each other.

When she isn't writing, she is climbing rocks, working at the Renaissance Festival, and trying to become a wood witch.

Find Me:

Follow me @avrahwrites on social media. For news and updates, please subscribe to my newsletter at abigailiswriting.com!

Did you love this book? Please do me the favor of reviewing on your preferred platform!

9 798990 054608